Words of Praise fo

"The lives of today's young peo₁ ____ ___ __₁ and the challenges they face are unusually cruel, and can mean life or death. Duane Smith understands this and uses **The Nubian** to teach them how to triumph..."

- Bethany Campbell
Curator, APEX Museum

"Though Smith has created a fictional setting with mystical events to tell his story, this book never the less is a real life testament of our times."

- about...time magazine

"...(Mr. Smith's) work is quite a tall accomplishment for a writer's first outing. It's a passionate story that raises some serious questions. I highly recommend it!"

- Fredrick D. Robinson
Creative Loafing Newsmagazine

"...the story (is) unique, pioneering, and critical for all people who desire to understand the African mind, and especially for those who are seeking to find their own African consciousness again."

- Dr. Na'im Akbar
Author, scholar, psychologist

"**The Nubian** is an exciting novel! Duane Smith has faced the daunting challenge of incorporating historical information and cultural lessons into the contemporary experience..."

- Dr. Asa G. Hilliard, III
Fuller E. Calloway Professor of
Urban Education
Georgia State University

About the Cover

The massive sculptured likenesses of Pharaoh Ramses II survey the desert landscape from the Temple of Ramses at Abu Simbel in Nubia. The temple stands one hundred and seventy-four miles south of Aswan.

Historians have wondered why Ramses II, one of the most powerful and revered of Egyptian monarchs would locate such an awe-inspiring monument some three hundred and fifty miles south of the seat of Egyptian monarchy at the time. Certainly, there was the political need to demonstrate the dominance of the Egyptian throne to the Nubian inhabitants, who were at the time subjects of Egypt.

More importantly, Pharaoh Ramses was paying homage to the immense debt that he as the head of state owed to the Nubian civilizations that *spawned* Egyptian civilization thousands of years *before* his birth. In remotest antiquity, Nubia was the seat of power of the ancient Cushite Ethiopian Empire, of which Egypt was one of its first colonies.

Our modern world owes so much as well to these Cushite Ethiopians, these Nubians, including the cultivation of crops, the calendar, the natural sciences, and the disciplines of mathematics, engineering, and architecture. The Nubians have endowed our world through the brilliance of the civilization they introduced, and that was refined by subsequent Egyptian monarchies.

Most of the physical evidence of the greatness of the Nubians has been drowned beneath the waters of Lake Nasser, which resulted from the construction of the Aswan dam. History has both ignored and forgotten such wonders of these originators of civilization.

This is the story of one man who understands...and remembers!

Duane Smith

Temple of Ramses - Abu Simbel - NUBIA

The story our world's been waiting for!

The Nubian
a novel

Azimuth

The AZIMUTH PRESS • College Park, GA. 30349

foreword by Dr. Molefi Asante
edited by Myra B. Moon

The AZIMUTH PRESS
3002 Dayna Drive
College Park, GA. 30349

Library of Congress Cataloging-in-Publication Data

Smith, Duane, 1953-
The Nubian: a novel / foreword by Molefi Kete Asante;
edited by Myra B. Moon
p.   cm.

ISBN 0-9632074-0-7 $12.95

Manufactured in the United States of America

About the Author

Author, educational consultant, and motivational speaker, Duane Smith has emerged as one of the compelling new voices in African-American literature. A graduate of Cornell University, *The Nubian* has been critically acclaimed as "...a fascinating blend of political intrigue, culture, and spirituality."

Mr. Smith first became aware of the issues surrounding African-American studies while at Cornell. Throughout his professional career, he has continued to study African culture, artistic expression, and spirituality. He has appeared on radio and TV in New York, Philadelphia, Washington, D.C., Chicago, Detroit, Houston, and Atlanta, and is a popular workshop presenter and keynote speaker. His writing emphasizes the African based cultural experience in contemporary literature, an area he feels has been sorely neglected by writers as well as readers throughout the country.

His other works include the *Multi-Cultural School Kit*, a structured learning laboratory for middle and high school students, and the soon to be released *Abubakari's Gold*, which takes up the historical issues of the African presence in the Americas before Columbus.

ACKNOWLEDGEMENTS

Grateful acknowledgement goes out to the Fulton County (GA.) Commission, who has provided partial funding for this project, under the guidance of the Fulton County Arts Council.

Literary acknowledgements to Adolf Erman for his work, *Life in Ancient Egypt* , and to U. S. News and World Report, for their April, 1990 article, *Lost Empires of the Americas*.

Special appreciation goes to the late Alex Haley, and his illustrious subject, El Hajj Malik el Shabazz, for concepts brought forth in *The Autobiography of Malcolm X.* We are also grateful for ideas introduced in the works of Carlos Castaneda. We thank the Mayor of Washington, D.C., the Honorable Sharon Pratt Kelly for ideas introduced in her speech to the National Urban League Convention in Atlanta. Finally, a very special thanks to my editor, Myra B. Moon for her insightful suggestions and thoroughness, in helping to see this project through.

FOREWORD

There is an expression in the tradition of the Wolof of Senegal that says, "Wood may remain in water for ten years..... but it will never become a crocodile." In this powerful novel by the new writer, Duane Smith, we see the move toward an understanding of just how such a concept applies, when considering the historical experiences of African people in the United States.

Often we are confronted with the enormity of what we have lost in terms of our cultural and social heritage. In *The Nubian,* Mr. Smith pulls together historical and contemporary themes to introduce values such as self-reliance, discipline, integrity, faith, and loyalty. In this novel, we see how characters interact on the basis of values. Although they have been transformed by the American society (names, positions, certain attitudes) they remain essentially rooted in the fundamental traditions, which cannot be ignored.

Emanuel Castle and his uncle, Derek Alston, interact in such a way as to have a profound impact on their family. In many ways Derek is the keeper of the traditions..... in a significant fashion. He carries with him the power of the great *nyangas* and *babalowas* and *houngans*. He is the root worker, the maker of sense, the creator of the word, and the giver of instructions. Actually, what Duane Smith shows is the ever present need for spirituality in the trials of life.

As the youngest member of a well-to-do family, with a father who is a first term U.S. Congressman and who is absent from the family in Washington, D.C., doing the country's business, Manny finds that his uncle is his only mainstay in culture. His mother, a lawyer, while active in the family and her profession, is unable to give the insights and cultural history provided by the rather eccentric Derek.

Indeed, Derek should not be seen here as a negative force, but as a counter to the negation of life in America without an anchor. In a real sense, the power of this book is the fact that Derek represents continuity and power, and this tradition should not be viewed as negative. Thus, the novel, with its emphasis on the values and principles which have governed African life in America for a long time, is an insightful look at disintegration in the personal and family sense, as well as the value of using what we (intuitively) know.... to overcome the difficulties of such disintegration.

Manny goes through personal trauma and psychological problems in much the same way as African Americans may be said to have gone through a series of traumas and problems. However, the only way out of these difficulties is the appeal to the centering values of the traditions. Thus, a bond is developed between the young man in personal trouble, and the uncle with the key to the centering process. It remains the <u>only</u> way back to ourselves, and away from the disillusionment and hopelessness..... to which we as a people, all too often succumb. The door is wide open, and we must not lock ourselves out of our own sanity....... by refusing to touch the base of our tradition.

In the end, we know that the traditions, the teachings, the philosophy of Derek, represent the wisdom that has been handed down from generation to generation. In *The Nubian,* Duane Smith, in his first novel, explores this most powerful element of connectedness. The lesson that **must** be learned is that we are only victims if we allow ourselves to be victims; we are chosen.... if we choose our traditions.

Dr. Molefi Kete Asante
Chairman, Department of
African-American Studies
TEMPLE UNIVERSITY
Philadelphia, Pennsylvania

CONTENTS

Duane Smith

Temple of Ramses - Abu Simbel - NUBIA

The story our world's been waiting for!

The Nubian
a novel

Azimuth

The AZIMUTH PRESS • College Park, GA. 30349

foreword by Dr. Molefi Asante
edited by Myra B. Moon

Prologue

Narrative: 2016 A.D. Manny, age 36

 Even today, almost twenty years later, the headlines still seem scandalous. **'SENATOR'S BROTHER-IN-LAW CONVICTED FOR INTERNATIONAL DRUG TRAFFICKING!'** It's so ironic..... how things turned out for him. The media has always manipulated events for their own purposes, and in so doing, established the tenor of the times. After all, what they do _is_ a business; their mission is to generate interest on the part of the masses. His intent was to help those who couldn't, or wouldn't, help themselves. But the people who had him put away, those who were strongly influenced by this same media, knew nothing at all about the man. But I knew Derek!

It seems funny now. The recollections of him are stronger than ever. But it's not so much the person I recall; it's more his presence, that tremendous sense of wonder he exposed me to.

I haven't seen Derek for more than eighteen years now, and to this day I still have no idea why he didn't appeal his conviction. I know Asia and Mom thought he was a lunatic. But I never did. He always seemed perfectly normal to me. I guess what struck me most about him was the way he carried himself; he had a regal kind of quality. Despite that, he was the most humble, down to earth person I know.

We could talk for hours on end. Actually, Derek would talk and I would listen, which wasn't an insignificant accomplishment by any means. At that age, my attention span was..... well.... let's just say I wasn't an active listener. But the moment he began to speak, it was as if I became absorbed.... enthralled..... in some kind of trance. For sure, I asked lots of questions. And I didn't always understand his answers. Yet somehow, something inside me felt compelled by his words, even though at the time I had no way to comprehend the enormity of the truth we shared.

"Manny", he'd say capturing me with a most serious gaze, "things are not always what they seem. Look beyond the obvious.... beyond what's presented to you, and you'll discover a world that's entirely different from that of everyday perception." Over the months we spent together, he progressively sensitized me to the limitations of our normal experiences. And in so doing, he created in me a sense of expectation; a lively anticipation of even the most mundane activities of each new day.

Some of the things he did appeared clairvoyant or magical to the others, and I know that unnerved Mom and Gloria immensely. But what he was dealing with had about as much in common with magic..... as the oceans have with a reflecting pond. Technically, I guess you could consider them both bodies of water. I guess. But that's right about where any comparison ends.

Everything wasn't esoteric or obscure with him either. Derek had a practical side, too. He enjoyed working with his hands, and seemed to be most content digging in the garden with Enrico. I was never interested in gardening; I was too busy becoming the next Michael Jordan. God, how I loved basketball! I remember asking him one day why any intelligent human being would ever want to be a farmer. Well.... it was one of the few times that I ever recalled him scolding me, saying I should "... never.... ever be ashamed to work the land, to work with your hands. This country was built on the sweat and backs of our people, and the highest form of work.... is the ability to produce something of quality, to create." I haven't forgotten.

It was five years ago that I came out of my wheelchair. Understandably, the doctors were amazed. There was no way I would ever walk again, according to the body of medical science. But it didn't surprise me. Derek always said that once we learned how to 'Grip the Spirit', and bring that plane of existence.... into the world of material things, then nothing was impossible!

And not only were all things possible but it was, in fact, essential for us to understand the basic relationships between the spiritual and physical realms..... in order to fulfill our potential as human beings. This is particularly true.... 'for one to meet the demands of manhood, in a society desperate for the creative power of true men; men who comprehend the totality of their existence, who possess the courage to act on what they believe, and recognize the significance of their history and culture.' He spoke of these things with such conviction, such complete abandon, that it was clear he was absolutely persuaded of their validity.

Derek treated me like his own son. It was his nature to instruct me in the ways of the real world, and it becomes more apparent everyday what an effective job he did. The lessons of cultural fellowship, the principles of spiritual power, and our essential nature as creative beings have become vivid to me. He remarked once that '... liars surrounded by the truth will eventually show themselves..... for what they are.' Conversely, Derek stood for truth, amidst the deceit and misunderstandings of those who were as close to him...... as his own family! He knew that a man with vision, a spiritual man, could accomplish the things he set his mind (and heart) to.

Through it all, he sought to reconstruct for me the broken strands of our history, with the indelible ties to our African culture. He knew that along this road was a crucial sense of cultural identity. Today, that sense of identity provides me with a self-conscious role in history and above all, a sense of my own worth....... as a man in this society. Now...... I've got to raise my own son. And I'll deliver to him the messages of his culture, the wonders of this life, the responsibilities of his birthright, and the glorious history of his people, just like Derek did for me.

He even made science and principles governing the physical world alive and interesting. I wish I'd paid more attention to his instruction in physics, and the nature of materials. Looking back now, he was completely ahead of his time in understanding vibratory patterns of matter, and the manipulation of object resonances. I'm sure he'll arrive at a way to perfect the inverse synthesis technique..... right there in his cell.

Derek took pride in his relationship to the forces of nature, not in any academic accomplishments or achievements. The entire process he developed..... was a classic example of applying spiritual insight to a real life problem. Lord knows he's a brilliant man. Probably, he should have received a Nobel Prize.... or something. Instead he ended up incarcerated...... like a common thief. I guess he knew better than anyone the contradictions that we face in this life.

Even Mom and Dad seem to have the beginnings of an understanding of what he was trying to accomplish. Actually, I think he had the most impact on my father. Once he retired from the Senate, Dad travelled on lecture tours, speaking at colleges and inner city schools..... about the importance of education as well as taking pride in our heritage. It's amazing to me! After all he's been through....... the politics, the scandal, Derek's trial and the accusations, that entire Washington scene, Dad's become very popular with the younger generation. I don't quite understand it.

All I know is that Derek helped me develop the courage to deal with my existence in all of its manifestations, never asking for anything of his own. I remember him saying, "Manny, it is important for a man of knowledge, a man of culture, to understand that all our actions occur within a spiritual context. Self-importance has no place in the life of a man seeking true knowledge; the only thing that is relevant.... is courage. Courage develops self-discipline. Self-discipline is necessary.... in order to live your convictions, to challenge the immediacy of your own death. By facing the impending nature of his death, the man of knowledge loses his sense of self-importance.'

'Once self-importance is overcome, you are on your way to a life of true freedom. Such freedom empowers you to comprehend your relationship to the whole realm of existence, to become aware of the truth in all things. Understanding the truth.... forces you to live creatively. We have been made in the image and likeness of the Creator. It is our duty to live this truth to the fullest; to be creative."

I know now that he was right!

Sometimes I wonder what I'd say if I ever saw him again. But whether I do or not really isn't important. He's shown me how to face my life with an openness, with a grounding and a heart of love, for myself and my people. The life I now lead..... is invigorated........ by the power of the cultural imperative we all share. I owe him so much.... and yet, he would tell you..... I don't owe him a thing.

It's sounds strange, but the most gratifying compliment I could ever receive, would be for someone to say to me......... that I remind them of my Uncle. That I'm just like him. *A man of culture....... a man of vision....... a Black man!*

Oh........ and by the way, he did know something about basketball! Even though he didn't talk all that much with me about it, I'd watch him from my room at night, practicing on the goal in the backyard, alone under the floodlight. I can remember it vividly. He'd start slowly just walking around. All of a sudden he'd spin to his left, fake as if someone were covering him, then go up and let it fly..... so smoothly, perfect rotation. God, he had one of the nicest jump shots I ever saw!

I miss him.

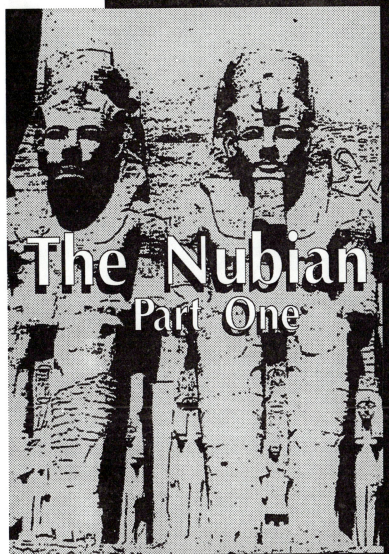

The Nubian
Part One

Atlanta: 1991   Manny, age 11

The Arrival

Normally, Tuesdays are nothing special around the Castle household. But **this** Tuesday was different.

The children were off from school, the result of a teachers convention, and for Manny it was great..... to not think about dealing with Ms. Summers in his math class. Gloria was in the kitchen making dinner, which wasn't very unusual except that for some reason, Manny didn't mind having liver. That was strange...... because he hated liver! The smell of onions was already making him wince. But Gloria promised she'd discovered a new recipe which was certain to make their Tuesday evening meal a delight. And he believed her. Talk about gullible!

There was one other thing that was a bit extraordinary that Tuesday afternoon. Asia and Manny were sitting, quietly, in the rec room watching a news program, and for once they weren't at each other's throats.... over who was going to see what on TV. The reason for their rapt attention was their father Edison, who was scheduled to be interviewed regarding his Chairmanship of the Congressional Subcommittee on Energy. As the moderator prepared to introduce him, Edison kept muttering something about superconductors, and their impact on the environment. Apparently, this was something of a big deal, as Edison was serving his first term as a Congressman from the great state of Georgia. Deidre, their mother, told the children no one thought he'd be able to hold his own with environmentalists, and lobbyists for the utilities, given he was a rookie legislator. So that afternoon's interview was his first public opportunity to prove his worth. Just as they were ready for the introductions, there was a commotion outside the house. Then the doorbell rang.

Even though Manny was anxious to hear his father's talk, he couldn't help but wonder what was happening out front. He and Asia fell into a mild debate over who would open the door, but before they could decide, they heard their mother's voice in the vestibule. "Derek! Derek! Hi Babe........ how have you been? It's so good to see you!" Manny wondered where she had come from. He knew something was strange, because his mother always waited for Gloria, or one of them, to answer the door. It was as though she appeared out of nowhere.

"Hi Family," Derek said cheerfully, stepping briskly inside. It was a beautiful spring day, clear and warm. "How is everybody?" he continued, giving Deidre a big hug. When Asia and Manny heard his voice, they rushed out to see what was going on.

There was their Mom, neatly dressed in one of her expensive tennis outfits. "I was just on my way over to the club," she announced as Asia and Manny burst in. Derek is Deidre's younger brother. Manny thought him to be in his thirties, although he didn't look like he was almost middle age. And even though Derek wasn't that tall, his broad shoulders gave him the appearance of a football player, or something. With deep set eyes and high cheekbones, he reminded Manny of a Black Indian. Not that he'd ever met any Native Americans mind you; but he HAD seen pictures. But, come to think of it, none of the Indians in the pictures Manny had seen wore a BEARD....... a scraggly one at that.

Asia would joke about the fact that she couldn't believe her mother and Derek were really part of the same family. Where Derek was dark and wide with big bones, Deidre was tall and slender, with flawless amber skin and warm brown eyes. Her hair was shiny and dark, and with it pulled back into a ponytail beneath her tennis headband, she had the appearance of a young college co-ed. Asia told Manny that their mother was a model at one time, and had done some magazine layouts before he was born. Manny always wondered what *kind* of magazines she'd modeled for. Anyway, he reasoned that they **were** related because his mother's name was Deidre, and it made sense to him that his grandparents would call their male child Derek, and their female child Deidre. Made perfect sense to Manny.

Asia would throw up her hands in disgust whenever Manny raised this theory. Because she was older (and loved to gossip), Asia just dismissed his ideas as immature and juvenile. Actually, everything Manny knew about his Uncle was courtesy of his sister. Derek had visited them once before when Manny was still a baby, but they hadn't heard much from him since. His mother spoke very little about him; Asia said that was because Derek and their father didn't get along very well. But it was obvious that a real bond existed between brother and sister.

By this time, Gloria had joined their welcoming committee sprawled about the foyer. Manny guessed Gloria was in her forties. She was still a pretty woman, with smooth brown skin, light eyes, and slightly graying hair. Asia told him Gloria was a track star in her younger days, and had made the Olympic team. She was a sprinter...... from Trinidad, he recalled.

That was always quite interesting to Manny...... because Gloria has such a big chest! He could just imagine how she must have flopped around while racing down that track, juggling as she went. He knew that women athletes now wore special bras to restrain their breasts while competing. But Gloria would need a full corset, just to be able to get into her starting blocks!

Deidre told her daughter that Gloria experienced a lot of misfortune in her life. She was married to a boxer who died of injuries he received while in the ring. He left her with little of nothing. Gloria had always wanted to be a teacher, but fortunately, she loved cooking too. Manny wasn't quite sure how she came to be with them, but his mother said they were very blessed to have her. She and Deidre really got along great; more like old and dear friends, than employer and employee. Gloria didn't stay in the servants' quarters like Enrico. She had her own bedroom there in the house. Deidre said she would like to help Gloria get her degree in education, which Manny thought was very commendable of his Mom. But he didn't know what they would do around there if she ever took another job. His mother couldn't cook a lick!

Gloria worked on keeping herself in good shape. She had an exercise bike in her room, and subscribed to a lot of health and fitness magazines. And she loved to walk around in workout clothes. No aprons or maid outfits for her! Her favorite getup was a pair of purple sweats and matching top, with hot pink high top Reeboks. Manny always wondered what her legs looked like.

"Wow, Ace! You've become quite a young woman," Derek exclaimed when he saw Asia, giving her a warm hug. "There was a time when I could pick you up with one hand; you were a 'Little Ace' then." Manny couldn't help but laugh when he heard that. Derek sounded so sincere, yet he was quite hilarious.

"Don't embarrass me, Uncle D," Asia retorted. "I'll be seventeen in November."

"Don't worry, Missy," said Gloria in her direct, matter-of-fact sort of way. Manny remembered his Grand-dad telling him that people from the Caribbean have a knack for '....cutting through all the crap...' and 'getting right to the point'. Well that description certainly fit Gloria nicely. "We're your family," she emphasized. "It's too late for you to try and act embarrassed in front of us. Isn't that right, Derek?" Gloria shot a furtive glance at him and winked. Her little act seemed to put them both at ease.

Asia was really quite attractive, even for a sister. Of course Manny would never let her know he thought so. She looked a lot more like their father than Manny did. She had more of his features and mannerisms. And Asia definitely got along much better with Edison, than she did with her mother. Daddy's little girl and all that. She had some very fine friends, too. But.... alas, to them Manny was just a kid, just Ace's kid brother. What a drag for him!

Before he could fully lament his kid brother status, Deidre unceremoniously interrupted Manny's little pity party. "D, this is Emanuel," she said, introducing her son. "He was just a baby the last time you saw him." Manny hated her calling him 'Emanuel'; it seemed so formal.... like he was being introduced as a speaker at a benefit, '.....and now, ladies and gentlemen. Please join me in welcoming the Atlanta businessman of the year..... the Honorable Emanuel Aaron Castle......."

It WAS a nice name, he mused; Grand-dad once told him that Emanuel meant 'GOD with us' in the Bible. Great! But what bothered Manny most....... was that there weren't any BASKET-BALL stars named Emanuel. At least none he'd heard of.

Derek reached out and shook Manny's hand. Those deep set eyes fixed on him, and for a moment Manny had the strangest sensation, as though his uncle were looking right through him. The feeling took Manny completely by surprise. While he was still absorbed in this stupor-like condition, Derek greeted him. "Manny, it's REALLY great to see you. Deidre has spoken about you so much! I can tell you're becoming quite a young man. Make your Mom proud of you!" Again, it amazed Manny how sincere his uncle seemed. He'd been around grown ups before who would say things like that, just to be nice. Mostly his mother's friends, who were always more worried about how one looked or how one dressed. All that formality got on Manny's nerves. C'mon people.......... GET CURRENT!

But Derek immediately made him feel as though he accepted him just the way he was..... which was great because at the moment Manny looked like a bum; cut off jeans, old sweatshirt, hi-tops; LIKE A BUM! "Manny..... I've got something for you," Derek said, becoming more animated. Quickly, he pulled a videocassette out of his bag. "Deidre says you enjoy basketball, so I thought you might like this."

WOW! It was Michael Jordan's newest highlights video. Manny had wanted to tape the Chicago-Atlanta game on TV the night before, but he couldn't get the VCR to work properly. He LOVED Michael! Manny also liked the commercials he did with Spike Lee. But this video was supposed to be the HYPE!

"Thanks a lot, Uncle D!" he gushed. Out of the corner of his eye, Manny noticed Asia squirming nervously. He could tell she was hurt.... because Uncle Derek hadn't brought her anything. But that wasn't his problem, was it? "Mom, can I go look at this? PLEASE?" Manny was ready to see Michael right away, and he must have sounded as though he were pleading with her.

"Of course, dear. Derek would be disappointed if you didn't." Manny always felt his mother liked him more than Asia. Part of it was something of a rivalry that develops between a Mother and a Daughter...... around the time the Daughter thinks she's become a woman. It affects the Mother because she remembers how beautiful and innocent she was at that age, and she secretly resents the emerging womanliness of the Daughter, since it makes her feel old and past her usefulness. And the Daughter feels it's her right of passage to out-woman the Mother..... just to show she's arrived. Manny received all this carnal knowledge courtesy of his friend, that renowned ladies man Haskell Lee Jones, who told him he read all about it...... in the latest issue of his Mom's Essence magazine.

"I didn't forget you either, Ace," said Derek, smiling as he revealed a large spray bottle of women's cologne from his black leather bag.

Now it was Deidre's turn to be envious. She really loved that stuff. "Don't you worry, Missy; we'll be sharing that cologne," she snapped at her daughter.

"But Mom....... Uncle D brought it for ME," Asia protested.

"Yes he did. But you know that any cologne that comes into THIS house..... has to be tested by me, personally."

Derek was shaking with laughter; Gloria was just shaking her head; and there were Mother and Daughter fussing over that stupid bottle of smelly perfume. *Women are SO strange,* Manny thought. As for him, he was ready to see Michael soar across his TV screen! Derek vainly attempted to intervene on behalf of his niece.

"Deidre..... you should leave Ace alone. She's a young woman now, and you can't continue to treat her like a child."

Manny never called his sister Ace. *That's a good name for a truck driver, but not his sister!* Deep down, he really liked her. But for the past few months it seemed like she and Deidre would start arguing over the least little things.

"We'll discuss this later, Missy," Deidre grunted, temporarily ending the controversy. Asia always hated it when her mother called her Missy; she thought it was such a childish thing to be called. It was OK for Gloria to call her that though. Well..... maybe she didn't like her saying it either, but Asia KNEW Gloria didn't care whether she liked it or not. *Boy! WOMEN! What a HEADACHE! They're even worse when they're not really women, when they just think they are. SEMI-WOMEN!* Anyway, Asia felt she'd earned a minor victory. As she left, she merrily sprayed the cologne, as though it were air freshener.

Immediately, Gloria turned her attention to their new guest. "Derek, you must be HOT in that getup," she said, looking him up and down, her light eyes flaring.

Derek couldn't help but laugh. He was dressed in a black canvas jump suit, with velcro snaps at the neck and across the chest, heavy black leather boots, and gold zippers all over. "This is my motorcycle outfit," Derek answered, attempting to reassure Deidre and Gloria. "I've been riding all night, and it gets pretty cold out there on the open road."

He looked like he belonged on the Space Shuttle or something. Manny noticed white streak marks on his sleeves and shoulders. It looked like the kind of white residue which results from something burning, maybe ashes. He quietly wondered what could have caused that, but quickly decided he'd already missed too much Michael-time.

"See you later, Big D; thanks for the tape," Manny said turning to depart. He didn't know why he had called his uncle that.

But Derek laughed it off and said, "I'll see you later Manny!" Manny took an immediate liking to his uncle. He couldn't tell exactly why, but Derek just seemed to be very relaxed and easy to talk to.

As the welcoming committee dispersed, Deidre's inquisitiveness took over. "So Derek Andrew Alston, why don't you tell me...... what brings you to Atlanta?" she said, taking Derek's arm as they walked toward the living room. Gloria went back to her affairs in the kitchen. "Mother said a few months ago that you might be coming this way."

"Well, Dee-Dee," Derek answered "after all that's happened the past year or so, I felt the need to relax and wind down a little, so I decided to take some time off. I got this brainstorm to come down...... and visit you for the summer. Do you mind?"

"Well..... you at least could have called first." Deidre was so formal about people dropping in, even family. She always had to have everything in order.... just right. Even her mother always called to be sure it was OK. Not Derek. But she WAS glad to see him, since he was her baby brother and hadn't seen him in years.

"Actually, it'll be nice to have a man around the house. With Edison gone so much I....... Oh, Dammit D!" she exclaimed. "I forgot all ABOUT Edison. Come on upstairs. I was taping an interview of his when you came!" Deidre took off up the stairs. Derek grudgingly followed.

The house was very elegant, what with its long winding staircase and oval foyer, in the great Southern tradition. At one time it belonged to the Hinton family, one of the country's first Black millionaires. Deidre's taste was impeccable; a large crystal chandelier hung from the second story ceiling into the foyer. Original relief sculpture and tapestry graced the walls. The floors were waxed and spotless. Gloria was a supreme housekeeper, as well as a loyal and trusted friend.

Outside was a mess. Enrico, the gardener, had been ill off and on for months and hadn't been able to keep the grounds in order. This really bothered Deidre. She couldn't stand the lawn not being meticulously manicured. The property was enormous; almost ten acres, with large groves of dogwoods, and a small forest of pines in the back, beyond the servants' quarters and the bath house. The rows of weeping willows in front gave the house the look of the old Antebellum mansion it once was.

Derek didn't have much use for Edison. He thought politics was a needless profession, followed closely by law. He felt Deidre could have done much better for herself in the soul-mate department. Never mind the fact that Edison's father was one of Atlanta's most prominent lawyers, and that he provided for Deidre and the children very well.

However, Deidre was no slouch herself. Summa cum laude graduate from Spelman; J.D. from Emory Law School; a growing real estate law practice in Buckhead. Their father was a professor of engineering and physics at Drexel University in Philadelphia. If anything, it was Deidre's intelligence, savvy, and yes, good looks that helped Edison get to where he was. Most of all, Derek quietly resented the fact that Edison didn't spend much time with Manny. Though he never discussed it, Derek always wanted a son... but his marriage broke up before that could happen.

Deidre did know how tough the divorce had been on him, which was one of the reasons she agreed to let him stay. She also knew that Edison wouldn't appreciate Derek being around their house for any length of time. Even though Deidre dearly loved her brother, she was aware of how strange he could be, and to an extent could understand why her former sister-in-law left him. She was determined not to allow Derek's eccentricity to get the best of her.

But Deidre also wanted someone to talk to about the things on HER mind. About the fact that she really didn't enjoy the political life, and that she suspected Edison had another woman in Washington. She could always talk to Derek..... because he was such a good listener. She appreciated an objective male perspective, not someone who would pay attention to her simply because they had more carnal intentions on their mind.

Meanwhile, Manny was hard at work, absorbed by his video. He decided to call his boy, Haskell, to come over and enjoy it with him. Haskell was slightly older than Manny and although they were pretty good friends, Haskell's agenda was oriented more towards pretty girls..... than point guards.

"Hello?" It was a woman's voice at the other end of the line, but it didn't sound like Haskell's mother.

"Hi, this is Manny. Is Haskell there?"

"Just a minute, Manny. Has-KELL! Telephone!"

A lot of people thought Haskell was such a nice guy and a gentleman, but Manny knew better. "Hello, this is Haskell Lee Jones speaking."

Manny couldn't understand why he tried to sound so damn important all the time. "Yo, Has...... this is Manny. My uncle just came down and he brought me the new Michael Jordan video. Why don't you come over and check it out?"

"Manny, I ain't got time for that now. Man, if you want to see some videos, I found a couple of my Dad's X joints and..... I'm over here havin' a GOOD time. You ought to see these tapes

Manny! They're doin' everything..... screwin'..... and suckin'..... and big titties and.... everything.......YEAH!"

"But Has man...... this is MICHAEL. You can watch that X-rated stuff anytime."

"Manny..... GET A LIFE! I can watch Michael Jordan anytime! You need to be over here with me. You could learn something. Then Asia's friends might treat you with a little more respect.... if they knew, you knew, how to sa-TIS-fy their needs....... like I know!"

"Haskell...... you're drunk..... if you believe any of those high school girls think about you for more than three seconds. Anyway, you certainly don't have anything they want..... or can't get! Don't waste your time! Later, Haskell Lee." CLICK!

Manny was tempted to call Haskell's mother and let her know he was sneaking his Dad's videos. Then it occurred to him ..... that SHE might not know his father had 'em. Oh well...... that wasn't his problem. Oooooo.......... a 360 degree, double pump, left handed slam..... DO IT Michael!

While all the activity accompanying Derek's arrival was taking place, Edison had been expounding on the virtues of the energy committee's initiatives on superconductor research during his interview. As Deidre watched intently, Derek picked up the conversation. "You know, Dee-Dee, Edison sounds like he knows what he's talking about," he said in a more than slightly sarcastic tone. "Does he really have any idea?"

"Of course he does!" she responded, defending her husband. "Actually, he's got a staff of advisors who make sure they keep him up to date on the latest research information." Deidre knew quite well of what she spoke. For the past several months she had been spending time off and on with Lance Powell, one of the key members of Edison's advisory staff. On the surface, it was to keep abreast of Edison's activities, but lately she'd realized that she found herself very much attracted to Lance, and enjoyed his company.

Suddenly, out of the blue, Derek said, quite matter-of-factly, "I understand this Lance Powell is supposed to be a real hotshot on Capitol Hill."

Deidre was shocked! The comment startled her so much she completely lost track of what Edison was saying. How the hell did HE know about Lance? She quickly searched her mind for some clue as to how Derek could have any idea of who Lance was. Deidre thought that perhaps one of her friends, whom she confided in, had leaked some information. *I'll bet that HEIFER Carmen told him we had lunch the last time I was in Washington,* thought Deidre. *Wait a minute, Derek doesn't know Carmen, does he? What the hell is going on here?* Deidre reasoned with herself.

Derek continued, as if anticipating her questions. "Don't worry, Dee-Dee, I won't say anything.... just be careful. I care about you. I don't want to see you get hurt." He paused to survey her reaction, then mentioned softly, "I'm going downstairs to take a shower. See you later."

Deidre's expression was left somewhere between amazement and embarrassment. Her initial reaction was to ask Derek how he knew so much about Lance.... but she didn't want to give herself away. Frankly, she didn't know what to do. There she sat, mouth agape, as Derek disappeared down the stairs. Edison's interview didn't seem the least bit important anymore.

Downstairs, Derek stopped in on Manny, who was still watching the video. "Man-NAY! How's the tape?" Derek gave him a high five as he sat down.

"This is great, Uncle D. Do you know anything about basketball?"

"Well..... I used to play a little when I was younger."

Manny continued to talk, ignoring his response. "I tried to get my friend Haskell to come over, but he said he was too busy."

"Yeah, Haskell is too busy looking at GIRLS," Derek replied. He stopped for a moment to catch Michael slam down a monster tomahawk dunk. "You know, Manny, did you ever think about...... what it must feel like...... to **be** a basketball?" Derek looked over at him with a very unusual expression.

Manny realized Derek was right. Haskell WAS too busy thinking about girls. He liked girls too, but they seemed to be more trouble than they were worth. Just then, it occurred to him that Derek didn't know Haskell, he couldn't know Haskell. How could he? Manny had just talked to him, maybe ten minutes ago.

But before Manny could voice his question about Has... he felt a strange sensation overcome him. Everything seemed to move in slow motion. He felt as though he were being stretched..... twisted.... like a rubber band, and drawn toward the television, where Michael was performing his magic. The next thing Manny sensed..... was that suddenly he was in the hands of Michael Jordan, bouncing..... and bouncing..... up and down..... just like..... a BASKETBALL!

WAIT a minute! He was just watching Michael on the videotape, and now...... Manny felt like he was being dribbled, up and down like a basketball. But Michael was on TV! Then it dawned on him. Somehow, someway he had been drawn..... into the TV set...... as a BASKETBALL! *Too Weird!!* It was a very strange sensation, to say the least. Manny could tell he was awake, but he had no orientation. Yet he didn't get dizzy, or feel any pain. There was just an awkward feeling..... of inflation.

"Don't let him DUNK you, Manny!" He could vaguely make out Derek's figure in the rec room through the TV screen, yelling at him (not to get dunked). Derek was jumping up and down, laughing and screaming wildly.

Before he knew it, Michael took him (the basketball) behind his back, then between his legs, and with a graceful sweeping movement, cuffed him at the wrist and took off from the foul line..... up..... up..... up and whipped him down....... through the hoop!

The next thing Manny remembered was waking up from what seemed like a deep sleep. When he awakened, he could see that he was still in the rec room sitting next to Derek, with a Bo Jackson NIKE ad flashing across the TV screen.

"SOME tape..... huh Manny?" laughed Uncle D.

Manny looked around the rec room. Everything was normal, but all he could think of was the sensation of feeling inflated, like a basketball. But then he wondered, did that really happen? Or was he dreaming? And what about Haskell? Derek doesn't know Haskell. How could he? Meanwhile, Derek was getting a big kick out of Manny's obvious perplexity, and laughing his head off. "Manny, I'll see you later," he said between guffaws. "I'm pretty rank..... and I need a shower." That said, he was gone.

Manny kept wondering how he got inside the TV, and on that tape. And he couldn't forget about Haskell. He felt very confused.

He was certain about one thing though...... Derek had something to do with all this!

Just then, Gloria's voice rang out, "DINNER EVERY-BODY!"

At that moment, Manny really looked forward to Gloria's liver. It seemed like the only thing that was immediately familiar (albeit distasteful) to him. But the smells from the kitchen were different than usual. Good smells. In fact, Manny couldn't ever remember smelling cocoanut, or curry, or the aroma of garlic so thick in the air.

The arousal of his hunger momentarily made him forget about the basketball business, about Haskell, **and** Derek. Gloria was right! Manny was completely psyched for this liver dinner. And he was so HUNGRY. He felt like he'd just played a tough game of one-on-one. In a strange way, he really had!

When he got to the kitchen, Asia was already there gossiping with Gloria about Mrs. Burris down the street. Boy! Asia certainly smelled good. She had taken a bath and tried out some of her cologne. It was so nice! Deidre came in looking very angry. Manny was ready for her to start in with his sister about the cologne, but she didn't even notice how good Asia smelled. Her mind was definitely elsewhere.

Just as everyone finished saying grace, Manny noticed two bruise marks across his forearms. He couldn't figure out where they came from..... until he recalled the basketball scene and the video. Then the events of the afternoon returned and Manny couldn't contain himself. He started telling everybody about watching Michael on the tape, and the basketball, and how Derek read his mind about Haskell.... and everything!

Asia and Gloria were laughing and laughing. They thought the excitement of the new tape had become too much for Manny

They didn't believe a word he said. "Maybe you need to see a psychiatrist, my brother," kidded Asia. Her semi-serious tone even made him laugh out loud. But Deidre wasn't laughing. No one could tell what was bothering her.

Finally, Gloria decided to ask, "What's wrong, Ms. Castle?"

"Oh, Gloria, it's that DAMN Carmen. You think you can confide in friends, but you really can't trust anybody these days." Unlike Manny, Deidre had convinced herself that Derek wasn't a mind reader. Somehow he had discussed Lance Powell with Carmen. But she couldn't figure out how Derek knew Carmen. Could she be an old girlfriend, or something?

"Well, one thing's for sure Ms. Castle," Gloria replied, quickly changing the subject. "It's surely been interesting around here..... since your brother arrived!"

Right then, Derek wandered in, wearing scraggly jeans and a T-shirt. "Hi, family! How is everything?" he asked with a broad smile flashing across his face. Everyone just looked at him. Gloria offered Derek a seat and invited him to taste her liver.

"Thank you, Gloria, but I'm a vegetarian." Derek went to the refrigerator and pulled out an apple. "Dee-Dee, do you know you forgot your tennis match?" he said, shifting the attention to his sister. Deidre didn't say a word. All she could do was stare..... as though she didn't want to say anything in front of the rest of them.

Finally she blurted out, "At least eat some vegetables. It's impolite to sit at the table...... and not taste what has been cooked. Your manners are terrible Derek!"

"You're right, Deidre," Derek acquiesced, avoiding any further controversy. "Please forgive my manners Gloria." He then turned halfway toward Manny and whispered, "You know Manny, your Mom is such a BUPPIE. But I love her..... like my own SISTER!"

Manny wasn't quite sure what a buppie was. He was about to ask, when the phone rang. Asia sprang up to answer it, thinking it was for her. "It's for you, Manny," she said as she sat down.

Manny was on the phone for a couple of minutes. When he returned to the table, Derek inquired, "Well, who was it Bud?" He had a strange looking smile on his face, like he knew exactly what Manny was going to say.

"It was Haskell," he announced as if on cue. "His mother caught him with some adult videos, and put him on punishment for two weeks." Derek and Manny both broke into hysterical laughter. The two of them laughed so hard they nearly choked. Manny felt that no one else saw the humor in the whole thing, although he noticed Gloria covering her mouth, and her chest jiggling along with them. That only served to make the scene that much more hilarious to Derek and his nephew.

Deidre, still preoccupied, had seen enough. "I'll leave you here...... with the two children, Gloria," she said, smirking at Derek and Manny as she got up.

"Mrs. Castle, you haven't finished your dinner," Gloria protested.

But Deidre was determined. "It'll have to wait. I'm going to call that hussy Carmen, right now, and give her a piece of my mind."

It was all Derek could do to get himself together, he was laughing so hard. "I love her dearly, but that woman is such a BUPPIE!" Derek repeated as Deidre went on her way. Now Asia joined in the laughter and before long Gloria was right in there with them, just laughing her head off.

Manny had to admit to Gloria that the liver did taste great! And he also had to agree with her, that things certainly had become quite interesting since Derek arrived. Every time Manny thought

about Haskell, he just CRACKED UP. It was really a great day.
And somehow he knew..... that all this was only the beginning!

Chapter 2

The Importance of Culture

The return to school was something of a drag for Manny, even though a lot was happening. It's amazing how relaxed one can get in a week and a half off. The teachers informed the students that examiners from the State would be in to observe, and they should be on their best behavior. On top of that, achievement tests were going to be administered, to determine how effective the faculty had been..... in shoving all sorts of information down their throats. Manny's best subject was history, but history wasn't on the California Achievement Tests. Mostly English and math.

Things got pretty intense those first couple of weeks back. Now Manny knew why students were given a spring break. Everyone needed a rest, just to make it until the end of the school year.

Besides everything else going on around him, Manny was trying out for the basketball team. Even though it was May, Coach held tryouts to identify the players he wanted in the fall. He then made sure they enrolled in basketball camps or summer leagues to prepare for the upcoming season. Manny was trying to make the team as a guard. It was the first year he was eligible, and he was determined to make it. Manny could handle the ball well enough, but his shooting needed work.

While home one afternoon, he was out back practicing, shooting at the hoop his father had constructed for him, when his uncle happened by.

Since he'd arrived, Derek had made a point of working on the grounds because Enrico hadn't been able to as a result of his illness. Derek always seemed to be grimy from digging and handling so much yard work.

"Hey, Bud. What do you think you're doing?" Derek asked innocently enough. Manny was sure his uncle knew he was trying out for the team, but he played along anyway.

"Uncle D, there are only a few days left till spring practice starts. I'm trying to make our JV team this year. It's my first chance to tryout. I've got to practice my shooting and ball handling."

Derek watched for a few minutes. Then he put down his roto tiller, and looked at Manny very seriously. "Manny, how do you expect to get any better playing in your backyard? You need some competition."

"Well, Haskell and I play sometimes. And when Asia's boyfriends come over, they play with me. How about you, Uncle D? You know how to play don't you?" Manny thought he would attack his ego a bit.

"Manny, Haskell and Asia's boyfriends are not what you need. Aren't there any playgrounds around here? Don't you ever play ball with guys like..... the Glider, and Snake, and Savannah Red, guys with nicknames.... on the PLAYGROUND? That's where you really learn the game."

Manny thought for a moment. The nearest public basketball courts were in Kellum Park, but he never recalled seeing anyone playing out there. "There aren't any playgrounds nearby. The closest one is in Kellum Park, and there's never anyone out there. I guess I'd have to go downtown, Uncle D."

"Well, all I know is you won't be ready to make your team playing around back here. Besides, who put up this basket? I'll bet your father did it, didn't he?" Derek stared at the goal strangely.

Manny hadn't paid attention before, but he immediately noticed the rim of the basket was tilted to the right. No wonder his shooting needed work. "How am I gonna get to the playground?" he asked, not really expecting an answer.

Derek had picked up the roto tiller, ready to go back to work. "Ever hear of a bus, Manny?" With that, he was off to defeat another dried up flower bed.

Manny kept practicing that evening, but what Derek said stuck with him that night and the next day in school. He was coming out of the cafeteria line when he heard someone call, "Manny, Manny, over here!" It was Haskell and a few of his friends. He really didn't feel like being bothered with Haskell, but since he'd already seen him, he felt obliged to stop.

"Manny , this is Carl and that's Big Dog," announced Haskell as he made the introductions. Carl was a tall, muscular, dark skinned guy, very athletic looking. Big Dog, on the other hand, was small and kind of scrawny. Manny wondered where he had gotten his name from.

"What's up, Haskell.... I haven't seen you in a while," he asked, just to break the ice. Manny knew he'd been on punishment since the video incident, but he also knew Haskell wouldn't let his boys know about that.

"I've been laying low for awhile," Haskell responded, lying through his teeth. "I'm trying to get prepared for these achievement tests. My Dad said I can get a motor bike if I do well. Carl and Big Dog are actors; they're trying out next week for the production of Othello."

"Yeah," grunted Big Dog. "All the women like guys with talent, right CarlTON?"

Carl nodded, as he inhaled half of his cheeseburger. Manny changed the subject quickly. "Coach Anderson is gonna let me try out for the spring team. I'm working on my game. We need to play some one-on-one Haskell." Even as he said that, Manny was still thinking about Derek's advice.

"Manny, I'm gonna be real busy this week. Plus, I'm going to a party Saturday. One of Big Dog's friends' sister. Sorry, I ain't gonna have any time for basketball. By the way, how's Asia?"

Manny thought, good ol' Haskell. Same one track mind, as always.

"Who's Asia?" Carl asked, taking a break from his fries. He was pretty soft spoken for a big guy.

Normally, Manny would have gotten angry at Haskell for starting with him about Asia, but he was too preoccupied that afternoon for Haskell to bother him. "She's my sister. She's a junior in high school."

"And fine as she can be," offered Has. "I think she likes me, too." He smoothed the little growth on his upper lip. "It's the moustache ya know, fellas." Even Carl and Big Dog thought that was funny. They all started laughing at the same time.

Big Dog jumped on his case right away. "Yeah, right Haskell. You're such a powerful ladies man." Everyone was having a good time..... at Haskell's expense.

"Hey Manny," Carl broke in, "there are some good runs downtown; off Ralph McGill, near the Civic Center. You ought to go down there after school sometimes. Tell them Carlton sent you."

Manny liked Carlton. He seemed to be more serious than the other two clowns. Of course, Manny didn't want to let on that he had never been downtown by himself; that he really didn't know how to get down there. And he thought Carlton might have sensed his dilemma.

Right on time, Carlton started giving Manny the directions. "Just take the subway down to the Civic Center stop. The park is three blocks away, on Ralph McGill, just past the Civic Center. Maybe I'll see you there." Carlton was a nice guy, really helpful.

"Maybe I will see you, Carlton," Manny answered. This was pretty exciting. The playground had been on his mind since last night with Derek. He decided he was going down there tomorrow after school.

Just then a girl came up to the table. "Hi, Haskell, how are you?" she cooed, smiling sweetly. "You haven't called me in a while. Where have you been?"

"Well, fellas, time for me to get moving," Manny announced as he got up to leave. "Nice meeting you guys." He couldn't resist the urge to spill some dirt on Haskell, so Manny leaned over to the young lady and whispered, "Ask Haskell about his videos." She looked at him rather strangely. As Manny walked away, he could hear the laughter from Carl and Big Dog, while Haskell pitifully attempted to explain what Manny had mentioned.

"I'm gonna get you for this, Manny!" Haskell yelled across the cafeteria. All in all, Manny thought it had been a good lunch.

The next day right after school, Manny hopped the bus to the Brookwood MARTA station. The train ride was very pleasant, down through town past Lenox Square Mall, and the Arts Center station and finally, he got off at the Civic Center stop. Interestingly enough, as Manny was coming down the ramp, in the parking lot he noticed a black Mercedes coupe with a maroon interior. It looked just like his mother's car! He was petrified. She was the last person he wanted to see. She would never understand what he was doing downtown on a Wednesday afternoon.

Manny raced through the parking area, dribbling as fast as he could. He stopped at the corner of Piedmont and Ralph McGill. Manny looked back and saw his mother and a man getting into her car. As soon as the light turned green he took off, sprinting toward the park. He hoped she hadn't seen him.

At the park, several groups of guys were shooting around, getting ready to play. Manny wandered over to one of the side courts. There were five guys there and they needed a sixth for three on three. "Hi," Manny said somewhat timidly. "You need one more?" No one said anything for a few minutes, they just kept shooting, joking and ribbing one another. Finally, one of the taller guys came up to him.

"Yo, Homeboy..... you got a game?" He was tall and wiry, with long arms. "You must be nice, with those new Air Jordans...... and that new ball."

Deidre had bought Manny the sneakers a couple of weeks ago. He hadn't worn them much. It was then he remembered the conversation at lunch the day before. "I'm Manny. Carlton said that there were some good runs down here."

The tall guy broke into a big grin. "I'm Snake. Carlton is my cousin. He sent you down here, huh? Awright.... you're gonna run with me." He turned to the others. "Yo! Let's run," he said. "This is Manny. Me, Manny and The Glider against Kev, Savannah, and Money. Twenty-one game. Let's go!"

Manny was amazed. It was obvious Snake was the leader of the group. He seemed to be older than the others. Everyone was bigger than Manny. But what Derek had told him was pressing on his mind. These were the same names his uncle mentioned a few days ago. How could he know who these guys were? Manny hadn't told anybody about his conversation with Carlton, or about his plans to come downtown.

Just then The Glider came over and said, "Snake and I can score. You play good defense and stick Savannah..... and we'll win." There were more players coming. Soon it would be three deep out there. If you didn't win, you sat down.

Manny was a little surprised by how he played. Snake and The Glider were smooth. Manny ran and hustled. He got a couple of steals, and worked the ball inside whenever he could. "Good pass, Man-NAY!" exclaimed Snake on a behind the back bounce pass Manny made after a steal. This WAS a lot different than playing at home.

They split the first two games. In the third game, things got more intense. Manny was fouled by Savannah on a drive. "FOUL," he called.

"We don't play that funny stuff down here, pretty boy. No harm, no foul," Kevin commanded. "Take it up top!"

Manny thought he had been fouled, but he wasn't going to argue, so they continued to play. There was more banging and shoving as the game got close to the end. Savannah stole the ball from Snake and was driving to the basket for an uncontested layup. Manny reacted, went up and fouled him pretty hard across the head. "Good foul, Man-NAY!" he heard The Glider say.

Savannah didn't feel the same way. Before Manny knew it, Savannah turned and swung a wild right hand at him. He caught Manny right in the eye. "What's the matter with you man?" Snake glowered at Savannah.

Savannah was hot. "Come on, let's see what this punk knows!" Manny's eye obviously ached, but his pride hurt more. He wasn't quite sure what happened next, but Manny flung himself at Savannah, punching, and screaming, and biting. Savannah landed a couple of good shots, but he whirled around and kicked him..... right in the balls! The next moment, it seemed as though the entire playground had jumped in the fight. Bodies were flying everywhere. Manny remembered being in a big pile. Then he felt someone take a sneaker off of his foot.

At that point, he felt someone pulling him out of the pile. It was Snake. "Yo, Manny. You better get out of here, now man!"

"But somebody got my SHOE," Manny protested.

"Forget it, Manny." he implored. "Just get out of here. I'll hold Savannah and the rest of them off. You played a good game. Now BEAT IT!"

Manny gamely made it back to the MARTA station, just as the train arrived. From the platform, he could see police cars pulling into the park. He was a mess. One shoe, blood running down the side of his face, a big hole in his shirt. Right then, Manny realized he had left his basketball. Even though he was sore, Manny was more disturbed by the thought of having to explain all of this when he got home. And he'd lost his basketball!

It was nearly dark when he got to the house. Inside, Gloria was warming up dinner. Deidre had called to say she would be getting in late. She'd met a client downtown, and was going to stop for drinks. Asia was at her girlfriend's house.

Manny decided to sneak around the back of the house, and climb up onto the veranda. From there he could make it to his room and get himself together. The plan worked perfectly. Or so he thought. Just as he got to the bathroom, there was Gloria.

"My goodness! Man-nay, what happened to you?" She made it sound as though his head had been torn off. Then he looked in the mirror. His left eye was swollen and bleeding and beginning to shine. He did look pretty bad.

"I'm OK, Gloria. I was in a little fight." The pain was starting to get the best of him. "We don't have to mention this to Mom, do we?" Manny was groping for any way possible to avoid facing his mother, at least until he got cleaned up a bit.

"Your mother has been worried sick about you," Gloria confirmed. "She's been out this evening with a client, and she's already called three times, wanting to know where you were. Where HAVE you been?"

At that moment, Manny heard a car pulling up in the driveway. In his heart, he knew it was his mother. Uh-oh! The shit was about to hit the fan!

He had to think FAST. Gloria had cleaned him up pretty well and stopped the bleeding. "Please, Gloria, don't mention what happened to Mom. Just tell her..... I don't feel well and I'm lying down. Please. Thanks, Gloria." With that, Manny was off to his room. He jumped into bed, with half his clothes still on.

"Gloria..... Gloria," Manny heard Deidre calling from downstairs.

"Hello, Mrs. Castle. How did things go with your meeting?"

"Fine. Have you heard from Manny? This isn't like him, not to call and let us know where he is. Did you check at Haskell's?" Manny knew she sensed something was wrong.

"He came in about ten minutes ago. Said he didn't feel well, and went upstairs to bed." Manny thought, *good job Gloria! Perfect! I hope she buys it.*

"Well, that's strange," Deidre wondered out loud. "He was fine this morning. You know Gloria, this afternoon I was downtown, and I could have sworn I saw Manny at the MARTA station. I was..... wait a minute! Wait a DAMN minute!"

Manny could feel the vibrations of his mother charging up the stairs. His only hope was to pretend to be in a deep sleep. He rolled over on his left side to hide his shiner. When she walked into his room, Manny sounded like he was snoozing comfortably.

Deidre wasn't buying it. The lights flipped on. "Manny.... Manny.... wake up. Wake UP!" She shook him pretty hard.

"Hmmm.... Hmmm, Mom? Oh hi, Mom. I don't feel good. I need to sleep." He was really proud of himself. The screen actors guild would be recruiting him next. The performance appeared to be working.

"Son, what's the matter? Tell your Mother." Sometimes Manny thought she may have missed her calling. She'd make a great nurse. Deidre rubbed his head and the back of his neck. "C'mon..... tell me what's wrong." With that she tried to turn him over to talk to her, but Manny wouldn't budge from his left side. He mumbled that he didn't feel like talking, that he just needed some rest. "All right then." Deidre seemed satisfied that he really needed to sleep. *WHEW, home free.* Or so he thought. "I'll be back to check on you later." But as Deidre got up to leave, she noticed some blood on his pillow case. She grabbed Manny and pulled him up by his shoulders.

"My God, Manny! What HAPPENED to you? Gloria! GLOR-I-A!!" Deidre was screaming at the top of her lungs. The eye was swollen nearly shut now, and the bleeding had started again.

Gloria arrived with some gauze and medication. After she and Deidre stopped the bleeding, they bandaged Manny up. "All right, young man. I want the truth. What is going on here?" Whenever his mother called Manny 'young man', he knew she was serious. He had no choice but to come clean. He told her everything; about his wanting to make the basketball team, and how Derek had advised him to find some better competition, about Carlton, and Snake, and Savannah, the fight..... everything.

Deidre was incredulous. "You mean to tell me you went downtown, by yourself and didn't let us know? Manny, that is so dangerous! You could have gotten mugged, or worse!"

"But Mom, Uncle Derek is right. I DO need to play against good people if I expect to get any better!" What did he say THAT for!

His mother jumped up and nearly jerked him out of the bed. "Come with me! NOW!" she commanded. Gloria looked at him with pity. Deidre was livid.

When they got downstairs, Deidre pulled Manny into the kitchen; Gloria followed close behind. "Derek!...... DEREK........ DER-EK!!!!" she screamed out the back door. "DEREK..... GET IN HERE!" About that time, Asia and her girlfriend Geri came in the front door.

"Hi. What's going on?" inquired Asia innocently. Gloria motioned for her to keep quiet for a moment.

Geri spotted Manny's eye. "WOW," she exclaimed. "Look at your brother, Ace!"

By now, Manny's ego was hurting as much as his eye. They were all standing around the kitchen when Derek came in. He had been out in the woods near the edge of the property, and had run all the way. He looked kind of comical in his baggy work pants and sweatshirt, and he was covered with dirt from head to toe.

"What's the matter?" he panted, bursting in. He zeroed in on Manny immediately. "Wow, Manny. You got yourself quite a nice shiner there. What's the problem, Dee-Dee?"

Deidre lit into him. "What do you mean, what's the problem? Can't you see? Look at his eye! Manny says you told him to go downtown to the playground, and look at what happened. They stole his sneakers and took his basketball. He could have been killed! It's dangerous down there!" Manny felt his mother was exaggerating the situation; it wasn't Derek's fault he got into a fight. But she kept pouring it on. "Manny looks up to you. But he's a little kid! He shouldn't be running around downtown by himself. We put the basket up in the back.... so he wouldn't be in the streets all day."

Derek sighed. He squatted down and said to Manny quietly, "OK, tell me what happened, Bud." When Manny told his uncle the story, his wide smile indicated Derek wasn't mad at him. He seemed particularly amused at the fact that Manny kicked Savannah. "So.... you kicked him.... in the chungatas..... huh Manny? Good job!" His laughter was infectious. Asia and Geri started cracking up. Deidre wouldn't have any of the humor.

"Dammit, Derek! This is not funny! Wait till I tell your father, young man. And you're not going to school until that eye goes down. I'm not sending MY son to class looking like.... like.... Ray Charles!" Geri and Asia thought that was so hilarious.

"We're going to call you Ray-Ray from now on," said Asia. They were really enjoying themselves now. "Ray-Ray, Ray-Ray, Ray-Ray," they cackled.

"HUSH, Asia!" demanded Deidre. "And you're going to be responsible for Manny while he's home, Mr. Derek Alston," she proclaimed. "Gloria is too busy to keep up with the two of you. Manny felt Derek knew it was useless to argue with his Mom. She was on a roll. "Manny, eat your dinner, then get your little butt upstairs to bed. And no TV or VCR for a week, Mister." She went away muttering, "Wait till I tell your father....." Gloria put a sympathetic arm around Manny. From upstairs everyone could hear Deidre yell, "... and Derek, get your filthy behind..... out of my kitchen!"

"Good night, Ray-Ray!" the giggle sisters squawked as they left.

Fortunately, Derek was encouraging. "You really kicked him in the balls, eh? I like that. Don't worry about your Mom, Manny. She'll get over this. I'll see you tomorrow."

Upstairs, Deidre got on the phone. She couldn't get over the fact that Manny would risk his life, just because Derek said it was a good idea to practice ball at the playground. And she couldn't stand the thought of embarrassing herself in front of her friends if any of them saw Manny with his eye like that. But deep down, she was troubled most by the fact that Edison wasn't ever around to spend time with his son. Deidre acknowledged the importance of his role as a Congressman, and she was aware of the demands on his time when he got into politics. But the children needed their father..... and she needed a husband! The phone in his office rang and rang.

Finally, someone picked up. "Representative Castle's office. Can I help you?" The voice on the other end was warm and strong.

"This is Mrs. Castle. Is Edison there?" Her voice was edgy and impatient.

"Oh, hello, Mrs. Castle. This is Lance Powell. Your husband was called into a late subcommittee meeting and should return in about an hour. I was next door, working on some research. If you need me to, I'll go see if he can break away to take your call."

It was LANCE. Deidre was momentarily distracted. His tone was courteous and quite soothing. She calmed down immediately. Lance was about twenty-six and not long out of graduate school. Edison liked his drive, enthusiasm, and ambition for the political life. Lance was good, and Edison relied on him immensely. And Deidre thought he was quite good looking. Not dashing or disarmingly handsome, but quietly attractive, with a sophistication beyond his years.

"No, Lance. Don't bother him now. I was just a little upset, that's all." She really wanted to talk, but Lance had work to do.

"Is it about Manny?" Lance inquired cautiously. Deidre was quite surprised by his comment.

"How did you know that?" she responded with amazement. She was beginning to feel more relaxed now.

Lance continued, "At lunch today, Representative Castle was discussing Manny with me. He's quite proud of his son, and would love to see him enter politics when he grows up. It was a lucky guess on my part. I know I could really upset my mother when I was young. It must be hard for you, with your husband as busy as he is."

Deidre was impressed with his sensitivity. "Thank you very much Lance, for your concern. I'm sorry to interrupt your work. Please tell Edison I called."

"No trouble at all, Mrs. Castle," he responded. "I'll be certain to let the Congressman know." Deidre knew she had better get off the phone. Lance was quite a charmer.

"And Lance, please..... call me Deidre."

"Most certainly, Mrs. Cas.., I mean er, Deidre. It was very nice talking to you again. Have a good night!"

The next morning, Manny was awakened by the pounding of a hammer out back. Dinner wasn't much fun the night before, so he was starved once he woke up. His eye felt a bit better though. Manny washed and dressed quickly.

Gloria had left a couple of waffles and links of turkey sausages that Manny warmed up for breakfast. She also left him a note saying she'd be gone all morning. Deidre called to check on Manny about 9:30. He told her he was OK. She advised him to take some Tylenol if his eye started to bother him. Deidre also wanted to know where Derek was. Manny explained that he was repairing one of the posts supporting the deck. Vainly, he tried to negotiate a reprieve from the VCR moratorium. His request fell on deaf ears. Deidre was completely serious. Gloria even hid all the videotapes. Deidre promised to call back that afternoon, which was fine with him.

Manny took his reconditioned meal out onto the deck. It was a pleasant, sunny day with a small breeze. Great to be out in the fresh air. His eye didn't even feel bad. Just then, Derek bounded up the stairs. He stalked around, jumping up and down, testing his repair work.

He was in a good mood. "Hey, Bud, how's it going this morning?" Without waiting for a response, he moved right along. "I want you to know, I was very proud of you last night. It took some real intestinal fortitude to go down to the playground like you did. I hope you apply that same determination to your schoolwork."

It was reassuring for Manny to know his uncle didn't think he was crazy for getting into the fight. However, the connection between the playground and his classes wasn't at all apparent. But he thought.... so what? It was a great day. And the waffles and turkey links didn't taste too bad either.

"We're having achievement tests next week," he answered between gulps of breakfast. "I'd feel a lot better about them if there were questions on history. I like history; I'm just so-so in English. But these tests are mostly math and English."

"So, you're a history buff, eh?" Manny noticed Derek's eyes begin to shine ever so slightly. "Well..... that's good, because history may be the most important thing..... you could ever become interested in."

Derek's comment caught Manny off guard. He liked the subject, but it wasn't THAT big a deal. "Why do you say that, Uncle D?" Derek had peaked his interest.

"Because, Manny, a man without an appreciation for his history..... has no identity." He paused, to let Manny swallow a gulp of waffle, and to reflect on what he'd said. "Without an identity, he can have no direction. Without direction, you have no purpose. Without a purpose, there can be no freedom. And without freedom, you cannot live as a man. Culture is what gives history its texture, and makes it a compelling, active force."

The sun was shining brightly now, and it had gotten pretty hot. Derek was wearing a gray tank top, and his brown skin glistened in the sunlight. He had taken off his carpenter's belt with all the nails and screws and tacks in it, and sat down on the deck. Derek seemed to be enjoying the warmth of the day even more than Manny. Manny was mesmerized by him. "Go on Uncle D," he said.

Derek continued, "In the dictionary, culture is defined as 'the pursuit of breeding or education, or alternatively as the collective set of customs, beliefs, and achievements of a civilization.' It's important to know that great and complex societies, or cultures, arose in six ancient areas of the world, dating back over five thousand years to Mesopotamia and Egypt.

"The interesting thing is that these six independent civilizations were far more advanced in many ways than modern man, and all six of these great cultures arose in areas of the globe...... which today are considered 'Third World' countries."

The heat made Manny thirsty for some cold orange juice, but Derek was so interesting, he didn't want him to stop. "I never heard about any of this in my history class, Uncle D."

"I know, Manny. But that doesn't make it any less true! Sometimes you've got to be hungry and thirsty for knowledge. It's important to go beyond the obvious, to gain a real understanding of yourself and your culture. Are you thirsty, Bud?"

Manny wasn't quite certain what his uncle meant by going beyond the obvious, but this culture stuff was fascinating. As for his thirst, he WAS (thirsty)...... for something cold to drink. "Well Uncle D, I don't know about the quest for knowledge. But I could really use some cold OJ. Can I bring you something?"

Derek laughed, a deep hearty laugh. "Sure Manny," he said in a jovial tone of voice. "I'll have a nice big glass of Coke, with lemon and ice please. And when you get back, we'll explore these six cradles of civilization together."

In the kitchen, Manny found a pair of Asia's sunglasses. It was very bright outside now, so he decided to put them on. He took a tray from the cupboard, and poured a tall glass of orange juice for himself, and an oversized Coke for Derek.

When Manny stepped back outside on the deck, he was completely taken by surprise. Derek was gone. Standing over against the rail with his back to him, was a man dressed in a long, purple robe embellished with gold dragon-like patterns, and a small pillbox hat. He had a thin, braided ponytail that dangled from beneath the hat. Just as Manny was about to ask what had happened to his uncle, the mysterious visitor turned around. It was DEREK! He was transformed; sporting a thin Fu Manchu moustache and narrow eyes, but it was Derek nonetheless. He was an Asian emperor, but black. Manny almost fainted and nearly dropped the tray with their refreshments.

"Ah, Honorable Manny-san," he said as he bowed deeply. "Our first stop on the tour of ancient cultures.... is China." Manny managed to put the tray down on the table. He couldn't believe his eyes! He thought perhaps it was Asia's glasses causing him to hallucinate, so he yanked them off. But there was Derek, his uncle..... Chinese Derek, taking a long sip of lemon-fresh Coca-Cola.

"Around 1800 B.C., a rich Chinese culture developed and flourished. Some of the achievements of this age were the refinement of elaborate textile production techniques, incorporating some of the world's most valuable fabrics like fine linen and silk; a comprehensive understanding of health and wellness approaches that included such procedures as acupuncture and T'ai C'hi; and the cultivation of medicinal herbs like ginseng. Modern medical science is just beginning to appreciate the benefits of these wondrous ancient remedies."

Manny sat there, his mouth hanging wide open, unable to speak. Before he could think of what would happen next, Derek cleared his throat, arched his back like a lion, and spun around three times. On the third turn, he was transformed...... into an Inca Indian Chieftain!

"The Andes region on the Pacific coast of South America was the home of the ancient Inca civilizations, beginning around 2100 B.C....." Derek said. From there, he gave Manny a personal guided tour of each of these six great civilizations: China, 1800 B.C.; the Andes region and the great Inca civilizations, 2100 B.C.; Central America, home of the Maya and Aztec civilizations, beginning 1200 B.C.; the Indus Valley, 2500 B.C.; Mesopotamia, 3500 B.C., and finally, the great Egyptian dynasties, starting in 3200 B.C.

"Undoubtedly," Derek continued, "the greatest of these ancient cultures, both in terms of duration and influence on Greek, Roman, and ultimately Western civilizations, were the Egyptian dynasties. For some 3000 years until the conquest by Alexander the Great in 324 B.C., the Egyptian cultures dominated the politics, arts, and sciences of the world. Most of the principles governing math, physics, and the applied sciences can be traced to Egypt. The glories of its art and architecture are well documented.

"What is not well known, is that for the 500 years prior to conquest by Alexander the Great, Egypt and the regions today known as Sudan and Ethiopia were ruled by a people of completely African bloodlines. They were from the area just to the South, known to the Egyptians as Cush, or Nubia. From about 800 B.C. to 324 B.C. the Nubians defined what we know today as Egyptian culture. Their influence was felt in the development of Greek and Roman civilizations which emerged around 500 B.C. Historians speculate that the Nubians would have ruled Egypt indefinitely, were it not for their involvement in a dispute between Persia and Assyria which ultimately led to their overthrow by Alexander the Great. Come, Manny, let me show you what I am talking about."

He beckoned Manny to join him at the railing that ran around the edge of the deck. Manny was still quite dumbfounded by this guided tour of the ancient world, but he couldn't resist the urge to see what would happen next. He walked toward his uncle, half excited, half cautious. Derek put his left arm around Manny's shoulder and gestured with his free hand exclaiming, "Behold..... the glory of Egypt!"

As he spoke, the yard and the forest that stretched before them was transformed..... into a bustling scene from the Nile valley where tremendous activity was taking place. Large crews were hard at work on the construction of a temple. In the foreground were four large obelisks, square columns that tapered as they moved upward, that were crowned with small pyramids at the top. Off in the distance were the Great Pyramids of Gizeh, coated in a golden icing, shimmering brightly in the Egyptian sunlight. To the east were great and magnificent sphinxes, guarding the entry to the tombs of royalty; half man, half lion. The picture was so revealing; the sphinxes were made in the image of the black man, with a broad nose and thick lips. Manny was completely in awe. It was all he could do to absorb the panorama unfolding before him. The entire scene was breathtaking!

Without a word, he turned to Derek. His uncle's clothing had now been transformed into the attire of Egyptian royalty; a linen wrap-around skirt with gold borders and embroidery, an oval shaped gold necklace, and a gold and silk ceremonial headdress that was crowned with the sculpted image of a golden hawk with outstretched wings.

It was then that Manny noticed that he was different too! Dressed elegantly in the finery of a Nubian prince, right down to the headdress, he felt as though they had stepped right into the middle of history! What a wonderful trip! This was great!

Derek picked up his narration. "The Nubian rulers of Egypt were conquered around 324 B.C. by Alexander the Great. Many of the vanquished who escaped fled to the South and settled in Ethiopia. Subsequent generations of the dispersed Nubian culture settled in various parts of Africa. Migratory patterns even led many as far as the western coast of the Continent, from which our forefathers came to this country, at the hands of slave traders. Manny, most of us don't know our tremendous cultural legacy, and the glory of our heritage. You need to know."

Manny's mind was racing now.... with questions about the nature of this ancient civilization and the reasons why none of this was ever mentioned in school. Just as he finally felt able to voice himself, the phone rang. He could hear it ringing faintly, as though from a great distance. They were only right outside the kitchen on the deck, but it seemed as though they were far away, in a separate reality.

"You'd better get the phone, Bud," Derek instructed him. "It could be your Mom."

At that moment, Manny really wasn't interested in anything other than the wonders of the Egypt they were investigating. "OK, Uncle D," he answered. "But don't go anywhere, I'll be right back." Derek laughed a silly kind of Derek laugh, and assured Manny he'd be there when he returned. As Manny took off inside, he was so excited about what had happened that day, he couldn't contain himself. He picked up the phone. It was his mother. Manny had completely forgotten about his eye, the Tylenol, everything. Deidre could barely get a word in edgewise as Manny recounted what had transpired.

Unfortunately, Deidre didn't share his enthusiasm. "That Derek is out of his mind!" she screamed into the phone. "I'm coming home right now. He's not going to turn my son into a liar!" Needless to say, she was very upset.

"But, Mom, I'm telling you the truth," Manny protested. It was no use. Before he was able to hang up, Gloria walked in.

Overhearing Deidre scream through the phone, she rolled her eyes heavenward in a gesture of resignation. "NOW what has Derek done?" she asked. "Have you two gotten into trouble again.... already? I've only been gone a few hours. Manny, you shouldn't upset your Mother so."

"I didn't do anything, Gloria," Manny retorted while briefly reviewing their trip around the world and the visit to the ancient civilizations. He could tell she didn't believe him either. But they couldn't dampen his exuberance. Manny rushed back outside.

There was Derek, in his work garb, putting on his carpenter's belt. "Time to get back to work I guess, eh Bud?" he announced. Everything had been restored to normal; Egypt was gone and Manny wanted to know what had happened.

"Those explanations will come later, Manny," Derek assured him. "Right now, it's important for you to remember the lessons of our travels today. Everything that affects our lives is not always apparent to our senses. Human beings operate in several planes of existence, concurrently. Many factors are important in comprehending the totality of our existence; beliefs, faith, reason, intellect. But the thing that enables us to keep all these in perspective...... is an appreciation of culture.

"The importance of culture...... lies in the fact that it gives each of us a wholistic view of the interdependencies of our lives; our relationship to one another, and even our role in, and dependence upon nature. Always remember to respect the cultural background of someone, even if that person doesn't appreciate it for themselves. Culture provides the proper context within which we can understand ourselves and our experiences.... as well as the experiences of others."

Manny was going to tell Derek about his conversation with his mother, about the fact that she was angry again and thought they were crazy and everything, but somehow he felt his uncle already knew. "Don't worry," Derek said. "Your Mom will get over it." With that he was off down the stairs and into the yard.

Just before Manny turned to go inside, he heard Derek call him as he bounded right back up the stairs. "Manny, I forgot. I've got something for you," he said, and with a playful grin on his face, he pulled a basketball out from behind his back. It was a beautiful, brand new leather ball, with deep ridges; it had a great feel in Manny's hands. It was an official NBA model, one of the autographed versions. When Derek tossed it to him, Manny turned it over and noticed the signature that was on the ball. Where he expected to see Michael Jordan... or David Robinson.... or Patrick Ewing, it said.....'Emanuel Castle'. At first, Manny wondered who in the NBA was named Emanuel Castle? Whoever he was, he certainly didn't deserve an autographed basketball. Then it dawned on him! That was his name! Manny was completely shocked!

"Snake asked me to give that ball to you," said Derek, quite matter of factly. "He thinks you're a good ballplayer, and told me to tell you to go for it, all out, everyday. He says you don't have to worry about playing on the driveway with it, or in the rain. It won't get ruined; must be a special basketball!"

With that, Derek smiled that wide, bright smile of his....... and left his nephew there on the deck, speechless once again.

Chapter 3

Weapons of the Spirit

When Deidre got home, Manny was sure all hell would break loose, again. But he decided not to let that thought bother him. He knew he was telling the truth, even if his mother didn't believe him. Besides, how could she explain the basketball with his name on it? For that matter, how could he explain it?

Even though there weren't many logical explanations for what happened when he was with Derek, Manny believed in his uncle and was convinced he had his best interests at heart. So..... Manny decided he would go shoot some baskets, to get his mind off things. No need to let all these cares get him down. *Might as well look at the bright side.*

It was such a beautiful day, as the song says, and Manny's eye felt great even though it was still partially swollen. The basketball his uncle had given him was real nice, and..... after kind of just hanging out, shooting around for a few minutes, Manny began to notice something unusual. He tried a variety of different shots, from all over the court and every shot went right in. It was strange but..... it seemed as though he couldn't miss. *Hmmm.* He kept on shooting and shooting...... and shooting and.... kept making all the shots. Every one! He just couldn't miss! What a rush!

It was such an intense sensation, knowing that everything he put up would go in. Manny's confidence was soaring! Everything was right with the world as far as he was concerned; he was SO happy! This was HIS basketball; he knew that when he played with it, he couldn't miss. He wouldn't miss. All of a sudden, Manny couldn't wait for basketball practice to start.

It felt sooo..... good! He just HAD to tell somebody. Derek was gone; without thinking Manny ran into the kitchen to talk to Gloria.

When he got inside, Manny discovered Gloria and his mom sitting at the table, sharing a glass of wine and looking quite serious. He overheard his mother mention something about Edison coming home. Manny immediately interrupted them.

"When is Dad coming home?" It had been several weeks since he'd seen his father, but with everything that was happening, Manny really hadn't missed him.

"Your father will be here this weekend, Manny," Gloria volunteered. "Have you forgotten your manners young man? What are you supposed to do when people are talking?" she demanded.

Right away, Manny apologized. When Gloria was in a stern mood, you really didn't want to cross her. "I'm very sorry.... I should have said, 'Excuse me, but did I overhear you young ladies mention that Mr. Edison Castle was returning to the Atlanta area... sometime in the near future? Would you please enlighten me as to the date of his planned arrival?'" Manny sounded so ridiculous, he laughed aloud at himself.

They couldn't help but laugh either. It was good to see his mother enjoying herself a little bit for once. Manny wasn't aware of it, but Deidre had confided to Gloria that things weren't going so well with her law practice. Manny hoped his improvisation helped break the ice. He knew his mother was quite angry when she talked to him on the phone earlier.

"That was very good of you to inquire so earnestly about your Dad," Deidre replied. "You ought to be that courteous all the time." She didn't seem upset at all. Just then the subject changed. "Where did you get the basketball, Manny?" she asked.

Her question rekindled the excitement Manny had entered the room with. He told them all about Derek giving him the ball, and how every shot he took would go in, and how anxious he was for basketball practice to begin, and everything. They looked at one another ever so strangely, as if he was crazy to be talking that way.

On the other hand, Manny was still fired up. He was determined to show them he knew what he was talking about. "Well if you don't believe me," he bellowed, "come on out back..... and I'll show you, both of you!" Immediately, he launched himself outside. His two skeptics followed, clutching their glasses of white zinfandel as they came.

They stood on the deck as he made shot after shot, even some ridiculous attempts from behind his back. Once, Manny actually drop kicked the basketball up, and it went in.

Needless to say, their faces were tense with amazement. They stared at one another momentarily, then Gloria disappeared into the house. She returned directly with the bottle of wine from which they were partaking, and eagerly refilled their empty glasses.

"I don't know how it works, but...... it works!" she volunteered somewhat tentatively between gulps of the vino. Manny could tell she was hoping for a logical explanation of his display. Deidre was more defiant.

"Let me see that basketball," Deidre growled, as she charged down the stairs, kicking off her black designer pumps. "Something's fishy here. Derek probably put a magnet of some kind inside.... to make it attract the metal rim. Yes, I'm sure that's what he did. I'll show you!" She was determined to prove that there wasn't anything at all special about Manny's basketball.

The entire scene was riotous. Here was Deidre in her silk blouse and pleated skirt, with no shoes on, laboring mightily to put the ball in the basket. Meanwhile, up on the deck, Gloria guzzled glass after glass of wine while cheering her on. Manny had to admit he was having the time of his life, with these two.

Try as she might, Deidre wasn't having any luck imitating Michael Jordan. Occasionally one would drop for her, but for the most part, she couldn't make enough baskets to validate her magnetic attraction theory.

Manny's utter delight and enjoyment couldn't be restrained. He even wished Asia and her friends were here to see this one. "I told you.... it's MY basketball and with it..... I can't miss!" he gleefully exclaimed. "See! You two wouldn't believe me." Manny sensed they were groping for an answer.

Suddenly Deidre exploded. "Where's that DAMN Derek!?! I've had enough of him! I'm going to get to the bottom of this.... if it's the last thing I do." Manny couldn't understand why she became so upset. "Manny, get your little behind up to your room! NOW!"

"But Mom, what did I do?" he protested. He really wanted to see what would happen when she found his uncle. But thinking quickly, he decided to use this opportunity as a bargaining chip. "OK, Mom. I'm going. But is it all right if I watch a video or two? Please......?"

"All right..... all right. Just let me find Derek. We're going to have a long talk." As Manny turned to go, he could see her heading for the servants' quarters where Derek stayed. She had his basketball under her arm.

Even though he thoroughly enjoyed the afternoon's exhibition, Manny couldn't help but wish he was able to give his Uncle D some warning...... that Deidre was heading his way. She was in a strange frame of mind. Despite that sense of concern for Derek, it had still been a great day. Manny was so excited he even decided to call 'ol Haskell and tell him all about it.

It bothered Deidre greatly that Derek chose to stay in the servants' quarters instead of the house. She was concerned that some of her friends or business acquaintances would find out that her own brother was living with the servants. She couldn't stand the thought of being ridiculed like that.

Gloria stayed at the house with the family; the only one living in the servants' quarters was Enrico. And he hadn't been around for the past couple of weeks. After a recent discharge from the hospital, he'd gone to stay with his sister in Savannah to recuperate. Enrico loved the ocean, and was convalescing on Tybee Island; just sun, sand and surf. Meanwhile, Derek had moved into the suite adjoining Enrico's, and seemed to be doing just fine. Derek always seemed to be doing just fine.

As Deidre walked, her thoughts turned to Edison. She was silently thankful he was coming home after more than three weeks away. Her concern about Manny was growing, and the events of the past few days had her confused. Things weren't going so well at the office, and to top it off, she really needed the touch of a man. *It's tough being a woman of the 90's,* she mused thoughtfully.

But what disturbed her most was the relationship that had grown between Manny and Derek. It seemed that whenever they were together, strange things happened.

Worst of all, she felt Manny had lied to her about the things he and Derek did, all this stuff about ancient cultures.... a trip around the world.... and the magic basketball! Enough was definitely enough. She decided she was going to let Derek have it! As soon as she found him.

He wasn't in his room. She headed for the woods beyond the servants' quarters. The fallen pine needles pricked her bare feet as she went. *If only I'd put on my sneakers before coming all the way out here....* it occurred to her. Walking on, Deidre realized she'd missed the last appointment for her bi-weekly pedicure. Things were definitely out of sync. The momentary daydreaming wasn't enough to cause her not to notice how her pampered tootsies were beginning to ache.

At last, she found Derek out beyond the woods at the edge of the property. He was working on the wire fence that ran along the top of a grassy ridge. The ridge dropped off sharply into the tiny creek that was the legal property line.

Deidre had been in such rapt thought that the sight of him actually startled her. It was interesting to her that Derek was much larger close up than he seemed otherwise. She was gathering her thoughts when he spoke, even though his back was turned, as if sensing her presence.

"Hi, Dee-Dee," he said in a most cheerful tone. "You trying to surprise me, huh, sneaking up like that. You're home a little early, aren't you?" The question was more of an observation than anything else. "I thought I'd repair this fence back here. It's a pretty steep drop into the creek. We wouldn't want any guests or kids falling in, you know." Derek knew something had to be on Deidre's mind..... for her to come all the way out there. "Is anything wrong?"

"D....... we've got to have a little talk," she said in a very serious tone of voice. "It's about Manny."

Derek looked alarmed. He was quite sincere in his concern, particularly when it came to Manny. "Well.... let me finish tacking this fence," he responded, "and we'll go sit under a shade tree and talk. Is that all right with you?"

She thought to herself how amazing it was that Derek had a queer way of making people feel at ease, even if they had no desire to be. In fact, it occurred to her that he could be downright charming when he wanted to be.

"Sure, Big D," answered Deidre with a reassuring tone in her voice, "just don't take all damn day with that." Years and years ago she used to call him Big D, when she wanted to butter him up. It never failed to get him into a good mood. She sat down on the basketball, watching quietly as Derek completed his work. She was impressed with the way he went about the job. *There is something appealing, something very masculine about a man working with his hands,* Deidre thought. And Derek was a competent craftsman. Before long, he was through.

"OK, Dee-Dee," said Derek taking her by the arm. "Let's talk." They walked over to the edge of the wooded area and sat down on an old tree stump. "By the way, how do you like Manny's new basketball?" he inquired teasingly.

His question caused her evil demeanor to resurface. Deidre's feistiness could not be averted. "Derek, I resent the fact that you are turning my son into a liar!" she blurted out, easing not so subtly into the issue at hand. "I mean Manny talked all day

51

about how the two of you were traipsing 'around the world' as he put it, visiting ancient cultures along the way, while sitting on the deck of the house. I can't...... I WON'T condone him making up preposterous stories like that!" Clearly, she was very angry.

There was a silence that ensued between the brother and sister, for what seemed to be an eternity. At last Derek spoke up. "Deidre, do you remember when we were young, and you used to tell me how Mom never gave you credit for having an opinion, for having your own thoughts? And I would say, 'Dee-Dee... it isn't her fault.... she just doesn't have much imagination.' Remember how we got the biggest kick out of all of that...... do you remember?"

At that moment, it crossed Deidre's mind that Derek always seemed to have more maturity than his age would suggest. She recalled fondly the times she would confide in him, about just those kinds of things, and how encouraging he was. "Yes D, I remember very well that particular conversation." she confessed, though not knowing why it was significant now. "Yes, I remember...... but what does that have to do with anything?"

Derek stood up slowly, his body seeming to unfold vertically as he rose. He appeared much taller than he actually was. As he peered down at Deidre, she noticed a strange, faint glow in his wide brown eyes. There was a clarity there, no ambivalence or confusion, and great power.

"Dee-Dee, I've discovered over the years... that imagination is one of the few traits of our human personality that can't be learned, or taught, or for that matter used up; it really can't be lost. But it can be stifled, or worse yet...... ignored. It's as individual as our fingerprints. Imagination spurs the power of creativity.

"Manny possesses great imagination, and insight. When he and I are together, it's as though his openness compels the force of the spirit..... to represent itself to him, in different ways. He's not lying to you Deidre. Those experiences he described are real.... as real as this tree stump you're sitting on!"

The directness with which he spoke stunned her. She couldn't fathom how Derek could speak of such things..... with such absolute certainty in his voice. Surely, he couldn't believe Manny's stories himself, although he appeared completely serious. Before she could gather her thoughts to respond, Derek began again.

"Perception is expanded, when we are able to free our sensory responses from the burden of validating the physical realm. That requires different frames of reference than the ones we're used to. Manny just naturally flows from one frame of reference to another, easily. I guess it's one of the qualities of childhood we should never grow out of.

"He implicitly accepts the possibilities of other realms of existence, possibilities which most of us are unwilling to accept. As a result, his perception is expanded. And what he perceives is **real**. All I'm doing is showing him how to discipline his awareness, and to comprehend that the capacity for understanding spiritual principles..... is rooted in his culture and history. To utilize the power of the spirit.... is his birthright."

Derek's words made Deidre vaguely uncomfortable. She was trying hard to absorb what he was suggesting, but it simply didn't make any sense to her. However, despite the intellectual foolishness of it all, there was a gnawing feeling in the pit of her stomach, that there might be some validity to what he was saying. Not knowing quite how to express her feelings made Deidre feel inadequate, and very frustrated.

"Well.... all I know is that this supernatural stuff you're talking about doesn't make any DAMN sense Derek," she snapped.

"You're full of it, that's what you are! And you're not going to fill my son's head with a bunch of nonsense! I know what's real and what's not! It's impossible to be in two places at one time, I know that. Go on, tell me again how Manny's not lying to me!"

They were so caught up by the tautness of their discussion that neither one of them noticed the clouds moving in, nor the breeze beginning to pick up. There was a storm brewing.

"Deidre," asked Derek curiously, "how is it that you are so certain of your own infallibility? Don't you know there are things in life you may not be aware of? All I'm saying is don't judge Manny solely on the basis of your own understanding. He possesses a sweet and vibrant fascination with life. That creativity is something to be treasured, and nurtured constructively."

Unfortunately, Deidre wasn't buying in to his proposition. "Dammit, Derek! What you're talking about isn't REAL! Besides, who are you to tell me about nurturing Manny? You're not his father! He's my responsibility, not yours. I'm not going to let him grow up thinking the world is just one big..... PLAY-GROUND! He's MY son.... and he's not going to end up crazy....... like you!"

The words hung thick in the evening air like enormous icicles. By the time Deidre realized what she'd said, it was too late. She really loved Derek, but it was clear she wasn't certain all his marbles were in place. She attempted to offer an apology, but Derek brusquely interrupted.

"Don't bother, Dee-Dee. It's not that important what you think of me. And you're right...... I'm not Manny's father. But I AM family.... and I'm interested in seeing him grow into the kind of person he's capable of becoming. The things that I'm describing to you ARE real..... even more real than the nose on your face. The realm of the spirit is where the active forces of life originate.

"And it's critical for Manny to know how to handle these forces for himself. To be prepared for the manhood that awaits, for the contradictions that this society will confront him with..... simply because of his color and heritage.

"Tremendous pressures lie ahead, and HE has to be ready to accept the responsibilities of his life; that's something none of us can do for him, as much as we might want to. He's got to have the attitude of a man of culture: a man who can lay aside the superficiality of false ego and deceptive materialism. A man who can look deep into the fullness of spiritual power, and mobilize those positive life forces. A man who, when all else fails, will believe in himself!

"You must understand Deidre, that what Manny faces is warfare; a warfare of the soul..... and of the mind and will, in a society designed to rob him of his cultural identity. I'm trying to equip him with the weapons he'll need for the battle........ the **only** weapons that will ultimately make any difference........ weapons of the spirit!"

Derek's words rang out with a sharp resonance, so clear.... so penetrating..... it nearly moved Deidre to tears. Yet, despite her intuitive agreement with what was expressed, she couldn't fathom how someone could speak so authoritatively about things so....... so...... other-worldly.

Deidre could recognize the sincerity that fueled Derek's passion. At the same time, her own mind and experiences would not allow her to validate the truth he spoke. Without an appropriate frame of reference, her instincts reverted to what she knew, which was to attack vigorously that which she couldn't understand.

"Damn it, Derek! I didn't make the world the way it is," she hissed, "... and Manny's got to understand it takes more than good looks and personality to succeed today. What about his education? Edison and I have worked hard to give him, and Asia, the opportunities to make something of themselves. And I don't intend to stand idly by while Manny pursues this fantasy of becoming a basketball player. He's going to be doctor, if I have anything to do with it..... and I DO!"

In the distance, an ominous rumbling of thunderstorms growled while the Georgia sky grew dark in anticipation of the rain. Down on the ground, the heat had become stifling. The tops of the tall pine trees swayed slowly as the wind played a summer ballad in the tiny clearing where these siblings sparred.

It was Derek's turn. "Education IS crucial Deidre. But you've got to realize Manny's education doesn't begin and end with school and college. There is an element of cultural.... and spiritual development he will never get from the educational system. We've got to be responsible for that. Can you trust that Edison even KNOWS what's best for Manny? After all, he has a political career to be concerned with."

Though he probably wasn't aware of it, Derek's suggestion about Edison struck a responsive chord with her. It crossed her mind that she should defend him. But.... Deidre really found it difficult to argue. Deep down, she was disappointed with the way responsibilities in Washington kept Edison away so much. And lately she'd found herself thinking about Lance Powell in more than just a professional context.

However, despite the disappointment and her own mental indiscretions, she missed Edison desperately. Derek's mention brought his person to mind. He wasn't a bad guy. It was just that the politics were turning out to be more than she bargained for. Deidre was looking forward to having him home again. She needed to share her concerns, frustrations, and fears with..... her husband.

Suddenly, a blinding crevice of light pierced the evening sky, followed immediately by a deafening crash of thunder. It was so loud, the wildlife emptied from the trees overhead. Before either of them could make a move, the sky opened up.

It wasn't just raining; sheets and torrents of water gushed violently from above. Cascades of thunder and lightning covered their pine forest. Snapped out of her suspended animation by the intrusion of nature, Deidre instinctively took off. *It wasn't safe there in the woods,* she thought, with the flashes of lightning illuminating the dark skies.

As she ran, Deidre recalled her own youth as a little girl, how she would run and play carelessly in the rain. She remembered how much fun it was to abandon yourself to the exhilaration of letting your body go, and the joy of adventure and imagination. To express yourself in dance and play with your friends. To get completely soaked in the rain, without being concerned about getting wet or what your hair would look like the next day. She felt free, so alive, as she headed back to the house in that downpour, bare feet and all.

Deidre was so engrossed in her own escape, she totally forgot about Derek. Turning to find him, she was able to vaguely make out his figure through the curtains of water. It was strange, but she thought she saw a wide smile on his face as he waved vigorously to her.

The most peculiar thing was that Derek wasn't running at all. He actually seemed to be enjoying the storm, not really trying to get out of the rain, but walking....... and dribbling Manny's prize basketball as he went.

Chapter 4

Physics, Chemistry, and the Material World

When Deidre arrived back at the house, Gloria met her in the kitchen. "My goodness, Ms. Castle! You're soaked! What did you and Derek do out there in this rain?" Gloria rushed to get her some towels from the downstairs linen closet. Deidre was so wet, she made a series of small puddles as she stood there in the middle of the kitchen floor. The journey back to the house seemed to have cheered her up.

"Well, what's been happening in here since I've been gone?" she called after Gloria. "Has Manny gotten into anything?"

Gloria returned with a couple of large beach towels for Deidre to dry off with. "Oh Ms. Castle..... you're such a kidder when you want to be. And a good friend and wonderful woman to work for, I might add." Gloria had a tendency to get mushy and sentimental when she had a bit too much to drink, and she had gone through a goodly portion of blush that afternoon. "It's not like you've been gone for several days, Ms. Castle...... you've only been out there for an hour and a half. Anyway..... Manny's fine, and Asia called to say she was at Geri's waiting for the rain to stop. They're both under a bed downstairs. She's so scary when it comes to thunderstorms, you know." Gloria laughed out loud thinking about Asia hiding under a bed.

Meanwhile, feeling quite uninhibited, Deidre wrapped herself in one of the beach towels and began to slip out of her wet clothes underneath. "I'm freezing," she remarked, as the effects of the air conditioning chilled her wet body and hair. "I'm going to take a nice hot bath, Gloria. If anyone calls, tell them I'm out."

Deidre waddled up the stairs, as she had not completely gotten out of her dampened panties. But she was anxious to get into the soothing, luxurious bath that awaited her. Gloria volunteered to help. "Let me take those wet things and put them in the drier for you." Gloria got all of her clothes together just as Deidre was making her way to the top of the stairs. "Oh.... and by the way, Ms. Castle," she called out. "Mr. Castle called a little bit ago. He said he'd like for you to call him back."

Deidre was delighted that Edison called. She was feeling kind of playful, and anxious for him to come home. "Did he say where he would be, Gloria?" she answered.

"No.... he didn't, Ms. Castle. I assumed he was at his office," was Gloria's reply. Although she respected Edison, Gloria didn't trust the man and secretly thought he might be cheating on Deidre. She would never let her opinion be known, however. At least not without provocation.

"Well I'm going to relax in my bath, and I'll call him a little later. By the way, please call Geri and tell Asia it's time to get home." The vicious thunderstorm had subsided and been replaced with a light but steady drizzle. The sun even made a final reappearance just before vanishing beyond the western horizon.

Settling into the tub, Deidre reflected on the day's events, particularly her conversation with Derek. Although nothing had really been resolved, she felt comfortable that she had at least voiced her displeasure to him. The warmth of the water combined with the massage-like motion of the jacuzzi lulled Deidre into a dreamlike state. Physically relaxed, her mind became clear and unencumbered, as though the rain had rinsed away much of the anxiety and confusion she'd felt. And it was satisfying to know that Edison had called.

Before long, her satisfaction began to wane. It occurred to her that Edison might be calling to say he wouldn't be able to come home as planned. He'd done that on several occasions in the past, but it would be a terrible time for that to happen now. *How awful it would be,* thought Deidre. *His timing was never the greatest anyway, and he WOULD allow something to prevent him from coming home. Dammit, Edison.... how could you do this to me?*

Her displeasure caused her to knock over the vase of bath oil crystals that so delightfully scented the bath water. The light crash of the vase on the floor startled Deidre out of the daydream she was in. *Why am I getting so excited?* she reflected as she started to calm down. *I haven't even talked to him, and already I'm condemning him for something he probably isn't even thinking about.* The little pep talk she gave herself seemed to help, and before long, she returned to a more positive frame of mind.

The fluffiness of the terry cloth robe felt wonderful against her body as she emerged from the water. The summer sun had darkened her skin to a golden brown, and she smoothed moisturizer all over. She spent a little more time completing her beauty treatment by removing the polish from her nails and toes, dressing her cuticles, taking a quick honey almond mask, and finishing up with the floss and toothbrush. Deidre felt clean and relaxed. She was finally ready to call Edison.

Just as she was getting settled in her room, there was a knock at the door. It was Gloria carrying a tray with some dinner. "I thought you might be hungry, Ms. Castle," she said with a warm, wide smile. "And I brought you a small carafe of wine to go along with your meal."

"Gloria, you're such a sweetheart," laughed Deidre. "What would I ever do without you! Were you able to get in touch with Asia?"

"Yes.... and she said she'd be home in about a half an hour. Geri's brother is supposed to be showing them a new dance. You know how teenagers are, Ms. Castle." Gloria liked Asia, and took up for her whenever there was a chance Deidre might get on her case.

"Yes, I guess I do Gloria. You go and relax now. You've got to be worn out, trying to keep up with all of us."

"Well, you know I don't mind looking after you at all," Gloria sighed, turning to go. "I just wish I could keep up with that husband of yours." With that, she headed downstairs.

Deidre didn't know what to make of her comment. But she was hungry, and her appetite diverted her attention away from what Gloria said. Digging in heartily, she finished most of the meal in a few minutes. Now comfortably reposed in her gown and upright in the bed, she picked up the phone and eagerly dialed Edison's office.

She waited patiently through a fourth, a fifth, and a sixth ring. Finally, it was answered.

"Hello. Representative Castle's office.... Lance Powell speaking."

"Well.... hello yourself, Lance. This is Deidre Castle. You're working a little late tonight, aren't you?" *What a pleasant surprise,* she thought, to have the opportunity to talk to Lance.

"HELLO Ms. Ca... I mean Deidre. How are you? It's been a while since we've talked." Lance, too, seemed to be excited by her call. "I've got to get your husband ready to leave. He's very excited about coming home for a little vacation. Do you know where you guys are going?"

Whew, sighed Deidre silently. *At least Edison was still planning on coming to Atlanta. But he hadn't said anything about vacation. Hmmmm.... I wonder where we'll be going? Maybe Bermuda, or Trinidad-Tobago, or how about Barbados? Now that would be nice!*

"Edison and I haven't had a chance to discuss the particulars." She waited to see if Lance might have any clue as to where Edison was going to take her. "Did he mention anything to you...... I mean, about where he might want to go?"

At this point, Lance realized he may have inadvertently opened a can of worms, so as diplomatically as possible he changed the subject. "Well.... not really, Deidre. By the way... how is everyone there? Manny?"

"Everyone's fine, Lance. Very nice of you to inquire." Deidre really liked him, but it was obvious he wasn't going to give out any more information on this vacation idea.

"Your husband is on the other phone," Lance said somewhat nervously. "I'll let him know you're holding. We've been in and out of committee hearings all week."

It occurred to her that Lance seemed slightly stressed out, maybe even overworked. "Listen, Lance, don't disturb him now. Just let him know I called and have him call me as soon as he completes his conversation. And Lance, you sound like you may need a vacation yourself. Don't you and your girlfriend have any plans..... to get away?" she inquired devilishly.

Surprisingly, her comment incited a huge laugh. "HA....
Who's got time for a girlfriend? Things are too busy on the Hill
for me to worry about my social life. But it would be nice to get
away to the beach for a while. Maybe when the Congressman
returns, I'll take a few days off."

"Well.... you know what they say about all work.... and no
play, Lance," Deidre playfully taunted. "I won't hold you up
anymore now. Please let Edison know I called.... and remember
what I said. A female companion would be good for you."

"I'll most certainly keep that in mind. It's really nice
talking to you again, Deidre." Lance was feeling a bit guilty about
the way he enjoyed talking to his boss's wife, and he knew he had
to stop. "Hopefully, I'll see you soon. And don't worry. I'll make
sure the Congressman boards that plane on Friday. Have a good
night!" CLICK!

Lance had to re-focus his attention to the business at hand.
He was working feverishly to prepare transcripts of the congressional hearings on alternative energy sources. Edison planned to
review some of the transcripts while on vacation. The papers were
considered confidential and restricted in that the government had
been conducting research in several controversial areas of the
African continent. Edison and key members of his staff, including
Lance, held the proper security clearance to have such documents
in their possession.

Part of the government's effort involved the use of merce-
naries to secure several excavation sites where a rare mineral ore
was being extracted from the foothills in Namibia. Researchers
believed this material could be used in the fabrication of new and
highly powerful superconductors. The experiments were encoun-
tering costly delays due to the activities of nationalists and anti-
apartheid groups who were raiding the mining compounds. These

raids resulted in the theft of valuable fourth generation explosives and firearms. 'Without the use of the mercenary groups, the research could not proceed, and millions of tax dollars would be wasted,' the reports contended.

Meanwhile, in an adjoining room, the Congressman was in the midst of a vigorous debate. His adversary was a young woman named Camille Ferguson. Camille was a local community activist and ardent supporter of embattled Washington, D.C. mayor, Adrian Lowery. The good Mayor was indicted on charges of racketeering, tax evasion, and perjury. Edison was quoted as saying he felt the Mayor '.... had let the people of the District down, and was a poor role model for the children, not only of the city, but of the nation as well.'

His comments were made at the dedication of a new community center that opened in the Southeast section of D.C. only a week before. The center was the first of several inner city facilities underwritten by legislation Edison had co-sponsored in Congress. Beside local substance abuse clinics and counseling facilities, the center would also accommodate child care for parents who were unable to afford private day care. The intent was to provide an incentive for single parents so they could enter the workplace. Plans were also on the drawing board for a homeless shelter in the complex.

The issue of the Mayor came up when a media person remarked that his conspicuous absence again raised the question of his viability as D.C.'s chief executive. Edison responded instinctively, saying essentially what he really believed. For a politician, honesty simply is not always the best policy.

He was challenged, right there at the press conference, by Camille. She was one of the thousands of D.C. residents who had prospered under the leadership of Mayor Lowery. In fact, it was as a result of Mayor Lowery's efforts and visibility that D.C. had been chosen as the inaugural site for the rollout of the community centers.

Interestingly enough, Edison immediately became fascinated by Camille. She was a captivating woman, and he was impressed by her fire and commitment, no matter how misplaced he felt her fervor for the Mayor was. He instructed one of his aides to be sure to get her phone number, and promised to call, at his 'earliest opportunity'.

However, consistent with her style, Camille took the initiative and found Edison's office number. She called for three consecutive days, not daring to leave a message when she was unable to reach him. She was determined to speak directly to Representative Edison Castle, person to person. Camille finally got through that evening as Edison and Lance were preparing his departure for Atlanta. Because of everything that was happening around there the past few days, Edison initially didn't remember who she was. But soon the voice and manner in which she spoke so passionately of the '... entrapment of Mayor Lowery....' clued him in that it was '.... that fine woman who shouldn't be so damn worried about what the no good Mayor was or wasn't doing...' as Edison had privately characterized her.

He attempted to explain that his comments were taken out of context; what he really meant was that if the Mayor were found to be guilty, then it <u>would</u> be a shame and an embarrassment for his constituents. At this point, Edison acknowledged, it was up to the courts to determine guilt or innocence. Even though he held some strong opinions on the matter, Edison was having trouble concentrating on the subject under discussion. Camille's feminine, yet assertive approach, along with her smoky, tender voice completely excited him. He could tell something was up...... when he began to stutter.

It had been over a long period of time, but Edison learned to overcome a serious speech impediment that had troubled him since his youth. In fact, when he decided to begin a political career, he had a desperate concern that he would have trouble speaking in public. After years of training and group experience, he was finally able to feel comfortable in front of crowds. He hadn't experienced any more trouble from the stuttering..... until that moment.

He couldn't help himself; he was turned on by her. They had been on the phone about a half an hour, when Lance entered with Deidre's message.

"Excuse me, Ms. Ferguson," Edison gently interrupted, "but I.. I.... I.. ve g... g.. got to take a c... c... ca... call on another line. Please excuse me, but I... I.... I'd l.... ll.... love to continue our discussion at a later time."

"Don't try that Ms. Ferguson stuff here. My name is Camille, and yes, I would very much like to continue this conversation." Above all, she stayed true to form. "When are you going to be available again?" Even though Camille didn't condone his views on the Mayor, she was not so unconsciously attracted to Edison, too.

"Well, Camille, to tell you the truth I'm going to be on vacation in Atlanta for a couple of weeks. Could we get together when I get back.... for lunch perhaps?" His stuttering crisis had momentarily subsided.

"You can call me when you get back in town, and we'll talk about it then. My number is Anacostia 8-6344. If I'm not here, be sure to leave a message." Camille wanted to see him, but decided she would wait to see if he was going to call back, before committing to anything. *No use frustrating myself if he's not serious* she thought. "Is that acceptable to you, Mr. Congressman?" Camille challenged him.

"That's fine w.... w.... wi.... withhh.... with me, Ms. Ferguson. I'll see you wh.... wh.... whe.... en I return. Thanks for your call." CLICK.

Edison briefly reviewed the message Lance left for him. Quickly re-orienting himself, he dialed Deidre. It was getting late, and he wanted to speak to her before she fell asleep.

The phone rang twice. "Hello." It was Deidre's voice.

"Hello, Love. It's your husband. How are you?"

"Edison!" Deidre had begun to doze off, but hearing his voice caused her to perk up. "Hi baby, when are you going to be home? I miss you!"

"Well, I'm scheduled to leave National early Friday morning. I should be at Hartsfield around 11:00 A.M. You know Dee, I was thinking how good it would be good for us to get away for a little while. Do you think you could stand a little trip?"

WOW! thought Deidre. *He's trying to fake me out, talking about a 'little' trip. I bet we're going to Bermuda, or Aruba.... or Hawaii. God, I could use a nice relaxing vacation.* Her mind was racing away in anticipation. But she didn't want to seem too anxious. "Well, sure baby. I could go for a 'little' vacation. Anywhere you think would be good.... is alright with me, Edison. I just want to be with you." She was setting him up, or so she thought.

"That's great! I've asked Lance to confirm reservations for us at Carroway Gardens for Friday night. We can take a nice drive down there once I get home from the airport and get settled. We can talk on the way down. Oh Dee..... I'm really looking forward to getting away, just the two of us, for a while. How about you?"

There was a strained silence at the other end of the line. Deidre's bubble was burst. Here was a classic case of differing expectations. Carroway Gardens WAS a beautiful place to go, for a day trip, or a picnic. It was definitely not the exotic, second honeymoon type of resort Deidre had in mind. Somehow, with all she felt she was dealing with at home, her practice, the house, Manny and Asia, and most of all Derek, Deidre felt entitled to more than just a weekend outside of Columbus, GA.

"Deidre.... Deidre.... are you there?" Edison thought they had been disconnected. Everything was so quiet. "Deidre!"

"I'm right here, Edison," Deidre finally spoke up. "I'm sure we'll have a wonderful time." Inside, she was crushed.

"Baby, it's not Hawaii, but it'll be good for us to get away...... by ourselves for a while. You know how romantic we can get..... with a little quiet time on our hands." Edison sensed her disappointment and was trying to be encouraging.

Well, at least he knows I can use some loving, Deidre silently reflected. Slowly, her spirits began to rise. "I miss you Edison. I need to talk to you about Manny........ and about Derek."

The mention of her brother's name was like someone scratching a blackboard with their fingernails to Edison. Certainly, there was no love lost between the two of them. He remembered how, once he and Deidre got engaged, Derek had gone so far as to write her a letter suggesting that he wasn't the right type of man. Over the years their relationship had been one of mutual dislike, but tolerance. It was hard for Edison to forget what Derek had said about him though. "What's going on with Manny and your brother?" Edison snapped.

"Well, Honey, it's just that you're away so much, and Manny looks up to Derek and.... well.... I just think Derek is a little weird, that's all." Deidre was hoping to get Edison to spend less time in Washington, although she was trying to be realistic about it. If there was anyone who could cause him to be concerned about something, it was Derek.

"What do you mean a LITTLE weird?" Edison shouted. "That brother of yours is an absolute NUT if you ask me. He hasn't tried anything with my Asia has he? I wouldn't put it past the son-of-a-bitch to try and molest her. Horny bastard!" Edison was getting excited and angry.

"EDISON! Derek may be a little different, but he's no rapist. I know that. How could you SAY something like that about him." It annoyed Deidre that Edison worried about his daughter first, and Manny always seemed to be an afterthought with him. "That's his niece. Don't worry, Asia is fine."

"Well Dammit, Deidre. These days you never know about people, even family members. You just have to be careful. Asia is an attractive young woman. And you have to admit, Derek IS strange."

The conversation was becoming a drain on her. "Listen honey, let's discuss this when you get here. Be sure to let me know what time you're arriving, so I can meet you. I love you. 'Night." CLICK!

"Good ni...," Edison heard the line go dead in his ear. *I wonder what she's so upset about,* he thought to himself. *I'm just telling the truth about Derek. And while he's a guest in my house, I have the right to express my opinion about him and my children, don't I? Of course, I do.* Edison's thoughts enabled him to justify his feelings. He even thought about calling Deidre back, but decided to give her some time to sleep on what he had said.

Shortly, his thoughts returned to the lovely Ms. Ferguson. *God, I wonder how it would feel to be with her. I'll bet she feels WONDERFUL....* He was beginning to drift into an erotic, lust induced fantasy...... when Lance knocked on the door.

"I've got those transcripts ready, Congressman," he announced.

"Oh... that's great Lance." Edison stammered, momentarily snapping out of his sensuous daydream. "Why don't you get out of here? Go on home. I'll see you in the morning. Thanks for all your help."

"No problem.... no problem at all," he responded. "See you in the morning." Lance packed up his things and headed for the door. He lived near a section of the District known as Adams-Morgan, which wasn't too far from Malcolm X park. He owned a car but rarely used it since he had access to the staff car for Congressman Castle, and the train was so convenient to the office. A short METRO ride up to 16th Street, an even shorter bus connection and he was home. Walking in, he flipped on the TV, waiting for the start of Arsenio. Lance was dog tired.... and this evening he actually looked forward to another night alone..... with a glass of sherry, and several deep lines of cocaine, to get him ready for the next day.

With the events of that afternoon and evening still on his mind, Manny was having trouble falling asleep. On one hand he was excited by the prospect of basketball tryouts starting and yet he looked forward to the end of the school year in a few weeks. However, he was disturbed about not knowing what went on between his mother and Derek. Also, Manny secretly didn't like thunderstorms any more than Asia, and she at least had Geri around..... to be scared with.

Manny decided that the only way to resolve all this was to find out what happened for himself. He pulled on his pants over his pajamas and slipped quietly downstairs, past Gloria's room where he could hear Arsenio getting ready to begin, and out the back. He was headed for Derek's.

He knew he'd get the real story from Derek. It was still very wet all over from the rain, and some large branches from the pines had been broken off. The pool was a mess, with pine needles swimming around on the surface of the blue green water. The clear sky, complete with a canopy of stars and a full moon, gave the warm night a quiet and relaxing peacefulness. Manny thought how interesting it was that Nature could so quickly resume its normal countenance, after such a violent demonstration of its power.

Once he got to the servants' quarters, Manny could see a faint glimmer of light coming from Derek's room. It was funny, but he hadn't been inside these quarters in years. He knocked on the window. "Uncle D..... Uncle D..... it's me, Manny!"

Derek came to the door and let him in. "What are you doing out of the house so late, sport?" he asked quizzically. "Does your Mom know you're out here?"

He wore a pair of olive green boxer shorts, decorated all over with tiny red Christmas trees, and a Mandela T-shirt. A candle glowed on an end table near the corner and incense burned nearby, giving the room a pleasant and serene atmosphere. The jazz station from the Atlanta University campus sang quietly in the background. "Please, Uncle D, don't tell Mom I'm here. It was just that I was worried about you..... and couldn't sleep."

He broke into that wide, comforting grin of his. "Don't be concerned, Manny. I'm not going to tell your Mom. But why would you be worried about me?"

"Because Mom was really upset when she came out here to talk to you earlier, and I didn't want to see you get in trouble.... over me."

Manny's anxiety caused Derek to have the biggest laugh. He put his arm around Manny's shoulder. "Manny," he said. "I hope you never lose that sense of caring, of compassion for people. Your Mom and I had a little talk, that's all. She loves you very much. And you know that you're my Bud.... right Manny-san?"

Manny-san! The name made him recall the day they spent on the deck, and his uncle's lessons on the importance of culture. "Yeah, Uncle D, I know that." Derek had such a calming effect on him. He didn't seem to get overly excited, or bent out of shape.... the way his parents did. Derek really made him feel much better. "By the way, you weren't busy, were you?" Manny said apologetically. He was hoping he hadn't disturbed his uncle. "What were you doing?"

Derek turned to Manny and said softly, almost in a whisper, "I was in meditation and prayer, Manny. Would you like to watch TV or something?" Then he walked over and sat down, cross legged on the rug, in the middle of the floor, like an Indian. He had this tremendous gleam in his eyes, as though contained within were some intense power that was being channeled through those two apertures just below his forehead.

"No.... no, Uncle D, I don't want to watch TV. But can I ask you something? What is it about prayer..... that's so important? I've wondered about that for some time now."

Derek smiled slowly as if he were pleased Manny had brought the subject up. "That's a good question. To answer it properly, let me describe several principles to you." He took out a piece of paper and on it drew a large triangle. Across the triangle he drew two horizontal parallel lines thus dividing it into three sections. He laid the paper out in front of Manny.

"Manny," he started, "we are created by God as three part beings, mankind. We all consist of the spirit, the soul, and the body. The bottom portion of this pyramid represents our spirit. Each of our individual spirits has the potential to become 'connected' to the Spirit of God, which permeates all things. God's Spirit is the source from which all life forces emanate.

"The uppermost portion of this pyramid represents the physical manifestation of those life forces, our bodies. As a result of the interaction between the spirit and the physical body, the soul came into being."

"That's the section of the pyramid in the middle, right Uncle D?"

"That's right, Manny."

"But what's the difference between the spirit and the soul?" Manny asked eagerly. He had never heard of people described this way before, and the description intrigued him.

"Well.... you might think of the spirit as the access point where the creative power, alive in the universe, becomes available to each of us...... although properly speaking the movement of the spirit transcends any limitations of time and space. We are all equipped in our own spirits to partake of these forces.

"The soul is somewhat different. It is the realm of the mind, of the will, and of the emotions. It is the essence of a person that determines each individual's unique personality. And everyone IS unique. You could think of the spirit as a generator....

capable of producing enormous power. The Spirit, God's Spirit, is always on. The Soul is the mechanism which can direct that power, focus it, or if applied negatively, diffuse it."

This was getting really interesting. "You mean the soul is kind of like..... that light switch on the wall, right? And the body is like that lamp on the table over there? The power company, the spirit, supplies the power, but nothing happens until I flip the switch, huh Uncle D?"

Derek's eyes shone brightly as he could see Manny was catching on to the concept. "Very good Manny, very good. Although I guess not **all bodies** are like lamps." At that moment he winked quickly at Manny and bowed his head deeply. "Some bodies could be stereos...." As he spoke, Derek raised his head and on top of his shoulders where his head should be, there was A STEREO COMPONENT system! Manny was shocked! Before he was able to express his surprise, Derek stood up. "Of course, others of us could be.... a color TV!" As the words came from his mouth his stereo 'head' transformed itself into.... a color TV. "And then again some of us...... are like huge refrigerators!" He spun around two times, and before Manny appeared William Perry, the infamous 'Refrigerator' of Super Bowl fame.... number 72 for the Chicago Bears. HE WAS MASSIVE!

Well... all Manny could do was sit there with his mouth wide open. Derek the 'Fridge sat down next to him. Before Manny knew it, they had both broken into a wild laughter just thinking of all the types of bodies in this crazy world.

Once they calmed down a bit, Manny realized Derek was back to his 'normal' self. He continued to explain. "The reason prayer is so important is because it's essential to the proper growth and development of our spirits, the same way we stimulate and develop our minds through reading and study, and our bodies through exercise. You can think of prayer..... as exercise for the spirit."

It took a few minutes for the things Derek told him to sink in. He had never before heard these concepts described in such a way. The clarity of it all made a tremendous impact on him. In his mind, Manny tried to equate what Derek said to his own experiences. "If we can exercise our spirits, Uncle D, is it possible to over exert ourselves praying?" Manny asked in all sincerity. "All I know is I get tired in basketball practice after about five wind sprints."

The literal nature of his question caused Derek to laugh out loud. "Honestly, Manny," he said, "I don't know if you can exhaust your spirit through prayer. But I do know there's plenty of capacity for the spirit to accommodate. It's up to us to discipline ourselves to give our spirit the proper attention it deserves; and to train our mind, will and emotions to allow the power of the spirit to flow. When the process works properly, nothing is impossible for a man who believes in the potential of his own spirit.

"On the other hand, we just can't spend all our time in prayer. We have to work, you have to go to school....... there are things to do in this world."

His explanation was quite straightforward, very simple. "You know, this seems so understandable to me as we sit here talking about it," Manny confessed. "Why aren't these kinds of things ever brought out like this in church?"

Derek arched his back and stretched his arms and shoulders like a big cat, preparing for the prowl. "Manny," he looked at him, his eyes wide with emphasis, "what I am telling you is the way the process of life works. The urging of the spirit gives rise to creative impulses in the soul. The soul then translates these impulses into action in the physical realm. That is the proper order of life. Most of the time, what you hear in church...... is dressed up in religious double-talk that, at best, confuses the issue.

"The modern world has, unfortunately, come to be dominated by the influence of Eurocentric 'culture'. As such, we have moved away from an appreciation of the primacy of the spirit, which is integral to the lessons of our own cultural heritage. So much of modern understanding is conditioned by the sensory environment; what we can see, touch, taste, feel. Without an appreciation of the spirit..... the intellect, emotions, and the physical realm get unduly exalted, and cause the true nature and meaning of life to become distorted, out of context.

"This concept is evident in the way most Americans tend to focus on themselves, on the almighty I; it shows up in the drive for material successes and individual competitiveness..... at the expense of others. These manifestations are contrary to the instinctive yearnings of our own culture."

Derek paused at that point, as if to examine Manny..... to see whether or not he was following him. Manny responded dutifully that he was, although something had caught his attention that was quite distracting. Manny noticed that the room seemed to fade into the background and he couldn't seem to focus on anything except Derek or himself. Everything else was a blur; vague and nondescript. Manny wanted to ask what was happening, but Derek picked up his narrative before he could open his mouth.

"What I am telling you even reveals itself in the visual arts. If you were to examine paintings or murals from traditional European cultures and those of say, Ancient Mayan, Egyptian or other Afrocentric cultures, you would notice some marked differences, differences that reflect exactly what I'm describing to you.

"In the visual representations of the so called 'third world' cultures, the imagery is very much flat and two-dimensional. There is no representative distinction between foreground and background. This type of imagery suggests the uniformity and oneness of people, a unity of individuals with their environment and surroundings.

"When you look at paintings from various Western cultures for example, there is much more emphasis on the distinction between foreground representations versus that of the background. The concept of focus and depth of field are used to give the illusion of three dimensional reality. These more 'realistic' representations psychologically reinforce the ideal of the individual as distinct and apart from the surroundings and the environment. The almighty I. Any understanding of the essential relationship of the unity of mankind, of man's fundamental dependence upon and harmony with nature, is lost in the process."

He picked up the drawing of the pyramid and laid it down between them. Then he used the pencil to sketch another one, right beside it, but turned upside down.

"The result is that today we live in a world that is out of sync with itself; a world that is rapidly becoming dysfunctional..... the pyramid has gotten itself turned upside down." Derek circled the inverted pyramid and marked a large 'X' at the tip, which was now on the bottom. "As you can see Manny, the second pyramid is much less stable since it is balanced very delicately on its apex rather than on a wide base, as is the case when the pyramid is properly oriented.... as in our original picture. It is critical that men and women re-orient their lives according to the power and flow of the spirit so that our society can be restored to a true stability. That can only happen as we begin to deal with truth, the truth of the spirit and its expression through culture. It's only a matter of time before the current world structure gets completely reordered..... from the precarious position it is in today.

"We talked the other day about the importance of culture. The reason I brought that up is because the cultures described historically as 'third world' have, as their basis, a fundamental appreciation of the relationship between the spirit and the material world. Somehow, through the influence of Western (Eurocentric) 'cultures', the role of the intellect and the fascination with physical experience has come to dominate the role of the spirit, in the manifestations of the material realm."

Needless to say, all this fascinated Manny. It had never occurred to him that there was anything other than what he experienced in this world at work. But he was having trouble digesting everything his uncle was saying. Derek must have noticed Manny's quizzical expression, because he started up again in anticipation of his dilemma.

"Don't worry, Manny," Derek reassured him. "What I am describing to you doesn't always make sense to our minds. In fact, the power of the spirit is really a concept foreign to the intellect. It requires an awakening of the spirit in each of us.... to fully grasp the meaning of what I am telling you. Jesus, as recorded in the Bible in John 3:16, referred to the process of spiritual regeneration as being 'born again'."

It occurred to Manny that maybe the forces of his spirit could overcome any failings of his mind at school. "Gee, Uncle D, are you saying I don't have to worry about schoolwork?" he eagerly inquired.

Manny's question got a big smile from his uncle. "Sorry, Bud, but that is absolutely NOT what I am saying. Education is critical. And education is also a lifetime process that needs to incorporate a wholistic view of our lives, in terms of spirit, soul, and body.

"All I'm saying is that you shouldn't rely solely on intellectual development to give you an understanding of the issues of life. Culture is the key, and the urging of the spirit cannot be ignored. The eyes of a spiritual man are clear, like a deep pool of understanding. He may not be bright or articulate in an intellectual sense, but he knows how to mobilize spiritual power for himself. But the spirit in and of itself is not all that is necessary. Your education is crucial too."

Manny still wasn't convinced. "Why is that important?" he asked perplexed.

"Well, Manny, it's important because the principles of the spiritual world have their manifestations in the material world. Without proper educational development, you can't correlate the expressions of the spirit..... with the physical world. The sciences and mathematics are particularly important in the process of describing the phenomena of life as they gain expression in the material realm."

Now, Manny was getting a little nervous. His best subject in school was history, and he liked foreign languages somewhat. But he was a lost soul when it came to mathematics and science. Asia, as much of a pain as she could be sometimes, did help him through math. And next year Manny was supposed to take biology. Now Derek was telling him how important it was to understand science. Although Manny was hesitant to continue this train of thought, he nevertheless felt compelled find out how the sciences fit into the scheme of things.

"Probably the most relevant scientific disciplines, as far as the expression of the spirit is concerned," Derek stressed, "are physics and chemistry. Yes..... physics, chemistry, and the material world." He repeated the words several times, as if to be sure Manny understood the significance of the terms. Derek's own vigor seemed stimulated by the contemplation of the principles these words suggested.

"Physics is the study of the laws governing physical existence.... action and reaction, gravity, cause and effect, velocity and acceleration, frequency and resonance. These are concepts you should become familiar with. Similarly, chemistry is the study of materials, their interaction and the rules describing the states of existence.... solid, plasma, liquid; chemical reactions that occur when different types of materials act upon one another."

Derek was writing on the piece of paper as he spoke. He paused and looked up, his deep brown eyes staring right through Manny. He knew by Manny's expression and glazed stare that his nephew didn't know much of what he was talking about. Derek returned to scribbling briefly, then resumed his instruction.

"A while ago I mentioned the nature of the so-called 'third world' cultures, and their emphasis on the oneness of humanity and harmony with nature. It's very much of what I'll call a wholistic approach to living, an intuitive understanding of the interrelationships of all things.

"We also discussed the preoccupation of Eurocentric culture with intellectualism and individual achievement. Western scholarship has chosen to distinguish various scientific disciplines as distinct fields.... like biology, astronomy, geology........ physics, and chemistry. Moreover, an entire educational system has developed around this approach which, of course, bestows certifications and degrees upon those who study these disciplines and comply with rigorous academic requirements. This is not wrong. You must understand that we live in a society which requires and honors an individual's credentials..... these credentials are a key to successful living today. That's why it's so critical to get an advanced education.

"But, in reality, the wholistic approach is much more relevant to the true nature of life. All these varied and sundry scientific distinctions can ultimately be resolved into two areas.... physics and chemistry. And these two are the key to understanding the representations of spiritual law in the material world. Mathematics is also important in developing useful models of the scientific principles in our physical realm. You know, there are even fields such as BIOchemistry, and NUCLEARphysics, and ASTROphysics, and NUCLEARchemistry, etc., etc., etc.

"Interestingly enough, one of the most brilliant thinkers of modern times, Albert Einstein, mathematically validated an intuitive insight of the 'third world' civilizations, when he articulated something called the theory of relativity. Have you ever heard of it Manny?"

The question caught Manny off guard. He had fallen into a semi-trance state while listening to his uncle. Once Manny regained his attention, he told Derek that the theory wasn't familiar to him. "Can you explain what it is?" he asked.

"Well I'll try," Derek grinned, as he proceeded to describe what was completely Greek to Manny. "Einstein's theory points out the interdependent nature of the material realm as governed by chemical reactivity, and the physical laws of force, motion, and acceleration." Derek stood up suddenly, and as he did a blackboard mysteriously appeared out of the air. Even more strange was that the board just floated there.... with no stand or supports, nothing. Derek continually amazed Manny with the things he did.

"I needed some room in which to illustrate this principle Manny," he explained almost apologetically. On the board, he drew a large capital 'E' with an equal sign. Next to the equal sign, he wrote a small 'mc' and then a two, raised up slightly next to the small 'c'. "Einstein stated that energy E can be expressed by the mathematical relationship of matter m, times a constant of acceleration c, squared. $E = mc^2$. What this means is that any form of energy (which is a physical principle) can be derived from the acceleration of matter in just the right way, resulting in a chemical reaction..... transforming the matter   Have you ever taken algebra, Bud?"

"I'm supposed to have that next year. I'm really not looking forward to it. I don't like math or science, Uncle D."

Ignoring his comment, Derek continued. "From a spiritual point of view, everything we experience as physical in the material world is really a crystallization of different forms of energy. The inverse of this equation can be developed by dividing the expressions on both sides of the equal sign by 'c²'. Energy divided by the constant of acceleration equals matter, 'm'. Easy, huh Bud?"

Manny was completely lost. Despite his ignominy at not knowing quite what Derek was talking about, he marvelled at his ability to convey what had to be enormously complex ideas in what seemed to be such a simple way. He either had the most vivid imagination of anyone Manny had ever met, or he was a genius.

"One of the early applications of the theory of relativity was the development of the atomic bomb. You may have heard of the term 'atom smasher'. Atoms are the basic models of physical existence. In applying Einstein's theory, devices known as atom smashers were developed. By utilizing the process of centrifuging, a technique that highly accelerates the motion of the atomic structure, scientists were able to break down the atom. Breaking the elemental atomic model down releases tremendous energy. This is what is known as radioactivity. Unfortunately, such tremendous energy has most often been used for destructive purposes.

"Most of us are limited in our experiences by the frames of reference we rely upon to interact day to day in this world. I've referred to something called the constant of acceleration, 'c'. Another description for this constant is the speed of light. A key principle of physics is that light travels at the speed of 180 million miles per second. If, somehow, it were possible for us to 'accelerate' our physical state of being comparable to the speed of light, our frame of reference in experiencing the physical world would change, and our perception of the world would be completely different."

"Different in what way, Uncle D?" Manny asked breathlessly. Candidly, Derek had him on the edge of his seat.

Derek sat back down beside Manny. As he did, the floating blackboard disappeared. He spoke slowly, for emphasis. "What we would experience then Manny," he related, "would be the convergence of the spiritual and material worlds. We would be able to perceive the true nature of being." Derek paused to allow the import of what he'd said to linger for a moment. "Needless to say, we would never be the same again."

They sat there in silence for a long time. Manny really couldn't comprehend the significance of all of these things, but he could sense there was some part of him that, somehow, understood exactly what Derek was saying. Finally, Manny asked about the spiritual world. "Uncle D, what does the spirit look like?"

Derek glanced over at him. Putting his arm around Manny's shoulder he said, "It's getting late now, Manny, and I've talked your head off. That's a subject for another time. Right now we both need to get some sleep."

"Let me ask you one other thing," Manny gasped as a wide yawn broke through. "Why are you so concerned with spiritual things?"

"Well..... because, Manny, it is time for mankind to return to the truth. And the right relationship of spirit, soul, and body is the key to unlocking the truth, the meaning of life. As an individual, I simply refuse to live beneath my birthright as a man. We are all created in the image and likeness of God, and it is our unique privilege and responsibility as a species...... to manifest our God-likeness in this world. Our world is desperately in need of the creative power of the spirit...... to become apparent in a society out of sync. We must have the discipline, and the understanding of our identity as a people, to lift ourselves from the petty, the hateful and the destructive. We can work together to bring about the restoration of our culture, a great heritage hidden and lost among the fascination with Eurocentricity. Once you've come to realize these things, you'll refuse to live below your privileges too."

Derek looked at Manny sternly, then said with a reassuring warmth, "It's late sport. Time for bed." As Manny got up to go, Derek motioned for him to wait.

"Manny, don't forget your basketball. Your Mom left it out in the rain tonight." Derek ran over to the closet in the hall. Returning quickly, he flipped it over to Manny. "Don't worry, Manny. You won't be able to remember the things we've said tonight. But you'll recollect them at the right time. The spirit brings all things to our remembrance.... at the right time."

Having his ball again made Manny smile. "I know," he said grinning, "I don't know why...... but I know you're right."

Chapter 5

Mr. Boyfriend

"Manny..... Man-ny! Get up, Manny!" Asia's shouting abruptly shattered the otherwise peaceful silence of his very restful sleep. "You'd better get out of that bed, or you're going to be late for school. You know Mom doesn't like that." Nag, nag, nag. It was bad enough Manny had to put up with his mother and Gloria telling him what to do. Now Asia was acting like she was so grown. Sometimes it was a real pain..... being the youngest in the house.

At the foot of the bed was his basketball. Manny couldn't remember how it got there. The last he'd seen of it was when his mother took it and stormed off to attack Derek yesterday. He thought he remembered talking to Derek himself last night, but he wasn't sure. The recollection was unclear and that bothered him. Did he really talk to his uncle, or was it a dream?

Jumping up, Manny headed for the shower, his mind cluttered with images of the things Derek had said, or he had dreamed.... or both. The diagram of the pyramid, divided into three parts was vivid. And he recalled something about an Albert Feinstein and a 'theory of relatives', or something like that. Everything else, whatever else there was, was fuzzy. Manny was annoyed by the thought that he couldn't explain what happened, or whether or not anything had really happened at all.

When he got downstairs, Gloria told him Deidre had to leave early for work. Asia was in a hurry and couldn't wait for him to get to the bus. "I think your sister's got a new boyfriend," Gloria volunteered. "I remember when I was her age, and how big a crush I had on this cute boy, and how much I wanted to be around him!" She seemed to be enjoying her little stroll down memory lane, and Manny didn't have the heart to tell her he could care less about Asia's boyfriend. As long as it wasn't Haskell.

The thought suddenly scared him. "It's not Haskell, is it Gloria?"

His concern made her quake with laughter. "Oh no Manny, I don't believe Asia's interested in Haskell," she giggled. "You don't have to worry about him."

"Well, what makes you so sure she's even got a boyfriend?" Manny asked defiantly. He was sure Gloria would give him some off-the-wall answer about how..... 'women just know these things,' and he was determined not to go let her get away with it.

"Women just know these things, Manny," she responded, as if she read his mind. "I can tell by the way Asia was so anxious to get out of here. She looked very nice. And that's not just because she likes school, is it?"

Gloria was right. Asia was an okay student, but she wouldn't have gotten out of there so early unless there was a reason, and the boyfriend sounded as good as any. "Tell me, Gloria," he taunted, "what ever happened to the guy you were stuck on when you were young?"

Gloria looked at Manny, then down at the floor. She was pensive for a moment. It was obvious there were some painful memories that he'd inadvertently prompted her to recall. Abruptly, she began to speak. "We used to play hooky from school and go down to the beach in the middle of the day. It was so beautiful, watching the waves meet the shore. In those days, my mother would have my hide if she knew I was seeing him, and not going to school. In Trinidad back then, schooling was a precious luxury for most of us. She worked hard to give me the chance to even go. Most young girls my age dropped out early to go to work. Everyone had to pitch in to support the family's needs.

"You and Asia don't know how fortunate you are..... to have parents that care so much about your education, and provide so many opportunities for you both. Anyway, Hilliard.... that was his name, Hilliard Renfroe, wanted to get married. At least he said he did. But my mother was against it from the beginning. She felt the right thing was for me to finish my schooling, and to get a chance to go to college in America..... she always wished one of her children would graduate from an American university. It was about the time I had begun to compete seriously as a sprinter. I was selected for the Olympic trials in 1967. It was obvious Hilliard and I were headed in separate directions. He had a good job as a head waiter at a luxury hotel in the cafe district. And I met my husband at the Olympic trials. He was a boxer, a good one. But he just couldn't seem to avoid getting hit. I think I was infatuated more than anything else. Following the games in Mexico City in 1968, we were married. I was nineteen. He died three years later."

Boy! This was getting pretty heavy for Manny to relate to at 7:45 in the morning. A real tear jerker. He was surprised she wasn't all on the floor bawling her eyes out. He would have been! Gloria was so good to them and he really felt sorry for her. He didn't know what to say. Fortunately, she wasn't waiting for him to give her any encouragement. After a moment, she continued with her soliloquy.

"I guess the irony of the whole thing," she related, "was that I really loved Hilliard the entire time. And I knew it. Although he asked me to marry him, I didn't think he really loved me. I believed he was more in love with the idea of being married, than being with me. Men don't know what they want.... not until they're much older. They're just grown up boys Manny, like you. But I've always known what I wanted. I let my mother convince me of something different."

Well thanks, Gloria, Manny thought silently to himself. He always thought men were men and boys were boys. Women think they know everything about life.

"He got married shortly after I left for Mexico, and I've never seen him again." She paused to look at her watch. "My goodness, Manny.... it's after 8:00. You'd better get going!"

"Gee, Gloria," he tried to empathize. "I'm real sorry you and Hilliard didn't get together. You probably would have made a nice couple."

She smiled warmly and gave Manny a little hug. "Manny, thank you for listening to a lonely woman's lament." To his surprise, she released a loud laugh. "What do you think we ought to do about Asia's new boyfriend? You know your mother's very sensitive about her and the company she keeps."

As he was turning to leave Manny said the first thing that came to his mind. "Well, maybe you should have Asia invite the guy over for dinner. That might be a good way for us to get to know him. And Gloria, you shouldn't feel lonely.... you've always got us!"

Gloria looked at him with those huge amber colored eyes of hers, marvelling, "You know something Manny. I think Derek is right. You are wise for your age. Thank you for being such a good counselor!"

Manny could hear the horn of the school bus sounding. "See ya later, Gloria," he yelled, dashing madly out of the house. As he boarded the bus, Manny couldn't help but think what else was in store for him that day, after such a notable morning..... complete with true confession!

The sun was still low in the eastern sky over the Potomac River as Edison strode up the steps of the Capitol. He was out and about early, on his way to a breakfast meeting with several members of the energy subcommittee, and he was trying to focus on business at hand. He'd been thinking about Ms. Camille Ferguson until late into the night, and that wasn't good for one's attentiveness at an early morning meeting. Besides that, he was anxious to get home to Atlanta for a little rest and relaxation, and already he couldn't wait until the day was over.

Some of the other subcommittee members weren't planning to be very accommodating to him. There was resentment among a few key players over the fact that Edison had been selected to head the group in the first place. The post was considered a nothing job four months ago when he was named. No one on the Hill made much of an issue of it then. But now, with the antagonism growing in Namibia, and the information from research teams of the presence of super conductive materials there, Edison was getting tremendous visibility and good press. Some of his colleagues were impressed with his preparation and knowledge of the issues. The media had even begun to seek him out for his opinions on the questions of alternative energy and ecology in the country.

Of course, he relied completely on his staff, and Lance in particular, even though he was one of the youngest members of his team. The problem was that Edison particularly enjoyed the limelight, and was given to taking a not-so-subtle delight in the development of his reputation. Unfortunately, he was also creating several political enemies in the process, some powerful ones that would haunt him for years to come.

Meanwhile, the alarm clock in Lance's condo blared violently, or so it seemed to his aching head. This electronic wake up call was something other than music to his ears. Struggling over to the night table out of his stupor, he finally succeeded in turning the damn thing off. "Oh no," he lamented. "I'm late!" Rolling out of bed, he made his way into the bathroom and the shower. Moments later, with a thick lather of shaving cream reflecting at him in the mirror, Lance's thoughts wandered back to what Deidre had said to him the night before. *I wonder if she's really concerned about me...... or just being nice. Edison doesn't really know what he's got in that woman. A beautiful, intelligent, caring, lovely....... successful lawyer, for God's sake! What I wouldn't give to have a woman like that!* Lance felt himself becoming aroused, the more he thought about her.

C'mon, man.... get a grip! This is the boss' wife you're talking about! he told himself. Despite his silent protest, the stiff manhood between his legs convinced him that there was no way Edison could satisfy..... such a fine woman the way he could.

Half an hour after the alarm clock buzzed in his ears, Lance was ready to hit the morning rush. Well, not quite. On a small table near the door Lance kept a little stash of cocaine. He took three deep hits. Moistening the tip of his index finger, he dipped it in and ran the finger up inside his mouth, over his gums. Breathing deeply, he licked his lips once and wiped off his

moustache. "Lookout D.C.! Lance Ro-mance.... is good to go!"
he shouted triumphantly. Moments later he was out the door and
down the stairs, his long, throbbing erection still intact.

Later that day, Asia and Geri met at school for lunch. Geri
was uncharacteristically bitchy, even for her. "Hey Ger," Asia
greeted her, "what's the matter?"

Geri looked at her with disdain. "Why does something
always have to be wrong, huh Ace?" she snapped at Asia. "I'm
just a little preoccupied that's all." Asia thought it might be that
her time of the month was approaching. Geri was one of those
girls who had a tough go of it with her period. She really got
uptight during the days leading up to it. She had tried some of the
newer PMS treatments, to no avail.

But this behavior was a little different. She seemed despondent, almost depressed. They sat there silently for several minutes, Asia digging heartily into her tuna hoagie. Geri picked
absently at her food. Suddenly, Asia spoke up. "Alright, Geri,
what's going on? You've been acting strange for the past week,
and I want to know why. You're supposed to confide in me, I am
your friend, aren't I?" She was expecting Geri to tell her about
some family crisis, or that she was concerned about her grades,
and whether she would pass on to the twelfth grade. Or, maybe
she was pregnant!

"Well, if you must know what's bothering me," Geri began,
"I'll tell you. You're bothering me, Ace. It's you!" The air
between them was so thick, you'd have trouble cutting it with a
knife. It never occurred to Ace that SHE was the problem. They

had been such good and fast friends since the ninth grade; Asia confided in and trusted Geri thoroughly.

Her response took Asia totally by surprise. "Tell me then, Geri, what am I doing to upset you so much?"

"Ever since you met this Jason guy, you haven't even given me the time of day. I thought we were friends Ace. But now, every time we're supposed to do something, you just DIS' me. And I don't appreciate it, not one bit!"

So.... that was it. Asia never paid attention to the fact that Geri resented the time and attention she paid to Jason. Ironically, Asia first met him at Geri's house. Her brother Miles and Jason were just completing their freshman year at Morehouse, and Miles had him over one evening when Ace and Geri were there, just hanging out after school. "But Geri, you KNOW you're my best friend," Asia protested. "Why would you think that would ever change?"

Jason was from New York City, the Bronx to be exact. Ace thought he was a lot of fun, just as crazy as he could be. He was a good student, studying pre-med, and that was sure to impress her mother, Asia rationalized. Jason wasn't at all anxious to return to the City for the summer. He had come to enjoy Atlanta, and somehow was more interested in what Ace was going to be doing, rather than going home to the streets of Bronx, N.Y. He would tell Asia stories of the gangs and street wars he'd seen growing up. He even claimed to have known Mike Tyson before he became famous. She thought he was such a great guy, really interesting and fun to be around. There was only one problem: Jason liked to get high. He didn't do it around Asia or Geri. But he liked getting high. Jason was spending the last two weeks on campus taking a preliminary course on advanced biology before he returned to New York for the summer. Asia wanted to spend as much time as she could with him before he went home. In the process, she had neglected her friends, especially Geri.

"Wha'da ya mean, why do I think our friendship was GOING to change?" Geri exclaimed with a look of amazement. "It already HAS changed. Ace, all you think about is Jason this.... Jason that, he's all you want to talk about. You know, I thought you were more mature than that." Geri was digging the knife in deeply now. "But this guy, I mean you act like he's........ like he's........ BIG DADDY KANE, or something! I don't know about you anymore Ace, I just don't know."

Geri's disillusionment was beginning to sink in as Asia heard the bell for fifth period ring. "I don't feel like eating anymore," Asia said. She gathered herself up to head for her English class.

"Yeah.... I guess it's time to write some love letters to JASON, huh Ace?" snapped Geri, her tone dripping with resentment and sarcasm.

"Geri, I'm real sorry you feel this way," Asia responded in an attempt to placate her feelings. "No matter what you think, you're still my friend. My best friend, no matter what." Asia turned to go. As she left, Geri felt a tear form in her eye then slide slowly down her dark brown cheek. She couldn't control her emotions and that made her even angrier. She was quite a sight leaving the cafeteria.... cursin' and cryin', cryin' and cursin'.

By the time she arrived at home later that afternoon, Asia was distraught. It greatly upset her how personally Geri was taking her interest in Jason. She sat down in the kitchen, staring blankly at the woods beyond the pool when Gloria walked in. "Well, hello Asia," Gloria greeted her cheerfully as she peered into the microwave to check on the turkey she was preparing. "Your father is coming home tomorrow and your Mother wanted me to get as much cooking done today as I could." Asia didn't answer, didn't acknowledge her presence at all. Gloria knew something was wrong.

Sitting down beside her, Gloria put her arm around Asia's shoulder. "Tell me, baby..... what's bothering you? Are you having trouble with your boyfriend?"

Her question startled Asia out of her reverie. "How did you know, Gloria?" she whispered, completely surprised by her insight.

"You know, I've was a young woman once, in my time," Gloria told her comfortingly. "Now tell me.... what's wrong?"

Asia hesitated at first, but slowly opened up as Gloria gave her her full attention. "His name is Jason," she began. "And he's a lot of fun, really an interesting person, you know, Gloria. But he's leaving for New York next weekend to go home for the summer."

"To go home?" Gloria inquired quizzically.

"Yeah, he's a freshman at Morehouse. He isn't all that attractive you understand, but we get along well together, you know?" Asia seemed to be trying to justify him to herself.

"Well isn't he coming back in the fall?" Gloria reasoned with her. "Don't worry, the summer will go by fast. Before you know it, he'll be back."

"Yeah, I'm sure you're right Gloria. But, truthfully, it's not Jason that's worrying me so much. It's Geri. She thinks I've DISsed her, for him. And that's not true, it's just not true! She's my best friend!" The anxiety and frustration that had built up since lunch couldn't be contained any longer. Asia burst out in tears. "She's my FRIEND!"

Gloria looked upon, and treated Asia just like the daughter she'd always wanted, but never had. "Now, now..... don't you cry my Asia," Gloria comforted her, taking Asia's head into her arms of reassurance. "Now listen to me," she continued with Asia crying profusely in her lap. "Sometimes, girls don't understand..... when their girlfriends become interested in boys. They can get upset, even jealous. But don't you worry. In time, Geri will realize how much you care for her, how much you value her friendship."

"But Gloria, what can I do? I don't want Geri to hate me for the rest of her life. What should I do?"

"All you can do is be true to yourself and what you believe Asia. You know how you feel about this young man, and how you feel about Geri. Be true to your feelings. Learn to trust your instincts. You won't always be right, but you can at least be consistent..... with the people you care about. And I know you care about Geri. Try to do your best. That's all you can do, baby. That's it."

Asia continued to sob heartily, as Gloria lovingly stroked her thick, dark hair. "I do know of something else you can do," Gloria whispered softly into her ear. "You can invite your young man over here for dinner next week, before he goes home."

That certainly got Asia's attention, and she sat up straight vigorously wiping the tears from her eyes. "Do you really mean it, Gloria?" she gasped, wide eyed. "I've been thinking about that for a while, but I was afraid to ask Mom. You know how she acts with me sometimes."

"Don't you worry about your mother," Gloria said confidently. "I'll handle that end of things. You just take care of getting... er... um..... what's the boy's name again?" she stammered, slightly embarrassed to have forgotten so quickly.

"JASON. His name is Jason!" Asia laughed out loud. "Oh, Gloria, thank you so much for listening to me. You're the best! Sometimes I wish you were my Mom."

"Hush that up, Asia. Your mother is a wonderful woman. Now you get going and let me get some work done. And don't worry, I'll handle things around here for you!"

Asia gave her a long, warm embrace and kissed her lovingly on the cheek. "Gosh, I feel so much better now," she gushed and went up to her room..... to call Jason.

Gloria went back to her turkey roast, the tears of joy and tenderness streaming down her face. *I guess you see a lot of yourself in that girl, huh Gloria?* she thought to herself. *Well she's Ms. Castle's child.... and not yours. You're just the house-keeper...... so don't torture yourself this way. Just mind your own business.... for a change.* Her self chastisement couldn't keep Gloria from succumbing to her own feelings. She loved the Castles, and Asia in particular. And if she wanted to cry about it, well then she thought, that was her perogative. So she did.

Who should happen to walk in at that moment, but the happy go lucky Emanuel Castle, a.k.a. Manny, arriving from school after a strenuous basketball practice. Manny was in a great mood! The coach had asked him to try out for the team in the fall! He wanted Manny to attend a basketball camp that summer.... which started in about three and a half weeks; Manny thought that would be enough time to convince his mother to let him go.

Of course, the sight of Gloria bawling her eyes out as she stood staring at the microwave oven caused Manny to think she had been pining over Hilliard there in the kitchen all day long. "Hey, Gloria, it's me, Manny," he said loudly trying to get her attention. "Come on, cheer up. We love you!" The words made her weep even more uncontrollably. Manny was really getting concerned that she was having a breakdown or something. Fortunately, at that very moment the phone rang, and grabbed his attention. It was Deidre.

"Hi, Mom!" Manny cheerfully greeted his mother. "Boy, am I glad to talk to you!"

"Hi, Honey, what are you so happy about? How was school?"

"School was great!" His enthusiasm surprised Deidre. Manny had never been so adamant about his schoolday before. Abruptly shifting the conversation, he called her attention to Gloria. "Mom, I think you need to talk to Gloria."

"Well.... sure, honey, I'll talk to her. Did she finish cooking? Your father will be home tomorrow and I wanted to have the smoked turkey ready for him. Why don't you let me speak to her?"

Manny handed the receiver to Gloria. She frantically tried to pull herself together, wiping the tears from her brown face with a kitchen towel. Deidre grew more concerned the longer it took for Gloria to get on the line. She could tell Gloria had been crying.

"What's wrong, Gloria? Why are you crying? Are you sick?"

"No.... no, Ms. Castle, I'm fine," she gasped, nearly in a whisper. "It's just that I'm so.... I'm so.... happy, it made me cry."

Manny thought to himself how completely illogical women were. It crossed his mind that he could never see himself living with or being married to one, having to put up with such an irrational and emotional person, day to day. And he LIKED Gloria.

Deidre was at a loss for words, not knowing what could have possibly brought on such an outburst from her. Gloria was normally the most even keeled woman one would ever meet.

"Ms. Castle, next week is the end of the school year for the children. I thought it 'd be nice to have dinner here for Asia and a few of her friends. Would you mind terribly if we did that?"

Gloria was so smooth in her delivery, it caught Deidre unaware. "Don't you think that would be a good idea?"

"Well... um.... yes, I guess so," responded Deidre weakly. "But you know Edison will be here and I don't know what he'll have to say about it. Don't you think we should check with him?"

"Oh, Ms. Castle," Gloria began softly, "I was recalling today how, when I was a young girl, my mother never really let us children entertain back at home. She was ashamed of our little house, I guess." As Gloria related her story the tears returned, and the quiet sobbing discernible over the phone was just too much for Deidre to argue with.

"Listen, Gloria," she interrupted, "tell Asia I said dinner next week is fine; it's OK with me. I'm finishing some work on a deposition, so I'll be home a little late this evening. And please, Gloria, don't cry anymore. You know we care about you."

Having accomplished her mission, Gloria's smile broke through the cloud of weeping. "Thank you so much, Ms. Castle. I'm sure Asia will be pleased. And the turkey's almost done! You have a good evening." CLICK!

Manny pulled a cold Coke from the refrigerator and sat down at the table, amazed at Gloria's persuasive power. He even thought he might enlist her assistance..... to help sell his parents on going to basketball camp.

Gloria looked knowingly at him. "You know Manny, this has been such a happy day for me," she commented wiping her face gently. "How was your day?"

Manny returned a furtive glance. "You know, Gloria," he replied with the utmost sincerity, "it's days like today that make getting up every morning..... such an adventure!" His comment incited the biggest laugh from her.

"It's amazing," she chuckled, "you sound more and more like your Uncle every day!"

In Washington, the congressional workday had just passed its midpoint. Edison spent all morning in meetings at the Capitol. Afterwards, there was a luncheon appointment with several lobbyists and a brief stop in the congressional registrar's office in the basement of the Capitol building.

Boarding the underground train that linked all of the legislative offices on Capitol Hill, his mind returned to Camille Ferguson. She would make a good legislator, or even a lobbyist, he thought as the tiny shuttle wound its way beneath SE 7th St. He was headed for a late afternoon meeting in the Dirksen Senate office building. Lance was to join him there in the office of John Torch, State Executive Assistant to Sen. Dunn of Georgia. *Hmmmm... maybe one of my esteemed colleagues can use someone of Camille's ability on their staff*, Edison wondered to himself as the car pulled into Dirksen.

He hopped on one of the elevators reserved for the legislators and rode up to the 6th floor. Torch had asked Edison over earlier that week, but he had been tied up in his subcommittee meetings. He thought he'd better see John before he left town, however. It was quite important for him to maintain a good relationship, both publicly and privately with the Senator. And Edison liked and respected Senator Dunn, as well as John Torch. Besides, he aspired someday, in the not too distant future, to succeed the distinguished Senator Dunn, who headed the powerful Senate Armed Services Committee.

Emerging sprightly from the elevator, Edison immediately spotted Lance pacing nervously up and down the hall outside John Torch's office. "What's wrong?" Edison inquired of his aide as he walked up.

"I'm terribly sorry, Congressman," offered Lance apologetically, "but I completely forgot to tell you that John phoned the office late yesterday to cancel this appointment. Apparently, Senator Dunn had something he needed him to do this afternoon. I tried to let you know this morning, but I couldn't locate you."

Edison was actually relieved to have the meeting off his schedule. However, he was careful to make sure Lance thought he felt more upset by the situation, than he really did. That was a key to being a good manager. His father had always told him that to be really successful, surround yourself with talented people, give them their own space and responsibilities, but always seem more dissatisfied with lapses or poor performance than you really were. That way, you would be able to assert your position of power without being viewed as domineering or aggressive.

"Well... it's a damn good thing you got here to let me know what was going on," Edison chastised him. "I could have been sitting around wasting a lot of time, kibitzing with the secretaries and such!" Lance looked genuinely distressed by the whole affair. Edison decided that it might be advisable to let him down easily. "I'm sure that all John wanted us for was to let us know about the Senator's next fund raiser," he said in a sincere effort to calm Lance down. "Make sure you get in touch with his secretary and inform her I'll be out of town next week."

The color began to return to Lance's cheeks. "Yes sir," he responded eagerly.

"What about my tickets for Atlanta?" It was very interesting how well Edison could move so quickly from one subject to another, without missing a beat.

"I've got them right here," Lance answered triumphantly. "The limo will pick you up at the townhouse at 8:30 in the morning." Lance felt better and more focused now, and was glad he could discuss the travel arrangements, which he was right on top of. "Oh, and Congressman, you received a call from a woman named Camille Ferguson. She sounded very nice over the phone." Lance paused, perhaps to see if his comment engendered some type of reaction from the Congressman. No such luck.

"Well........ was there anything special she had to say?" Edison scoffed with just a slight bit of disdain in his voice.

"No.... not really," Lance countered. "She simply said she'd speak to you when you returned." He suspected that there was more to this encounter than Edison was willing to disclose, but Lance decided the proper course to take at that point was to just drop the subject, for the time being.

"You know Lance, I'm pretty beat today," confided Edison. "I think I'm going to head over to the club, get in a workout and have some dinner. Have my files ready for me by 8:00 P.M. I'd like them dropped off at my house this evening. And Lance, I expect you to stay on top of things next week while I'm out of town." Edison seemed relieved his official workday was over. And despite the momentary impatience with his protege, he clearly relied tremendously on Lance's judgement.

"I'll have the papers ready at 8:00 sir," Lance replied half-heartedly. "See you then." As he turned to leave, Edison poked his head into John Torch's office to flirt briefly with the secretaries and female staff aides inside.

Lance departed quickly and headed straight for the office. He knew that several hours of work lay ahead of him in order to get all the papers into a format Edison could use while on the road. Although he really enjoyed his job and the whole congressional scene, Lance secretly couldn't wait until Edison got on that plane the next morning!

The day dawned brightly in Atlanta on Friday. Deidre awakened early and helped Gloria get the children off to school. Gloria left the house about 8:30 A.M. She took classes on Mondays, Wednesdays, and Fridays, and would be gone until about 4:00 P.M. Deidre decided to take a warm bath, and afterwards dressed slowly, enjoying a leisurely morning in her own company.

Edison was due in around 11:30 A.M. and she wanted to look her best. From her lingerie drawer she pulled out some beautiful silk underwear. Out of the closet came a lovely flowered print sun dress which she coordinated with white sandals. A touch of blush and eye shadow, followed by hot pink lipstick, completed her sultry summer look. Gazing fondly into the mirror she mused softly, *alright Edison, let's see if you're ready for me.... after hanging around all those single women in Washington!* She looked quite fabulous, with a perfect bronze tan enhancing her skin. Her long and shapely legs were prominently displayed by the sundress, as was her back, which was exposed by a daringly low cut design.

The ride through downtown to the airport took about thirty-five minutes. It was a glorious day; the sun shone brightly as it reflected off the tubular glass tower of the Peachtree Plaza Hotel, and the shimmering emerald cube of the Inforum. Deidre felt great.... and she really surprised herself at how excited she was to see Edison again. It had been nearly three weeks. And it wasn't much fun sleeping alone, even if you didn't have to deal with a man snoring, most ungraciously, in the bed beside you.

His plane touched down right on time, Gate 23, Concourse A. Edison made it a point of flying first class whenever he could. He hated the congestion and bustle that routinely took place when it was time to deplane. From his aisle seat, it was an easy hop off the flight to the jetway, and out into the concourse.

Inside the airport, Edison could feel the warmth and humidity so characteristic of summer in Atlanta. He loved it. As he came around the check-in desk at the gate, his eyes were drawn to a young woman approximately fifteen feet away, tall and bronze skinned, facing away from him. She was quite stunning, at least from the rear. Her back was fully exposed, with shapely legs, and outfitted in a lovely print sundress, with a white hat and matching shoes. A perfect southern belle, he imagined silently. His attention thus arrested, Edison momentarily forgot that Deidre was supposed to be meeting him.

Just as he looked at his watch, the mystery woman turned around. Edison was shocked! It WAS Deidre. "DEIDRE!" he shouted, almost involuntarily. "My God, I didn't recognize you!"

"Hello, honey," she calmly replied, "did you have a good trip?" They launched themselves toward one another, and locked into a deep embrace complete with a long, wet display of passionate kissing, right there in the midst of the mild crush of humanity that was scrambling to make their flights.

Two young men walking by stopped to gaze at the middle aged lovers. "Yo, check these two out!" said one of the youths to the other. "Atlanta must be a great place to get together."

His buddy joined in, "Yeah, you're right...... it must have been a long time since HOMEBOY last saw his old lady!" The two of them high fived, and laughed heartily as they made their way to the gate for Delta 107, bound for New York.

"Well, bigboy," Deidre gasped when they finally broke their clinching. "Is that a pistol in your pocket.... or are you just glad to see me?" she teased him. She was in a good mood and couldn't resist the urge to needle her spousal unit. Edison smiled sheepishly. He felt embarrassed once he realized that everyone in the concourse had been thoroughly enjoying his impromptu tete-a-tete. Several couples were actually applauding the two of them.

He grabbed her arm and they quickly made their way, as discretely as possible, down the concourse and on to the train that would transport them to the baggage claim area. "I'm sorry, Dee," Edison apologized as they boarded the airport subway. "I didn't mean to act so foolishly back there. It's just that you...... you.... look so WONDERFUL, I couldn't control myself!" Even for a person as polished as he was at stroking someone's ego, Edison was quite sincere in his comment. And Deidre was loving every minute of it!

"So.... you didn't remember you had a wife worth looking at, did you Buddy?" She took positive delight at his self-consciousness because she knew he was entirely unprepared for her reception.

He tried to change the subject. "Well, how are you Deidre? Are things going smoothly around the house? How are Asia and Manny? You know it's been very hectic the past week or so in Washington."

"Things are going pretty well Edison. I'm having a little trouble with a couple of my clients, holding up payment for some work I've performed, but nothing really too disturbing. Gloria's been acting a little strange lately, though."

The mention of Gloria, and any talk of her not being upright and normal surprised him. "What do you mean, she's been acting strange?" Edison wanted to know.

"She was having this crying spell yesterday," Deidre explained. "And she wants to have dinner at the house for Asia and her friends next week, once school ends. You do realize your children get out of school Wednesday, don't you?"

Of course..... not. Edison didn't have the foggiest idea that the school year was about to end, and summer vacation set to begin. "Maybe Gloria's feeling a little blue. A dinner party might be nice," he pointed out. "We haven't entertained at home in a long time, in fact not since the last time your Mother was here." Deidre looked at him with a scornful glare in her eye, and there was an edgy silence for the remainder of the ride. Shortly, the train arrived at the baggage claim area. They took the escalator ride up to the main terminal, and picked up his bags. Within twenty minutes, they were on the way home.

In the car, their conversation returned to small talk, centering around his activities with the energy subcommittee. Although the topic was something he was altogether familiar with, Edison couldn't get his mind off Deidre and how great she looked. And she smelled heavenly. She was radiant and in a cheerful frame of mind Even some of his joking, which she normally considered to be in poor taste, didn't seem to bother her that day. Soon, they were pulling into the circular driveway in the front of the house. "Boy, what's gotten into Enrico? The grounds haven't looked this well kept in months," Edison remarked noting the improvements in the landscape since the last time he was home.

"Enrico's in Savannah with his sister," answered Deidre. "The doctor suggested he get some rest, so he's been convalescing on the coast for the past few weeks. He's no spring chicken anymore you know."

"Well, who's been working on the yard? Did you find a new gardener?" he inquired, totally out of touch with the goings-on of his own household.

"Never mind that now," she countered, not desiring to discuss the fact that Derek had been managing the grounds in Enrico's absence. Deidre thought it might be better to avoid any discussions of her brother with him right then. "Just bring your things inside," she instructed him as she whirled to open the door.

Once upstairs, Edison began to unpack. He removed a folder marked 'READ FILE: VERY IMPORTANT' from a small valise in one of the bags. Setting it down on an end table, he returned to the suitcases. Then he pulled a small case from his bag. Before going to the airport, he'd stopped and picked out a diamond tennis bracelet for her. Just then, Deidre came in. She was wearing only a silk camisole and a pair of lace panties. She carried a tray with two champagne glasses, filled with what appeared to be a cranberry colored version of the bubbly. "I thought you might want to relax with a couple of Charley Parkers after your trip," she said softly. Edison could feel his excitement rising, and nearly forgot to give her the gift. After a long sip of his drink, there was no way he could contain himself any longer.

He nearly ripped off his clothes, as the rush of passion absorbed him. They made love there in the brightly lit bedroom urgently, savagely, for the better part of an hour. It had been a while, for Deidre particularly, and she was letting herself go, biting his neck, trying to swallow his tongue, digging her nails deeply into his buttocks, as their rhythmic thrusting built to a heated climax. When they were finished, a wonderful state of relaxation settled over them, coupled with a sense of quiet satisfaction in the room.

It was just after 2:00 P.M., but the fact that it was the middle of the day seemed only to enhance their sensuousness and excitement. As they lounged there in bed, legs locked in a casual embrace, Edison abruptly turned over and grabbed the telephone. Startled, Deidre sat up. "Who are you calling now honey?" she wondered aloud.

"I'm calling my travel agent, Dee-Dee," he answered with an air of enthusiasm. "I need to check on something." Her instincts immediately sensed something was wrong. She felt betrayed that he would be thinking of business at a time like that, but something in the back of her mind told her to hold her tongue, despite the difficulty of restraining herself at that moment.

"Hello, Kyle? This is Edison Castle. Do you have any seats left on that three day excursion to Cancun? Yes, that's the one. You do.... great! Please book the trip for two...... I'll pick the tickets up at the airport. How's everyone at home? That's wonderful. Listen, I've got to run. Thanks for your help." CLICK!

Edison rolled over on top of his startled wife, and kissed her eagerly. "Well Baby," he spoke up, "how would you like to go to Mexico?" Deidre's surprise at her husband's offer was nearly too much for her to handle. She didn't answer right away. "Dee.... are you all right? What's the matter? I thought you loved Mexico?" Edison began to feel as if he'd said something wrong.

"No, nothing's wrong," she was finally able to respond. "It's just that the last time we discussed this, we were going to Carroway Gardens.... that's all."

"Well.... doesn't a man have the right to change his mind every now and then? Now c'mon, we've got to get busy. The plane leaves at 4:00 P.M. Don't forget your bathing suit."

"But, Edison," Deidre protested mildly, "the children won't get home until a quarter of. Don't you want to see them? You haven't seen your son for over three weeks."

Edison was reassuring, but firm. "Of course I want to see them honey! But we'll be back Monday night, and they can wait a few more days. Besides, Gloria will take care of the house while we're away. You could use a vacation, Deidre. Trust me!" Without another thought, he hopped out of bed pulling on his briefs, and went back to his suitcases to repack for the weekend. Deidre simply shook her head and headed to the closet to get her bags. He was right about one thing, she sure did need a vacation. As she started pulling out a few outfits for the trip, Deidre recognized she needed to freshen up. Immediately, she ran into the bathroom for a quick shower, closing the door behind her.

Meanwhile, Derek had been working vigorously outside in the heat since 11:30 that morning trying to repair a feeder valve to the underground sprinkler system. He'd finished all the ice water in his thermos and decided that it was probably a good time to take a break, so he went to the house for some refreshment.

Upstairs, Edison heard Derek moving around down in the kitchen. "Deidre, Deidre," he whispered anxiously, "Someone's in the house. I think it's a burglar!" She was inside the shower, and couldn't hear what he had said. Without waiting for an answer, Edison went to his wardrobe and pulled a thirty-eight revolver from a private compartment behind a small shelf inside. Immediately, he headed for the stairs.

Quietly, cautiously, Edison crept down the staircase, convinced there was an intruder in the kitchen. At the landing he paused, careful that his motions were not detected by the burglar. He slipped unnoticed into the dining room, readying himself to pounce savagely on his unsuspecting prey. Derek, preoccupied by his perusal of the interior landscape of Deidre's refrigerator, was bent over, completely oblivious to the stalking actions of this most merciless of predators.

Carefully, Edison maneuvered into position for the attack. He checked his revolver to be sure it was loaded, and the firing pin released. Everything was in a state of readiness. Now was the time to strike!

"All right, you thieving motherfucker!" shouted Edison the Enforcer, as he leaped into action. "Get out of that damn refrigerator, and put your hands up over your head where I can see 'em! NOW! I've got my weapon trained on you!"

Uh oh, Derek thought to himself, Edison's finally gone off the deep end. Stepping back slowly, he stood up straight, revealing a plastic container of tuna fish salad in one hand, and a clear decanter of orange juice in the other. "Gee, Edison," said Derek quite seriously, "I know I'm not one of your favorite people, but I didn't think it had gotten to the point that you wanted to gun me down!"

The sight of his brother-in-law at once both relieved and annoyed Edison. "Derek! What the fuck are you doing in here?" he remarked, thoroughly exasperated. "Can't you ring the damn doorbell.... like a normal person?"

After hearing the commotion, Deidre came dashing down the stairs. "What's going on?" she wanted to know, as she came rushing in.

"Well.... I can see I've interrupted quite a heated little interlude here," Derek said, slightly embarrassed. Edison was standing there in nothing but his Calvin Kleins, and all Deidre had on was silk and lace underwear. "Please accept my apology. I'll go crawl back under my rock," Derek snarled, not the least bit sarcastically. "By the way, Edison, you need to watch your mouth," he reprimanded. "All that profanity is unnecessary. Children pick up those kinds of things you know."

Edison didn't appreciate Derek's comment one bit. "Just be glad I didn't SHOOT your black ass," he bellowed at him. "Deidre, you need to tell your brother how to mind his own damn business," he said turning for the stairs to finish his packing. "I'm ready to go! Let's get the hell out of here!"

"What HAPPENED?" Deidre inquired anxiously of her younger brother. "What in the world did you do, to set him off like that?"

"What do you mean, what did I do?" he asked incredulously. "Deidre, did it ever occur to you that maybe you're married to a bona fide maniac, a real madman?" Derek's tone was earnest. He held a genuine, but private concern that she was at risk to Edison's violent outbursts. But he'd promised himself years ago not to interfere with his sister's marriage, once she made her decision. His own hadn't been quite a smashing success, to say the least.

Ironically, Edison and Deidre shared the same concern about Derek's own sanity, or lack thereof. And the influence he could have on Manny. Although in truth, Derek had never pulled a gun on anyone as Edison had done. After a few moments, Deidre and Derek both calmed down enough to speak more civilly to one another. "Dee-Dee," he began "all I did was come in for a tuna sandwich and something to drink. The next thing I knew, your husband, the gunslinger, had his piece drawn and ready to fire. I'm sorry, but I didn't know you two were even here. I guess he thought I was a burglar or something."

Deidre could only shake her head resignedly. "I'm going to hear about this all weekend now," she lamented softly. "We're going out of town this afternoon Derek. We'll be in Cancun until Monday. When we get to the hotel, I'll call to let you and Gloria know where we'll be staying. And please, D, take good care of the house and the kids while I'm gone. Do you think you can do that for me? Huh?"

Derek's spirits seemed to perk up when she mentioned their impending trip. He resisted the urge to say good riddance to his brother-in-law, and simply answered her with, "Of course, I'll be sure to take care of things while you're away. What do you want me to tell the kids when they get in?"

"Just tell them we're in Mexico for the weekend and to listen to Gloria. I'll call this evening. Please, D, don't make any trouble, OK?"

Derek was a little annoyed that he was perceived as having caused any trouble, but he didn't say anything. "You have my word, Dee-Dee," he responded dutifully.

"Well, let me get back upstairs and finish my packing," she said. "We've got to get to the airport. I'm glad we had a chance to talk."

Just then, Edison's voice rained down with emphasis, "Deidre, let's GO!"

"Well, sports fans..... I guess that means we're out of time for today!" Derek scoffed at his brother-in-law's verbal notice by demand. "By the way, Dee-Dee," he remarked as she was leaving, "you've got on some hellacious underwear there, girlfriend. No wonder Easy Ed is so beside himself!" They both went their way, laughing heartily at his observation.

Half an hour later, Deidre and Edison were ready to load their bags into the car. She scribbled a note for Gloria and left it in the kitchen on the counter. Edison had the READ FILE folder in his hands when they came down the stairs. Inadvertently, he left the classified information on a chair in the dining room. In his haste to depart, he completely forgot the papers. At 3:05 they were on their way to Interlude Part II, Cancun.

Around 3:45, Gloria arrived home from school and her errands. After a brief stop to unload her packages, she changed clothes and headed for the kitchen to prepare dinner. She was somewhat surprised things were so quiet around the house. She knew Edison was scheduled to arrive that morning, and it usually got very lively when he was around.

Gloria pulled the roast turkey she had prepared the day before from the freezer, and was about to pop it into the microwave when she found Deidre's note. As she read it, a small chuckle livened up her demeanor. She found it amusing that Deidre had been able to convince him to take her somewhere other than Carroway Gardens, or so she made it seem in her note to Gloria. An impatient knock on the glass door that separated the kitchen area from the deck interrupted her. It was Derek.

Gloria started to tell him the news about Edison and Deidre, but he motioned to her that he already knew what was going on. Before he could fill her in on HIS story of everything that had taken place that afternoon, in walked Manny, followed shortly afterward by Asia.

"Well, isn't this a treat?" Derek jokingly remarked. "Our prize students, home from school together. Must be a special occasion for you two to be here so early, on such a beautiful day."

"Where's Mom and Dad?" Asia inquired of her uncle and housekeeper.

"Well, we're all here," Gloria responded, as if it were her responsibility to deliver some kind of awful news, "but your parents have gone away for the weekend. According to your Mom's note, they'll be back Monday night. She says that you're under my care until she returns. I'm sorry Asia." Her tone was laced with a touch of disappointment, not for herself, but for the kids. She felt a little sad that Edison and Deidre had run off so quickly without notice, but she also realized Ms. Castle needed the rest and relaxation.

Asia and Manny looked quickly at one another. A barely perceptible smile graced Manny's lips. Asia, on the other hand, seemed a little dejected. "I guess you're pretty disappointed not to get to see your Dad, huh Ace?" instigated Derek, as he reached into the refrigerator for a cold apple.

"Actually," said Asia, "I was hoping to catch Mom. I've got two free tickets for a concert tonight at the Lakewood Amphitheater, and I was hoping she would let me go."

"Well.... you heard what your mother put in her note," Derek reminded her. "We're all under Gloria's care until your Mom gets back."

"Hey, that's right!" Manny chimed in. "Since Mom's not here, you ought to be asking Gloria if you can go. What do you say, Gloria?" Manny asked, speaking up for his sister who seemed abnormally reticent.

Gloria could tell something was amiss with Asia other than getting permission for the show. She tried to draw it out of her.

"Asia, it's fine with me if you'd like to see the concert. Is there anything else wrong?"

The emotion and disappointment were clear on her face. "It's Geri," she finally confessed. Tears began to form in her eyes. "The reason I wanted the tickets in the first place was so she and I could do something together. But she doesn't want to do anything with me ever again..... she hates my guts!" Her exclamation came as something of a shock to Manny and Derek, who had no clue as to what the problem might be. Gloria, of course, had a different perspective on the situation since she was aware of the type of trauma girlfriends faced over boys. Asia wept softly in her arms.

Manny and Derek could only gaze at one another and shrug in confusion. Geri and Asia were best friends. What could have come between them? In an attempt to change the mood, Derek spoke up. "Who's performing tonight, Ace?" he asked his niece. Wiping her face, she told him that the show was called 'Hip-Hop Renaissance', starring her number one hero and idol, Big Daddy Kane! Geri loved him too, but now she didn't want to go, and without her friend the show would be a complete drag. Things were pretty serious.

"Well.... I've got an idea," Derek said with a distinctive gleam in his eye. "Gloria..... why don't you go with her? You haven't had a chance to get out too much lately, and who knows..... you may run into some old friends there." He looked at Gloria with an urgent expression, as if it were somehow crucial for her to be at this concert. "Is that alright with you, Ace?" he asked. Immediately, Asia brightened up.

"Now wait a minute," Gloria protested. "Who says I haven't been getting out much lately? Besides, I have no idea who this Big Daddy person is. And what are you going to do out there with a woman old enough to be your mother, Asia? In fact, I'm nearly old enough to be your grandmother! I like Johnny Mathis, Harry Belafonte, Nat King Cole...... and Luther Vandross! What is Hip-Hop anyway?" The more Gloria talked, the less convincing she was. They all stood there silently, with expressionless faces that told her she wasn't being persuasive, not in the least.

"Please, Gloria," Asia pleaded. "It would be great to have you go with me. We'll have a wonderful time!" It was obvious her enthusiasm had returned. Having a chance to see 'Big Daddy' live and in color was a once in a lifetime opportunity as far as she was concerned.

Gloria cared so much for Asia that she hated to disappoint her. Finally, she relented. "Well.... OK, if you insist, I'd be happy to go with you."

"All-right!" crowed Derek and Manny as they exchanged high fives with one another.

"I guess you girls better go freshen up before showtime," advised Derek. "Don't worry about dinner, I'll rustle up something for Manny and me." Determined not to let his sister receive all the benefit of Gloria's generosity, Manny promptly requested he be allowed to spend the night at Haskell's. "But I thought you and I could get around to some real male bonding while they were out," complained Derek mildly.

"Wish I could, Uncle D, but there's an all-star basketball game on tonight, and I told Haskell I'd come by if I got the chance. Can I get a rain check?" It was apparent Manny wasn't too keen on hanging around the house if Asia was going to be out.

"Well, I guess it'll be another quiet night back at the ranch..... for this old cowboy," Derek said matter of factly.

"You won't be lonely will you, Uncle Derek?" inquired Asia, very sincerely.

"Of course not," he replied. "Besides, someone needs to be here when your mother calls. Don't worry, I'll be fine. You kids go on and enjoy yourselves!"

Taking his words to heart, everyone was off to prepare for their evening within a matter of minutes. Dinner was one of the things forgotten in the wake of their impromptu social planning. Somehow, a most improbable day, complete with the excitement generated by Edison's 'stick-up' of Derek, seemed as though it would have quite a mild ending. The unusual events of the afternoon had taken their toll, so Derek decided to return to the servants' quarters for a well deserved rest.

By 6:00 P.M., Gloria and Asia were ready to go. Before they departed, Gloria made sure to leave a note for Derek saying they were going to drop Manny off at Haskell's house. Haskell's mother met Manny at the door, greeting him warmly. "Hello, Manny. Are you hungry? We've got some hamburgers on the grill. They should be ready in a few minutes."

The thick aroma of barbecue sauce had already disclosed that fact, and Manny's drooling taste buds predetermined what his answer would be. "Gee, Mrs. Jones, I'd love one!"

"Well, give me your bag and I'll put it upstairs for you. Haskell is down in the rec room."

Manny quickly waved good-bye to the girls. His voraciousness thus aroused, he followed his nose inside, anxious to sink his teeth into a juicy cheeseburger. Seeing Haskell had clearly become a secondary objective. Gloria pulled the car out of the driveway and headed for the show.

Derek arose from his nap around 7:00 and showered. By that time his appetite beckoned him to seek some dinner. Since he was alone for the evening, he gave serious consideration to dining out. He had trouble deciding, however, which direction to pursue in pursue in satisfying his gourmet tastes. Finally, he settled on ordering a large mushroom and onion pizza, thick crust version.

Within thirty minutes, the meal was delivered to the house, piping hot and aromatic. He was ready. Two Lite beers discovered at the bottom of the refrigerator would help to wash down the cheese and tomato sauce. Even though it wasn't your real restaurant setting, Derek treated himself to seating that night in the Castle's dining room. At least it would seem more formal in there. His plan was to get something in his stomach, then head over to the video store for an action-adventure movie, to kill the remainder of the evening.

Just as he was about to sit down for his Italian-American repast, the phone rang. It was Deidre. She and Edison had arrived safely, but they were having trouble with the hotel. Edison was embroiled in an English-Spanish, Spanish-English confrontation with the hotel's manager over their reservation, or lack thereof.

"Don't worry, Dee-Dee," Derek said in an effort to calm his sister. "I'm sure Edison can work it out."

"I guess you're right," she sighed begrudgingly. Derek explained that everyone was gone for the evening, and that Asia had taken Gloria to the rap concert. "What's Gloria going to do at a show like that.... with all those kids?"

Derek paused momentarily, then answered with earnestness. "Actually, I think Gloria's in for a big surprise tonight, whether she knows it or not." His tone of voice suggested that he knew something Deidre obviously didn't. But there was too much confusion for her to focus on Gloria at the moment. The Mexican standoff between Edison and the hotel was becoming quite heated. Her concern moved quickly to Manny.

"Derek, I'm counting on you not to let anything happen to Manny. He's my baby, and I love him dearly! I don't want him to get into any trouble. I'm counting on you and Gloria to take care of him while I'm gone. Please be sure to check on him tonight. Listen, I've got to go," she explained when she saw Edison emerge from the manager's office. "I think he's gotten something worked out with the hotel. Now don't you forget what I said D!"

Although he knew her sentiment was genuine, Derek felt that Deidre was really overdoing the bit about looking out for Manny. After all, she was only going to be gone for three days, and Manny was just over at Haskell's house, not downtown in some bar. However, since he didn't want to provoke anything with his sister, Derek restrained himself from giving her a piece of his mind, no matter how needful it may have been. Besides, he was starving, and his pizza was getting cold. "I'll be sure to contact Mrs. Jones," he obliged. "Have a good weekend....... with Billy the Kid! I'll see you when you get home. So long." CLICK!

Returning to his economy banquet, Derek popped open a can of beer, poured it into a large tumbler, and eagerly grabbed a slice of thick crust mushroom and onion. Relaxing, he pulled out the chair next to him so he could prop his feet up. Lying there on the seat of the chair was Edison's folder.

Derek's curiosity was sufficiently aroused by the label 'CONFIDENTIAL AND RESTRICTED' on the front. Against his better judgment, he couldn't resist the urge to open the file. Inside, he found a CIA report on the superconductor research project underway in Namibia, about 250 miles north of Cape Town. The initial quote of the opening paragraph was startling. It read, '.......support of the U.S. research team and their work must be protected from Namibian rebel forces who have been threatening the research camps for several weeks. These forces, should they obtain possession of the mineral samples being uncovered by the research teams, could unleash an uncontrollable series of

events. These materials are believed to have enormous supercon-
ductivity potential, and in the wrong hands represent a significant
military threat to our interests in Africa. Of particular concern is
the prospect of an alliance between Namibian rebel forces and
South African anti-apartheid groups. Such an alliance would
represent a serious threat to the interest of the South African
government, and jeopardize Western access to the considerable
mineral wealth of South Africa. Any further activity on the part
of Namibian rebels must be undermined..... at all costs!'

Immediately, Derek's mind and attention were drawn to his
brother-in-law's weekend reading. The hunger that was so
compelling such a short time ago was consumed by his interest in
the complete report, and research findings contained in the
document. And the idea about the video store had gone, as they
say, out the proverbial window.

Meanwhile, Asia and Gloria had arrived at Lakewood, and
found their seats in the loge center section. A handsome, semi-
enclosed auditorium with lawn seating just behind the covered
area, the amphitheater is built on the site of the old Lakewood
Fairgrounds where, years ago, the weekend happenings were
huge cattle and stockyard shows, and the state fair.

Hip-hop fans were out in full force and (rare form), rocking
and dancing all over the grass. The mood was infectious, and soon
Gloria was totally involved in the festivity and excitement. About
half an hour after they'd arrived, she got up to get some refreshments from the food court adjacent to the amphitheater. Asia

wanted some popcorn and a Coke. She stopped at a Fat Tuesday stand and ordered an Island Girl for herself.

Meandering back to her seat, she heard a man call out, "Glory.... Glory.... is that you?" The words stopped Gloria in her tracks. Turning around, she was confronted by a handsome middle aged man in, maybe, his late forties. The sight of him caused her to spill her Island Girl on the ground.

"My goodness," she gushed, "I haven't heard that name in years. There's only one person that ever called me that. Hilliard Renfroe! Is that you, Hilly?" She stared at him in amazement.

"Of course it's me, Glory!" Hilliard exclaimed. "I knew it was you the moment I saw that walk of yours. I'll never forget that walk." It was obvious that Hilliard was overjoyed to see such an old and good friend. He leaned over and gave her a warm hug. "God, Glory, it's wonderful to see you!" Gloria was having trouble believing her eyes. It had been at least twenty five years since she'd last seen Hilly Renfroe. Being with him again caused a flood of memories to fill her mind. Exotic, romantic memories, that she thought would never be rekindled.

Breaking his clinch, Gloria wanted to know what in the world Hilliard was doing in Atlanta. He explained that he was there for his daughter's graduation from Spelman College, and that she had persuaded him to come out to hear the rappers. "I came to Atlanta about seven years ago for the first time," he told her. "I fell in love with the city! When it was time for my daughter to go to college, I encouraged her to come to Spelman. She'll be graduating on Wednesday!" Hilliard had the look of a proud father on his face. "And what are YOU doing here...... my dear Glory?"

Gloria paused for a moment as she reflected on how nice it was to see her Hilly again. He had the same broad shoulders and thick chest. But he looked so much more mature and polished then the way she remembered him. He was almost dashing. "I live here. I came to the show with the daughter of the woman I work for," Gloria told him. "She's a wonderful girl, just going through some boy problems right now. I certainly remember how those can be.... don't I, Hilly Renfroe?"

He laughed a hearty, deep throated laugh, and gave her another warm hug. Hilliard was a big man, about 6'4" and over two-hundred pounds. He was very gregarious, and smiled and laughed easily. He was clearly enjoying Gloria's company. "Glory, we need to get together and talk about old times. I'll be here till Thursday. Maybe we could have dinner. How about that?"

The thought aroused Gloria's senses. How wonderful it would be to spend time with him again, after all these years. "Hilly, that sounds very nice," she admitted, "but what about your wife?" The question caught him a little off guard.

"I've been divorced for years, Glory, so she doesn't matter. Besides, after seeing you again, I'm glad I'm not married any-more. And how about you? The last I saw of you, you were headed to Mexico for the Olympics. 'Heard you married some athlete or something?"

The memories came furiously to Gloria now. Her husband didn't treat her well. There were instances of physical abuse, frustration, and alcoholism. It had been a most unhappy period of her life. Yet, she recalled the regret and extreme sadness she experienced when he died. Since then, there had been several men in her life, but it had become hard for her to trust another man, for her not to be skeptical. But despite all her experiences, her romantic sarcasm, seeing Hilliard again excited her beyond anything she had felt..... in a long, long time.

"I'm a widow, Hilly," she said directly.

"Oh, Glory, I didn't know. I'm very sorry."

Gloria was determined not to let her personal history destroy this opportunity. "Listen, Hilly, I have an idea. Why don't you and your daughter come out to the house and spend an evening with us? I'm sure Asia would love to meet her, a 'mature' college student and everything. What do you say?"

"I'd enjoy that, Glory," Hilliard answered quietly. "I'd enjoy that very much!" They exchanged phone numbers quickly, and he kissed her softly on the cheek. "I'd better get back. My baby will think I got lost or something. Be sure to call and let me know what the plan is, Glory. Be good!"

"You be good yourself, Hilly Renfroe!" Gloria yelled as he left. She was in such a nice mood, she decided to go get herself another Island Girl, and get back to Asia. Just as she was about to re-enter the seating area, it occurred to her how wonderful a surprise it was to run into a dear old friend like..... she stopped in mid-thought, dropping her Island Girl again. DEREK! His expression, his insistence that she come tonight, his comment about her running into some old friends. Derek KNEW! But how could he have known?

A shudder ran through her as she considered how it was possible for Derek to have known about Hilliard. It wasn't possible though, it couldn't be possible. She was able to finally reassure herself that the whole occurrence..... was one big coincidence, you know, just one of those things.

But something inside of her, not her mind but something else, knew better. It WAS more than a mere coincidence. There was no way she could articulate it, but she was convinced deep down that Derek knew this would happen. From that moment on, Gloria was secretly afraid of Derek.

South of the border at Cancun's Puerta de la Azure resort those two weekend runaways, Edison and Deidre, were settling in. Following the day's excitement, Edison was winding down. After a little rest, he and Deidre were dressed and ready for dinner. At the restaurant, they enjoyed a positively charming evening; oysters and steamers for appetizers, blackened marlin with a luscious clam-spinach sauce, dessert and champagne. They were seated at a table on a balcony overlooking the Caribbean. Delightful! Waves lapped serenely up to the shore in a stately, rhythmic procession. Over the horizon a blue-gray moon hovered perfectly, its reflected light creating a shimmering, glass-like runway on the water.

"Thank you so much, Edison," Deidre told her husband. "I needed this very badly. I think I'll just relax and sun myself all weekend..... and drink champagne!"

"That's great, Dee. I think we both needed to get away. Washington's nice, but it gets very intense at times." Edison, when he tried, was quite charming. A crazy day had turned into a very romantic night. "I've got some reading I must do this weekend, but that won't affect any......" He trailed off as he realized he hadn't seen the folder when he unpacked his bags earlier. Panic set in immediately. "Deidre, have you seen a folder of mine since we checked in?" he urgently inquired of his wife. "It was marked 'CONFIDENTIAL AND RESTRICTED'?"

Deidre told him she hadn't noticed anything like that since he'd arrived in Atlanta. Needless to say, the romantic mood had been broken. Edison was distraught. If that material got into the wrong hands..... he didn't even want to think about it. He had to find that folder! Leaving the restaurant, they raced back to the hotel. Edison tore apart the suite looking for the file. Not there. He called for Lance and paged his beeper. Nothing. Mentally, he retraced his steps that day. He remembered taking the folder out of his suitcase at the house. He had it with him as they were about to leave for the airport. But he didn't have it now! He must have left it somewhere in the house. "Deidre, didn't you call the house this evening?" he demanded.

"Yes, of course I did. Gloria and Asia went to a concert and Manny is spending the night with Haskell."

"You mean there's no one home?" he agonized.

"No, Derek was there," she said.

Edison's heart sank when he heard that Derek was the only one around. After the events of that afternoon, he was hesitant to call the house and suffer the embarrassment he was sure to receive from Derek. On the other hand, he couldn't take a chance on Derek discovering the file. Because Edison didn't trust his brother-in-law, the entire situation represented a gigantic security risk. It was a dilemma of immense proportions for him, and he felt helpless. "Well.... what did you tell him?" Edison questioned her. His tone was filled with a feeling of gnawing impatience.

"I told him to take care of Manny, to be sure to check on him at the Joneses tonight. Why, what is the problem?"

"That folder contains government restricted information," he confided. "It's top secret material..... that I'm responsible for. If word ever gets out that I've misplaced something like that, my name will be mud on Capitol Hill. My reputation will be ruined. Everything I've worked for will go right down the drain!"

"Edison, it's obviously not here, so that means it must be somewhere in the house," Deidre reasoned. "Why don't you just call and ask Derek to look around for it?"

"Dammit, Deidre," he screeched at her, "I don't trust that conniving, freeloading brother of yours as far as I can throw him, that's why!" He was growing increasingly paranoid. "He'd LOVE to use something like this against me!" Despite the fact that he was in this fix as a result of his own oversight, Edison loathed being in the position of having Derek control his immediate destiny. However inadvertent the circumstances, he was convinced that Derek had somehow conspired against him.

"Honey, if it makes you feel any better, why don't we wait a little while, and I'll call and ask Gloria to look for it, OK?" Deidre sought to calm her husband down. She also didn't want the latest confusion to spoil their weekend getaway. "I'm sure it's in the house, Edison. Why don't you sit down over here and let me rub your shoulders for you," she said in a seductive tone. "I'll order a nightcap from room service, and we'll get quiet for a bit."

After considerable coaxing and stroking, Deidre was able to calm Edison down. About two hours later, she called the house. The phone rang and rang. Finally, someone picked up. It was Gloria. "Oh, Gloria," she sighed. "I'm so glad it's you!" Quickly explaining the situation, she had Gloria search around for the folder. Edison wouldn't allow Deidre to hang up until Gloria completed her sweep of the downstairs. Coming around to the dining room, she was about to keep going but noticed a beer can at the edge of the table. Picking up the empty can, she spied Edison's file on the chair, exactly where he'd left it.

"I've got it, Mrs. Castle," Gloria announced triumphantly. "I'll put it safely away until you and Mr. Castle get back!"

Deidre was relieved. "Now we can get on with our weekend. Listen, Gloria, I'm going to give you this phone number, but don't use it unless it's absolutely necessary. Do you understand?"

"I understand completely. You two have a good time! And tell Mr. Castle I said he's getting a little messy, leaving empty beer cans sitting around in the dining room."

"Don't worry. He'll be so thankful you found that folder, he'll do anything you want. Tell the kids I love them. Have a good night." CLICK! Deidre relayed the status of the folder to Edison and not surprisingly, she could see he felt a great deal better. After a couple of glasses of champagne they both got comfortable, and after some playful tussling, they were sound asleep within an hour.

The next morning dawned brightly in Atlanta. Gloria rose early. She was still excited about seeing Hilliard the night before. It was all she could do to keep herself from calling the number he gave her. Mulling over a cup of coffee, she spotted Derek out in the yard. "Derek," she called to him. "Can you come in for a minute? I need to talk to you."

Obliging her request, Derek came on in, grabbed an apple and sat down to a glass of orange juice. "Hi, Gloria," he greeted her innocently. "Did you enjoy the show last night?"

She circled around, eyeing him suspiciously, like a predator sizing her prey for the kill. Suddenly she blurted out the thought that was weighing on her mind. "How the hell did you know I would run into Hilliard last night?" Gloria was staring intently at him, anxiously awaiting his response.

Derek looked absently at her, genuinely unaware of to whom she referred. "Who's Hilliard, Gloria?"

"Hilliard Renfroe..... you know perfectly well who I mean. My old boyfriend!" She was convinced that Derek knew Hilliard, and had somehow spoken to him yesterday while she was out, telling him she would be at the show with Asia.

"Hmmmm," Derek nodded slowly. He had a big chunk of apple poking his cheek out. "So that was it," he answered.

"That was what?"

He stood up and motioned for her to have a seat. "Gloria," he said deliberately, "I had no idea exactly what was going to happen last night. I just knew something significant would occur. That's why I suggested you go with Asia."

This was beginning to sound stranger than the events at the concert. Gloria was unsure whether she really wanted to hear his explanation or not, but she didn't stop herself from asking. "Alright, Mr. Smarty, I'm listening. How could you be so sure something important was going to happen to me?"

Derek sighed softly and rolled his eyes heavenward. He knew she wasn't going to believe the things he was about to tell her. But he felt he owed her an explanation, no matter how obscure it might sound. "Gloria, people exist in two different states simultaneously. In the material realm, we exist as flesh and blood, physical beings. On another plane, however, our same flesh and blood existence has an essential nature of pure energy..... our bodies are made up of vibratory energy flows. These vibrations flow in distinct patterns, or resonances. I know this sounds strange....... but yesterday I was able to perceive that your normal vibratory pattern..... was dramatically distorted. That indicated something important was about to happen. I had no way of knowing what it was; I just felt it was necessary for you to be at that show!"

Derek was right. Gloria simply sat there, looking at him in disbelief. She was even more stunned by his explanation than by last night's happenstance. She didn't know what to say; actually she couldn't say anything. And she was afraid to ask him anything else. It was too crazy. His explanation defied logic... at least anyone's logic other than Derek's. Even if this vibration business had any truth to it, how could it be possible for anyone to 'see' something like that? Secretly, she was interested in how he could have seen what he said he saw. But she was afraid. Derek finally spoke, breaking the strained silence.

"I know what you're thinking," he said. "The answer is that a spiritual man 'sees' into all things. He lives in a state of heightened awareness, a state where perception extends beyond the five senses, a state of expanded intuition. A spiritual man 'sees' into all things, even though he may not understand the experience in an intellectual sense. But heightened perception reveals the true nature of things... it is actually much more reliable than the experience of physical, sensory living. It goes beyond factual understanding, and leads one into the realm of truth."

What amazed Gloria was not only what he was saying, but his demeanor. His tone wasn't boastful or self-important. In fact, he was quite modest and unassuming. He spoke with a quiet authority, as though he knew precisely what he was talking about. Derek was a very unthreatening presence. Yet what he described couldn't be real, could it? She wished she hadn't said anything to him at all.

"Listen, Gloria," he said cheerfully, "I've got some work to do today and I need to run down to Home Depot for some materials. Let me know if you'd like to talk more." As if to snap her out of some type of trance, he abruptly changed the subject. It was like a slap in the face. "By the way, when are you gonna have this ex-boyfriend of yours over to the house? He seems to have made quite an impression on you. I'd really like to meet him!" With that, Derek turned and left, loudly munching his apple.

Gloria, of course, thought none of this was very funny. In an attempt to clear the confusion in her head, she poured herself a large cup of coffee. Oddly, the warm caffeine liquid had a soothing effect on her nerves. The cobwebs were beginning to clear from her mind when the phone rang. It was Hilliard!

"Good morning, Glory," said Hilliard pleasantly. "I'm glad you were in. I hope you don't mind my calling so soon, but I needed to speak with you."

"Of course I don't mind you calling me, that's what telephones are made for. What's on your mind, Hilly?" The response was positive, but half-hearted. Her initial reaction sensed something was wrong, that she wasn't going to get a chance to see him again. Maybe he had another woman in town. The thought made her uneasy.

"Well, Glory, I certainly appreciated your inviting us to dinner this week, but we're going to be pretty busy until the graduation on Wednesday. I'm finding out that there's a lot more to do than I thought. I don't know if we'll get a chance to come by. Is there any other time we could do it?"

Gloria suspected there was another woman in the picture, but she didn't want to miss the opportunity to spend more time with him. She also didn't want to come across as being too anxious about all this. Then it occurred to her that Deidre and Edison wouldn't be back until Monday anyway. Why not have them over tomorrow? "Why don't you and your daughter come by tomorrow, Hilly? I'm sure we could throw something together by that time." Gloria surprised herself with the impulsiveness she was displaying.

"Well, actually..... that would work well for us Glory. Are you sure we won't be a bother though? I really don't want to impose. I know we just saw one another last night, but I really would love to sit down and get reacquainted again."

"Believe me, Hilly Renfroe," she crowed, "this will be no trouble at all. By the way, tell your daughter to remember to bring her bathing suit. Here's the address," as she quickly gave him directions. "And you'd better show up, on time."

"Don't worry Glory, Glory... we'll be there. 'Bye." CLICK!

Her spirits lifted, Gloria ran out onto the deck in the back and screamed at the top of her lungs, "DEREK! You'd better clean out the pool. We're going to have a party!" Sticking his head out of the servants' quarters, Derek could only marvel at the voice that woman had on her! He surmised that Hilliard must be coming.

The night was beautiful and breezy in Mexico. Edison and Deidre had spent a glorious day sight-seeing and shopping. They even took the ferry over to the island of Cozumel for an afternoon of snorkeling. Back at the hotel at last, Edison was looking forward to a quiet evening. They decided to order a romantic dinner in their suite, complete with candlelight and soft music.

Deidre was enjoying herself, she loved feeling relaxed and feminine in such an exotic place.

Interestingly, they had decidedly different ideas about how the evening would unfold. Edison, even though they were dining privately in their own quarters, showered and dressed in a dinner jacket and bow tie. Deidre, on the other hand, sat down for her meal in a striking, low cut sheer evening dress that practically crossed the line from evening wear into the domain of lingerie. Edison had a difficult time carrying on an intelligent conversation...... with her so tantalizingly arrayed.

Deidre was positively radiant. She wished the holiday didn't have to end. "You know, honey, we really needed some time away like this. I mean, I've been feeling such a strain on our relationship the past few months. It's good to just spend some time alone, you and I, to get to know each other again." She was being completely candid and honest.

Edison also felt looser and open. "You're right, Dee. With so much going on in Washington, I haven't had a chance to focus on you and the kids lately. I'm sorry for that." His sincerity was genuine, and Deidre was seeing a side of Edison she hadn't seen in quite a long while. "I'm just glad Gloria found my papers.... it absolutely took a tremendous load off my mind, Dee."

"Well, I'm glad she found them too," said Deidre emphatically. She didn't want anything to disturb this weekend. "By the way," she casually mentioned, "Gloria told me to remind you about leaving things lying around. She said you're getting messy.... leaving empty beer cans in the dining room. I'm surprised at you myself, Ed."

"What.... what beer cans? What are you talking about?"

"I forgot to mention it last night. Gloria said she found an empty beer can next to your file in the dining room. She figured it belonged to you."

Edison was livid. "You FORGOT?" he shrieked at her. "I didn't have any beer before I left!" He paused for a moment, searching his mind for some correlation of the events. It didn't take long for him to tally the results. "DEREK!!!" He screamed the name at the top of his lungs. "That low life brother of yours read my file, Deidre!" He was up, pacing back and forth, room to room muttering to himself. Deidre made a vain attempt to calm him down, but there was no placating him. "We're leaving on the first flight out tomorrow!"

Deidre's heart sank. "Edison, don't throw away a perfectly good vacation over something like this. Just because she found a beer can...... doesn't mean Derek read your file. And even if he did, we'll be home on Monday. Please, Honey....... don't DO this," she pleaded.

But it was no use. His mind was made up. Edison couldn't concentrate on anything else but that damn file. And Deidre was left to contemplate what might have been a perfect evening, after such a perfect day in Mexico. It was a tense and restless sleep for her that night. From that moment on, a growing resentment sprang up in Deidre toward Edison. A resentment she would unknowingly hold her brother responsible for.

Chapter 6

Enrico's Song

The Sunday morning dawn had an ominous appearance. A misty fog hugged the ground, and the air was thick with humidity. It felt as though a heavy rain was on the way. Despite such warning signs, Derek arose early and started working to prepare the pool area for guests. Gloria had been adamant about that, and Derek wasn't going to create any more controversy, if he could help it.

He went meticulously about his task, carefully removing pine needles and leaves from the water. He cleaned the filter, and even loaded new chlorine into the tank. As the morning wore on, the fog was beginning to gradually burn off. By the time he finished, the clear, aquamarine water looked quite inviting. And by 11:30, despite the cloudiness, the heat of the day made it seem all the more so.

In the kitchen, Gloria was a whirling blur; fresh seafood salad, onion dip, celery and cucumbers, chicken fingers, deviled eggs, hamburger patties for the grill, desserts. You name it, she had it. There was going to be one hell of a picnic at the Castle residence. The overcast day couldn't dampen her spirits. Obviously, she loved a good party. And that's exactly what she was preparing for. Upstairs, Asia was on the phone telling some friends how to get to the house. And Manny even told Haskell to stop by.

Meanwhile, those lucky vacationers, Edison and Deidre were checking out of their hotel. The cab ride to the airport was memorable, only for the lack of conversation that took place. Their driver vainly attempted to make small talk in a distorted English-Spanish dialect that was impossible to understand. Deidre of course, was still offended at having to return before she was ready. Consequently, she was *too through* with Edison; she didn't even pay attention to what was happening, much less have anything to say.

Actually, Deidre was of a mind to let him return alone; she could continue hanging out by herself for a few more days. That would certainly put him in his place! But for some reason, the thought of not having her man with her made the idea less appealing. So Deidre resigned herself to the fate of sitting in the rear of a dilapidated old Volkswagen beetle, listening to the endlessly unintelligible banter of the cheerful old Mexican driver, while remaining thoroughly pissed at the whole situation!

Edison, of course, was determined. They were going home, and he was going to straighten out his brother-in-law, once and for all. *Who the hell does he think he is... reading my files*, he thought silently. As soon as they reached the airport, he tried calling Lance. No answer. He considered trying the house, but decided against it. He would surprise old Derek, that sonofabitch, by showing up early. And what of Deidre? *She'll get over it,* he rationalized. *Deidre will realize how important this is to us, in the long run.* After all, it was a matter of national security. Edison did an excellent job of justifying his actions to himself, and that was all he needed. Within three hours, they would be back in town.

By 4:00 P.M., things were rocking in Atlanta. The sun finally broke through around 2:00, and the afternoon was simply marvelous, thank you. And hot! Hilliard arrived a half an hour or so early, with his daughter and her boyfriend. Several of Asia's friends stopped by. Even Geri came over and seemed to be having a good time. Of course, with the weather so obliging, all the girls were anxious to see the guys in their bathing suits. And vice-versa. Never one to disappoint, he-man Haskell was showing off a new pair of authorized Lee Haney 'Mr. Olympia' posing briefs. Only problem was he didn't quite have the physique to fill out his swimwear in any significant way.

Manny and Derek pitched in as the designated servants, helping out in any way they could to make everyone feel at home. They did such a great job, Gloria could easily have been mistaken for the lady of the house. She was glowing and radiant, enjoying the company and graciously accepting compliments on everything from the grilled shark steak appetizers, to the bottled salad dressing she picked up at Kroger. Everyone seemed to be thoroughly enjoying themselves.

Taking a momentary break from his duties, Derek sat down at a table with Hilliard and Gloria. "Hilly, I'd like you to meet Mrs. Castle's brother, Derek," she said in introduction. "You and Manny have been great. Thank you so much!" Gloria was having a good time, and privately felt she owed Derek a lot...... for encouraging her to go to the concert. She knew she would never have encountered Hilliard otherwise.

"Gloria says your daughter is graduating this week," commented Derek. "I think that's great!" he continued, sounding very complimentary. Gloria was amazed at how sane Derek came across at times. But she still believed he was crazy, and consequently was wary whenever he was around that he might do or say something strange. But the two men seemed to be hitting it off quite well. The day had turned out to be very pleasant after all.

"Tell me, Derek," Hilliard asked, "what do you do for a living? Glory tells me you're visiting for the summer. But you must have a line of work, a profession. Am I correct?" Derek stared at the ground momentarily, as he pondered the best way to respond.

Before he could answer, Gloria joined the inquisition. "Yes, Derek, just what is it..... that you do? Mrs. Castle never told me what kind of business you're in."

Derek acted as if some terrible, dark secret had suddenly been uncovered. His expression indicated there was something so unpleasant about his vocation that he couldn't, or wouldn't, share it with anyone. "I don't make this widely known," he whispered slowly, leaning over his lemonade, "but I'm an investment banker by profession. I work for a firm out of New York that specializes in international finance, primarily looking at the viability of developing nations and what type of investments make sense for our clientele in those areas. Right now, I'm on leave to.... just relax... spend time with my family... to get my head together. I've been very discouraged recently by developments in the financial markets."

Well.... you could have knocked Gloria over with a feather! It never occurred to her that Derek was a banker. She thought he might be an engineer or an architect or something, because he was so handy around the house. Interestingly enough, she wasn't any more prepared for what she was about to discover next.

"And what about you, Hilly?" Derek inquired, changing the focus to her dinner guest.

Gloria's interest immediately shifted with the question. "Yes, Hilly Renfroe," she kidded him. "The last time I saw you, you worked in that restaurant on the beach in Port Cayman."

The memory of those days brought a roaring guffaw from Hilly. "You know, that seems like so long ago," he commented. In fact, it had been a long time ago. But he didn't allow his sentimentality to take over. "I work for the Ministry of Trade and Tourism in Trinidad," he said. "I'm what you might call..... our country's chief lobbyist." He gestured toward Derek. "It's my job to see that people like yourself view us as 'desirable' from an investment standpoint, and to make sure that our domestic financial resources aren't misapplied." He paused then, and couldn't help but notice Gloria's shocked expression.

"You do WHAT?" she exclaimed, not wanting to believe what she had heard. Gloria was stunned! The big, hunky kid she'd left bussing dishes in a beachfront restaurant..... had grown up to become a big, hunky Ministry official. At home, next to the Prime Minister himself, the Bureau of Trade and Tourism was the most powerful organization on the island. And her old flame was the head lobbyist! She couldn't believe it! This was too much. Her mother always warned her that Hilly would never amount to anything... he was too easygoing, no drive she said. Now here they were... Gloria a domestic servant..... and Hilly a government official. Just goes to show you. Life certainly is a beach!

Derek flashed a furtive glance at Gloria, then back at Hilly. He was enjoying every minute of this. One of the things he'd told Manny was to never underestimate the potential of human beings, particularly yourself. And here was a first hand example of what he was talking about. Of course, Derek wasn't privy to all the background Gloria had on Hilly's upbringing. But it was quite apparent that no one would have ever guessed that 'ol Hilly had anything like this in him.

"Interestingly enough," Hilly continued, "one of the projects I'm currently evaluating is an Olympic training complex. International athletic competition has long been a source of extreme pride on the part of our people." He stole a quick look at Gloria. "I don't know if you are aware of it, Derek, but Glory here was a member of our Olympic team in 1968.... isn't that right, Glory?" Hilly was having a good time himself.

Not waiting for her response, he plowed ahead. "One of the things I'm doing while in town is talking to some potential investors," he said to Derek. "By the way, did you know that Atlanta is making a bid for the summer Olympics in 1996? That would be wonderful for the city. The former Mayor is getting involved, I understand. Personally, I think Atlanta is a great place." Hilly was certainly well informed about Atlanta's civic activities. Before he got too far off track, however, he returned to matters at hand. "You don't know of any interested bankers I might contact here, do you Derek?"

The conversation had come full circle. What started out as a casual chat about life, love, and the pursuit of happiness, had turned into a fairly serious business discussion. But then again that's how many business deals are transacted, at cocktail parties... on the golf course.... in hotel suites. It's the American way!

"Well.... truthfully Hilliard, I haven't developed many contacts down here. As I mentioned, I'm on sabbatical. But I would be happy to call several of my people in New York..... to find out who you might speak to here. I'll be sure to let Gloria know. Actually..... it'd be great for you to meet my brother-in-law. I don't know if Gloria's told you but..... he's a U.S. Congressman. Obviously, he spends a lot of time in Washington, but I'm sure you two could swap some great stories... about politics, and lobbying, and..... things. It's too bad though. He's out of town right now. They're in Mexico for the weekend, and won't be back until tomorrow. I'm sure he'd love to meet you!"

"Well, please convey my fondest regards to him and his wife. Anyone who cares about Glory the way they obviously do.... must be special people!" Gloria, still mystified by the things she discovered during their conversation, just sat there....... her mouth agape. Derek, noticing the action picking up with the kids, excused himself to go back to his role as unofficial 'house' chaperon.

In those few moments, the festivities had really livened up. The music of rappers Heavy D, Queen Latifah, and the one and only Big Daddy..... had everyone slammin'... and jammin'..... on the edge of their seats. Most of the activity centered around the pool area, which was full with friends and neighbors and acquaintances...... from all over town it seemed. Amidst such frivolity, no one noticed the car pulling up in the driveway out front.

"Well," sighed Gloria, finally snapping out of her trance. "I simply had no idea that you were such a worldly, man-about-town, my dear Hilly!" Her mood quickly changed from one of absolute surprise, to a somewhat dour tone of self-effacement. Gloria knew that Hilly probably met many glamorous women all the time. It affected her self-confidence. "You DO realize that I'm just a servant here..... I work for Mr. and Mrs. Castle. I'm sorry, Hilly, but I don't get much chance to spend any time..... with the jet-set crowd."

The blaring music and clamor immediately caught the attention of the late arriving guests. Circling around to the back, they were shocked to find the yard swallowed up by such a raucous horde of merrymakers, most of whom they didn't even know.

"Mrs. Castle!" shrieked Gloria, with a semi-pleasant surprise in her voice. "How are you? I didn't expect you until tomorrow evening!" Needless to say, their early return was a shock for everyone, Deidre included.

"Who are all these people?" demanded Edison abruptly. "And what the hell are they doing here?"

Sensing the predicament that was about to ensue for Gloria, Hilly stood up and introduced himself quickly. "I'm afraid that I may be the cause of all this," he said, trying to divert attention away from her.

Before Hilly could tell his story, Asia spotted her parents. At once, she jumped out of the pool and ran to greet her father. "Daddy!!" she cried, overjoyed at seeing him again. Her low cut bikini made Edison all the more wary of that afternoon's happenings, particularly with those young brothers at poolside lustfully eyeing his daughter.

"Hello, baby," Edison said, and without thinking embraced her in a warm hug, completely soaking his clothes.

"Isn't this great, Daddy? Gloria invited Hilly over for dinner, and since we were going to cook out, I invited some of my friends..... and Manny did too.... and we're just having a wonderful time. I'm so glad to see you....... and Mom. How was your trip? We've had so much fun since you've been gone. I hope you're not upset with us, are you Daddy?"

Edison didn't stand a chance. He was like putty, silly putty as a matter of fact, in Asia's hands. He melted right away. "No, honey, I'm not upset at all. I'm glad you're having such a good time. Your friends seem to be enjoying themselves, too. Let your Mom and I finish talking to Gloria and her guest. I'll see you later."

"You know, Gloria," Deidre whispered to her housekeeper, "the least you could have done was call me and tell me what was happening. That way I could have prepared Edison."

Thinking quickly, Gloria placed the ball right back in Deidre's court. "Mrs. Castle, you know that normally I would have called. But don't you remember...... you told me explicitly not to call unless there were an absolute emergency. This certainly doesn't fall into that category, does it?"

"No, Gloria, this isn't the type of emergency I had in mind," she sighed softly. "You all must have been busy around here; no one even bothered to pick up the mail." Deidre laid the contents of their mail box on the table.

Scanning the pile quickly, Gloria noticed a letter addressed to the entire family. "Here's a letter from Enrico," she announced. "We haven't heard from him in weeks." Opening the envelope, she quickly read the contents. "He says he misses everyone, and that he'll be back from Savannah next week," she said, informing the group. "It'll be good to see 'ol Enrico. I've missed his face around here." He had been gone almost two months.

"Don't worry about Enrico right now," Edison gruffly commanded. "Did you put my file away, Gloria?"

"Under lock and key, Mr. Castle. It's quite safe.... I can assure you."

"That's good. By the way, where is Derek?" Edison was still preoccupied with his brother-in-law, and the thought that he may have examined the contents of his confidential information. In the clamor accompanying their surprise arrival, however, Derek seemingly had disappeared.

"I'm not sure where he is," Gloria responded.

"Yes..... he and I were just sitting here talking before you came," Hilly added pleasantly. "I really enjoyed his company.... he seems like a very genuine person."

Such unsolicited praise of Deidre's brother..... was like someone putting mayonnaise in his morning coffee for Edison. He couldn't stand it. "I certainly appreciate your opinion", he said sarcastically. "I'm sure he's around here, somewhere. I'll find him." As Edison turned to search for Derek, the shrill whine of a police siren stopped him in his tracks. "NOW what?" moaned Edison quietly, as two of Atlanta's finest entered his yard.

"Evening, ma'm..... gentlemen. We've received reports of disruptive disturbances going on here," they told Deidre. "We're going to have to ask you to tone it down a bit...... or we'll be forced to give you a citation." The officers were pretty nice about the situation as it turned out. And in truth, it was VERY loud back there. Edison gazed at his wife, as if to say 'I wonder who would call the police........ on US?'

"Good evening, officers," Edison said confidently. "I'm Congressman Edison Castle, and this is my wife and our guests. I appreciate your coming out here, but I believe we've got the situation under control."

The officers looked at him, quite unimpressed. "Very nice to meet you, Congressman," they responded. "You've got a lovely home here..... but you've also got neighbors that have a right to their peace and quiet. I'm sure you understand. Please be certain to take care of things. Sorry to interrupt the festivities. 'Evening folks." The patrolmen turned ceremoniously and left. Interestingly enough, the music continued to blare in the background. But the police had gone, and the distraction momentarily caused Edison to lose focus on his search and destroy mission for Derek.

After getting Manny to turn the music down, Edison was about to resume the hunt for his brother-in-law, when the phone rang. It was Lance. Apparently, a special session of Edison's subcommittee had been called for Tuesday morning. The President's chief advisor on energy was going to convey the Cabinet's perspective on the activities in Namibia. And, of course, it was crucial for Edison to be there. Edison related the saga of the missing file folder to Lance, and chastised him for not being available when he'd tried to reach him from Mexico. Nonetheless, it was apparent his Atlanta vacation was going to be more short-lived than he expected.

Meanwhile, Derek had followed two of the young guests out into the woods. They moved quietly, not suspecting that anyone noticed their departure from the pool area. Soon, they reached a clearing where there stood an enormous tree stump, the same spot Derek and Deidre had their earlier encounter about Manny. The two were Geri's brother Miles, and his friend Jason, Asia's newfound love interest. Jason pulled a small vial containing a white powdery substance from his shorts. He had picked up some cocaine before coming over to the house, and was going to turn his boy Miles on. The pair quickly became consumed with the snorting, and the momentary sensation of power that flooded their senses. So absorbed were they, that they didn't notice the imposing visage Derek cast as he stared menacingly at them.

"You two having a private party out here I see," he barked threateningly. His voice crackled through the serenity of the woods, despite the background music from the pool. The startled Jason dropped his vial abruptly.

Immediately, Miles began to plead for mercy. "Please, Mr. Alston! Don't tell my parents. I was just trying this out. I'm not a drug addict! Please don't tell them!" Derek didn't respond right away, and his reticence made the boys all the more uncomfortable.

Jason made a feeble attempt to retrieve his contraband, but Derek moved quickly and stepped squarely down on the vial, crushing it under foot. "Hey, man!" Jason shouted. "What's wrong with you? Are you a narc..... or something?"

Derek looked at him with a wild eyed stare. The anger contained inside was bubbling over now. "Son, you better be glad I'm not a narc. There were two Atlanta police officers here not ten minutes ago. You could have been on your way downtown, charged with possession with intent to distribute. Do you think THAT might have spoiled your day? I'm SICK and TIRED..... of what people are allowing drugs to do to them! And you two ought to know better!"

The fact that Derek had destroyed his opportunity to get high, and wasted a sizable amount of his money on the ground at the same time made Jason wax defiant. "Who the hell do you think you are," he screamed ".... my father?"

"Let me tell you something, son," Derek said leaning over nearly face to face with him. "You had better not come around here anymore with that FILTH..... and you'd BETTER stay away from Asia...... do you understand me?"

"Oh yeah?" he answered angrily, "you and who else are going to MAKE me stay away from Asia?" At this point, Miles was frantic. He knew the two of them would start fighting, right there in front of him. Oddly enough, Derek suddenly became quiet and seemed to regain his composure. Jason felt as though he had shouted the old man down. He flashed a confident glance at Miles, as if to say, 'I guess I showed him something.... didn't I?'

Calmly, Derek motioned with his arm and said simply, "Let me introduce you to a friend of mine. I think HE'LL help me keep you away from my niece." Literally out of nowhere, he pulled from behind his back..... an absolutely menacing...... nine millimeter sawed-off shotgun!

A look of complete terror seized Miles' expression. Without any wasted motion, Derek snatched Jason by the collar and ungraciously slapped the shotgun down hard on his shoulder, with the barrel close to his ear. Miles nearly passed out, so convinced was he..... that Derek was about to blow Jason's head off!

The frightened teen was paralyzed with fear. He couldn't speak. "You know, Mr. Excitement here doesn't like tough guys like you," Derek exclaimed as he cocked the trigger slowly. "Especially young punks.... who think these drugs are so cool!" Jason's bowels couldn't hold up under the pressure, and he let go of a load in his pants, just as Derek fired. "BOOOOMM!" The roar was deafening in his ear. Miles didn't believe this was happening. He'd hid his eyes so as not to witness the execution of his friend..... over a little cocaine no less!

Of course, Derek didn't kill Jason. But he certainly shook both of them up.... something terrible! Jason was so thankful to be alive that the moment his feet hit the ground he took off running as fast as he could, followed closely by Miles. Fortunately for them, that was the end of their casual drug use days..... and the last that was ever seen of Mr. Jason by the Castle household.

Derek watched the two banditos scurry off for a few moments. Then he turned to make his way back to the house. Oddly enough, the shotgun he had brandished so threateningly just minutes before, vanished into thin air! Literally. It was as if the firearm's reality was defined..... by the exigency of the moment. Once the need for intimidation was over, the gun's existence terminated. And it disappeared!

Before he left though, Derek found the smashed vial of cocaine near the tree stump. With his foot, he ground the white powder vigorously into the grassy soil beneath. But rather than harbor thoughts of satisfaction with his "bust", Derek's mind could only focus on the scope of the drug problem and the enormous devastation it was inflicting on today's youth. There was nothing satisfying or humorous about that. Uncontrollably, tears started to flow as he walked, and vainly he attempted to control the fury of the emotions that overtook him. It was no use. His compassion simply got the better of his rationality. All he could do was to continue on his way, weeping quietly into the warm summer breeze.

The next morning, Edison rose early to pack his things. He was scheduled on an 11:00 A.M. flight back to Washington. Truthfully, he was somewhat relieved that duty had called. The lost weekend turned out to be a flop for him and Deidre, and the tension created at their abrupt return from Mexico was still thick between them. She'd already left for her law office. Meanwhile, his thoughts returned to the intriguing Ms. Camille Ferguson, and how much he looked forward to returning to D.C. Hopefully, he would be getting to know her much, much better. The preoccupation with Derek and the missing file was gone now, and Edison's focus was squarely on how to prepare for the subcommittee meeting.

Lost in the commotion of the previous day's frivolity was the letter from Enrico. He was writing to let the family know that he planned to return to Atlanta that week. Gloria looked forward to his coming home. Before he became sick, he was such a fun loving, generous person. And his cheerfulness had always been a comfort for her.

His full name was Enrico Melendez y Stevenson, a Cuban by birth. Enrico was a tall and slender dark skinned man, with wide, round eyes that were black as coal. His low, raspy voice belied an extreme gentleness that was quite disarming. For the early part of his fifty plus years, Enrico worked in the fields of sugar cane, harvesting crops that were turned over to the government owned processing plants.

After coming to this country in the late sixties, he worked for some years as a porter on the Southern Rail Line, finally settling in Atlanta. But his first love was always the land. The cultivation, the planting, the nurturing..... and ultimately the gratification of the earth bringing forth the fruit of his labor. He had worked for the Castles as their gardener for the past seven years, and had done an exceptional job.... until he began to battle with illness that befell him nearly a year ago.

His inability to maintain the grounds for his adopted family had made him despondent. He took much pride in his agrarian pursuits. Enrico's only surviving relative was his younger sister who lived in Savannah. After several stays in the hospital, his doctors had prescribed a prolonged rest, and he went to stay for a time with her. Apparently, the ocean convalescence had helped. Now he was on his way back to the Castle homestead.

On Thursday afternoon, he arrived. The cab pulled up in front of the house just after lunch. Gloria, answering the door, greeted him warmly as he came in. The two acted like long lost family, even though it was only a few months since they last saw one another. As it turned out, much had transpired in both their lives over that short period of time.

The two friends were relaxing with a cup of coffee when Derek happened in. He was grimy from digging post holes for a fence, and he'd come in to get a drink of ice water. "Enrico Stevenson, I'd like to introduce you to Ms. Castle's brother, Derek," said Gloria as they sat at the kitchen table.

"Very nice to meet you Enrico," offered Derek cheerfully. "I've heard so much about you. I hope you don't mind, but I've been staying in the servants' quarters while you've been out of town." Enrico's shiny eyes studied Derek carefully for a moment. Then a broad smile flashed across his face, revealing a mouth full of perfect white teeth, oddly accented by a gold cap around one of the incisors.

"I'm honored that you would want to stay with me in the servants' quarters," Enrico commented, measuring his words slowly. "Likewise, I've heard much about you too, Derek."

Laughing out loud, Derek answered playfully, "Don't believe the things Gloria says about me." He shot an evanescent glance her way. "She thinks I'm a little weird." Though something of a joke, his observation was really more of an understatement.

Enrico's expression indicated he was thinking of another reference. "Well, Gloria did mention that you've been helping out around here since I've been away," he started. "A few weeks ago, I received a lovely letter from Manny. He was nice enough to inquire as to how I was progressing..... but he also wrote quite a bit about you. He admires you very much, Derek. That's one of the reasons I was anxious to return. I very much wanted to meet you..... for myself!"

About an hour earlier, Deidre had sat down to a sumptuous lunch at an exclusive Buckhead restaurant. She was in the company of one Carter Henderson, local real estate magnate and president of the Fulton County Realtors and Development Association. Carter had long been an admirer of hers, as well as a sometimes adversarial business associate. His interests were more than professional, however. A widower in his mid forties, Carter was fascinated by Deidre, and had told her so on several occasions. He'd been after her for over a year to have dinner with him, or a drink, or anything! There were even offers of expense paid trips to the Caribbean. He was infatuated, and he had it bad!

But Deidre always maintained her distance, resisting the sometimes heavy handed advances he would try. Over the past few weeks, Carter had backed off a bit. So, he was completely shocked when, during his call two days ago, Deidre suggested they get together. Not knowing quite what to expect he offered to take her to lunch, to which she heartily accepted. More than anything else, her latest frustration with Edison had her wondering seriously about his commitment to the marriage. She wanted some caring and attention. And she wanted it.... NOW! Besides, Carter was a very handsome man, considered a real catch by most of her friends. She really wasn't clear at all about how far this would go, but she knew she needed a male's companionship. They had a delightful time that afternoon..... and Carter did in fact succeed in arousing her feminine sensibilities.

Over the next couple of weeks, Enrico and Derek became good friends. Still weak from his ailment and medications, Enrico couldn't do much serious work on the grounds. But he would talk to Derek about his fascination with the earth, and share some of his ideas and gardening techniques. Derek never seemed to grow tired of the coaching and almost endless banter. Actually, they were a matched pair..... Derek loved to work with his hands, and spending time with Enrico made him more cognizant of the vision he (Enrico) had for the Castle property.

One evening after dinner, the two of them were enjoying the day's twilight out in the woods, not far from the scene of the Miles and Jason 'cocaine war'. Derek noticed Enrico pulling a photograph of a beautiful young girl from his wallet. "Who's that?" Derek inquired, almost as a reflex.

"This is my sister's daughter," he responded softly. "Her name is Sardis." There was a pregnant pause then, as if the mention of her name dredged up some long simmering bitterness. "She used to be such a beautiful girl... intelligent... happy-go-lucky." His tone naturally caused Derek to probe further.

"What do you mean, she used to be...... what happened to her?"

"About three years ago," began Enrico, "her father, who was in the merchant marines, was killed in an unfortunate accident on a cargo freighter while docking in Savannah. My sister Jocelyn was understandably distraught and frantic. This went on for several months, and obviously had a negative effect on both of them. During this time, an old acquaintance of her husband's, who had sailed with him on several voyages to South America began hanging around whenever he was in town. Initially, Danny was a comfort and a help to Jocelyn and Sardis. In her weakened condition, Jocelyn eventually grew to depend on him. They began sleeping together and, she believed, had fallen deeply in love.

"What started out as something seemingly good, turned into a situation that was dreadfully wrong. Jocelyn was unaware that Danny was a heavy cocaine user. Of course, warning signs were all there..... but she chose to ignore them..... in favor of catering to her own physical and psychological needs. She justified this by saying she had to re-establish stability for herself..... and Sardis.

"First, Danny was able to get her to become a casual user. As time went on, they occasionally would bring Sardis in on their 'get high' parties. Things got rapidly worse. What began as a random thing grew into a daily occurrence. Sardis was becoming quite popular around school with the wrong crowd because she had access to some 'good blow' on a regular basis. After a while, her mother began to come to her senses and see what was happening to their lives. But Danny was able to persuade Sardis that it was OK...... that she was helping to support them by dealing drugs."

By this time, Enrico was fighting back the tears. It was clear that he had not discussed this with anyone, and it was painful for him to open up and disclose what was tremendously difficult for someone to see happen to their family. "Sardis was hooked by this time, and that son of a bitch Danny would trade supplying her with cocaine..... for sexual favors. Jocelyn finally threw the bastard out, but at that point, Danny had no more use for her anyway. He got what he wanted from my niece. She was fifteen. As Sardis' habit grew, her day became consumed with either finding drugs, or selling enough to support her habit. She dropped out of school and began using crack, which was more available than the purer cocaine she was accustomed to.

"Fortunately, Danny met an untimely demise not too long after that. One night, upon leaving late from one of his favorite beer joints, he was hit by a car, not far from the docks where my brother-in-law died. Hit and run. They never found out who did it. I've often wondered since then whether or not Jocelyn herself was driving that car. But I never asked her.

"When I arrived there a couple of months ago, I wasn't aware of all that had transpired. Jocelyn tried to reach Sardis, to reason with her about how she was throwing her life away in the streets. She would come by the house at night, in search of food and money. When Danny boy bit the dust, her primary source of supply went with him. She was pathetic now, even selling her body to keep up with the demands of the crack. Twice I went to the county jail to get her out. The second time she was being held on prostitution charges." Enrico was crying now, and the depth of the pain in his voice captivated Derek. It was an experience that moved him more than he would realize, although not until many years later.

But just as the despair had come through so clearly, there was an unexpected change in Enrico's tone, as he continued his account. "It was after the second visit to jail that the county arranged for us to get counseling at a local social action agency. I remember meeting the young woman who ran the agency. She couldn't have been more than thirty or so, maybe thirty-five..... she looked younger. Anyway, at our first meeting, I was very impressed with the way she described an approach to helping Sardis. She talked about.... 'the importance of dealing with such problems from a cultural as well as a psycho-sociological perspective.' She said that..... 'without a cultural frame of reference, psychological disorders create confusion. Treatment programs typically address only symptomatic conditions, and rarely effect any significant change in attitudes, which is the key.'

"Of course, it all SOUNDED very impressive, this clinical talk. But what really shocked me was when Jocelyn asked when we should bring Sardis in, the young woman told us not to worry about that. She said she would go find her. She then explained that not so long ago, she was in the same situation, on the streets of Savannah. A young woman, much like herself, reached out to help. She said that, 'it was time for her.... to return the favor.'

"Derek, I'm here to tell you. I couldn't believe it! I had become so disillusioned with people, so disgusted seeing my sister suffer the way she did. And here was this young woman, who didn't know us from Adam, willing to get involved in our lives. I mean she gave us HOPE! Well, she kept her word and found Sardis. And you know what..... she's getting cleaned up! The counselor helped her get into a detoxification and rehabilitation program. She also helped Sardis enroll in a state funded equivalency program in Glynn County, near Brunswick. Now she goes back to school three days a week and attends rehab the other two.

"Just before I decided to come back up here, Sardis came in early one evening. She walked up and put her arms around my neck and told me, 'Thank you, Uncle Enrico. Thank you so much for caring about me. You know.... I never paid much attention before. But the world is such a beautiful place! There is so much we have to live for. I'm beginning to understand how big the world really is..... and there is so much to see out there. I was living locked up..... in a world of madness, a slave to filthy habits. Ultimately, I've got to be responsible for myself. But now I have hope. You've helped to give me another chance. I'll always be grateful to you for that.'

"I mean, Derek, I got so choked up. You could see the sincerity and hopefulness in her eyes. She now expects good things from life, and from herself. I guess she'll always be a recovering addict. But Sardis knows that someone cares about her. And I'll always be grateful to the young woman at the crisis counseling center. It didn't have to turn out this way. My niece could have been dead by now, or worse. You know, I've never been very spiritual or religious. But now I've had a first hand experience. Human compassion is such a powerful force. People who really care.... they can change the world, can't they Derek?"

The question was a rhetorical one. Enrico's summation required no additional commentary. Derek simply nodded in rapt agreement, his own instincts confirming the voracity of what Enrico had so eloquently stated. The two men gathered themselves to return to the servants' quarters. On the way back, they were intercepted by a sprinting Manny. "Uncle D..... Uncle D," he shouted as he ran.

"Hey Bud, slow down," Derek cautioned him. "Now, what's going on?"

"Uncle D, Mom says I can go to basketball camp! I've got to be there this Sunday. It's in North Carolina. Dad won't be back until next week. Will you take me? Please?"

The two men looked at one another. Then Enrico nodded affirmatively toward Derek. "Sure, I'll take you Manny!" answered Derek. "It'll give us a chance to talk on the way. We'll have a great time!"

With that settled, the three made their way toward the house, and the hearty, home cooked meal awaiting them.

Chapter 7

On Becoming a Warrior

It never crossed Manny's mind that his mother would be so agreeable to his attending basketball camp. School had been out only a little more than a week, and Deidre gave him such a hard time before, whenever he brought the subject up. Manny thought that maybe she and Gloria were already tired of the kids hanging around the house all day long. And now that Derek was going to drive him, Manny couldn't wait to go. Michael, James Worthy, Sam Perkins, Johnny Dawkins, Tommy Amaker.... all those ex-ACC ball players would be there. Manny was ready for a def time!

Asia was going to Philadelphia for the summer, to stay at their Gran's house. Actually, Manny was kind of proud of her. She had gotten into a two week theater workshop at the University of Pennsylvania. Asia held such grand illusions of becoming a star that Manny didn't have the heart to tell her she couldn't act her way out of a paper bag! But somehow, someone believed she had talent. And really..... who was he to critique her theatrical performance?

Manny also thought about how good it was to see Enrico again. When Enrico told him how much he enjoyed the letter,

Manny didn't fully understand. After all, what was a letter? No big deal. He said it made him so happy that Manny cared enough to write. He always liked Enrico, and before Derek arrived, Enrico was the one who kept Manny on his toes. It was interesting, to see how well Enrico and Derek got along together. It was almost as if they were brothers... or something.

Deidre sure had been grumpy lately. She certainly had not been herself since the party. Although she talked on the phone for hours at night, Manny did not believe she was speaking to his father. Sometimes he would pass her room and peek in. Manny was pretty sure of one thing... she was talking to a man. He was convinced of that because of the way she acted. Deidre told Manny she was driving Asia to Gran's next week. He wondered if she planned to stop in Washington on the way back, to spend some time with his father. Maybe that would help them get themselves together.

Gloria got a letter from Hilliard the previous week. Apparently, old flames die hard. She had been acting so giddy since his correspondence.... one would think the guy had proposed to her or something. Manny thought again how strange women are. God must have put them here..... to keep men humble. One would never know.... how a woman is going to act! Manny then began to wonder why anyone would ever want to get married. Then again, he was sure he would find out for himself.... someday. But not this summer. This summer it's going to be..... the breathtaking..... earth shaking.... slam-jamming.... sky-walking.... mad Manny Cas-tle! Look out, North Carolina...... the kid is READY! Manny couldn't wait!

Speaking of women, Manny thought about one special evening a few days before when he and Derek were sitting out back, gazing lazily up at the starlit sky. For some reason he brought up the fact that women seemed to be so different from men. He remembered how impressed his uncle was with this observation. Derek told Manny that it was perceptive of him to recognize one of the major sociological truths modern man has wrestled with for decades..... or longer.

"Women are one of the most precious gifts to man on God's green earth," Derek said in response to Manny's question. "Unfortunately, it's becoming increasingly rare.... to find a man who can fully appreciate that fact." He paused for a moment, and looked at Manny with a mischievous grin. He had been around his uncle enough to know Derek was about to share some insight with him. "However, to be truthful with you Manny..... this precious gift is so often proffered in such an undesirable manner..... as to make the acceptance of such...... tantamount to a bad case of hemorrhoids. You know....... a real pain in the ass!"

The statement shocked him. He had never heard Derek use profanity before, although Manny didn't tell him ASS seemed pretty tame compared to some of the things he heard in school. But then, Manny thought, he really shouldn't have acted so surprised. Derek made things quite interesting around their house. And he was a lot more fun loving than anyone gave him credit for. Particularly Deidre. Derek somehow managed to keep Manny's attention with his lighthearted manner, even about the most serious things. How could one not like a guy like that?

"Seriously Manny," he said laughing, "if you ever figure out how to deal appropriately with a woman, please let me know!" Apparently, he'd experienced his own frustrations trying to deal with the opposite sex.

"As far as I'm concerned, Uncle D," Manny responded, "I don't know if I'll ever get married. I think it's better just to keep several girlfriends.... all the time. What do you think?"

Derek glanced at Manny with that 'do you know what you just said?' type of look. It seemed as though he purposely delayed answering... to give Manny a moment to reflect on his statement. Finally, he spoke up. "Well, Manny, I'm not sure if a bunch of girlfriends is the answer. What would you do with them all anyway? Think about it. How are you going to keep track of all the birthdays? And what about Valentine's Day? That's a lot of Godiva chocolate to have to pay for. Not to mention all the money you'd be shelling out at Christmas. These days.... women have very expensive tastes. I know that diamonds are a girl's best friend and all that, but believe me..... guys like you.... the jewelers would love to see walk into the store!"

The images his words conjured up were hilarious. But he was right! Manny began to see how it could become a problem.... keeping things straight. It could get embarrassing not remembering the right names.... or worse, getting people confused. He had to admit he'd never thought about it in quite that way. That was another reason Manny liked Derek. He seemed so practical!

"Besides, Manny," he continued, "despite all the hype going around today..... the truth is that all you really need is one, anyway."

"One... what, Uncle D?"

That quizzical look of his momentarily returned. "One WOMAN Manny. All you need is one woman. With the right woman in his life, there is nothing a man can't accomplish."

That was a very bold statement, Manny thought. To say that with the right woman a man could accomplish anything. But Derek was given to bold statements. Without thinking, he heard himself ask, "How do you know when you've met the right one, Uncle D? I mean, there seems to be a lot of beautiful, intelligent women around. Isn't that the type of woman I'd want?"

The question caught Derek a little off guard. He paused to gather his thoughts, then said, "You'll appreciate the things we've talked about more as you get older. Certainly, physical attractiveness and compatibility are factors, as well as intelligence.... and personality for that matter. Ultimately, though, what it comes down to is trusting in your own instincts. And having patience. Don't ever allow yourself to feel rushed into..... matters of the heart. And be certain that you make up your mind for yourself. Remember, it's your life.... not mine, not your parents', not anybody's...... but yours!"

Manny listened attentively. He understood what Derek was saying, and it was good advice..... yet he felt a little disappointed. Derek was normally more direct than that. More revealing.... more insightful. Manny believed there was something more to this, something Derek wasn't letting him in on. However, before he could express himself, Derek started again... as if reading his mind.

"There is one other thing, Manny," he said in an dramatic sort of tone, "..... that a spiritual man will recognize about a woman..... which is fundamentally important." At that moment, Manny looked directly at his uncle. Derek's eyes flickered with a luminescence that had gone unnoticed before. The words were everything now..... all other contexts dissipated. There was a complete focus of all of his senses on what Derek was saying..... it suddenly seemed that the totality of what could be recognized as real .... was bound up in just the two of them there..... closely connected by the power of his verbal construction.

"A spiritual man always observes the eyes of a woman. I don't mean just noticing the color.... although that will sometimes attract your attention. Learn to study the eyes Manny! What most of us don't realize is that the eyes are windows to the soul. In the past, you and I have spent time discussing the role of culture.... and the importance of the spirit..... as it affects the material realm. The eyes of a person, particularly a woman, can reveal to you the essence of the soul. And the content of the soul is what ultimately determines the degree of spiritual power that can be brought to bear on this world."

"What specifically should I be looking for..... there in the eyes, Uncle D?"

"It isn't always clear to your mind what's there. You have to rely on the urging of your own spirit. So, I guess what I'm saying is..... you won't be able to recognize this particular quality, at least not intellectually. But I can tell you that what you're 'looking' for.... are..... the eyes that let you know the woman has the.... soul of a warrior!"

The pronouncement struck Manny.... and arrested his attention. Truthfully, he didn't have a frame of reference for what Derek said. Yet, it somehow seemed completely sensible. "To be sure, Manny," Derek added, "when you find a woman like that..... then you'll really have something!"

It was a smooth, pleasant evening in Washington that greeted Edison and Lance as they left the steps of the Capitol. The two had enjoyed a good day on the Hill; now thoughts were turning to their respective evening plans. For Lance, that meant drinks with friends downtown. Afterwards, he'd probably head over to Kilamanjaro to catch ladies' night. If he was lucky, he might even catch a lady..... to spend the rest of the evening with. Just in case, Lance was ready with a small vial of cocaine.... in the event that his prospective 'date' indulged. Even though it was the middle of the work week, the balmy summer weather made for good refreshment, good conversation and hopefully, good fun.

Edison had other ideas. Specifically, one Ms. Camille Ferguson. Ever since he'd met her at the press conference, his fascination with her style and presence, had developed into an out and out lustful desire. Since he'd been back in D.C., they'd spoken on the phone several times, completely professional interests mind you. But even then he found himself turned on by the sound of her voice. He'd decided he just HAD to have her. Of course, in his job he was around articulate, attractive women regularly. And he'd had his share of overnight stands and weekend flings. After all, that was simply executive privilege in his business. But Camille was a different situation, and he knew it. And he knew, she knew, he knew it.

However, there had been a breakthrough! She agreed to have dinner with him. The plan was for her to meet Edison at 7:30. Camille was working as a volunteer in the campaign of Eva Pratt Christian, a lifelong D.C. resident and lawyer, who was emerging as the dark horse favorite to succeed embattled incumbent Mayor Adrian Lowery. Eva's 'clean house' campaign rhetoric seemed to be reaching the District's voters. Despite her previous outspoken support of Mayor Lowery, Eva's platform was certainly a breath of fresh air to a heartfelt community activist like Camille.

At any rate, Edison came up with the bright idea to pay Ms. Ferguson an unannounced visit. Stopping at his club, he took a quick steam bath, shaved, showered, and dressed for the evening, all within an hour. Summarily, he headed for the campaign office. The ride wasn't far from the Capitol, just across the Whitney Young bridge into the Anacostia section of D.C. As he arrived, a flurry of activity was underway.

The candidate herself was there, as were several news reporters from TV 3. Despite the confusion, Edison was not difficult to spot, pulling up as he did in his steel grey Mercedes, with the congressional ID stickers prominently displayed on his windshield. The reporters assumed he was there in support of Eva, and immediately approached the car as he got out. Normally, he relished the attention and publicity. But this wasn't the time for an unscheduled interview. He began to mentally kick himself for deciding to come in the first place, as discretion is always the better part of valor. Particularly when you're trying, as Edison hoped, to carry on an affair.... without public scrutiny.

The commotion caused by Edison's presence outside attracted the attention of the workers in the office. Finishing with a phone call, Camille got up to see what was going on. When she saw Edison holding court on the sidewalk in front of the small neighborhood storefront, she could only shake her head in mock disgust. *What an ASShole.....* she whispered to herself, *but he is kind of cute.* While it was entertaining to watch him squirming with the reporters, explaining why he was there, Camille began to wonder the same thing. *What WAS he doing there?* Then she remembered that they were supposed to get together for dinner. It had been such a hectic afternoon, she'd forgotten about their date. Realizing he obviously ignored her instruction to meet at the restaurant, she immediately became irritated. "I'm going to have to train him," she said, not so softly.

Just then, the candidate herself entered. "Get WHO trained?" Eva inquired of her campaign co-chairwoman.

"Oh.... I was just referring to my dog," Camille trailed off, awkwardly trying to change the subject. Eva noticed Camille's pained expression, as well as the fact that her attention was riveted on the scene outside.

"And who's this?" asked Eva tapping lightly on the window-pane.

"That..... Camille responded matter-of-factly, "....is Congressman Castle.... from Georgia."

"So.... that's Edison Castle. I've heard about him before. I should think I'd like to meet the Congressman. Do you think you could introduce me?"

Camille hesitated momentarily, then decided that now was as good a time as any for Eva to meet him. After all, Edison couldn't make any more of an ass of himself than he already had. "Well, OK...." answered Camille begrudgingly. "Let's go."

As they headed for the door, Eva mentioned to Camille teasingly, "Some dog you've got here!" The two looked at each other..... and both had a real good laugh as they stepped outside.

Things were beginning to really trouble Deidre. Certainly, her marriage wasn't in the best shape. The tension still lingered between she and Edison from the whole Cancun mess. But it wasn't that she lacked for male attention. Carter was a most doting and caring companion. He did everything he could to please her. And he'd proven himself to be an adequate, if not heroic, lover on the several occasions they'd met for an afternoon interlude. Carter questioned Edison's commitment to her while pledging his own undying love. But she knew Carter wasn't what she wanted...... in the long term.

Deidre wondered often about Lance. She consciously thought of taking him as a lover. That would really shake Edison up! Realistically though, Lance was too close to her husband for her to seriously entertain a tryst. Nonetheless, he held a playful fascination for Deidre's more carnal instincts.

Besides everything else, the annual Delta Sigma Theta formal was approaching. It was very important for her to be there, as she was this year's Chairperson. But she wasn't sure if Edison would be home, and Carter had to go out of town. Deidre didn't want to attend something like that with Carter anyway. No use letting those newsy women speculate about her personal business. At the same time Deidre knew she couldn't show up without a date. That would just be too humiliating! At any rate, the formal certainly presented her with a dilemma.

But what troubled her the most was Derek. It seemed that her life had been so much simpler, so much less intense before he arrived. Although she couldn't put her finger on it, she was convinced Derek was the cause of her problems. And Manny's growing confidence in, and relationship to her brother was more than she could stand. Yet Derek really hadn't done anything overt, and he certainly was a great help around the house. It was this curious imbroglio that bothered her so. He slept on the floor like an Indian! He never seemed to want to go out and socialize. He was always dirty and grimy from working in the yard. Yet Manny loved him! She didn't know what to do. But she knew she had to do something...... before he completely ruined her life!

"The eyes of a warrior," Derek explained to his nephew, "reveal the essence of power..... the power that resides in the spirit. The quality that makes this power active..... is relentlessness."

Their silver Caravan moved out smartly as they traveled around I-285, toward Spaghetti Junction and I-85 North. They were on their way to basketball camp in North Carolina, and the bright sunny afternoon had them both in a good mood. The two had just completed lunch in transit; Manny had an cheeseburger with fries, and Derek an apple with black coffee. "You should cherish this time of your life, Manny. It's great to be young," Derek mentioned jovially.

"Why do you say that, Uncle D?"

"Because you can eat all that cheese, and red meat and not even think about your weight..... or your cholesterol count, that's why!" Derek released a hearty laugh, and Manny could only look at him with an air of satisfied indifference. Cholesterol counts were the last thing on his mind at the moment. Derek enjoyed his nephew's company enormously, even more so than most of the adults he found himself forced to spend time with.

Gulping down the remains of a tall Coke, Manny alluded to the fact that Derek had never really explained what exactly it meant to be a warrior, and what relentlessness was. "After all, Uncle D," he said, "how can a woman ever fight like a man?" Derek's earlier comments about the eyes of a woman had stuck in his mind.

"Well, actually, Manny.... there have been civilizations where women were, in fact, the dominant gender. The legends of several civilizations that developed along the Amazon River in South America..... have given rise to the stories of a race of women, physically superior in most ways to men, and clearly dominant in the field of battle. Amazons. But when I refer to the nature of a warrior.... I'm not necessarily talking about combat and the battlefield. That is simply one of many venues where the heart of a warrior can be manifested." Derek paused as he slowed the van to a stop. He lined up behind a row of vehicles that were queuing because of an accident.

"You know, I've never been anyplace where there were so many wrecks, every day!" Derek said incredulously, referring to the Atlanta traffic patterns. Manny was surprised by his uncle's impatience. He had never known Derek to react like that..... to actually lose his temper. Slowly, the line of traffic moved along. As they approached the scene of the accident, the luminescence of an ambulance's flashing blue lights and several police emergency vehicles came into full view. Two people were lying on the ground in a small pool of blood, while nearby a young girl on a stretcher was being carried to an ambulance. The distorted wreckage of crushed automobiles recounted the story of a violent collision that claimed at least two lives, and threatened another. Manny's rapt attention to the scene of destruction was interrupted by the sound of Derek's voice, as he suddenly resumed his instruction.

"The nature of the warrior that I'm referring to has much more to do with an attitude..... a sense of self and a comprehension of our potential..... as conduits of the spirit." Derek looked over at his young nephew as they passed through the accident area. He could recognize the despair Manny felt for the injured. Although it was clear Manny wasn't paying close attention to him, Derek went on with his thought. "One of the first things a warrior learns to deal with in his life....... is his death!" The juxtaposition of terms snapped Manny out of his momentary silence.

"What do you mean, Uncle D?" he wondered aloud, looking to his uncle for understanding. Derek accelerated now, and the accident scene was quickly left behind as they moved through Gwinnett County and on up I-85.

"All of us," Derek began "are concerned at some point with the uncertainty that death presents. Yet we are all certain that death awaits us. This is one of the central contradictions of life. The average person treats this dilemma in one of two ways; either they resign themselves to the inevitability of their death in a casual sort of way, and live their lives according to their 'fate'. Or, they develop an almost paranoid preoccupation with security, physical comfort, and material attainment in order to..... 'get the most out of life'.

"Interestingly enough, both approaches are manifestations of the same perception, namely, that death is preordained and final. And there is nothing at all that we can do about it. This is the way the average person, either consciously or unconsciously, comes to grips with his own mortality." Derek paused, allowing the impressions his words brought forth to germinate inside the cabin of the van. The lack of response from his nephew let Derek know that Manny assumed, even at his age, that the inevitability of death was just a given.... that it was, in fact, inevitable.

"On the other hand," Derek resumed, "the attitude of the warrior is different. A warrior identifies death not as a forgone conclusion..... to be experienced some time in the future, but rather as an immediate, impending eventuality. But the recognition of the impending nature of death is not approached in fear, and therefore recklessly. A warrior comprehends the immediacy of his own death, and uses it as a motivator, a positive, active facilitator in the experience of life. He (or she) looks for opportunities to inject life into every situation. In so doing, a warrior actually learns to keep death at bay..... to deal with this entrance into eternity...... completely on his own terms.

"Most assuredly, the life of a warrior is one of discipline..... the discipline required to remain ready to meet the intrusion of death at any moment, and to turn it away. The intrusion of death, by the way, can take many forms. Affliction, disease, sickness, disability, emotional disorder, depression, insecurity; these are all different aspects, or degrees, of death..... in the experience of the warrior.

"For this reason, warriors are vitally concerned with their history. That's why we've spent so much time discussing the heritage and culture of our African roots.

"For the average person, such discussions are important in terms of providing a sense of identity. This sense of identity enables the individual to measure himself against the past, in order to find justifications for present or future behaviors. At best, such a motive can only provide the basis for a personal or interpersonal commentary on human conditions; race, economics, politics, etc.

"The intent of the life of a warrior, however, is to go beyond mere commentary on the human condition. The warrior seeks not to comment..... but to act; to create a new existence, a new set of conditions...... both personally and by extension to others, collectively. Because of this, the examination of the past is for the purpose of understanding how other warriors (of his culture) have dealt with and applied..... the immensity of the power of the Spirit.

"The reason I've shared some stories of great Nubian warriors of the past is not only to give you insight into your history and lineage...... but more importantly...... to prepare you for an application of spiritual principles in your own life. By recognizing the power of the spirit and seeking application in the day to day world, the warrior transcends simply facing his own mortality. He actually learns something bigger and more important. He learns to come to grips with his own...... immortality! A man of culture recognizes the eternal realm in his own existence. It's what men of culture refer to as..... GRIPPING THE SPIRIT."

Derek glanced over at his nephew, whose rapt attention was disturbed only by the irresistible urge to relieve his bladder. "Don't worry, Bud," said Derek cheerfully. "You won't have to become a spiritual man...... just to use the bathroom!" The hearty laughter they both enjoyed caused Manny even more urgency in his need for relief. They got off the interstate at the Braselton exit, and headed for a Burger King about a quarter of a mile down the road. "I wonder if we'll run into Kim Basinger," mused Derek thoughtfully.

Manny looked at him quizzically. "I don't know who you're talking about," he said anxiously, "but if she's got the key to the men's room.... she's my kind of woman right now!" The two smiled at one another, and made their way to the closest relief station they could find.

Deidre's face reflected the concern she was feeling as she brought the Delta Sigma Theta committee meeting to an official close. Gaining final agreement on specifics for their annual formal event had been more of a challenge than she ever thought. But while that process was drawn out and tedious, what she really dreaded was ending the meeting. Deidre knew that she would then have to face several of her less than discrete sisters, and their endless attempts to pry into her private life, nosy hussies that they were.

Of course, what she did was really none of their business. But since she was Chairwoman for the affair, Deidre knew all eyes would be on her. And now she felt particularly vulnerable.... not because arrangements were late, or tickets weren't being sold. As silly as it may seem, she felt awkward because...... she still didn't have a date! If she didn't do something soon, she'd be the laughingstock of Atlanta. Even as the thought ran across through mind, the predators were already circling about, awaiting the chance to strike.

"Well, Sister Castle, I'm glad to see things are going so well with our affair for next week," squawked Emma Carson, a plump, cherub faced psychologist. Emma was known as the unofficial leader of 'Gossipers Anonymous'. "You know Deidre," Emma went on, "my husband and I were wondering if you and Edison would care to stop by for cocktails before the ball gets underway. It's been so long since we've all had a chance.... to get together."

"Oh, I don't think so, Emma," Deidre responded weakly. "There will be so much to do.... prior to the ball, I sincerely doubt that I'll...... uh... I mean..... we'll.... be able to get by your house. Thanks just the same for your offer."

Emma's cat eyes glazed over with delight. She could tell from Deidre's reaction that she'd struck a nerve. Emma had heard through the rumor mill that things weren't too tidy with their marriage. Now was her chance to get Deidre to squirm. "Oh honey, believe me..... I didn't mean to pry," smirked Emma. Her smugness made Deidre want to pull the little chubby's hair right out of her head! But she thought better of it and decided not to let them get to her.

"Oh, you weren't prying," answered Deidre sweetly, biting her tongue.... to keep from slapping the little bitch's face off. "As I said, there's just too much to do beforehand."

Not willing to leave well enough alone, Emma continued the attack. "I know it must be hard, you know, getting an escort for something like this..... with Edison away so much." Emma the Cat's fangs were flaring now, and she waited for Deidre to break down and admit that things weren't very kosher at home. This was the nectar that the gossip gods longed for!

"No, not at all Emma," lied Deidre. "In fact, I've invited my brother Derek to go with me. He hasn't had a chance to get out much since he's been in town. I thought it would be a good opportunity for him to meet some people. Edison's been to so many of these events, he'd just as soon relax at home anyway. Who knows Emma? Derek may even be interested in meeting you."

She paused there. Emma couldn't hide her surprise. Deidre's brother? She wasn't aware Deidre even had a brother. Noting the shock on Emma's face, Deidre moved quickly to gather her things. "If you'll excuse me, I've got to be going now..... ladies." As she turned to leave, she gazed at the stout, diminutive Ms. Carson. "You know... on second thought, Emma," Deidre yelled making her way to the door, "somehow, I DON'T think my brother would be very interested in meeting you. I'm sure he's got better taste. Good Night!"

Deidre was surprised at how good it felt..... beating Emma at her own game. Once she reached her car, however, the satisfaction she enjoyed from shutting up Miss Busybody, soon gave way to an uneasy mood of apprehension. In her momentary frustration, she'd committed to showing up at the formal with Derek. *How could I do something like that?* she wondered silently. Deidre realized she didn't know what to expect from Derek. And with some notable, local dignitaries expected to be there, her choice of an escort represented even more of an exposure.

He's so damn strange. He acts so.... so.... indifferent every time it comes to any type of social event. He probably won't even want to go... she muttered aimlessly to herself. I'll sit down with Edison when he comes in this weekend. Maybe I can convince him to change his schedule.... and HE'LL go with me. Interestingly enough, the thought was somehow more distasteful to her than the prospect of being escorted..... by an eccentric brother! Clearly, the seeds of resentment sown in Mexico were beginning to sprout into a thick hedge of bitterness..... and a particularly solemn indifference.

The weight of her expectations so preoccupied Deidre that she neglected to get off the expressway at the proper exit. It was another two miles around I-285 before she even recognized her error. *OK honey.... let's get a grip here*, she moaned unconsciously, making her way to the nearest U-turn and heading for home. *Why do I think Edison would want to be part of anything that interested me anyway? All he cares about..... is Washington and his damn political career. Sometimes, I wish I knew...... why I even married the man in the first place!*

In actuality, her self-admonition was purely rhetorical. Deidre knew exactly why she had married him in the first place. And it was a realization she still had trouble coming to grips with...... even after all these years!

The evening turned out to be a lovely one for Edison and Camille. Following the impromptu news conference outside Eva Christian's campaign office, Camille succeeded in luring him away to a quiet dinner at Cafe Atlantico, a small restaurant known for it's Caribbean cuisine. Afterwards, it was on to Cities, a vibrant Adams-Morgan nightspot for some drinks and dancing. While they were having a good time, Camille managed to keep their interactions friendly and semi-professional, even though Edison clearly had more intimate things on his mind.

Oddly enough, Camille knew there was a strange sexual attraction Edison held for her. It wasn't the typical 'pretty boy' type of attraction however. More than anything, Camille could see that despite his charm and professional stature, Edison was not all that polished when it came to the interpersonal dalliances..... of dating. In fact Edison, at times, was awkward..... well, actually he could be downright clumsy, both figuratively and literally. Yet the contradiction he represented...... the powerful, Congressional persona on the one hand, and the urgent, almost adolescent panty pursuit on the other, intrigued her. She was the type of woman that enjoyed lovemaking with a man who wasn't too good..... not refined or very expert. Camille was really looking forward to the sexual experience she would derive from him. But not tonight!

For his part, Edison was simply spellbound by her. He was so impressed that a single mother who worked full time and was raising two children could find the time to get involved in the local political scene. And she was so knowledgeable about a variety of topics, from the variances in pricing on the commodities exchange, to the state of affairs in the Middle East. Needless to say, Camille was very well read. But what impressed Edison beyond everything else...... was the commitment she exuded, a commitment to her candidate, but more importantly, a commitment to her beloved D.C. She was born and raised in the District, and Camille was determined to see a better future for her children. She really believed in building a better city.

Of course, there WAS one other thing that captured Edison's attention. Even though she lacked the Cosmopolitan magazine looks, Camille did have the kind of body any man would kill for; the kind of firm, tight, hourglass shape that so delicately filled the clingy, knit one-piece dresses that are so popular these days. Each time they danced Edison brushed against her, feeling the firmness of her thighs.... of her breasts. The sensations were nearly too much for him to stand!

After all was said and done, however, the highlight of the evening for Edison had to be..... THE ELECTRIC SLIDE! In spite of his clumsiness, both real and imagined, one of the true qualities Edison did possess...... was a distinct lack of any dancing ability! While not all that difficult, the Electric Slide did require SOME coordination, on the part of the individuals, and in conjunction with a group.

The party people that night were an eclectic gathering of lawyers, government employees, school teachers, business persons, and assorted tourists, each soaking up the unique ambiance of the club. The low murmur of mingling and social trivia from earlier in the evening had given way to a funky, infectious jam session that reverberated sensuously in the balmy night air. Through it all, Camille managed to convey to the good Congressman what the 'Slide' was all about. Before long Edison was Electric, and they spent the rest of the evening gaily spinning..... and dipping..... and Sliding their way into the night.

While riding home after dropping Camille off at her car, (and managing to at least get a good night kiss) Edison reflected on the evening. He couldn't recall the last time he'd had so much fun. Suddenly, the importance he placed on the affairs of the day...... simply weren't important. At that moment, he was lighthearted, exuberant, contented. It was a sensation he wished would never end. Although not yet aware of it, Edison was experiencing that wonderful, lyric, intoxication...... of a man in love!

Unfortunately, he would have to discover how ill equipped he was to handle THIS kind of drunkenness.

"The objective of the life of a warrior is clarity. Such clarity is requisite for a proper orientation and handling of the urgings of the Spirit." Manny and Derek were crossing the state line into South Carolina, and the late afternoon sun was giving way to a spectacular twilight canopy above the Cherokee foothills. "You know, Manny," Derek continued serenely, "the Native Americans of this part of the country believed that there were places of power in these hills.... places where the manifestations of the Spirit would become apparent, if one were able to tone down the internal dialogue..... to become clear enough to experience the powerful flow of life. Maybe we'll explore a few of them...... when I pick you up."

"Really, Uncle D?" Manny responded excitedly. "That would be great!" Fanciful thoughts of old Indian trails and tribal artifacts danced about in his head.

"You see, Manny," emphasized Derek, returning to his narrative, "the purpose of all our discussions of the past few months has been....... to familiarize you with the rudiments of your total being, to give you some insight into the necessity of mobilizing the tools of creative living for yourself. That's the essence of the life of a warrior...... a life of pure creativity. For a man of culture, a warrior, to ever have the capacity to handle the unspeakable power of the spirit for himself, he's got to learn to conserve energy; for it takes a tremendous amount of energy for one to emerge from the constrictions of everyday living. The absolutely most effective way to stop the endless dissipation of one's energy..... is to achieve internal clarity; to relieve the constant interior messaging that characterizes the thoughts, emotions, and willfulness of man. There is a biblical reference, as it is expressed by the Apostle Paul in the twelfth chapter of the Book of Romans:

> '.... be not conformed to this world..... but
> be transformed.... by the renewing of your
> mind, that you may prove what is the good
> and acceptable and perfect will of GOD.'

"For the warrior, this renewal of the mind begins when we cease to rely solely on its dictates; rationality, intellectualism, emotionalism, doubts, worries, and the like. Truly, what is required is a retraining of our mental processes...... to bring the endless activity of thoughts under the direction and guidance of one's spirit. We've discussed prayer, and how praying is exercise for the spirit. Listen to how it is worded in Biblical terms,

> 'For the weapons of our warfare are not
> carnal..... but mighty through God to the
> pulling down of strongholds...... casting down
> imaginations and every high thing that exalts
> itself against the knowledge of God.... and
> bringing into captivity..... every thought unto
> the obedience of Christ.'

A strained, almost grim expression overtook Manny's face. It was clear that Derek's words unsettled his nephew to no small degree. The smoldering confusion inside him flared suddenly into a stream of distressed pleadings. "Why are you doing this to me? Why do you talk so much about this warrior stuff, Uncle D? I'm just a kid. I don't want to fight anybody. I'm not running around with gangs or messing with people. I mind my own business. All I want to do is play basketball!" His face was flushed now, as he tried hard to collect himself. Manny was somewhat embarrassed for acting so emotional in front of Derek, whom he admired immensely. But the weight of his despair was too pronounced to contain. "Why do you talk so much about negative things, so much about..... war?"

The silver van hummed along easily as they approached Charlotte, N.C. It was just another thirty miles or so to the basketball camp. A brief silence settled into the cabin as Derek and Manny both recognized the need to allow the tenseness in the air to subside a bit. Slowly, Derek began to speak. "There are three primary reasons I speak to you of the warrior's mantle..... each specifically associated with our collective past, the present, and then future experiences..... of your life. From a purely historical perspective, you must come to a working understanding of the greatness of our heritage and ancestry. From the glories of our beginnings on the Continent, through the deportation of our forefathers to this country... the terror and indignities of slavery..... the displacement and slaughter of millions of Native Americans, and the myriad of mixed blood we've undergone since coming here. These are the essentials of our identity..... who we are! Many of us, like myself, have white, black and Indian bloodlines. Yet there is no need to escape our African ancestry. On the contrary, it is impossible to do so! It is in the examination of that very ancestry where we will find the platform that leads to deliverance from the delusions of this material, consumer minded existence.... to freedom! The important thing is to acknowledge and apply the lessons of our own culture, not that of Europeans.

"Secondly, because of that heritage, we must come to grips with living in present day America. The gang warfare of which you spoke earlier has nothing whatsoever to do with the cultural integrity of the life of the warrior. At best, gangs represent a perverted attempt at re-establishing the identity of the ancient tribal unit, a sense of community, of belonging. At worst, they facilitate those terribly destructive processes that eat away at our cultural and social fabric..... drugs, crime, a complete disregard for the sacredness of life."

The view on gangs thus presented by Derek was somewhat surprising to Manny. "Uncle D.... I'm not interested in gangs. What do they..... what does.... any of this.... have to do with MY life, anyway?"

Derek's normally pleasant facial expression yielded to a dismayed look of chagrin, as he considered his nephew's perspective. "Manny, the things that affect people of color... anywhere in the world.... affect you! We are all part of a great African Diaspora. I know it may be hard to understand.... but this concept of essential connectivity is at the heart of what I am laboring to describe. Truthfully, we can't be concerned with just our own lives as individuals, our own successes or failures.

"Of course, each of us must take responsibility for our own expectations of life, our own attitudes. And it does take a tremendous amount of discipline to resist the urge to continuously dwell on ourselves. But human beings are not created to be isolationists; we all have an indispensable connection to one another. It is the truth of the power of the spirit. By operating in the fullness of that truth.... we can work to enhance the quality of life for all people. We have got to deal with this critical social interdependence, if there is to be any hope for revitalizing the humanity of our world! To live..... selfishly..... is to be doomed to an existence that is empty, fruitless. And one that is completely self-destructive!

"Invariably, these things will become apparent in your own future. The basic nature of life's processes is cyclical; you know....'what goes around, comes around'? Well..... believe me, Manny, it's absolutely true in the realm of the spirit, and the spirit realm is what underlies and invigorates everything we experience in the physical world. There is nothing lost, nothing used up in the spiritual world. It is eternal. Ultimately, everything is accounted for. And every living thing exists, simultaneously, in both the spiritual and physical planes of existence.

"The fundamental challenge of the warrior is to bring to bear the power of the spirit on the circumstances of everyday living. To garner the discipline required to consistently focus the immensity of the spirit realm, in a positive way, on the events of this daily existence. To empty oneself of the excess baggage..... of undue emotionalism...... of too much intellectualizing, to become clear enough....... to give the truth of the spirit a chance to re-establish itself in our world!

"The warfare that is waged by a true warrior...... is not against physical foes. Rather, it's against the forces of destructive thoughts, of calloused attitudes, of self doubt, of insecurity, of acceptance of mediocrity. To walk as a warrior.... is to walk in the fullness of your manhood. Everything we've discussed these past months...... is to prepare you for the challenge of life...... that you will inevitably have to face. Make no mistake about it. The challenges that lie ahead are in fact..... spiritual warfare."

Derek's eyes burned with a fervor that revealed the totality of his compassion for the subject at hand. Manny could only sit there in a state of paralysis while he contemplated how these things could possibly affect his life. It was, after all, a bit much to expect an eleven year old to be prepared for such a compelling personality as Derek's.

"Manny," Derek said with a touching warmth and emphasis, "....I love you dearly.... like the son I never had! And what's at stake here.... is nothing short of your own life! But my passion goes beyond..... even my own hopes for you. It runs to the future of our people, of our world. I have seen and now comprehend that you have the capability...... to be a powerful creative force. You've got to learn to use that creativity, first in your own life, then in the relationships that you build.

"I mentioned earlier that we exist in both the spiritual and physical planes of reality..... simultaneously. Clearly, the physical is subordinate to the spiritual. The creative power available to all of us..... resides in the spirit. What is needful is a mechanism to activate this creative force in the physical realm. I call this process..... GRIPPING THE SPIRIT. The unique quality that separates mankind from any other living thing..... is the fact that human beings possess the ability to think, to reason, to will, to emote. All of these qualities are characteristics of the soul of man. Remember the diagram of the pyramid? Schematically, the soul resides between the spirit and the body, which is our physical presence in this world. The soul is where the warfare we've been talking about occurs. By far, the most effective technique for men to manifest the presence of the spirit in the realm of the physical world...... is with their WORDS! Words are the containers by which the power of the spirit..... is **shipped** into the realm of physical existence!

"Of course, a tremendous amount of discipline is required to control one's tongue. Over time, the spiritual man trains his speech patterns..... to reflect the life giving nature of this process. The bottom line is...... you can have, what you say you can have! And if you say something long enough, you'll believe it! Once you believe, it's only a matter of time before it manifests itself, whether it be good..... or bad.

"One of the reasons I've spent time talking about the Bible, and quoting Scripture..... is because it so concisely and clearly articulates..... the nature of the spirit realm. This is particularly true given our African-European development in this country. These are the words that need to find their way into our mouths........ not words of incompetence, of inadequacy, of despair, or defeat!

"The world of the spirit is all around us. And it has a structure and organization that, if anything, is more developed than the physical world we experience day to day. However, nothing from the spirit can be introduced into the material world without the involvement of a living, physical presence; a body. You've heard of demonic possession, of seances and the like. These are particular manifestations from the realm of the spirit. The common denominator in all this is the presence, yea, the necessity of physical bodies through which the various types of spiritual manifestation can occur. Manny, I tell you truly, what a glorious opportunity it is to be born into the world! The fullness and enormity of all possibilities lie ahead! What a tragic crime it is that men and women don't respect their bodies more!

"The essential challenge for the warrior, then, is to facilitate the flow of creative power from the spirit into the physical realm. As I've mentioned, the power of the spirit is all around us. We must actively search for opportunities to apply this power. Therein lies the ultimate purpose of life, namely, the application of the presence and power of the spirit...... to make the world the kind of wonderful place..... it was always intended to be. There are creative solutions to the problems facing modern man..... AIDS, drugs, neglect and abuse of children, despair, financial ruin. But these solutions are not to be found in ever more material consumption. They can come only from an experience....... of the illumination of one's spirit."

Manny fidgeted nervously, while Derek maintained the flow of this stream of consciousness. "In the Bible, the process of illumination of one's spirit is described as being 'born again'. I think it's significant to note the connection between spiritual illumination.... and the physical event of birth. In fact, the two notions are inseparable. As I have said, nothing from the spirit can be introduced into the physical plane...... without the intervention of a physical body. Therefore, the illumination of the spirit cannot occur without the agreement and decision of a person. This is important! The life of the warrior is characterized by a continuing series of quality decisions concerning the primacy of the spirit, despite the protests or doubts that are raised in his or her own mind.

"Such patterns of decision making lead to a spiritual integrity. This spiritual integrity ultimately breeds a life of impeccability. In a state of impeccability, the warrior reaches a point where there is free flow of energy from the spiritual realm...... into the physical. To the untrained eye, such experiences of this energy flow are interpreted to be...... magic! The fact of the matter is that the two have very little in common."

Manny immediately perked up with excitement once he saw signs indicating the approach to the 'Michael Jordan Flight Time' basketball camp. The recognition snapped him out of a dazed silence. "Uncle D, why is it that you put so much confidence in God...... and in the power of the Spirit? It doesn't seem that any of it matters today, that any of it makes any difference."

The sudden boldness of his nephew's question startled Derek. Gathering again his thoughts he answered slowly, "...because, Manny, any man who ignores the presence and power of

God, and his Spirit, who relies solely on his own understanding...... is a <u>fool!</u>"

Pulling into the winding driveway that led up to the camp headquarters, Manny's attention was now focused on the two weeks he would be spending in the company of REAL ballplayers. Getting his things together, he groped anxiously for the latch to unlock the van door. Before he could get out, he felt his uncle's firm grip on his shoulder as he attempted to open the door.

Turning quickly he looked at Derek, who, fixing a stern expression on his nephew, said simply, "nothing remains for us to discuss. What is left for you.... is only the experience..... of the power of the Spirit!" Derek paused, then added deliberately. "And always remember what I said, Manny. Don't you....... be no FOOL!"

Edison's flight arrived at Atlanta's Hartsfield Airport early that evening. Normally, the late day rush from Washington National headed south to Atlanta caused inordinate delays. The best description for that flight was a cattle car. Fortunately for Edison, Lance always had their travel agency book first class accommodations for the Congressman. It was OK. to be a representative of the masses, but to have to fly with them? That was another matter altogether.

At any rate, his plane touched down nearly twenty-five minutes early. Edison barely had time to finish his quiche, which, by the way, was quite delicious considering the whole thing was an 'add water and microwave' powdered concoction. Usually, this Thursday evening trip home caused him to be in an uneven mood. But the heavy intoxication of his evening with Camille lingered, and that remembrance had Edison in a pleasant frame of mind. It lasted all of fifteen minutes once he realized that no one was there to meet him at the airport. *Where the HELL was Deidre?* he thought to himself nervously as he paced up and down the arrival concourse. As much as I've done for that woman... the LEAST she could do is give me a damn ride home! Of course, all HE had to do was walk over to the west exit and pick up a cab or limo. But that was too simple. He was going to give her a piece of his mind before anything else!

The phone rang three or four times before a breathless Gloria managed to pick it up. She had been outside talking to Enrico when the call came in. "Hello, Castle residence," she said in a most courteous voice.

Edison didn't let her pleasantness disrupt his UNpleasant intent. "Where's Deidre?" he demanded angrily. "She KNEW I was coming in tonight."

Instinctively, Gloria tried to protect Deidre. "Well... Mrs. Castle didn't mention that she WASN'T going to meet you Sir. I'm sure something just held her up." Gloria wasn't really convinced that was the case, but she wasn't going to let him know that. It was all Gloria could do to contain her contempt for Edison. Conversely, she loved Deidre and thought that she could do much better for herself with someone else. She didn't understand why a woman with so much on the ball like Deidre... would ever put up with HIS mess. But Edison WAS her employer, and as such, commanded a certain measure of respect. "If you'd like, Mr. Castle, I'll come pick you up," Gloria offered, somewhat tentatively.

Her accommodating tone only served to further infuriate Edison. "No.... don't you bother," he muttered defiantly. "I'll find my own DAMN way home. And tell that wife of mine..... not to wait up for me!" CLICK!

Truthfully, Edison was the last thing on Deidre's mind at the moment. Her would be suitor, Carter, had captured her attention. She'd just left some cozy quarters in a smoky Buckhead cafe where he had been confessing his unwavering devotion to her.

"Deidre, you KNOW you don't love Edison," he emphasized. "And I realize that you don't love me...... yet. But I want you to understand Deidre. I can make you happy! I'm sick and tired of being out here...... you know..... of going from one woman to the next. I want to... no... I NEED to settle down with the right person. PLEASE, Deidre. I want you! Leave Edison..... and marry me!"

Of course, Deidre had heard all this before. Actually, Carter was a good catch..... he was well-to-do, charming, a decent sense of humor. Up until that point, their discretionary affair had been a matter of some convenience, and occasional satisfaction. Certainly, as men go, he wasn't a bad one. However, there WAS one small problem.

Carter was what Deidre so aptly referred to as a WANNABE. You know... I wannabe your man.... I wannabe your BA-by.... I wannabe your protector...... I wannabe your EVERYTHING! Trouble was, for all his admirable qualities, Carter lacked the excitement, lacked the charisma, lacked the personal POWER..... a woman like Deidre secretly craved. He just couldn't be..... what he WANNABE! To make matters worse, he was demanding that she give up on years of marriage and risk public ridicule as the result of a messy divorce action against Edison. No way! Obviously, her little fling had become more of a nuisance than she bargained for.

Beside such consternation over 'boyfriend', there was still the matter of the Delta Ball. Deidre hoped Edison would consent to go, but she knew how his distaste had grown to the point of antagonism with many of the people that attended the affair, even though most of them were his constituents. Moreover, he had been quite testy the past few times they'd spoken, and she quite frankly didn't feel like putting up with his nonsense.

Ironically enough, thinking about Edison's demeanor of late caused her to suddenly remember that his flight was arriving that evening. *Oh NOOOO,* she lamented while nearly driving her foot through the gas pedal of her Mercedes. *Why did I have to forget about his arrival..... tonight of all nights? Maybe it was late..... very late I hope,* Deidre whispered to herself, giving in to a fit of wishful thinking.

When she arrived at home, Gloria immediately filled her in on the conversation with Edison. "I sure hope he doesn't hurt himself, Gloria," she muttered quietly and sighed, resigned to enduring the night alone. *Lord... don't let him get drunk,* she said in silent prayer. *He can be SO clumsy.... I don't want him to break a leg.*

Despite Carter's pleadings, the one thing he'd said that stuck in Deidre's mind was the fact that she didn't LOVE Edison. While it had been presented as a taunt, or more properly, a challenge of sorts to her, the truth was that she had never really been in love with Edison. Their marriage was mostly the result of circumstances beyond her control, rather than any matter of the heart.

The Delta formal was only three days away now, and things hadn't improved very much for Deidre. After a week at home, Edison decided he should attend a dinner in Washington that was to be hosted by Senator Dunn, and regrettably couldn't attend her affair. Carter was behaving like a wounded puppy, whining and yelping as though she had beaten him with a stick. Since Derek returned from taking Manny to basketball camp, she'd hardly spoken to him. He spent all his time working in the yard and talking to Enrico. The only good news was that the children seemed to be enjoying their summer. Deidre was glad they weren't around while she was dealing with her 'adult days'. Asia had written to say she was having a great time in the drama program at the University of Pennsylvania, and had met an interesting boy that lived in her grandmother's neighborhood. Manny, of course, was in seventh heaven working with his idols.

The July heat in Atlanta was burdensome, so Gloria had resorted to whipping up batches of 'Summer Slush', a luscious concoction of whatever clear liquor was around the house, a mixture of fruit juices, and crushed ice. She popped this mixture into the freezer until it reached the consistency of sludge. Served in a tumbler with a squirt of ginger ale, it was a great refresher.

Late that afternoon, she and Deidre were having a little 'Slush' party on the deck. About midway through their third round of cocktails, the conversation inevitably turned to men, specifically to Edison. "I hope you don't mind my saying this, Mrs. Castle," Gloria cautiously began, "but I really don't see how you and Mr. Castle ever got together. I mean, you're so different from him."

Deidre knew what Gloria meant, and her 'Slush' induced frame of mind allowed her to speak more freely than she might have otherwise. "You know, Gloria, Edison doesn't respect me at all.... not the way a man should respect a woman who has supported him the way I have all these years. Sometimes I wonder how we're ever gonna stay together, what with him gone so much. And I don't like that whole Washington scene either!" She paused a moment in reflection, then continued. "But truthfully, I've got more immediate problems to think about. The Delta ball is only two days away, and I don't even have an escort. How do you like that? I'M the Chairwoman for the ball, and I can't even get a date!" Gloria didn't really understand why this was such a big deal, but she empathized with Deidre's predicament anyway, like a friend would. She knew about her involvement with Carter, but resisted the urge to bring his name up. She just let her talk, get things off her chest.

"Edison doesn't think MY interests are important," Deidre went on. "Even though he knows this is a big event each year for me, he won't be there. He always manages to find some official reason that prevents him from attending. You would think he'd go, just because I want him to."

Suddenly Gloria perked up, as if a small electric shock zapped her. "Well.... what about DEREK?" she said somewhat involuntarily. As soon as she spoke, Gloria realized how incongruous the words sounded, particularly to Deidre. Despite his eccentricity, Derek WAS likeable. She really thought Deidre was unduly hard on him, although Gloria privately was a bit afraid of him herself. But now that Deidre was in a jam, maybe she would look at the situation a bit differently. A pregnant pause followed while the question, although not rhetorical, hung in the air. She was surprised when Deidre began to laugh, not just a small giggle, but a hefty, hysterical, raucous laughter. Gloria looked down at her glass, mystified, wondering whether her potion was more than Deidre could sanely handle.

"It's so funny you would mention that," Deidre said, speaking through tears of laughter that were beginning to streak her cream colored face. "A couple of weeks ago at a committee meeting, I got frustrated with one of my sorors, who happens to be a busybody. She was bothering me about who my escort would be. I told her she could expect me to show up with my BROTHER. And now, here you are..... suggesting the same thing!" Gloria had a blank look on her face as she wondered why Deidre thought the coincidence was so hilarious.

"Mrs. Castle...... did you ever think it might be a GOOD idea?"

Calming down quickly, Deidre considered her comment seriously. "Gloria..... it's just that Derek scares me. I'm afraid he'll EMBARRASS me.... in front of all my sorors. You know how strange he can be. Besides, he's always such a mess! This is a formal affair we're talking about.... with the Mayor, the Council President, the County Chairman, even someone from the Governor's Office is going to be there.... not to mention the honorees and their families from all over the country. I can't have him..... acting the FOOL in front of these folks!"

The words were barely out of her mouth when you-know-who bounded lightly up the stairs to the deck, the trademark Cheshire cat grin sprawled all over his face. "I don't act the fool ALL the time, sisTER," Derek said with a flourish, his hands sweeping upward, head and feet askew in crude imitation of a court jester. "I haven't done anything sociable since I've been here," he went on. "Who knows, I just might enjoy your high society, BUPPIE crowd." Sneaking a playful glance at Gloria, he added "or.... they might enjoy ME!"

"Ooooooo.... that's so CRUDE of you, to eavesdrop on our conversation like that!" Deidre exclaimed. "And look at you...

you're a MESS!" He was. In his baggy coveralls, caked with mud and grass stains, scraggly beard, ragged shirt and baseball cap, he looked a lot like a black scarecrow. But as always, his eyes were bright and shiny beneath the sweat and grime coating his face.

The contradictions he embodied were more than her highness Deidre could take at that moment. "Sometimes you make me so damn MAD," she shouted, snatching up her 'Slush'. Storming into the house she yelled, "You'd BETTER not embarrass me, Derek Alston!" Quickly she added, "..... and make sure he gets a TUX-E-DO, Gloria! This is a formal affair we're talking about!" They looked at one another in momentary shock as Deidre disappeared inside. Then Derek motioned to Gloria for a high five, and the two of them couldn't help but laugh themselves silly at his sister's bad 'attitude'.

The phone rang not very quietly as the morning light was seeping into Lance's bedroom. His aching head and inflamed sinuses from the previous night's round of partying made just the **thought** of answering much too strenuous. Besides, that's what answering machines were made for, to screen calls at a time like this. So, he just laid there as his mother began speaking.... after the tone. "Lance.... this is your MOTHER calling. I know you're there. Please pick up the phone...... you KNOW how much I hate these stupid machines!"

Her familiar voice snapped Lance to attention. He figured he better pick up. She would never call him this early, unless something was wrong. Lance's father was deceased, and his mother lived alone now that her two sons and daughter were out of the house. She owned a nice two-story home in Mount Vernon, about twenty-five miles north of New York City. She called to explain that his sister, Angela, a pre-med student at Fisk University, was going to be honored for superior academic achievement at the Delta Ball this weekend in Atlanta. She had planned to go, but her brother, Robinson, was very ill and needed her help in Chicago. His mother wanted Lance to attend in her absence, because she felt someone from the family ought to be there to see the presentation to Angela. He was the logical choice, since Lance was much closer to his sister than his older brother, Foster, who lived in California.

Initially, the Delta Ball didn't hold much excitement for him. But as he thought more about it, he began to warm up to the idea. He hadn't been to Atlanta in a long time, and there were bound to be plenty of gorgeous women around, particularly at a sorority function. "Don't worry, I'll pick up my ticket first thing this morning, Mom," he answered dutifully. "It'll be good to see Angie again."

"And Lance.... don't forget to take pictures. I'd like to send some to your uncle. He loves Angela dearly, and the last time he saw her she was only nine years old. I honestly don't know how much longer he'll be with us. So this is important.... for all of us!"

Lance appreciated his uncle too, and always had a tremendous respect for him, so he understood completely his mother's feelings. He felt he could use a little break from Washington anyway. Besides, a weekend in Atlanta couldn't be too hard to take, could it? "I'm packing my camera right now. Tell Angie I'll be there for her."

"Thank you, Lance! You're a good son. Now be careful, and remember that I love you."

"Love you too, MOM. Take care of yourself and tell Uncle Robbie I said hello. 'Bye.'" CLICK.

It had been a bit of a struggle, but Gloria was finally able to find a set of formal wear that suited Derek's slightly unorthodox taste. They had shopped through all the malls on the north side of town, in and out of an assortment of formal wear establishments without much success. Finally, Derek spotted a tailor's shop off Peachtree Street where there were several previously owned garments for sale. He selected one that fit him nicely. Being frugal, the fact that it only cost thirty-five dollars, which was far less than he would have spent for a rental, made it even more stylish. And even though it was already cleaned, the shop owner agreed to press the tuxedo once more..... to Derek's specification.

The tailor explained that the suit once belonged to a Mr. Ernest L. Hickman, an African Methodist Episcopal (AME) Bishop, and one of the first trustees of Morris Brown College. The fact that the garment had been owned by a man of considerable spiritual and social impact was an important confirmation for Derek..... that he'd made the right choice. An hour and a half after they walked in, Derek was, at last, 'good to go'.

For her part, Deidre spent the day undergoing an extended beauty treatment. It began with a manicure and herbal facial mask, followed closely by a soothing mint pedicure. Afterwards, she rounded things out with a massage, and finished up with four hours in the hairdresser's chair. Her beautician recommended a daring new haircut, and Deidre at first resisted the idea, citing Edison's preference for long hair. However, he convinced her that a shorter style would look far more elegant, and require much less maintenance, particularly in the summer weather. When he was through and she saw herself in the mirror, it was 'shock at first sight'. Deidre could hardly believe it herself. Actually, she looked quite striking, and years younger. But a lot different.

That evening, the Castle house was in a mild uproar as Gloria rushed about helping Deidre prepare for the Ball. She had trouble deciding which earrings to wear with which necklace, to wear with which shoes, to wear with which purse... etc.... etc..... etc. Gloria could only marvel at the jewelry and other baubles Deidre had at her disposal. Finally, she decided to adorn herself with a glittering diamond cord necklace, punctuated by a small diamond-studded elephant pendant, and a matching pair of diamond earrings. The accessories perfectly complemented her shoulderless black gown and delicately sculptured lace shawl, which was highlighted by tiny studs that shimmered brightly when she moved. The effect was reminiscent of a clear midnight sky, with all the stars of the heavens on hand to take a bow. Deidre's hairdresser was correct. She was radiant, and the new 'do made her look every bit as elegant as he'd predicted.

But as much as Gloria and Deidre were able to impress themselves in the elegance department, neither of them was quite prepared for the shock they encountered downstairs. There, in the foyer, stood her date for the evening, Derek. But it was a Derek they had never known. This gentleman was nattily attired in a tastefully cut double-breasted tuxedo, a formal shirt with a slight lavender tinge which served to accentuate a barely noticeable piping of purple velvet that edged the lapels of his jacket. The look was completed by a striking kente patterned bow tie with matching pocket square.

However, what startled them the most was his grooming. They were accustomed to his dingy work garb and gritty, unkempt visage. Without any fanfare, it was obvious he had taken time to get himself together. Where once had been the scraggly, sparse facial hair there was now a neatly trimmed and brushed beard, replete with several specks of gray. On top, the coiffure was trimmed low and slicked back into a glistening pattern of subtle waves that reflected the light from the hall's chandelier. As always, the eyes were bright and clear, and were all the more impressive set amidst the smooth brown skin and evening attire. The complete look of surprise that was evidenced by their open mouths as they descended the stairs...... was confirmation that they both suddenly, and quite unexpectedly, realized...... that Derek was quite a handsome man, and something of a gentleman to boot!

"Your car is ready, madame," he said in a throaty imitation of a professional chauffeur. He had already pulled the Mercedes up to the front entrance, in anticipation of her appearance. The new look and demeanor of her brother had Deidre noticeably relieved and excited about 'hanging out' that evening. Taking his outstretched arm, Cinderella and her newfound Prince Charming were off...... to the Ball!

On the way downtown, they fell into a mild session of small talk. Soon, however, the conversation headed in more pointed directions. "You know, D," Deidre began ".... we haven't spent much time together, particularly since you came back from Manny's basketball camp. In a way, I'm jealous that Enrico gets so much of your attention."

"Well, Enrico's taught me a lot about the land, and the processes that control it. He tells me all the time how much he cares about you, Edison and the children."

"That's very nice, D, but is that any reason to spend all your time with him? Maybe if WE could talk a little more, we would understand each other better. Wouldn't that be good?"

"As a matter of fact, it would be good. But right now, I think Enrico needs someone to talk to..... someone who's interested in what he has to say."

"Doesn't he think we're interested?"

Derek looked at his sister and paused momentarily, so that the import of his words was clear. "Enrico is dying Dee-Dee," he said flatly. "He's giving me the benefit of his years here on the earth as a gift.... a gift of enlightenment. Frankly, I'm honored that he would choose me to share his understanding and tradition with."

Deidre was stunned. "I thought the doctors said he was on his way to recovery. We can't let this happen!"

"Dee-Dee, I don't know what the doctors have said. All I know is that he is making preparation for his death. And in that process, he's giving me insight into a powerful stream of consciousness."

"But if he's dying, he needs to go to the hospital! I'll make sure he's put in the care of a specialist. How can you know this..... and not do anything about it?"

"I AM doing something about it. I am granting him his desire.... of listening to the stories of his ancient homeland. Enrico's ancestors are descendants of the great Mayan cultures. He remembers the stories he was told as a young man, the purpose of which is to convey to younger generations the motivations, the hope and purpose of this life. Don't you understand? He's making his peace with this world.... by planting the seeds of his culture in me. He's getting his 'house' of mortality in order....... to pass on..... into immortality."

"Are you out of your MIND, Derek? We can't just stand idly by and let him die! I don't care if he is a descendant of Indians. He's got no right to die on us!"

The disappointment Derek felt at his sister's lack of understanding was obvious. "Deidre.... I didn't tell you this so that you would condemn Enrico..... or me. And I don't believe he's planning to commit suicide or anything grisly like that. I just want you to have some sensitivity..... to the matters of spiritual importance that are all around you. It's not up to us to determine how Enrico lives his life. All we can do is respect his right..... to express his cultural identity, even if we don't agree with him."

By this time, they were within shouting distance of the World Congress Center, the scene of the evening's festivities. Without warning, Derek abruptly changed the topic of conversation. "Really, Dee-Dee, you shouldn't concern yourself with Enrico now. I think you've got some aspects.... of your OWN history.... that you'll have to deal with tonight."

Deidre had an uneasy feeling of anticipation engulf her. The gleam that shone from Derek's eyes was certainly no reassurance. Arriving at the entrance to the Omni, a parking attendant rushed out to greet them. Once out of earshot of the valet, she snapped at her brother. "What the HELL could you possibly be referring to....... with that remark, Mister?"

"I'm talking about the one person you never discuss. I'm talking about..... Sam Case."

The name impaled Deidre, dead in her tracks. She hadn't heard it in years, though the memories were fresh, even now. How did Derek know about Sam? And what possible connection could he have with her Ball? They were just inside the ballroom entrance when Miss Busybody came rushing up to greet them.

"Hello," she said smugly, directing her attention toward Derek. "I'm Emma Carson. Aren't you going to introduce me to this handsome young man?" she said motioning to Deidre. Taking the initiative, Derek intervened, realizing his sister was still distracted by their brief verbal exchange moments before.

"Good evening, Ms. Carson. I'm Derek Alston, Deidre's brother. She's spoken fondly of you. It's my pleasure to make your acquaintance." His charm temporarily superseded the truth.

"GIRL...... they've been waiting for you up front," Emma said glibly, taking Derek by the arm. "Why don't you go on..... while I introduce your brother to some of the sorors." Without waiting for an acknowledgment, Emma was off, with a struggling Derek in tow. It occurred to Deidre that she ought to slap Emma's fat little face off for being so rude. But then, she thought, maybe the two of them might be better off in each others company for awhile, considering how WEIRD they both were.

Making her way through the crowd of dignitaries and well wishers, Deidre greeted everyone confidently. Clearly, she was in her element now. Casually, she delivered several vague explanations for Edison's conspicuous absence. The activity of the evening caused her to forget, for the moment, Derek's sobering prognostication. Before Deidre took her place at the head table, she stopped to greet the evening's honorees. One charming young woman, Angela Powell, a student at Fisk University, was very complimentary of the consideration she had received from the Deltas.

"Oh, Mrs. Castle, I just want you to know how grateful I am for this wonderful award," Angela gushed. "My family is so happy for me!"

"Well.... they should be proud of you young lady," a most gracious Deidre replied. "You've maintained a fine academic record. Are your parents here tonight? I'd like to congratulate them also." She thought back to the carefree days of her own matriculation, and the excitement she felt years before, at winning a national literary contest. Deidre might have been a great writer. But then she met Sam.

Angela's response startled Deidre out of the reflections of her own past. "No, my mother really wanted to be here," she sighed, "but she was called away to visit my uncle.... who's very sick."

"I'm so sorry to hear that," Deidre empathized.

"But my brother is going to be here tonight. If you don't mind, Mrs. Castle, I'd very much like you to meet him."

"Absolutely! When he arrives, please bring him by the head table. I'd love to say hello. As a matter of fact, I'm here with MY brother tonight as well," Deidre remarked thoughtfully. "What an interesting coincidence." She quickly explained that her husband was out of town on business.

Meanwhile, Emma was working the crowd with Derek dragging along. Heaven knows what HER husband thought about her antics, but Emma didn't seem the least bit inhibited by such a concern. For his part, Derek was attempting to politely remove himself from her company. Fortunately, he was suddenly aided by the sound from the evening's DJ, who started to liven things up a bit while many of the guests were enjoying their second round of cocktails.

Evidently, Emma was very popular among the men in the crowd. Quickly, she was swept up by a young man who led her out onto the dance floor. Boogie down! The vibration and the music began to magnetically draw folks out of their seats. Derek watched nearby, entertained by the variety of movement before him, relieved that he was free at last from the grip of Ms. Carson.

Emma was partying now, and the novelty of her newfound acquaintance with Deidre's brother rapidly dissipated. Derek decided it was time to blend into the crowd and walk around for a while, 'seeing what he could see', before returning to Deidre.

Outside, a dusty cab pulled up in front of the hotel, letting Lance out at the curb. He wasn't in the best of moods at the moment. Beside the lateness of his plane's arrival, he had been unable to secure any cocaine for the evening's use. His homeboy, Eddie Body, had assured him that there would be no problem picking up a bag or two once he got to Atlanta, so he didn't bother with his own contacts in D.C. before he left. But when he arrived at the airport, he discovered Eddie had been in a car accident and was in guarded condition at the trauma center of Grady Hospital. Worse yet, he didn't know anyone who could turn him on to any of Eddie's contacts, so he had spent two hours riding the streets of Atlanta (dressed in black tie and tuxedo) in search of some coke. Finally, recalling that his sister was awaiting him at the affair downtown, he grudgingly abandoned his unsuccessful pursuit. Consequently, his twenty dollar cab ride from the airport had turned into a seventy-five dollar summer misadventure. And he was pissed!

Once inside the hotel, Lance made his way to the restroom to regroup and freshen up a bit. Walking in, he noticed an older man at the sink beside him with the telltale sinus drain and impromptu nasal massage of a cocaine user. Boldly seizing the opportunity to transact business, he approached the gentleman and unashamedly explained his dilemma. Ten minutes later, Lance walked out of the men's room in possession of his weekend supply of good times, at last.

The ballroom was buzzing now, the dance floor flooded with party people, and the one-hundred dollar-a-plate tables filling up fast. Surveying the scene before him, Lance searched for the whereabouts of his sister. Spotting Angela across the ballroom, he waved madly in an attempt to get her attention, to no avail. When the music stopped, Lance headed determinedly toward her table. Unfortunately, his progress was ungraciously interrupted by a new flood of humanity onto the dance floor... in response to the 'ELECTRIC SLIDE'. Seemingly, everyone in the room got up at once.... to try out their 'Sliding' technique.

The inexorable surge caught up even the unusually stoic Derek in its wake. Before he knew it, he was out there with the rest of them, enjoying himself in the crowd. Diligently, Lance proceeded ahead, looking for his sister. Fighting his way through the lines of merrymakers, he ultimately made it to where Angela was seated, slightly embarrassed at the dishevelment he received en route.

"Sorry I'm late, Angie. My flight was delayed. By the way, congratulations! Mom sent this to you." He handed her a gold embossed envelope.

"Well.... I feel better now that you've finally gotten here. I was beginning to wonder if you'd ever show up. I've got someone I'd like for you to meet."

The effect of Lance's men's room tune up was beginning to take hold, and he started to pay attention to some of the lovely young ladies in attendance.... with their backs out..... shoulders bare...... in clinging dresses and gowns that displayed their more obvious assets. He was settling into the Atlanta scene now, and looking forward to the rest of the weekend. As a result, he barely listened to what his sister had said, simply nodding absently in agreement.

Angela proudly introduced Lance to the other guests at her table. Following their meal, she repeated her desire to introduce him to one of the women responsible for the affair. Still preoccupied by the scenery, Lance silently wondered why Angela wanted him to bother with one of these older women, when there was so much youthful talent around. Nonetheless, he complied with her request.

Approaching Deidre's position at the head table, Lance's obvious distraction continued unabated until they reached the place where she was seated. Engrossed in a conversation with a woman beside her, Deidre didn't notice the two of them walking up. The woman next to her motioned to Deidre that a young lady was there, trying to get her attention. As she turned around, Angela was about to introduce her brother when Lance also turned, suddenly recognizing who it was his sister had been referring to.

"Mrs. Castle!" he exclaimed in complete surprise. "I had no idea you knew my sister! It's good to see you."

"Lance, what are you DOING here?" Deidre said standing up quickly, as if pricked by something sharp in the seat of her chair. Her reaction was a discomfiting blend of shock and excitement at seeing him there.

"You two..... KNOW each other?" said Angela, taken aback by the happenstance.

"Well.... yes," Lance volunteered. "I work for her husband.... in Washington." Lance was once again struck by the fact that Deidre was quite an attractive woman, still very youthful looking for her age. And that night she was particularly elegant in her sequins and gown. For her part, the sight of Lance caused a leap of excitement in Deidre, that frankly, she could not explain. But she did have a vague recollection of feeling that way..... once before.

A moment of awkward silence followed as the three of them stood there, kind of gazing back and forth at one another, with Angela not quite certain of what to make of the situation. Into the midst of this unusual triangle walked none other than Derek, who was returning from a necessary trip to the bathroom. His arrival lifted the silence.

"Angela.... I'd like you to meet MY brother.... Derek Alston," said Deidre motioning Derek to shake hands. "And Derek, this is Angela Powell, one of our academic honorees. And this is her brother Lance." She paused briefly, then continued. "You've heard me speak of Lance before. He works on Edison's staff."

Derek, of course, knew who Lance was, although he'd never met him. "Very nice to meet you Lance. How was your trip down from D.C.?" Derek asked, attempting to engage him in some smalltalk, to help break the tension. Before Lance could fashion an answer, the DJ started up some funky sounds again. Immediately, Derek went into action.

"Pardon me Angela," he said. "Could I trouble you for this dance?" Not really waiting for a response he lightly grabbed her arm. "Don't worry," he said as they left. "I think your brother and my sister have some things to talk over anyway."

Once they were gone, Lance sat down in Derek's place beside Deidre. Oddly enough, he forgot all about his prior fascination with some of the lovelies present, and focused his attention on her.

"It's certainly a nice surprise..... seeing you here, Lance" Deidre offered. "I trust you've been well. Why didn't you call to let me know you'd be in town?"

"Well, this was really a last minute thing. My mother was planning to come, but my uncle's been sick up in Chicago and she felt she needed to be there for him. I just received a call from her this week. We're all very proud of Angie. She's really a good kid."

"Listen to who's talking. You're just a kid yourself."

A sheepish smile came to Lance's face, and it became obvious things were beginning to get cozy between the two of them. They talked and enjoyed each other's company over a couple of glasses of champagne. A few minutes later, Lance suggested that they take a walk outside to get 'some fresh air.' Deidre hesitated at first, then, allowing the champagne to get the best of her, decided to go along. They left the ballroom and headed for the plaza.

"How is Congressman Castle?" Lance inquired. It was a gorgeous summer night downtown, with the imposing silhouette of the Georgia Dome framed by a glittering starlit sky.

"Well.... don't you know? He left this week to return to Washington.... on 'important' business. Or so he said."

Realizing he may have inadvertently put his foot in his mouth, Lance recovered quickly. "Oh yes..... I do recall him mentioning that he was coming back to town. I haven't seen him though. I've been out of the office for a few days." Changing the subject dramatically, he returned to the object of his immediate attention. "You know, Ms. Castle, I don't want you to take this the wrong way.... but.... you look... SO enchanting.... in this moon-light. You know if you weren't married I'd........"

The cocaine and champagne flooding his bloodstream charged Lance up with a boldness that belied good judgement. Of course, Lance didn't know that Deidre wasn't the least bit concerned with Edison at the moment anyway. She too, was caught up in a champagne enhanced romantic sensation..... that was becoming increasingly hard to deny. Taking his hand, they wandered out into the evening air. "Lance... I've told you before.... call me

Deidre," she said reassuring him that she wasn't at all insulted by his 'pass'. On the contrary, out of sight of any other guests, Deidre turned slowly and embracing him firmly about the neck.... kissed Lance full on the mouth. A strong, wet, sensuous kiss. A rush of emotion ensued, with the two passionately locked.... for what seemed like an eternity.

When at last they came up for air, Deidre experienced what could only be termed the shock of her life. Opening her eyes, she couldn't quite believe what she saw. It was Sam! No, it was Lance. But what she perceived was Sam..... in Lance's clothes! She let out a shriek that could be heard for blocks..... and recoiled from him as though she'd been hit by a lightning bolt! Deidre simply couldn't believe her eyes!

Poor Lance! He didn't know what the hell was happening! One minute they're drooling all over one another.... the next minute she's screaming at the top of her lungs. Worse yet, he was worried that someone might come along, such as a policeman, and assume that he was trying to rape her! That would be all he'd need. To be accused of raping his own boss' wife! Lance's heart pounded in his chest. He could see his career passing... right before his eyes! Frantically, he tried to calm her down. However, all Deidre could see was Sam. The image was too much for her. Things were starting to swirl around in her head. It looked as though she was about to faint. Not knowing what else to do Lance reacted instinctively...... and...... POW!.... smacked her full across the face!

Miraculously, that slap seemed to do the trick. Immediately, Deidre calmed down and her visage of Sam disappeared. Lance was back, and she returned to a more normal state of mind. Good thing, too! One of the city's finest had just pulled up.

"What's going on here?" he demanded. "Are you alright, ma'am?"

Her sensibilities having returned, Deidre had the presence of mind to assess the situation and deflect any attention away from Lance. "Yes, Officer.... I'm fine. I was walking along.... and felt as though I was about to pass out. Fortunately, this young man came along to help me. I'm sure I'll be OK. Would you please walk me back inside?" she said motioning to Lance.

"Yes.... yes, of course," Lance responded courteously. Turning back to the policeman he said, "I'll make sure she gets back safely, Officer." Despite not being at all convinced that everything was what it seemed, the police officer nonetheless relented and returned to his patrol car, keeping a watchful eye on the two of them as they left.

"ARE you..... alright?" Lance asked her cautiously.

Deidre staggered momentarily, accentuating the drama of the situation, then replied in the affirmative. Her head was clearing up, and needless to say, their brief romantic interlude had passed. Wandering back into World Congress Center, the two of them received only cursory glances..... until they were about to enter the ballroom. Standing inside, directly in their line of sight, was Derek! His face was expressionless, motionless..... yet his eyes seemed to burn with a cogent awareness.... that Deidre was unable to escape. In that moment, she suddenly realized what Derek had meant earlier in the evening.... about dealing with her own past! Immediately, it became so clear..... the reason that she was so attracted to Lance. It was Sam! Lance reminded her of Sam.... and her own youth... and the love that had been so cruelly taken away from her.

But at that same moment an intense fear gripped her, a fear borne of the realization that someway.... somehow.... Derek knew what had taken place! That Derek had SOMETHING to do with all this! But how? It didn't seem possible. The only logical explanation was that.... it really didn't happen... that this was all some kind of dream. But that couldn't be the case; she was fully conscious and alert. Whatever the explanation, she DID know beyond a shadow of doubt, that she couldn't go on this way.... that she wasn't going to let HIM ruin her life. Why would he want to do such a thing to her? Her own brother. There was no other choice. Derek had to go..... before he drove her completely out of her mind!

A crystal clear day blossomed in the rolling hills of western North Carolina. The silver van rolled slowly into the visitor's parking area at the 'Flight Time' basketball camp. Derek had arrived to pick up Manny and take him home. However, his thoughts and attention were wandering elsewhere at the moment. It was a week since the episode at the ball, but all Derek could think about was the ride home that evening, and the subsequent accusations he received from his sister. Although he felt unjustly accused of conspiring to drive her crazy.... of attempting to ruin her life..... of trying to destroy her family, he felt most of all a tremendous sense of inadequacy; a sense of remorse. It was still hard for him to understand how people were unused to, or more appropriately, unwilling to recognize the operation of the spirit all around them, in their everyday lives. It was hard for him to accept the fact that his own sister could only deal with those things that were immediately obvious, that she could not accept the possibility that there were forces at work in life that were beyond her own ability to fully comprehend or understand. It was tough for him to face the fact that Deidre believed he was out of his mind, on the one hand, and on the other, somehow able to control these strange occurrences that she experienced.

Most importantly, Derek was depressed...... depressed because he knew he would have to leave soon. It bothered him greatly because he really loved them all...... Deidre, Gloria, Enrico, Asia,...... and especially Manny. Fortunately, he was able to convince Deidre to let him pick Manny up from basketball camp, so the two of them would have at least a little more time together. So, it was with a heavy heart that Derek met his nephew in the Carolina woods....... late that Saturday morning.

He had determined not to let on anything to Manny, but his demeanor clearly was not upbeat. Manny, however, was quite gregarious due to the excitement of the past two weeks of camp still fresh on his mind. As they rolled down Interstate 85, Derek didn't say much while Manny talked on and on about his experience.

"You know, Uncle D," Manny intoned at one point, "Michael himself, came to speak to us at dinner a few days ago. What he said that evening...... really made me think a lot about...... the things you've been telling me."

Perking up, Derek responded. "Just what did he say, Bud?"

"Well.... one of the guys asked him how he learned to do the things he did with the basketball..... you know..... where he got his moves from. He told us that the things he did weren't learned; that it was simply creativity that took over. But then he said that he felt fortunate, actually blessed, that God had given him this ability 'to express the creativity that was within him.' He said he believed that creativity 'was a gift and the power of the Spirit of God' and that we should all 'look for ways to express that gift..... in everything we do, not just sports.' It made me think of the things........ you've talked about, Uncle D."

Manny's account jerked Derek out of his doldrums. Refreshed and alert, he started talking again. "The biggest danger to a man of knowledge..... to a warrior..... is to dwell on self-importance. Self-importance is self-pity in masquerade. The instruction I have given you has been designed to familiarize you with the rudiments of the expressions of the Spirit. As I've told you, learn to choose your words carefully, for they are the keys that unlock the power of the spirit..... in this world. As we move away from the fascination with self-importance..... we leave behind the valuations of only our senses.... of the constructs of material existence.... and open ourselves up to the perception of the spiritual realm. We also leave behind the acts of homicidal egoism that self-pity gives rise to; acts of individual and collective stupidity, and wanton violence. I told you two weeks ago that our talking was through..... that all that remained was for you to experience the power."

Turning off the interstate in South Carolina, Derek followed a road that led into an area called the Cherokee Foothills. The late afternoon sun was still brilliant as he took a two lane route that headed up into the mountains. Strangely enough, this unusual detour didn't seem to bother Manny. He was fascinated by the palette of nature's decor. Finally, Derek stopped the van in a clearing about a quarter of a mile from the nearest paved road. He instructed Manny to get out and follow him. They walked through a quiet wooded area, and stopped around a bend at the base of a sheer cliff, overlooking a lake. It was a breathtaking view, with no one visible save the two of them, a scene from a postcard.

Derek squatted down, the trunk of his body low, knees up, with his back wedged tightly against the base of the cliff. Urgently, he motioned Manny to do the same, right next to him. They were facing the water in the distance below. The sun was beginning to dip down just to the left of the lake, and its reflection shimmered up from the water into their faces. Manny fidgeted uncomfortably as Derek started to speak.

"The Native Americans knew of various places where they believed that the intrusion of the spirit world occurred more boldly and dramatically than in other locations. They referred to these spots as 'places of power'. As preparation to become a warrior, it was the responsibility of the older men, the guides of the tribe, to familiarize the candidate with the experience of power. Great care had to be taken to ensure there was ample development of the candidate's awareness and sensitivity, so that the experience could occur properly. To effect the development of awareness, the guide spent time relating to the candidate stories of the generations... of their culture. Once the time was right the guide and the candidate went to the 'place of power'. It was here that the first 'tangible' experience of power took place."

As Derek spoke, the sun continued to sink lower in the sky. In so doing, it was beaming almost directly into their eyes and causing Manny to squint. Manny felt a strange warmth rising up his back. Derek told him to breathe deeply and slowly, bringing the breath up from his abdomen in a rhythmic flow. His legs had begun to tighten and ache from the pressure of the squatting position they held. Derek's voice, which had been so commanding and direct, gradually faded into a faint echo, and all Manny could really 'hear' was the sound of his own breathing. He suddenly became aware of the mechanics of his own body, particularly the beat of his pulse and the throbbing of the muscles in his legs. They became increasingly 'louder' until all of his senses were consumed with the pounding beat of his heart. It was a struggle to move now; his body felt like an enormous cramp.

Oddly enough, all of these abnormal feelings didn't cause Manny to panic or become fearful. Instead, he had the sensation of wonderment.... as though his mind and senses had been separated from his body. Glancing over at Derek, he couldn't believe what he 'saw'. Where Derek's body had been, there was now only a faint outline of him. Down near his abdominal area, Manny 'saw' a glowing oval of light that pulsated mightily with each 'breath' Derek took! Attempting to scream, he turned back only to realize that he, too, had been 'disembodied', in the same way as his uncle.

Shocking as all this was, when Manny turned his attention to the surroundings, he realized that they had also been 'transformed'. He could still perceive the sun's position in the sky, and the lake, and the trees, and the mountains. But their shapes, their substance had faded. What appeared to be a series of brilliant threads of light, tiny glimmers of fibrous light, permeated everything. It was these shining threads of light that dominated the scene, penetrating everything. When the glowing fibers reached an 'object' that Manny could identify, he could see how the fibers were more concentrated, almost clumped together, and the luminescence wasn't as bright. Yet these fibers of light weren't static; they were constantly in motion. They vibrated back and forth with movement of 'energy' along each strand. It was interesting to Manny that at the concentrations of fibers, the 'objects', motion was markedly slower and more deliberate. Manny could 'see' that everything was CONNECTED..... solid and liquid, animate and inanimate..... an enormous web-like network. Yet everything was in perfect order.

Suddenly, Derek's voice returned. "Manny, the life fibers are conduits for the movement of the spirit. They are the true 'nature of things'; this is the REAL world. Now, you are part of this continuum as well. As I told you before, nothing is lost in the realm of the spirit.... nothing ever gets used up. Focus your attention on a single fiber.... and watch what happens."

Following his instructions, Manny concentrated on a single light strand that ran right through him. As he concentrated, the strand glowed brighter and brighter. Unexpectedly, Manny felt the sensation of his own movement. He felt himself lifting off the ground, suddenly taking off in flight, as if shot from a gun. It was an experience like none other! Manny, in a state of heightened consciousness where normal perception was magnified.... could experience minute details of things he had no idea even existed. The sensation of traveling literally at the speed of light was so exhilarating Manny wished it would never end. He could 'feel' himself pass through trees and rocks, and 'fly' right over water.

Despite the utter fascination of the experience, Manny was still conscious of Derek nearby. "Once we're able to move our attention away from perception based on self-importance, we become aware of the potentialities of the spirit world. Once we can accelerate our own characteristic vibratory patterns up to the speed of light....... time literally stands still. You're doing fine now Manny. But you must be careful about ..... coming back into material form," Derek warned. "Imagine yourself as a large airplane.... easing down onto the runway for a landing. Fix that imagery in your mind....... and you'll be OK."

Unfortunately, Manny was too absorbed to heed Derek's guidance. Gradually, he 'felt' himself slowing down. But rather than follow the directions, he attempted to 'will' himself 'airborne' again. As quickly as it came, the 'power' seemed to simply shut down. When he regained consciousness, he opened his eyes to see Derek dousing him with a small bucket of water. Coming to, he recognized that they were about two hundred yards from the hills where they first began. Even though he was awake, Manny felt a disturbing inability to move a muscle..... his entire body seemed to ache, and he had no energy.... he was literally exhausted. It was dusk now; they had to have been there for several hours. But the entire experience felt as though it transpired in minutes.

Dragging Manny to his feet, Derek attempted a brief explanation. "I told you to watch out for those landings," he said. "The experience of power is just that..... the experience itself has the effect of absorbing any excess energy that it can. By not following my direction, you came in for a hard 'crash'. Literally, you were drained in the process." Manny could barely walk; Derek was nearly carrying him at this point. "Good thing I was with you," he joked. "That return jolt could have killed you. The power of the Spirit... is nothing to play around with. We had better get a move on.... before your mother has the entire state police force out after us."

The next morning Manny awakened refreshed. After a quick shower, he headed downstairs for breakfast. He wanted to spend some time with Derek so that he could more fully understand what happened to him the day before. Not that he really understood any of it to begin with. But he knew he had experienced something important.... something powerful that day. He decided not to bring this up to the other adults because he knew these stories created quite a stir around his house.

The mood inside was very quiet, almost somber. While in the kitchen finishing off some whole wheat pancakes and fish, he asked Gloria if she had seen Derek. Strangely, she didn't answer him. She just looked away. He thought he saw a tear forming in her eye. He knew something was wrong.

Rushing out of the house, he ran to the servants' quarters. There he found Enrico, sitting on a chair slowly rocking, his eyes riveted on a small crack in the wall across from him.

"Enrico... where's Derek?" asked Manny frantically.

Turning halfway toward the young man, Enrico said simply, "He's gone. He left early this morning, before sunrise. He told me to give you this." Leaning forward, he handed Manny an envelope with his name printed on the front.

Half fearful of reading it, Manny stumbled down the steps leading to the pool. He sat down and opened the letter.

"Dear Manny. I'm sorry to say good-bye to you this way, but it was important that I go. I want you to know, I'll miss you..... and everyone there. But it's in everyone's best interests...... that I leave.
You and I have shared many things these past few months, and I want you to know.... it's been a special time for me. I've learned so much. And please tell your Mom..... that I appreciate her allowing me to spend time with the family. Above all else, your family is most important, so remember that when the time comes for you to start your own. And remember the things we've discussed and the experiences we've shared.

"And Manny, wherever you go, whatever you do, always keep this in mind. In the words of the immortal poet, Maurice Haltom:

'To move...... is to change.
To change........ is to be flexible.
To be flexible..... is to adapt.
To adapt........... is to live.
To live............ is to be CREATIVE.
In the majesty of the human form, creativity may be boundlessly graceful.'

As the realization that Derek was gone began to sink in, Manny couldn't quite handle the ensuing flood of emotions which overcame him. He knew his mother had something to do with Derek's untimely departure, and he felt anger and rage building inside him toward her. Tears filled his eyes, and he was determined to find his mother..... to give her a piece of his mind concerning his uncle! Turning to head for the house, he suddenly noticed his basketball.... the one Derek had given him..... lying on a lounge chair. Picking up the ball, he started to dribble.

As he walked along, Manny noticed how good the grounds looked; how neat and manicured the flower beds and lawns were. He recalled how much of a mess everything outside was.... before Derek came. And now he was gone!

He was crying profusely now, and some of his tears fell on the letter Derek had written. Miraculously, the moment his tears touched the paper, the letter just dissolved.... into thin air!

Intuitively, Manny realized that this was a sign from his uncle..... a sign for him not to worry, not to fret. After all, as Derek had said, nothing was ever lost.... ever used up..... in the realm of the spirit. Everything was in perfect order! Suddenly, his exhilaration was restored. The ball felt magical in his hands so, he did what came naturally to him..... he started to shoot some baskets.

A broad smile captured his face as the feeling of confidence returned. And Manny proceeded to make the next fifty shots in a row, from everywhere! Like magic!

The Nubian
Part Two

Washington, D.C. 1998

Chapter 8

The Xenium Operation

Politics wasn't one of the things that held any particular fascination for a young Simon Harder while growing up in rural Georgia. In fact, the focus of his adolescence was to get himself off the farm his family had worked for generations. So, it was with a certain amount of pride that he reviewed the results of early returns at Georgia's U.S. Senatorial Primary. The polls showed him with a clear lead over his closest competitors, with nearly half the state's precincts reporting. Of course, the largest metropolitan areas, including Atlanta, weren't completely accounted for, but it was a very positive sign nonetheless.

Harder had gone on from his farm days to graduate from Georgia Tech, and receive a law degree from Duke University. Upon his return to the Peach State, he developed a successful labor law practice, held various municipal and governmental posts including a stint with the Department of Transportation, and three years ago was elected Lieutenant Governor. Through exposure to the various power players in the state's civic and business circles, he was able to garner the support necessary to mount a run at the junior Senate seat, vacated by the late Spike Dowler.

The fact that Georgia had adopted an open primary format, which eliminated the dual party primaries, made his early lead that much more important. Only the top three finishers would be on the ballot for the general election in November.

The other practical consideration..... was that the primary finalists would become eligible for federal matching funds, which would be crucial for the Harder camp in preparing their campaign against his principal foe, the Honorable Edison M. Castle, U.S. Representative.

In truth, Simon had his political work cut out for him. Though there was relatively strong support statewide for Harder's candidacy, Edison's years of experience on Capitol Hill, coupled with his concomitant celebrity-like status on a national level would be hard to overcome. This was particularly true when it came to the area of campaign spending, and specifically the cost of securing the all important exposure that he would need from television. Simon's generally unknown political background would require significant visibility with voters in the upcoming months...... were he to have any hope of defeating Congressman Castle.

As the result of a furious barnstorming effort over the past six weeks, Harder virtually assured himself a spot in the finals. However, he also knew Edison's people had maintained a purposely low-key approach to the primary, thereby saving their resources and clout for the stretch ahead. So, there was a curious blend of satisfaction, relief, anticipation, and wariness that filled the breast of one Simon Harder that evening. Deep down, he secretly questioned the extent he would be willing to go........ the extent he would have to go....... to become Senator from the great state of Georgia. As much as that thought bothered him, it was even more disconcerting for Simon to wonder the same thing about his opponent....... an opponent who was much more experienced at surviving in what had developed into an absolutely cutthroat world of national politics.

"CUT!" The sound of the director's voice echoed throughout the sound stage. Filming was being completed on the last of several campaign spots for candidate Edison. The format of the commercial was a series of candids of Representative Castle in action.... at work in Washington..... visiting the elderly in a rest home....... singing with a Baptist choir in church...... at a ground breaking ceremony for a federally funded AIDS clinic. After the vignettes, the camera bore in on the candidate himself in a studio setting, delivering a 'punch line' statement on how he was committed to an 'era of continued growth and opportunity' for Georgia, into the year 2000. Creatively, the entire episode most closely resembled one of the NFL's United Way public service announcements, ('Thanks to you..... it works for all of us..... the United Way') and thus far had generated about the same amount of enthusiasm.

"Edison, you're just not believable enough," a frustrated director lamented during a break in the shooting. "It's not simply what you say...... but how you say it. You have to come across completely sincere. That's crucial..... when you're asking for money.... or when you're asking for votes. C'mon Edison, you've got to be more relaxed..... let your human side come out!" He thought about how tough it was working with professionals; the egos and star syndromes and all that. But compared to this, it was a piece of cake. He wished he could have a stand-in for the real guy now!

For his part, Edison was trying very hard to look professional and maintain his composure (in particular, to keep from stuttering). Strangely, after all the years of public engagements and appearances, this one on one relationship with the camera was intimidating him.

"Let me see the video," Edison demanded gently. "Maybe I can see what's wrong.... for myself." Sitting down at the monitor, Edison studied his delivery...... the body language, the facial expressions, the eye contact, all along keeping in mind what the director had said about 'letting himself come through'.

Walking up quietly and gazing over Edison's shoulder at the screen, Lance casually suggested ".... maybe you should try to focus your mind on those things.... that make you feel most relaxed and comfortable."

Taking the words to heart, Edison's mind drifted lazily to the images of the times he'd spent with Camille. After a rocky start, they'd been seeing one another off and on for most of the past three years. He recalled those quiet evenings in front of the fire, gazing out at the picturesque winter scenery on the Potomac, voraciously making love into the night. He could feel the touch of her hands, the pleasant suction of smooth, full lips on the nape of his neck, his chest, his abdomen. He remembered the aromas of her cologne, the sensations of her full breasts and erect nipples on his tongue.

Beside the physical reminiscence enfolding him, Edison recalled how he talked to her.... of his family, of his youth, of the things that just came to his mind. He recognized how much he felt like himself in her company.... no pretense, no protocol, no personal expectations to live up to. He could just be with her... and let HIS hair down. She was certainly different from any of the other women he'd been with...... by a long shot.

"I'm ready now," he said purposefully to the director. "I know what I need to do."

Still skeptical, the director motioned the crew to get set again. "OK Congressman.... from the top. QUIET everybody. Let's roll 'em!"

This time, Edison had the focus he needed. He imagined himself telling Camille the truth.... how much she really meant to him, how comforting she was for him. Suddenly, he felt the honesty and sincerity, yet was professional and articulate in his delivery. In other words, he NAILED it.

"CUT!" The director shouted again. "OK everyone... that's a wrap. Put it in the can! We're outta here! Great job, Senator!"

"He's not a Senator... he's a Congressman," corrected Lance.

"Well..... if he performs like he did just then," answered the director, "he will be a Senator, no doubt about it!"

Several days later at a dinner strategy meeting in Washington, Edison's campaign manager, Kyle Robinson, pulled Lance aside. "I know Edison relies on your judgment a great deal," said Kyle. "We've gotten good support from some of the business leaders in Atlanta, and we're working on an endorsement by Senator Dunn. But I tell you Lance, Edison's got to watch the company he keeps. I mean, he's got to stop seeing this woman..... what is her name... here in town? The last thing we need is any sort of scandal..... to disrupt things. If Harder's people get wind of of Edison's running around..... well you know what that could mean. We've got to make sure the media focus is on Edison as a model citizen; not only a responsible leader.... but a committed and dedicated family man."

"I believe her name..... is Camille Ferguson," Lance interjected.

"Oh... well.... whatever her name is, the important thing is to get his mind off of her. I mean he's got the 'perfect' family... an attractive wife, a daughter who just got out of college, a son that is a good student and basketball prospect. We've got to make sure he doesn't let his penis get the best of him, and waste this opportunity. And not only for him, but for all of us.....you included. I know Edison has some bigger plans for you. But we've got to get through this election..... before any of those things can ever happen. Do you understand what I'm saying, Lance?"

Lance, of course, understood what Kyle meant. Edison's affair with Camille was only mildly discrete among those who had any interests in and around Capitol Hill. And Lance was always attentive to anything that had to do with fostering his own career aspirations. Though he'd done well over the years as Edison's Chief of Staff, there were still times when he wondered, for example, why Edison hadn't selected him to run his Senatorial campaign, instead of Robinson. However, despite any private resentment he might have harbored, Lance was astute enough to realize that Kyle was in a position to help him..... if he played ball.

"What do you want me to do?"

"Well.... we've got to get this Camille woman out of the picture. I plan to talk to Edison about it. But you know how bull headed he can be sometimes. So, I want you to get to her... and make sure she stays out of the way. We don't need any attempts by the media to draw any conclusions about his relationship with Ms. Ferguson."

"Just what do you suggest I say to her? I mean, from what I understand.... she's no bimbo-type."

"Frankly, I don't care what you tell her. We've just got to make sure that he doesn't see or hear from her until well after this election is over. Do whatever it takes..... just be sure you see to it. Remember Lance, we're counting on you!"

The next morning, Lance set about the business of undermining Camille (and Edison). He didn't let Kyle know, but Lance didn't care for her much anyway, and not because he necessary disliked her as an individual. He didn't know her on a personal level. But since she'd been in City Hall as an appointed head of the Public Safety Board, and a member of Mayor Eva Pratt Christian's inner circle, Camille had been largely responsible for the crackdown on drug trafficking in the District that had resulted in several of Lance's main suppliers going to jail. Beside the tremendous inconvenience it caused him, the price he now had to pay for cocaine had gone through the roof. Consequently, Lance was looking forward to the prospect of somehow upsetting life for Camille, at least to the extent that she had caused him his present hardship.

His challenge was to devise a reason that would cause Camille to not want to see Edison. He thought about telling her that Edison's family was moving to Washington, but decided that would be too easy to disprove. Mulling this over in his mind,

Lance happened to notice an old newspaper lying on his dining room table. Glancing down, he saw an article highlighting the latest in the treatment of AIDS patients.

'Over a year ago, researchers at the Georgetown University School of Medicine announced the first significant breakthrough in the treatment of AIDS,' the article read. The procedure called for the implantation of a small, triangular, metallic sliver just beneath the skin of a testicle in male AIDS patients. After a little over a year in clinical investigations, the results were remarkable, in that 100% of the patients thus treated..... had fully recovered from the disease. The key ingredient was an alloy that went into the fabrication of the implants. The substance, known as Xenium, was to be found only in the mountains of Southwestern Africa. The Xenium compound apparently '....... interacted with the male hormone testosterone...... to completely reverse the symptoms of the previously deadly AIDS infestation..... and rid the body of the HIV virus.'

The greatest hindrance was the cost of the preparation of implants. Because the raw material had to be imported from the Continent, it made the treatment prohibitively expensive for all but the most well endowed. A second drawback which appeared in several of the patients who had undergone the implant treatment..... was that impotency had resulted as a serious side effect. The most prominent of these was ex-basketball star Magic Thompson, who'd made a remarkable recovery from AIDS related complications just six months after receiving his implant. Sadly, his manhood was compromised in the recovery process. But, as he pointed out, that was a much more desirable fate than the alternative..... which was almost certainly an early death.

Camille might not believe that Edison was moving his family to D.C., Lance thought to himself, but he might be able to scare her away (from Edison). And this Xenium implant business was just the story he could use. Since he knew a few colleagues at Georgetown Medical School, Lance was determined to find out all he could about the status of the AIDS implant procedures. He realized that the more he knew of the particulars, the more effective he would be in executing 'Operation Xenium' with Ms. Ferguson.

As the final weeks of the election were approaching, the Harder camp was trying (harder) to portray their candidate as a man of the people of Georgia..... as in contrast with Edison, whom they attempted to show as a glory hungry jet-setter with none of the 'home folks' interests at heart. As interesting as that character juxtaposition was, real voter concern began building over the only substantive issue of the race: transportation.

Harder's platform called for a transportation initiative based on the development of new applications for that timeless mode of carriage: rail. The Harder team advocated adoption of some of the ultra high speed train technologies that had proven themselves so successful in Europe and the Far East, particularly with the operation of the English Channel rail tunnel, also known as the 'Chunnel'. Since its opening in 1993, the 'Chunnel' had been the principal vehicle fueling the growth of the European economic community.

Harder advocated a specific regional network of ultra high speed rail connections ,with a hub in Atlanta, connecting all the major and secondary cities in the Southeast, and by extension, the rest of the country. Some of the routes he envisioned were west to Birmingham, northwest to Nashville, northeast to Charlotte, and east to Savannah and the Georgia coastline. The proposed Harder program was to be financed on a three to one Federal to State funding basis, with the Federal government providing three dollars for every one that the State came up with. One of the responsibilities left to the State was to implement a one-to-one matching funds public/private package, where private industry would produce a dollar for every dollar the State provided. Thus, the entire plan would have resulted in the state of Georgia earning $3.50 for every $.50 of investment it provided.

The precedent for such a large scale public/private initiative was still fresh in the minds of Georgia voters. The 1996 Summer Olympic Games in Atlanta had proven to be not only an aesthetic triumph, but an economic boon to the region as well. Much of the credit for the overall appeal of the Games was given to a well thought out transportation scheme. The nucleus of the transport mechanism (and the genesis of the Harder initiative) was the Olympic Railway Station, opened late in 1995. The station was located at the site of the old Crossman Steel Mill, just a quarter mile south of the old AMTRAK terminal. Key civic leaders, led by Atlanta Mayor Brainard Faxon were instrumental in structuring an innovative public/private consortium to underwrite the cost of the Railway's construction. Initially, the Mayor was reluctant to support the venture, since he had been so instrumental in the growth and development of Atlanta's Hartsfield Airport. But with the demise of Eastern Airlines, and several failed attempts to attract a second major air carrier to establish a hub, Mayor Faxon was forced to entertain alternatives to spur commerce and travel.

In the years following the shutdown of Eastern, Omega Air Lines had established a de facto monopoly at Hartsfield. As a result, airfares into and out of Atlanta skyrocketed. In addition, the severe effects of the Great Recession, which began in the late 80's, were still being felt in 1994. The members of the Atlanta Olympic Committee recognized that the fundamental economic viability of the Games was tied to the number of people attending..... and the amount of money they spent as tourists. High attendance would drive more advertisement, hence, more commercial visibility for the broadcast media. With the state of air travel what it was, the focus shifted to rail transport.

There was one problem, however. The old AMTRAK station was barely functional, much less viable, as a port of arrival for an international sporting event the magnitude of the Summer Olympic Games. The old Crossman Steel Mill was the perfect site, inasmuch as its long since abandoned tracks spurred off the AMTRAK route and ran directly into the mill. Interestingly, the mill itself was an ideal structure for a train station; essentially it was a gigantic shed, with an enormous amount of clear space, reminiscent of an airplane hanger. With such a location at the city's disposal, the required construction was completed in just fourteen months. Estimates of the expanded attendance as a result of the opening of the Olympic Railway Station were in the hundreds of thousands. Connections to the MARTA system made travel to hotels, and any of the Olympic venues, a snap.

Mayor Faxon and Simon Harder had many consultations during his days as Lieutenant Governor. Though they were not close friends, and Brainard had not endorsed his Senatorial bid, Harder knew a good idea when he saw one. Unfortunately for Simon, the anti-rail lobby in the state, which carried a great amount of money behind it, was lining up with Edison. Politically, Harder's approach threatened several of the largest industries and employers in the state, as well as the Georgia Department of Transportation who had managed to have its own way with the building of new roads for more than twenty-five years. The spectre of high speed passenger rail travel caused a political galvanizing effect among these previously unrelated entities.

Despite such opposition, Harder pushed ahead with his platform. One of the most innovative (and controversial) aspects of the transportation program, was the proposed use of state prisoners as the labor force for the construction of tracks and bridges for the rail routes. Practically, Harder reasoned, one of the concepts that made rail construction economically feasible in the 1800's was the wide spread use of Coolies; Asian and Oriental work forces that provided cheap labor. In effect, the prison population could be used in a similar fashion..... to provide virtually free labor. Though it was a creative and innovative concept, it proved to be a political millstone around Simon's neck..... one which thrust him into a televised debate....... with a fully prepared and combative Representative Castle.

"Good evening voters. My name is Jason Gordon, your host for this third installment in WSON TV's series of broadcasts of CONFRONTATION '98, the Georgia Senate Election. This evening's debate is brought to you courtesy of Omega Air Lines, who reminds Georgians everywhere that '......we love for you to fly.... and it shows!'

"With us in our studios is the Lieutenant Governor of the great State of Georgia, the Honorable Simon L. Harder. Welcome, Mr. Harder. Joining us via satellite from his Washington, D.C. office is Mr. Harder's opponent, Congressman Edison M. Castle. Welcome Congressman.'

"Gentlemen, tonight's topic is transportation..... specifically the proposed construction of a statewide passenger railway system, popularly known as the 'Harder Initiative', after its author and chief proponent. Lieutenant Governor Harder..... let us turn to you for your opening comments".

HARDER: "To begin with, I'd like to thank WSON TV and Georgia's voters for giving me the opportunity to share my views.... in such an open forum. If you review the history of economic development in the state, even prior to the Civil War years, Georgia's economic destiny has been tied to transportation, and up until some forty years ago, rail transportation. Very simply put, the 'Harder Initiative' is designed to help return us to our economic and transportation roots. We have seen, in this decade of the 90's, the problems created by ever increasing burdens placed on our road systems; the metro area sprawl this has introduced, the economic paralysis thereby spawned in our inner cities through an erosion of the residential and business tax base, and the financial stress borne by commuters caught in the crossfire of escalating insurance rates, outrageous commuting time, and an uncontrollable DUI crisis.'

"The 'Harder Initiative' will foster growth in the tourist trade for Georgia's coastal areas, ensure the economic viability of the state's second tier cities, not just Atlanta, and enliven the quality of life..... for all Georgians. Thank you."

MODERATOR: "Representative Castle.... your opening thoughts....

EDISON: "I must admit an admiration for my esteemed opponent's eloquent comments concerning the ideals and objectives we share..... and with specific regard to the welfare of our State's voters from both an economic and quality of life standpoint. However, I feel duty bound to share some salient facts with the voters.... facts that Mr. Harder conveniently omits from his scholarly views.'

"Six years ago, the Federal government enacted a $151 billion transportation bill which, among other major provisions, called for $24 billion to go into a flexible surface transportation program, which was to be disbursed under the discretion of state and local officials. In addition, some $38 billion was earmarked for completion of a national highway system to feed the interstate highway system. Each of the States were permitted to transfer half of this money, or $19 billion to transit projects. On a fair share basis, Georgia was eligible for slightly less than 4% or nearly $2.5 billion dollars on a federally mandated 80-20 federal-state match. Of this $2.5 billion, effectively 70% was targeted to passenger rail and mass transit projects for the State. Beside these amounts, another $658 million dollars was planned for the development of a high speed rail prototype utilizing magnetic levitation techniques, as well as new transit starts and rail modernization.'

"Now, I was one of the more vocal Congressional supporters of this transportation bill back in 1991. Moreover, I chaired the House sub-committee on alternative forms of energy, which conducted extensive research and evaluation of super conductive materials.... materials which make the magnetic levitation technique..... used in high speed passenger rail feasible.'

"Given this background, I must say that I find it intriguing that Mr. Harder purports himself to be a champion of transit and rail initiatives, when the record shows that in the three years following the enactment of the Transportation Act, during which time he was head of the Georgia Department of Transportation, only a small fraction of the over $2.4 billion earmarked for rail and mass transit projects.... ever found its way into these areas. During that same period.... more than $3.5 billion was spent on roads.... roads..... and more roads! I think my esteemed opponent believes Georgia's voters.... are suffering from...... an extended bout of amnesia... regarding his transportation record!"

MODERATOR: "Mr. Harder?"

HARDER: "Well.... I didn't realize Representative Castle was so well read... regarding my record at the Department of Transportation. The fact of the matter is, we did spend money on the development of roads. During those years of economic depression throughout the State, I strongly felt that part of my job was to utilize such public works projects in order to provide jobs.... employment for out of work engineers, contractors, and suppliers. Therefore, a conscious decision was made to accelerate road projects, since they directly provided meaningful, long term employment to a large segment of Georgia's labor force.'

"Tell me, Congressman. How is it that someone like yourself..... with the significant financial support you receive from interested third parties such as tonight's sponsor.... fashion yourself as a leader in transportation.... other than airlines? After all, haven't you had your girlfriend.... flown around much of the country..... and the Caribbean, compliments of Omega Air Lines?"

MODERATOR: "Mr. Harder, let's stick to the issues at hand!"

EDISON: "Jason, I appreciate your attempt to give guidance to Mr. Harder. It's obvious he feels compelled to take up the voters' time..... with unnecessary slop and gossip. To get back to the facts; Mr. Harder pointed out the intent of all this road building was to put people back to work, providing jobs for the jobless. Mr. Harder fails to mention that two of the key contractors enlisted by the DOT under his guidance..... were indicted on fraud and tax evasion charges. One of them was convicted. More than $85 million was never accounted for, $85 million which certainly could have paid a lot of bills for out of work Georgians.'

"Most disturbing of all is the fact that Mr. Harder has now gone on record as saying that he advocates, and I quote, '........use of the incarcerated, the prisoners filling our jails...' as the labor force to carry out this 'new' transportation mission. Mr. Harder was unable to properly manage federal funds when he was directly responsible for them. Now he wants to loose criminals on the countryside and municipalities of our state..... in the name of cost-effective project management. If anything, the jobs that Mr. Harder says he was committed to four or five years ago....... are even more important to the State today. I say the Harder Initiative is a project whose time has passed, being promoted by a man who has demonstrated a proclivity to satisfy the whims of his professional cronies.... at the expense of our State!"

Needless to say, things went progressively downhill from that point on for the Harder camp. Simon stormed out of the studio, realizing the jeopardy his performance put his candidacy in. Once they were off the air, an interesting but brief exchange took place between the moderator and Edison.

"Representative Castle, could you stay on the line for a moment?" inquired the moderator.

"Well.... I've really got to get going, Jason," Edison answered, quite impatiently. "What do you need?"

"Well Sir, I'd like you to tell your daughter, Asia, that I said hello. We went out briefly when I first came to Atlanta as a freshman in college. Also, there was a gentleman I had the occasion to run into at a party you had at the house one summer. I believe he was your housekeeper or gardener or something. Anyway, he scared me away from some very destructive things I was doing to myself. If you know where that gentleman is..... please tell him I said thank you.... for helping me get my life together."

"I didn't know you knew Asia. She's living in New York now. I'll certainly pass your greetings along to her, but quite frankly, I don't know who this other person is you're referring to. Our gardener, Enrico, has been dead for more than six years now."

"Well... I won't take up any more of your time. I never found out who that man was, but I believe you must know him. He seemed to know your family. All I can tell you is that in retrospect, he did something for me..... something I wasn't able to do for myself. Good luck in the election Congressman!"

The conversation puzzled Edison somewhat, but he was more preoccupied by the reference Harder made to '...his girlfriend'. He had not heard from Camille for nearly three weeks, and couldn't understand why. He'd even called her office several times, but received a vague response that she was out of town on business. It occurred to him that she might be avoiding contact, but he didn't know what he could have possibly done to make her feel that way. Edison purposely stayed away from attempting to contact her at home, upon mutual agreement. But he was getting desperate to hear from her. Of course, Edison had no idea of the conspiracy underway by key members of his staff. The fact of the matter was that the Xenium ruse, concocted by Lance had clearly worked...... to a despicable perfection.

An anonymous envelope appeared mysteriously in Camille's office two weeks prior. Enclosed were two documents, suitably falsified by Lance and his cronies, which recorded a series of treatments Edison was undergoing for HIV. They even went as far as to describe the controversial Xenium technique, and showed a scheduled date for Edison to have the implant procedure which, if things had gone according to the documentation, should have occurred over a month ago.

Camille had one of her staff members check out the address of the Georgetown physicians. Because of the nature of the inquiry, however, the doctors' offices '...regretfully could not disclose any confidential patient information....'. She even did her own research through the Library of Congress on all current intelligence surrounding the implant technology. As Camille came to understand the subject more, she reflected on the last few times Edison had been intimate with her. Although he'd never been a particularly stud-like lover, Camille did notice the fact that there was a marked struggle for him to attain, and maintain, a decent erection. And she tried everything to help him.... massage, fellatio, you name it.... she tried it. And it was a medically documented fact that impotence was a potential side effect of the Xenium treatment.

Putting the pieces of the picture together, Camille did exactly what Lance counted on her to do..... she avoided Edison like the plague. She even travelled to an exclusive womens' center outside Philadelphia for testing to see if she had yet been infected with HIV. All of her results were negative.

But it was a small consolation as she, based on the evidence presented, assumed Edison had knowingly exposed her to the virus, thereby risking her life. It was a sullen bitterness that developed in her heart for him. She couldn't deny the consuming desire, the seething lust growing in her..... to see him destroyed, his public reputation shattered.

Edison defeated Simon Harder handily on Election Day.

Chapter 9

Notes From a Sleepwalk

One of the more successful community initiatives developed over the years by D.C. Mayor Eva Pratt Christian was the District's International KWANZAA Festival, which ran from the second week of December up until New Year's Day. Each of the key principles, or Nguzo Saba, of the KWANZAA season was observed by a day long series of events, speakers, and exhibits at various venues around D.C. While other cities held isolated festivals and celebrations between Christmas and New Year's Day, Mayor Christian had galvanized distinct neighborhood and cultural segments into a truly unified three week District event. In past years, distinguished guests included Winnie Mandela, Nigerian President Akar Henmenotep, and Ethiopian Minister of Information Kamali Undwasso.

Each of the principles of KWANZAA, of course, has a positive emphasis for African-Americans:

UMOJA (Unity) To strive for and maintain unity in the family, community, and nation.

KUJICHAGILIA (Self-determination) To define ourselves, create for ourselves, and speak for ourselves, rather than being defined, named, created, and/or spoken for by someone else.

UJIMA (Collective Work and Responsibility) To build and maintain our communities together and to make the problems of our people (anywhere) our problems and to strive to solve them together.

UJAMAA (Cooperative Economics) To define and maintain our own economic base, and to profit from this base together.

NIA (Purpose) To make our collective vocation the re-establishment of a cultural community infrastructure, thereby restoring our people to their traditional greatness.

KUUMBA (Creativity) To do always as much as we can, in order to leave our community more desirable and beneficial than we inherited it.

IMANI (Faith) To believe with all our hearts in the in-fallibility of this spiritual force in carrying out the work of cultural restoration.

Appropriately, the Mayor's office saw to it that profits from the Festival were plowed back into the schools, community centers, and recreation programs of the District's neighborhoods. Fortunately, the Festival was not only a cultural success, but a proven money-maker as well. Probably the single biggest economic boon of the three week affair, was the high school All-Star basketball tournament that preceded the formal observance of Nguzo Saba. The D.C. KWANZAA Invitational Tournament attracted the best high school players from all over the country to its round robin format. In the tournament, the country was divided into four regions, with the top players from each region competing. This year's Southeast contingent was led by a 6' 3" senior guard from Atlanta's Northside High School; Emanuel (Mad Manny) Castle.

Manny had gone on from his more humble days as a junior high school player, to become one of the top 5 college prospects in the country. He was a member of the PARADE All-America team as a senior. His nickname came from an ability to take over games in the fourth quarter, seeming to be everywhere at once. Characteristically, he would seize a rebound, charge (madly) full speed down the court with a completely wild eyed look on his face, and without seeming concern for life or limb, fling himself at the basket for a resounding slam. In truth, he played like.... well..... like he was crazy!

But what really made the moniker stick, was a story Manny once recounted to a local news coverage team. When asked how he had developed such good ballhandling skills, Manny explained that when he was younger, he had this "... out of body experience in which I found myself trapped inside a basketball..." during his viewing of a Michael Jordan video tape. Ever since then, Manny always had a special affinity for handling the ball, he felt, because he knew what is was like to BE a basketball. Therefore, he understood the subtleties of force, spin, rotation, and had developed some unusual passing techniques to take advantage of this knowledge. Of course, after that conversation, the media was absolutely sure that, although he seemed to be nice enough, all his marbles weren't in place.

Fortunately for him, Manny stayed away, for the most part, from alcohol or drugs. Occasionally, he'd have a glass of wine or a beer, but otherwise played it pretty straight. Other than his slightly unorthodox basketball reputation, Manny was a very well liked and well adjusted young man. Though not necessarily a scholarly type, Manny was a solid B student, and with his physical talents, was actively being courted by all the major basketball powers. He'd narrowed his choices down to Virginia, Georgetown, or Villanova since each of these schools was within driving distance of D.C. The KWANZAA Tournament was the last big opportunity for Manny to show his stuff in front of his principal recruiters.

Since Manny had to be in town for the tournament, Deidre decided the family should celebrate Christmas in the Capital. Asia and her boyfriend were coming down from New York, so it promised to be a very special holiday for them all. Deidre received a wonderful card and basket of pastries from Gloria. Once she finished her degree (with Deidre's help) in 1995, Gloria moved to Henry County and was now a principal in the school system there. And like the good friends they were, Deidre and Gloria always promised they would get together from time to time, although their schedules didn't make that proposition very feasible. But the holidays were a time they always got in touch with one another.

Manny was staying in a dormitory at the George Washington University in D.C. with the other ballplayers, about a fifteen minute ride crosstown to his father's Capitol Hill offices. The athletes were having a good time, with the camaraderie, the food, the coeds. Preparations were underway to move Edison into the Dirksen building after the holidays. Deidre had phoned to let

Manny know she wouldn't be arriving until the 23rd, and had instructed Edison to make sure he spent some time with Manny. For his part, Manny wasn't too concerned about seeing his father right now because of his focus on the upcoming game against the Northeast. However, on the day of the Northeast game, Manny received a call from his father's office.

"Hello," Manny answered.

"Hello, is this Manny Castle?" the voice on the other end inquired.

"Yeah, this is Manny. Who are you?"

"Manny, this is Lance Powell. I work for your father. He asked me to get in touch with you to see if you'd be able to have dinner with him..... after tonight's ballgame."

At first, Manny wondered why Edison didn't call himself. But then he realized there was a lot going on in his father's life after the election. He had been planning to go out with the fellas, but did consider it thoughtful of his father to want to spend some time with him.

"Sure, I'd like that," Manny answered.

"Look for a silver gray Congressional limousine outside the Capital Centre when you're through," Lance instructed him. "I know your father's looking forward to this. Good luck tonight!"

"Is my Dad..... going to watch the game?" Manny asked somewhat nervously. His father had only seen him play twice since he'd been in high school, and both times he played terribly. He didn't want to feel jinxed going into the game.

"Honestly, Manny, I don't know. But I tend to doubt it. I hope you don't mind, but I know he's got a tremendous amount of work he needs to get done before the end of the year."

"No... no I don't mind at all. I'll look for him after we're through." said Manny, relieved. "Thanks for your call." CLICK!

About two hours later, the phone rang in Edison's office. Lance and the secretary were both out, so the Senator-Elect picked it up himself.

"Hello. This is Edison Castle. Can I help you?"

"Yes.... you can help me. This is Camille, Edison."

Her voice was warm and sensuous. He hadn't spoken to her in weeks, and his mixed emotions were apparent in their brief conversation.

"Well..... what happened to you? I tried to contact you for weeks, but you were never around. The least you could have done was return my calls."

"I'm sorry Edison. I've just had some personal matters I needed to attend to. And you had to give your attention to the campaign. By the way, I guess congratulations are in order, Senator Castle."

"Camille...... I've missed you so much. Why didn't you let me know what was going on.... how you were doing? You know how much I care about you."

"You're right Edison. It wasn't fair of me to be so mysterious. But that's why I'm calling. I'm over it now, and I'd like to see you.... to give you my own, special, congratulatory present."

Edison was so thrilled to hear that she was anxious to see him, he nearly swallowed the phone. "Baby.... you just name the place..... and I'm there!"

"Meet me at Duke Zeibert's, six-thirty. We'll get a bite, and some drinks, have a chance to talk. Then maybe we'll go somewhere where we can be alone, and private. How does that sound?"

Edison knew he was supposed to pick Manny up after his game, and Deidre was coming to town in two days. But he wasn't about to let such considerations dampen his enthusiasm for spending some time with Camille again. Besides, Manny's game was bound to last until nine-thirty or so. He could still make it. "I wouldn't miss it for the world," Edison told her.

"Fine," she responded, "neither would I!" CLICK!

A cunning smile graced her lips as she hung the phone up. Camille had thoughts of seduction on her mind. And revenge! Little did Edison know he was being lured into the midst of a scheme worthy of the sting operations carried out by the FBI in the early 80's. And to help her pull it off, Camille knew just the person she would need.

An enthusiastic crowd looked on as the final seconds of the semi-final game ticked away between the Northeast and Southeast All Star teams. A tightly played game until the end, the Northeast earned a hard fought 102-97 victory over the Southern All Stars. In a losing cause, Manny was named the game's MVP on the strength of an outstanding performance: 35 points, 12 rebounds, 11 assists, and 3 blocked shots from his guard position. He was a shoo-in for the All-Tourney team. And he had certainly not done anything to hurt his scholarship chances.

In the locker room afterwards, talk turned to the evening's activities. Several of the players were headed to Georgetown for partying. Everyone was anxious for Manny to go with them, but he explained that he was meeting his father, and that they should go on without him. He would just as soon go with the guys, but he'd committed to have dinner with his Dad. Eventually, the locker room emptied, and Manny waited outside for the Congressional limousine he was supposed to meet. Fifteen minutes went by, then half an hour. The Capital Centre was nearly empty now, and Manny nervously wondered what could have possibly happened to Edison. He went inside and called the office. No answer. Next, he tried his father's townhouse, and got nothing but a taped recording from the PhoneMate.

Thinking he'd been stood up, and consequently feeling quite dejected, Manny headed back outside in search of a cab for a ride back to the dorm. The early evening had been drizzly, and now the precipitation was turning to snow. Walking toward the cab stand area, Manny noticed a car pulling up slowly beside him. He could tell it wasn't his father's limo, so he was cautious about stopping to see exactly who it was. Just then, he heard the horn of the car, and the driver shouting his name out loud. Startled, he turned to see his old friend, Haskell Lee Jones getting out from behind the wheel to greet him.

"Man-NAY! How you doin'?" yelled Haskell. "We watched the game tonight. You were tough my man, T-O-U-G-H! I waited to see if you were going to come out. I've got someone who wants to meet you."

Manny hadn't seen Haskell in almost three years. He was a sophomore at the University of Maryland in College Park, and had gotten tickets to the KWANZAA Invitational, when he heard that Manny was going to be playing. Manny never thought he'd say it, but it was good to see Haskell!

"Manny, what are you doin', standin' out here in the snow?"

Slightly embarrassed, Manny explained that he was supposed to be meeting his father, but he hadn't shown up. "I was about to get a taxi," he said sheepishly.

"Why don't you come with us?" Haskell offered. "We're on our way to a party out in Virginia. Besides, I've got someone here that wants to meet you anyway, Mr. Basketball All-Star," he repeated.

Sticking his head inside the car, Manny discovered two lovely young women. "This is Sharon," Haskell said of the young lady in front. Motioning to the back seat, Haskell continued the introductions. "And this is Sandra Whetstone. Sandra, this is Manny Castle."

"Very nice to meet you Manny," Sandra spoke up. "You played so hard tonight.... it was a shame to see you lose."

Well... thought Manny, maybe there is a silver lining to every cloud. Quickly, he related the fact that he was waiting to meet his father. "Not now, Manny," commanded Haskell. "Just get in. We'll drop you off later." Considering his options, Haskell's idea was clearly much more compelling. Hopping in back with Sandra, Manny joined the three of them, and they were off.

A glistening snow covered evening greeted Edison and Camille as they emerged from their dinner downtown. The two had enjoyed quite a pleasant meal, with splendid seafood entrees punctuated by several tall glasses of champagne. Camille even convinced Edison to have a snifter of cognac prior to departing, and the cold outside air could do nothing to temper the ensuing heat that churned inside him. Of course, Camille suitably stoked his amorous fires, with a black wool dress that conformed to every nuance of her shape, gracefully enhancing her otherwise obvious physical assets. Moreover, she had taken the time to have a new hairstyle installed and with some tastefully applied makeup, Camille was looking quite gorgeous. And Edison knew it. He was like a lost young puppy following his master around. Unfortunately, this stunning female presence concealed a heart full of sinister motivation, all of which would shortly be directed at him.

Hailing a cab, Camille cuddled warmly beneath his arm in the back seat, placing his hand on her lower thigh. "Well, where are we headed now?" Edison asked innocently. He hoped there was more to follow this initial advance, much more. Sadly, he was correct.

"Baby," she whispered in a sultry voice, her tongue lightly caressing his ear, "it's been quite a while since we've had a chance to spend time together. I've got a little surprise for you tonight.... to celebrate." She instructed the cab driver to head for Georgetown. The snow was picking up now, and the District took on a picture postcard beauty, beneath the blanket of crystalline flakes. Surely, it was a romantic enough evening, and Camille felt so good in his arms.

Shortly, the driver pulled up in front of a stately townhome, high above the city. Down the tree lined street was a breathtaking view of the Potomac River, clothed in a warm evening garment of snow. The snowfall caused a pleasant hush to engulf the area, as not much traffic flowed that night. Except for an occasional pedestrian, the street was eerily serene.

Arriving to greet them at the door was a beautiful middle aged woman. She looked, appropriately enough, quite dignified in a black chiffon evening dress and heels. "Edison," Camille spoke up as they entered, "I'd like you to meet my good friend, Antigua Gregory. Antigua.... this is Edison Castle."

"It's certainly a pleasure to make your acquaintance Senator," Antigua said earnestly, greeting him with a firm, yet warm handshake. "Please... come in and make yourselves at home." Antigua ushered them into the living room, which was tastefully adorned with two large Oriental rugs, and dominated by an oversized cranberry couch, which sat opposite an enormous, triangularly shaped fireplace. A roaring fire blazed inside, and without inquiring about their preferences, Antigua shortly joined them with a large snifter of cognac for Edison, and chardonnay for Camille. A very cordial round of smalltalk ensued, and Edison could feel himself becoming quite comfortable with the two women. He wondered what Antigua did for a living, to be as charming and articulate as she was. And obviously quite well to do.

As it turns out, Camille and Antigua were childhood friends, growing up about two blocks from one another in the Anacostia section of the District. Unbeknownst to Edison, Antigua was one of Georgetown's most successful (and discrete) madams. She had agreed to help Camille implement her plan of revenge on him...... and he could only think about how nice an evening it was turning out to be! Quietly excusing herself, Antigua left the two of them alone for a few moments. Almost imperceptibly, the lights dimmed... to the point that the flicker from the fireplace provided most of the room's illumination. Edison was pleasantly inebriated now, and the music that played softly in the background escalated his amorous mood.

"Where did Antigua go?" he inquired.

Cuddling warmly beneath him Camille replied, "She's gone to prepare your surprise, darling." She kissed him fully on the mouth, and her tongue made it tough for Edison to contain his excitement. Before things could get any more heated between them however, Antigua returned, this time clad in a clinging red mini-dress, so tight and short it barely covered the top of her panty hose.

Standing directly in front of him, she began to slowly caress herself, letting her hands flow lightly down over her hips, fondling her breasts, and grinding sensuously to the beat of the music in the background. The backlit glow of the fire obscured her features, causing Antigua's movements to appear as a silhouette; mysterious, enchanting, and so, so exciting. Edison nearly jumped off the sofa..... as her routine built in its sensual intensity.

Oddly enough, Camille slipped quietly out of the room, unnoticed by Edison, who was captivated by the evening's entertainment before him. In a nearby guest room, Camille picked up a small remote control-type device and pressed a little red button in the center. Out of thin air, the rectangular representation of a video monitor appeared floating, literally, in the air. On this instantaneous display, Camille watched the action unfolding..... between Antigua and her (ex) lover.

By prior arrangement, Camille had her son, who was an engineering technician for a D.C. television station, install three tiny video cameras in Antigua's living room. No ordinary electronic gear, these devices utilized the latest in holographic technology, which completely obviated the need for monitoring equipment. By depressing the red knob on her control console, the images being recorded (silently) to videotape could be projected (holographically) into the air, as though a screen existed. Such an approach was perfect for Camille's scheme, since it gave no clue to Edison.... that he was co-starring in her private, (and soon to be quite passionate) pornographic production. Ultimately, blackmail was Camille's game, and her unwitting prey was doing a superb job.... of getting himself implicated.

Grabbing her hair wickedly, Antigua rotated her hips, grinding the air hard, thrusting her pelvis up and out toward Edison, her thighs tight and muscular in front of him. By this time, his mouth was dry, his penis firm and erect. Leaning forward, he was less than a foot away from the evening's hostess. Taking his hands, she placed them on her hips, and he slid her dress up above her waist, revealing nothing but a neatly shaven and perfumed crotch, glistening with the enticing wetness of arousal. The sweet smell of passion overcame him and he began to slowly kiss her on the thighs, and run his fingers through her pubic hair. Antigua looked down at him, eyes flaring, and quietly commanded, "Take me."

Edison didn't hesitate another moment. He dropped his pants, and lifted her in the air as she mounted him. They fell back to the couch as he thrust violently inside her, fucking wildly, as though his life depended upon it. Antigua moaned softly; Edison groaned in pleasure. Inside, Camille watched attentively, conscious of herself becoming noticeably excited by the scene. Curiously, she felt very ambivalent about the action unfolding before her. Rather than anger or jealousy, she was intrigued by all of this in a very detached sort of way. Outside, Edison continued to pound away furiously at Antigua, completely oblivious to all else.

Suddenly, Camille reappeared, dressed only in a rose colored silk nightshirt. Standing directly over them, she knelt down beside Antigua, and taking Edison firmly by the back of the neck, shoved his head forcefully down between her legs, even as he continued pounding her girlfriend. This unorthodox threesome continued until Edison, nearly suffocated by the leglock applied to his head, succumbed to nature. His powerful orgasm caused him to shudder uncontrollably, then pass out, exhausted, in a heap on the floor.

As Edison snoozed peacefully like a baby, Antigua gathered herself and silently went upstairs. Once in the privacy of her luxurious bathroom, she carefully removed the oversized female condom from her vagina. Giving Edison's ejaculation a cursory glance inside the latex pouch, she quickly discarded it and took a relaxing shower, poured herself a glass of wine, and went straight to bed.

Downstairs, Camille rolled over, lit a cigarette and pulled out her remote control. She reviewed the tape, and acknowledged with satisfaction that it would make for great footage on the evening news..... and be an even greater surprise for the good Senator. "Sweet dreams, my poor scoundrel," she said softly as she wickedly replayed her production over and over several times.

The party was winding down in northern Virginia, and although Manny and Sandra were having a great time, he knew he needed to get back downtown. Tomorrow was the consolation game of the tournament, and he wanted to be sharp in front of the recruiters. Manny wondered, momentarily, about what could have happened to his father to prevent him from showing up, then quickly decided that he'd had a better time with Haskell...... and Sandra anyway.

For his part, Haskell was 'feeling no pain', having had too much to drink. Haskell also had developed a mild appetite for cocaine, and that made him feel as though he was in control of the situation, when he really wasn't. Despite his intoxication, Haskell didn't appear particularly incoherent or sufficiently disoriented to cause alarm. Still, Manny offered to drive several times, not quite comfortable that Haskell could 'handle it'. Sandra, however, convinced Manny that there were "....better things we could do with your hands...." than worry about driving the car.

Outside, the snow had tapered off a bit, but the temperature was falling rapidly. The roads were passable but slippery. Haskell insisted on taking the George Washington Parkway back into town rather than dealing with the Beltway. The Parkway was particularly scenic at night, and the snow covered woods that lined the road looked like something right off of a painting. Coming out of a turn, Haskell didn't notice a small dog crossing in front of the car. Swerving at the last minute to avoid hitting the canine, he lost control on the ice. The momentum coming off the curve caused the car to take off, as though launched from a rocket. They sailed up over the divider, clear across the Northbound lanes, and crashed through the guard rails. Finally, the car came to rest precipitously on a small ridge high above a sheer drop straight down to the Potomac River below.

Sharon and Haskell were flung unconscious from the vehicle just as it broke through the guard rails. Manny was partially stuck in the wreckage. Though injured, he was still conscious. He could hear Sandra shrieking wildly, "Man-NAY... Manny...... HELP ME! Please help MEEEEE!" Somehow managing to free himself from the wreckage, one leg bleeding profusely, Manny was able to crawl forward a few feet. There he discovered Sandra, literally dangling by her fingertips from a ledge about two yards below him.

"HOLD ON Sandra!" Manny commanded her. "I'll get to you in a minute!" Wrapping his left leg around a massive vine nearby to anchor himself, Manny stretched down as far as he could, extending his right arm. From her position, Sandra couldn't see exactly where his hand was, so Manny had to guide her verbally to make contact. The wind suddenly began to whip up, and the ensuing cold made the rescue attempt that much more difficult. Sandra's fingers were turning blue from the cold and frost, but Manny determinedly focused only on the life or death task at hand.

"That's it," he coaxed her. "I'm just to your left. On the count of three I want you to let go and reach up as far as you can with your left hand," Manny shouted to her.

"I can't, Manny!" she pleaded, "I'm too afraid. Don't let me fall... please Manny... PLEASE don't let me fall!"

Realizing there was no time to debate, Manny started the countdown. "One.... two..... THREE!" Involuntarily, Sandra shot up her hand, and miraculously, Manny caught her, a split second before she slid away. Her weight was almost more than he could handle, but fortunately, the vine held his leg fast. Slowly, he began to drag Sandra back from disaster. The pain in his right leg was unbearable, and there was a tremendous strain on his back as he lifted her, one-handed, up toward the ledge below him. Yet, he managed to stay focused on what he was doing.

Across the river, some guests at a house party overlooking the gorge happened to notice the car wreckage perched awkwardly on the ridge opposite them. One of the women could make out the figures of Manny and Sandra, locked in their survival battle. Rushing inside, she immediately called the state police, who arrived on the scene in minutes. Surveying the damage from above, the police radioed for an ambulance to pick up Haskell and Sharon, still unconscious from the crash. About two hundred feet below them was the wrecked car, but they couldn't see Manny and

Sandra from their vantage point. Fortunately, the woman who called was kept on the line, and she described how dire the situation was to the state patrol. Quickly, they made arrangements for a heavy-duty tow truck, in an attempt to drag the wreckage back up the slope.

Before the towing equipment could arrive, however, a stiff gust of wind swept down along the ridge. The car, which had teetered delicately on its side, suddenly flipped over at the behest of the sudden gale. The wreckage slid uncontrollably down the hill, rolling directly over Manny's lower back and legs. Screaming out grotesquely at the unbearable pressure of the car smashing into his spine, Manny couldn't maintain his grip on Sandra's hand. Falling, she made a vain attempt to grab hold again of the ledge, but her backward momentum was too great. She plunged, with Manny's name on her lips, to her death on the rocks below. Seconds later, the wrecked car cascaded down the gorge behind her, exploding into a mushroom cloud of flames that glowed brightly in the winter night...... amidst the river's splendid wardrobe of snow and ice. Except for the voices of state patrolmen up above, an eerie quiet engulfed the scene. Mercifully, Manny quietly passed out from the weight of the emotional and physical tragedy he'd endured.

The phone rang four times before Deidre could reach it. "Hello," she managed, wiping the sleep from her eyes. It was 2:45 AM.

"Is this Mrs. Castle?" the voice on the other end inquired.

"Yes... yes... this is Deidre Castle." Instinctively, she could feel something was amiss. "Who am I speaking to?"

"My name is Captain Ross, with the Commonwealth of Virginia Patrol. Mrs. Castle, I'm afraid there's been an accident. Your son has been seriously inju............"

The words trailed off in Deidre's consciousness. She began to hyperventilate. Dropping the phone she rushed into her bathroom, splashing cold water on her face in a futile effort to awaken from some type of cruel nightmare she found herself trapped within. Momentarily, her senses returned, and Deidre knew this was for real. Returning to the bedroom, an unusually composed Deidre resumed the conversation. "I'm sorry, Officer," she apologized. "Please... please.... tell me what happened."

Quickly, the Captain explained the situation. "I'll be on the next flight to D.C." she told him. "Has my husband been notified?"

"I'm sorry, Mrs. Castle, but we've been unable to reach him. I've got one of my officer's trying to get in touch with his Chief of Staff, a Mr. Powell.... I believe."

"Well..... thank you and your men for everything you've done. I'm sure that Lan..... I mean... Mr. Powell will get in touch with my husband. Thank you for everything."

"I'm very sorry.... to have to bring you this news, Mrs. Castle." CLICK

Slowly hanging up the phone, Deidre began to weep softly. Flinging open the French doors of her bedroom, she rushed out onto the small balcony. The Atlanta December night was crisp and cool. Grabbing the collar of her nightgown, she tore the garment apart violently, revealing her naked chest beneath. It was as if she were trying to.... symbolically.... rid herself..... of the despair and anguish that filled her bosom. Slumping to her knees, she raised her hands and eyes heavenward. "YOU'LL NOT ROB ME AGAIN!" she shouted at the top of her lungs. "Not THIS time, you won't!" Deidre's vow echoed into the night as she cried bitterly, collapsing in a pile on her balcony.

Edison awakened groggily. His feet and arms were numb, and his head ached. He was aware of being back in his townhouse, but he wasn't at all certain how he got there. He could vaguely recall the fine dinner he had with Camille, and he remembered her taking him to Antigua's. The rest of the evening remained a sequence of dull images in his memory, like a pleasant dream. Or, perhaps more properly, a sleepwalk.

Beginning to undress, he was interrupted by the phone. "Hello."

"Senator..... it's Lance. I've been trying to get in touch with you for an hour. There's been an accident Senator. Your son is in the intensive care unit at the Fairfax County Hospital. He was in a bad accident on the GW Parkway."

"WHAT? Oh my God!" Edison shouted into the phone as he leaped to his feet.

"I'll be right over to pick you up," Lance volunteered.

"Oh my God.... oh my God..." Edison repeated again and again. The gravity of the situation caused him to bring the details of the night into clearer focus now. He remembered that he was supposed to meet Manny after the basketball game. Instead, he'd gone on with Camille, listening to the urging of his.... That didn't matter now.

"Has my wife been contacted yet?"

"I think so Senator. The Virginia Commonwealth Patrol told me they were attempting to get in touch with her."

Edison realized there were many questions he would have to answer concerning his whereabouts...... as soon as Deidre arrived. He would have to enlist Lance's help in covering up for him. His mind worked quickly now, as it searched for a suitable alibi that would explain why he never picked Manny up. "Let me take a shower, Lance, and come get me in fifteen minutes," Edison directed him. He knew he had to get to the hospital before Deidre arrived. "And, Lance, don't take your time getting here."

"I won't dawdle," he answered dutifully. "But you know.... it's pretty messy outside, Senator."

"I don't care if there's an earthquake outside..... just get over here!" Edison shouted into the phone. The pressure of the situation was becoming too much to bear.

"I understand, Sir." Lance responded meekly, not interested in pursuing the issue any further. Fortunately, he hadn't been out all night partying, although he did have to explain to his female house guest that she had to wake up and leave..... at 3:00 A.M. Thirty minutes later, he and Edison were on their way to the hospital.

In the car, a heavy silence pervaded as Edison, gripped with anxiety, tried to calm himself. After wringing his hands for fifteen minutes, he finally spoke up.

"If any wants to know where I was tonight," he commanded his Chief of Staff, "you tell them we were together."

"Where do you suggest I say we were?"

"At a cocktail party..... for one of the President's Cabinet members."

Lance studied Edison carefully for a moment. "Let me get this straight. We were at a cocktail party.... together.... until three in the morning?"

"Yes, we were TOGETHER, do you understand? That's what I want you to say.... if anyone asks..... including my wife."

Lance could see the fear and desperation in his eyes, emotions he'd never before witnessed from Edison. The sight of the Senator in this state unnerved Lance greatly, and caused him to wonder whether Edison was more afraid for his son's life...... or of Deidre ultimately discovering..... that he was where he shouldn't have been, when something as tragic as this occurred.

Deidre's flight touched down at Dulles Airport at 5:45 A.M. The trip itself was somewhat traumatic, as the plane had to be rerouted to Dulles from Washington National because of the heavy snowfall and shorter runways there. She was able to hail a cab and arrived at the hospital at six-thirty. The activity in the lobby was surprising for it to be so early in the morning, and particularly during a holiday week. An orderly escorted Deidre to the intensive care wing. In the waiting area outside of Manny's room, Edison was going over the accident report with one of the state patrolmen. Lance noticed her first, and motioned to Edison that she had arrived.

"Deidre..... oh Deidre," said Edison, as he rushed to his wife and pinned her to his chest with a hug. "Manny's strong..... he'll pull through this."

She hung limp in Edison's arms, barely acknowledging him. "Where... is.... my.... Son?" inquired Deidre hoarsely.

"This is Doctor Lewis," Lance offered. "Manny's next door."

"Your son is unconscious, Mrs. Castle," the Doctor said. If you'd like, you can see him but he's not able to respond right now. He's been through quite a traumatic experience."

"I want to see him..... alone," Deidre said softly, almost in a whisper. Ushering her into Manny's room, the doctor returned to the waiting area with Edison and Lance. Deidre sat down quietly next to Manny's bed. A nurse entered briefly to preside over the review of his monitoring devices. Except for a barely perceptible hint of breathing, he laid there motionless, amidst the mangled series of tubes, hoses and catheters that were necessary..... to sustain his life.

Immediately, the scene transported Deidre back in time to 1974, to a hospital room much like the one she was in now, where her lover, Sam, laid in a coma from which he would never recover, the victim of another tragic car accident. Edison was there with her then, too. She had never forgiven herself for getting so upset with Sam that night. How could she know, that it would be the last time she would ever see him... alive? How could God be..... so cruel.... so unfair to her..... AGAIN?

Deidre remained inside with Manny for several hours. Edison, not daring to leave the hospital, dispatched Lance to his townhouse to pick up a change of clothes, and then on to the office for some files he needed. He hoped that by occupying his mind with work, he would be able to think more clearly. Lance stopped at his apartment before making the rounds, to refresh himself from the long night that just passed. On his way out the door he paused long enough to do three lines of coke, in an effort to re-energize himself and clear his head. He reached the Senate office just after lunch. Picking up the files Edison wanted, Lance noticed a package that had been left for the Senator by a courier service earlier that morning. There was nothing particularly unusual about the package, and Lance didn't give it a second thought..... until he noticed that the return address was for...... Camille Ferguson.

After four hours, Deidre finally emerged from Manny's room. Taking her off into a quiet corner, Edison wanted to know if there had been any change. Looking up at him, she could only burst into a new round of tears. Edison vainly attempted to console her, but she was too overcome by anguish. Finally gathering herself, she said to him softly, "Edison..... I want to believe..... I truly want to believe.... that you had nothing to do with this. You've never loved Manny like a father should have. I want you to know this, mark my words Edison. If Manny..... if my son dies...... I'm going to hold you responsible. And believe me Edison..... your life will become a living nightmare. You'll wish to God.... that you had never met me!"

Downstairs, just outside the window below them, a local children's chorus began singing a series of traditional Christmas carols. All around, a mood of joyous festivity embraced the onlookers. Christmas spirit filled the air. Sadly, it was a cruel juxtaposition for Edison and Deidre. Fortunately, for the rest of the world, the family tragedy unfolding in the hospital for the Castles.... was still a very private event.

Chapter 10

Still in Love with You

Haskell put his arm around Sharon and pulled her toward him. The road ahead was slippery and treacherous, but there was virtually no other traffic out at that hour. In back, Manny and Sandra cuddled cozily, and she remarked how romantic the snowfall had made the river look. As Sharon stroked his penis with her hand, Haskell turned and kissed her full on the lips. This was a questionable maneuver while driving at any time, but it was particularly foolhardy, given the slickness of the road surface that night on the George Washington Parkway. Of course, Haskell's more than moderate level of intoxication caused him to feel much more macho than advisable. Coming up for air after their brief embrace, Haskell noticed a small animal darting across the road in front of him.

Instinctively, he swerved to avoid hitting the animal. Unfortunately, they were heading into a sloping turn as he vainly attempted to regain control of the car. The icy road surface gave him no chance, so in a state of panic he hit the brakes. The ensuing skid only made the situation worse, and the car took off as if shot out of a gun. They skidded across the divider, crashed through guard rails, and started down a hill toward the gorge.

Manny was momentarily aware of the screams of the two young women as they slithered across the Parkway, then he passed out. When he came to, he could feel the cold of the snow on his face. He was partially trapped in the wreckage of the car, but all he could focus on were shrieks of desperation.... from Sandra. Her screams caused Manny's head to clear quickly, and struggling to free himself from the wreckage he managed to crawl forward about twenty feet. From there he could see her hanging on for dear life, high above the Potomac River.

"Hang on, baby...I'll get you," Manny heard himself yell. He wasn't sure how, but there wasn't any time for indecision. Surveying his options, he managed to wrap his legs in a nearby vine to anchor himself, and stretched down as far as he could toward her.

Straining mightily to reach him, Sandra couldn't quite grab Manny's outstretched hand. "Manny.... HELP ME... please HELP ME! I can't hold on much longer." The ice and cold only served to magnify the terror in her voice. Desperately, Manny swung one of his legs free for added leverage. Hanging by that one foot, he commanded Sandra to stick her hand straight up into the air.... on the count of three.

"OK.... here we go! One... two.... three, NOW!"

Frightened beyond imagination, Manny's shout riveted her but she let go with one hand, shooting it straight up into the air. Miraculously, Manny caught her outstretched hand, and this delicate chain of humanity dangled precariously above the gorge.

Slowly, Manny began to drag Sandra back to safety. They made steady progress until a stiff wind arose, rattling the wrecked car that teetered right above them. Manny, literally with his hands full, couldn't see what was going on behind him. Suddenly the wreckage swayed, then tipped over and slid down the ridge, rolling right across Manny's back and legs. His awesome cry of pain pierced the winter night, like a sabre slicing through the icy wind. The impact of the car caused him to lose his precious grip on Sandra's hand. Sliding back, she groped for any hand hold on the icy ridge, but her backward momentum was too great. Manny watched helplessly as she clawed desperately.... vainly..... to hold on. Then she disappeared into the gorge, screaming his name......

"NOOoooo!" Manny yelled out, loud enough to wake all the patients in the trauma ward. Frightened out of his coma by the graphic recollection of his private nightmare, he snapped upright in bed... as if shocked by a live wire. He was nearly choked by the kluge of catheters, tubes, and monitoring electrodes tattooed to his body. Drenched with perspiration, his heart pounded and his chest heaved.

"It's alright son..... it's alright. You're safe now." Deidre tried to calm Manny down. "Lay back down." His awakening startled Deidre out of her dozing. She hadn't left his side for upwards of three days, and at 1:15 in the morning she finally drifted off to a tentative sleep. Although shocked by his sudden eruption, she was nonetheless thankful that Manny had at last come out of his coma. "Come on Manny... lay back now. You're OK," Deidre repeated. She pressed the nurse station alert button, and shortly one of the staff attendants arrived.

Manny wasn't able to speak very well because of a drainage tube that lined his mouth to remove excess blood and fluid from his throat. After a few minutes, the two women were able to get him to lay back down, and the nurse administered a small dose of DARVON to help him calm down. Lying there, Manny's cognition slowly returned and he realized that this was no nightmare. On the contrary, it was all too painfully real. He searched his mind for the connections, for some continuity.... to assure himself he hadn't lost his mind. "Where's Haskell?" he at last struggled to say.

"Haskell's gone back to Atlanta..... with his family," Deidre responded. "I think he's going to be alright. He's got a broken arm, but other than that nothing very serious."

"And what about Sharon?"

"You mean the young lady?" Deidre inquired. "I think she'll be fine too." She wiped his brow, thinking that it was a good sign he was coherent enough to ask questions about the other occupants of the crash vehicle. "It's late now, Manny.... it might be better for you to just rest. We can talk all you want in the morning,." she said reassuringly.

Not daring to fall asleep again, Manny quietly laid there, unable to stop the events of that fateful night from scrolling through his mind. Silently, tears filled his eyes each time the image arose of a helpless Sandra descending to her death.... as it did again and again throughout the night. All Manny could do was lie there.... weeping the darkness away in silence.

The next morning Edison was up early, on the phone with his daughter in New York. Asia was furious that no one had told her before about Manny. She and her boyfriend were planning a visit for the holidays anyway, but the nature of the situation had completely changed her normally non-confrontational demeanor. Edison vainly tried to convince her that it wasn't a good time for her to come to D.C., but Asia would have none of that. Even though he was saying and doing the right things, he really hoped she would come and help him console her mother. Two hours later she was on the Metroliner, bound for Union Station.

On the way to pick Asia up at the train station, Edison's thoughts returned to the night of the accident. He felt ashamed that he'd allowed himself to forget Manny's basketball game. Further there was an overwhelming sense of guilt..... at the lewdness of his evening with Camille and Antigua. *"How could this happen.... to me?"* he wondered silently. It also bothered him that he hadn't heard a word from Camille since; in fact the entire evening had such a mysterious quality about it.... he really didn't know what to make of the whole thing.

But what troubled Edison the most was his realization that his son was lying in a hospital, possibly near death, and he had really missed Manny growing up. There was an empty feeling in the pit of his stomach; the truth was that he had not developed any sort of real relationship with his own son. Perhaps if he had.... this whole thing might never have happened. Certainly, that was what Deidre believed, even though it had never been voiced. Edison tried mightily to fight off the overwhelming sense.... that he'd betrayed his family; that somehow he had sold his soul. In the midst of such musings, he suddenly started to laugh. In wasn't a hardy or raucous laughter though. It was more of a hollow, cynical whimpering, as he realized that he was becoming acutely aware.... of his own conscience. Everyone knows a conscience is the last thing a good politician needs; presence, yes....... decisiveness, yes........ but a conscience?!? That could prove to be fatal to someone in his profession.

His spirits were buoyed when he saw his daughter descending the escalator in Union Station. Asia had grown up to be a radiant beauty, statuesque with good proportions, and a lovely smile. In addition, she'd inherited her father's strong-mindedness, having defied her parents wishes to return to Atlanta once she finished school at Rutgers. She was determined to pursue a career in drama, and after spending several years under the guidance of Garrett Johnson at Crossroads Theatre group in New Jersey, she packed up and moved to New York on her own. Being the practical woman of the nineties that she was, Asia found that her live-in involvement with the manager of the theatre where she worked part-time, was more a matter of prudent financial efficacy than real depth of emotion. If she were to be brutally honest with herself, Asia would have to acknowledge that it was nice to have those warm, thick male loins around to help her make it through those cold wintery nights.

At any rate, there was the unique joy Edison derived that only a father and a daughter share. Asia genuinely loved both her parents, but always held a special place in Edison's heart. And at that moment, she was exactly the hypodermic he needed.

The ride to the hospital took about thirty-five minutes. Downtown D.C. was bustling now, and in its winter finery the city looked more beautiful and festive than ever. There were even ice skaters out on the reflecting pool that stretched between the Washington Monument and the Lincoln Memorial. "You know, baby," Edison said earnestly, trying to establish some conversation, "I really love this city. It's so scenic." Asia wasn't in a very talkative mood, but to avoid being rude she did manage to grunt back her agreement with a barely discernible 'uh-huh'. That conversational high point reached, they made their way across the bridge and on to the hospital.

Only a hint of sunlight peeked through the soiled window shades into Manny's room. When Edison and Asia walked in, Deidre turned in grudging acknowledgment of their presence and looked back to her son. Manny had finally fallen to sleep after a

night of stirring and wrestling with his re-awakened consciousness. Deidre was understandably concerned that he'd relapsed
into a coma, but the sleepless nights at her son's side had also taken
a toll on her. Anger, bitterness, and the feelings of betrayal
clinging to her, were dulled by the numbing peacefulness that
comes from sheer physical exhaustion.

Asia walked up quietly, putting her arm around her mother
while speaking softly, "Why don't you let Daddy take you home...
so you can get some rest?" She gave Deidre a knowing look of
confidence that she could handle things until her mother rested a
bit. "I've already spoken to the nurses."

"It would be good to freshen up a bit," Deidre replied
hoarsely.

"Well... it's settled then," said Edison relieved. "I'll make
something for you to eat at the house." Deidre thought it a bit
charming that Edison would be so gracious as to offer to cook for
her. Lord knows, he never cooked when he was at home. She was
quite frustrated to think that he could be so nice..... at such a wrong
time.

"Please, Asia.... be careful with Manny. He's been through
a lot," Deidre said in a masterful understatement. She was trying
to cheer up, in spite of being drained by the emotions, the despair
of the past few days. "Here's your father's number at the
townhouse," Deidre said, instructing Asia to call her the moment
Manny awakened again. "Your brother may be disoriented when
he comes to. He's been through so much," she repeated herself.
Deidre looked dismayed at her son lying helpless in front of her,
and the disillusionment of the past was rekindled. Here she was,
an attractive, intelligent woman with a successful career and a
lovely home. But her marriage was a shambles, her family
disintegrating, and the one person she loved beyond anything else

was, now a needless victim of a tragedy none of them could stand, particularly at this point in their lives. *And Manny was such a good boy! Why him... why us.... why now?!?* The anguish overcame her again, suddenly, and the tears flooded her eyes as she broke down and wept bitterly.

Quickly, Edison gathered her up, and the two of them made their way downstairs to the car. Edison was careful not to take Route 123 through McLean and into Georgetown. That would take them right below the George Washington Parkway, not far from the scene of the accident. Instead he took Route 66 across the river, onto Constitution Avenue and back through downtown. Once at his townhouse Edison drew a warm bath for Deidre. At first she was hesitant, but his continued insistence dispelled any suspicions she held, and she allowed herself to relax enough to enjoy the tub.

True to his word, Edison made his way into the kitchen to prepare an early supper for his wife. When he returned, he found Deidre passed out, sleeping like a baby in the warm scented water. He decided not to bother her and went to the den to turn on something soothing by Mozart, which he knew she enjoyed. The sound cascaded softly into the sprawling bathroom. The piped-in music had an unusually sensuous quality, and prompted Edison to recall several of his more successful conquests. He couldn't help but reflect on how those seductions ended up with him and his guest sharing his ample bathtub, champagne glasses in hand.

Ironically, he knew the woman that excited him most, this Camille, would never fall for such lame chicanery. It wasn't just idle frustration Edison felt.... standing there among his memories. On the contrary, Camille had shown him what seduction was **all** about.... that fateful night of Manny's accident. On top of everything else he was experiencing, he felt awkward just thinking about how preoccupied he was with his erotic recollections, given the seriousness of the circumstances. He felt even more awkward when he realized that a very beautiful woman, his wife, reposed stark naked before him.... and he wasn't the least bit aroused. 'What's **wrong** with me?' he wondered aloud.

Edison didn't have long to consider his query. Returning downstairs, he happened to pick up a day old Washington Post. There, on the front page in the lower right corner, was the pronouncement: **'Basketball Star Son of Georgia Senator in Fatal Car Crash.'** Edison's heart sank. He had hoped to keep this out of the news until they could determine the extent of Manny's injuries.... and he could get him back to Atlanta. Now it was too late. The media would be all over him, asking questions he wasn't in the proper frame of mind to answer. More importantly, he wasn't sure what Deidre might say, given her condition. That was the last thing he needed at this point.... his wife saying something that could cause more trouble for him. He certainly didn't need any more publicity.

A day earlier, that same Washington Post story caught the attention of Camille in her office downtown. She wondered why she hadn't heard anything from Edison since the videotape was delivered, almost a week ago. Now things were beginning to fall into place. As she began to take stock of the situation that had been created for Edison, Camille had some misgivings about her vengeance campaign. The scorn and anger she felt for him was migrating itself to a mood of benign contempt.... of indifference. Although she really believed the man was pathetic, she actually found herself feeling quite sorry for him. At the same time, she could kick herself for ever having gotten involved with someone like Edison. She should have known better.... since her days with the good Mayor Lowery. In any case, she decided she wasn't going to follow through with her threat to go public with the good Senator's latest indiscretion at Antigua's. He had enough on his hands at the moment. But Camille knew she would have nothing to do with Edison ever again...... **ever** again.

The doctors had just arrived when Manny awakened. Immediately, Asia came to his bedside to encourage her brother. "How are you feeling, little brother?" she inquired cheerfully. Manny needed a few minutes to orient himself, as the last time he was conscious he'd seen Deidre there in his room.

"Where's Mom?" he asked semi-consciously.

"She went over to Dad's townhouse to rest and freshen up a bit. She's been awake for most of the past three nights you know, Manny." Asia's words provided a semblance of perspective for Manny. It was obvious now that he'd been mostly unconscious for the better part of three days, at least, but with every passing moment his sensory recognition improved. Manny asked Asia to crank up his bed so he could see everyone clearly.

"Well, young man," said Doctor Lewis, "it's good to see you up and awake. How do you feel?"

Manny felt terrible. His head ached, and his back was so sore. And he was hungry. "Well Doctor, I feel pretty bad. But the worst thing is...... I'm starved. Do you have anything to eat?" he asked earnestly.

The doctor got a hearty laugh out of Manny's statement. "That's a good sign that you are on the way to recovering.... a healthy appetite. I'll have the nurse bring you a menu." Looking over to Asia, he inquired as to the whereabouts of Mrs. Castle.

Asia quickly explained that her mother had gone to her father's residence for a brief rest. "I was about to call her," Asia said, indicating that she was under instruction to do so the moment Manny awoke.

"That would be a good idea," Doctor Lewis told her. "Manny, this is Doctor Robeson, our staff neurologist. I'd like him to run some tests on you but I'll make sure you get something to eat first. And I think we can get rid of some of these tubes now. How does that sound?"

"Sounds great to me, Doc," Manny mumbled in approval. He felt relieved to know they were removing the drainage tubes from his throat so he could speak and breathe normally again. "Could I also get a back massage?" he asked jokingly, citing the fact that his back throbbed with pain. Even though he had trouble putting up with the discomfort, and the hunger, Manny soon became aware that he didn't notice any pain in his lower body. In fact, he realized that he had no feeling whatsoever in his legs. Alarmed, he tried to move his legs, his feet, his toes..... nothing. "Asia.... Asia..... what's wrong with me?" he screamed in desperation. "I can't move... my legs!"

Quickly, the neurologist stepped in before his terror caused Manny to be restrained. "Calm down, son. Let's not get alarmed just yet. The numbness you feel could simply be a traumatized effect of the accident you've been through. It's really too early to tell. I'm requesting some blood samples and a series of X-rays to see if there's anything more serious. Right now, eat and I'll be back to see you in a few hours."

Though outwardly he had quieted down, Manny's mind raced away in panic. While he heard what the neurologist said, he knew there was something more to this than he dared to think about. Manny had never felt so helpless before. What was he going to do? Just a week ago his life was all ahead of him. And now...... and now..... what? Slumping back against his pillow, he cried bitterly.

Two days later, Doctor Lewis ushered Deidre, Edison and Asia into his office. The neurologist's tests were completed. "Ms. Castle," he began, "your son has suffered severe internal lacerations of the lumbar nerves in his lower back. Additionally, two of the discs in his spine have been severely damaged."

"He's been doing fine these past few days, hasn't he Doctor?" Deidre had a look of impending disaster on her face.

"Yes.... you're right Ms. Castle, Manny has been improving very nicely since coming out of his coma," Doctor Robeson interjected. "But that's not what we're actually referring to."

"Well, what **are** you talking about?" Asia wanted to know, the tone of impatience quite obvious in her voice.

"Ms. Castle.... I'm afraid your son is paralyzed from the waist down," said Doctor Lewis. "Frankly, given what he's been through, he's very fortunate to be alive. But based on what Doctor Robeson and his colleagues can tell, he'll be a paraplegic for the rest of his life."

The resounding silence was deafening in the room. A sort of group shock descended on the three of them like a dense fog. Manny had always been so... so.... healthy. Other than some childhood diseases, nothing like this had ever befallen him. No broken bones, no major injuries.... nothing! But now this! Deidre was so concerned with his recovery that it had never occurred to her anything like this was even a remote possibility. She could only close her head in her hands, as Edison tried vainly to comfort her. "Take your hands off me," she said to him discretely, not desiring that her distaste for her husband become so apparent in front of the physicians.

Doctor Robeson finally spoke up. "I know this is hard for you... for all of you... to deal with. But both Doctor Lewis and myself did not want to keep anything hidden concerning your son's condition. And believe us, this is not the end of the world for him. There are over twenty seven million handicapped people in this country, most of whom are active, vibrant individuals and make a tremendous contribution to the quality of life in America. There is no reason why Manny can't resume a rewarding, functional life. He seems like a nice young man, with a lot to offer. He needs you.... all of you to help him see the opportunities that lie ahead. I'm not suggesting that any of this will be easy going forward. But by pulling together, you **can** overcome this...... hindrance."

'I've put together a list of physical therapists and other specialists in Atlanta that you may want Manny to consult with. Some of the best people in this field in the country, are at the Shepherd Spinal Centre. Please tell them I referred you. Also, let me suggest you look into a specific type of wheelchair that's been prototyped there. It has a series of electrodes and tension rollers that continuously massage the legs, to help maintain muscle tone and lessen deterioration of muscle tissue."

Doctor Lewis picked up the discussion. "I can only echo Doctor's Robeson's sentiments. We all wish these sort of things would not happen. But truthfully, it's not the end of the world. Life can go on... for all of you. And other than his handicap, Manny is a healthy young man."

Pointedly, Asia very succinctly summed up everyone's feelings. "When everything else is said and done," she said, "all my brother wanted to do..... was to be a basketball player. And he was a damn good one too." Edison went to his daughter's side as the tears began to flow. "How is he ever going to reconcile all this? How can he give up something ..... he's always loved?" The words hung there, and as Edison looked over toward Deidre, his guilt at not picking Manny up that night resurfaced. It was a burden he knew he couldn't escape, a burden he'd have to carry.... for a long, long time.

Lance was getting very nervous about the package that arrived for the Senator from Camille. It had been more than a week, and he knew Edison would return to the office soon, even if it were just to gather some things for his trip to Atlanta. Lance was concerned because he didn't know **what** was in that package. *Perhaps Camille had discovered the elaborate ruse Lance concocted during the election. Was this evidence she planned to use against him.... with Edison? Maybe she'd already told Edison, and that's why he hadn't called Lance for days.*

The more he thought about it, the more his mind ran away with him. Lance considered taking the package home and privately seeing what was inside. He could then explain to the Senator that he'd opened it by mistake, once he knew what it contained. It then occurred to him that maybe she'd planted a bomb inside, triggered to explode the moment it was tampered with. The idea of being blown to bits.... made him wary of messing with it at all. He even considered having one of the Secret Service agents assigned to the building take it to their lab for testing.

Finally, he decided he had to know what was in that brown paper wrapping. He couldn't risk his career by allowing Camille to turn him in to the Senator. After all, he'd worked too hard.... for too many years... to have his reputation... crippled.... by one of these Washington mistresses. Picking up the parcel, he told the receptionist he had to leave early, and promptly departed from the office.

Once at home, Lance stared for a long time at the package that was sitting on his coffee table. The bomb threat idea had returned, and he wasn't sure what to do about it now. It would be much too awkward to try the Secret Service angle at this point, since he'd already left the premises. Still he wasn't real anxious to end up splattered all over his neatly decorated living room walls. Pouring himself a large snifter of brandy and filling his nostrils with cocaine, a newfound macho streak surfaced and he made up his mind..... that he was gonna' go for it.

Recalling a scene from one of his favorite films, he decided to proceed with extreme caution. Taking a pair of scissors, he meticulously cut through the tape that secured each end of the package. Once this first step was completed, he constructed a makeshift barricade pieced together from an ironing board and two wing chairs placed at right angles to one another. Rather than pulling or cutting open the top of package, he took a set of fireplace pincers and carefully grasped one end of the paper wrapping. With his free hand, he used one of the pokers from the fireplace to push the contents out of the open end of the wrapping. Opening his eyes, (and realizing there was no explosion) he discovered a videotape with a small note attached. It read: "To my darling Edison.... how do you think **this** will look on 'News at 11:00'?"

'Well... let's see,' Lance said to no one in particular while he popped the tape into his VCR. As the risque sexual drama unfolded, Lance could only watch in stunned disbelief. 'WOW! Look at that woman!' he exclaimed, noting Antigua's obvious talents and the robust manner in which she went about her night's work. After about two minutes of this, Lance found himself sitting there with his own penis throbbing, wishing he could dive into the film himself. Of course, his brandy cocktails didn't do much to sedate his prominent male organ. On the contrary, Lance searched for a way that would enable him to get the most out of his viewing pleasure. He momentarily thought of calling a female acquaintance over to join him. After all, this was much better than some of the porn tapes he'd paid for. Then he quickly realized that this wasn't for public screening. Suddenly, he broke out in a hideous laughter, at himself as well as Edison. 'Well, this wasn't quite the type of bomb I had in mind,' he remarked to himself, but it's certainly some explosive stuff... nitroglycerin... as far as the Senator is concerned.

As the end of the tape approached, a voice-over with Camille's sultry baritone arose. "My darling, Edison. I trust that you never develop the deadly effects of AIDS, and it appears as though you have taken appropriate steps to prevent that from happening. I don't suppose you felt I was worthy of confiding in.... about any of this. Nor do you seem to have any regard for MY health or well being. I honestly can't believe you would be so inconsiderate, so foolish. I mean people treat their pets better than that. But then again, I should have realized a long time ago... that you are what you seemed to be.... a spineless mongrel! I want you to know that I, at least, take my own life very seriously, and from this point forward I intend to take control of my own destiny. Listen to me, Edison... and listen well. If you ever try to contact me.... if you ever attempt to meddle in my life again..... I will send this tape to the TV reporters. Think what that will do to your reputation in this town! Au revoir.... mon cher!"

Shocked, Lance dropped his gold plated brandy snifter which smashed to pieces on the hardwood floor. It was beginning to dawn on him what a destructive response his little Xenium project had wrought! If this show ever hit the news, that would be all she wrote for the good Senator... and for Lance Powell! At the same time, he was also glad that he had decided to open the package before Edison saw it. He knew he had to destroy the tape, right away. But he also had to make certain Edison didn't bother Camille... and cause her to release the video.

How would he be able to keep the Senator away from her? Lance knew how strongly Edison felt about Camille. And he really didn't mind, except that now he'd gotten himself into a good mess, trying to do what he thought was the right thing.... helping Edison win the election. (And position himself for bigger and better things.) *Maybe he could have her killed?* Although seriously contemplating the idea, he summarily dismissed the thought. If, for some reason, that approach was unsuccessful, he reasoned, she'd be certain to head straight to the media. *What in the world was he going to do?*

As he pondered his next move, Lance noticed the time and date stamp on the video as it ended. Oh my GOD! he exclaimed when he realized that the production he'd just watched, took place on the same night....... as Manny's accident! *No wonder he wanted me to cover for him*, he thought, remembering Edison's instruction the night he drove him to the hospital. It occurred to Lance that the Senator, whom he admired, did seem to have a certain unerring knack for managing to get himself into some pretty awkward circumstances. But even for someone of his proclivity for disaster, this one was a real doozy! Even as that thought passed through his mind, Lance's attention quickly returned to how he would cover his OWN ass, given this mess. No matter what else happened, he had to be sure no one connected him with the Xenium fraud. Searching his mind for an angle that would divert attention away from himself, a small brainstorm began to emerge.

Wait a minute, he thought. *Maybe there's a silver lining in this cloud. Edison won't make a big deal of this whole thing..... not until after his son has recovered. He wouldn't want to draw any more attention to his whereabouts that night.* Rolling these issues over in his mind, Lance's confidence began to return. Maybe..... just maybe all Lance had to do was act as though.... nothing had happened, beyond the misfortune of the Senator's son, and continue to slide subtle reminders Edison's way about the mystery surrounding his whereabouts that night. *That ought to keep the old boy away from Camille's door... for a long time to come,* he thought with a gleeful smirk.

Satisfied that circumstances were beginning to take care of themselves, he pulled out his ever present vial of narcotic..... and activated the rewind button on his VCR. Playing back Camille's little epithetic postscript on the video, Lance felt a perverse sense of satisfaction at how completely convinced she obviously was, that Edison had the HIV virus. It was a strange sense of power he was feeling; power at his ability to very subtly, but very directly cause such disruption to Camille's life. Of course, in the process he'd exposed his own boss. But that couldn't blanch the exhilaration, the rush.... of his moment of mastery. His moment of power! Filling his nose with cocaine once more, Lance decided to watch the whole tape again, this time paying more attention to the details. Even though he empathized with the predicament Edison was in, Lance nonetheless was very proud of his boss.... for the way he pounded the pussy that night, screwing his brains out... as hard as he could! *Wish I could have been there, Senator.* With that, he gulped down another shot of brandy, getting quite comfortable as Camille's show rolled on.

From a purely physical standpoint, Manny's recovery progressed quickly. Three days after the interview in Dr. Lewis' office, he and his parents headed back to Atlanta. Manny didn't say much during the flight. He wasn't sure how he would adjust to his handicap. But more on his mind at the moment was Asia. She had been unusually comforting during the several days she was at the hospital. Unfortunately, she had to return to New York and couldn't accompany them back to Atlanta. He would much rather have her around.... than his mother and father right now. It was clear that their tolerance level for one another was minimal, at best, and now that he was conscious, Manny realized how awkward he felt in their company. He was saddened... as he began to recognize, sitting there on the Omega flight to Atlanta.... the disintegration his family had undergone over the years.

Before it had always been something that was there, but was always.... at least for him... below the surface. He had his friends, he had school, he had basketball. But now, given this cruel quirk of fate, Manny was forced to confront, as they were, the fact that each of them maintained an enormous depth of total *non-relationship* to one another. And Manny felt such anguish, he felt so sorry for them.... knowing that because of him, because of what happened..... his parents could no longer avoid coming to grips with themselves..... and their fragmented relationship!

Edison was determined to act like the head of his household, at least for the next few weeks. But this proved to be very difficult for a man who had been an absentee parent, much less someone who had virtually deferred the management of his homestead to his wife for so many years, to suddenly domesticate. He tried his hand at cleaning and fixing up around the house. He even went as far as to buy himself a completely new set of tools, and attempted to do some plumbing. Truthfully, he managed to do a respectable job, given that he simply wasn't the handyman type. But nothing he did moved Deidre very much.

She was preoccupied with caring for her son; at this point, the only person she cared anything about, including herself. She made plans to renovate the house to accommodate his handicap. The biggest change was the installation of a lift to enable him to move up and down. Unfortunately, in order to accomplish the task, their stately winding staircase had to be removed and replaced by an awkward modified ramp, which clashed dramatically with the graceful oval foyer into which it intruded. Surprisingly, Deidre didn't seem to care at all. Normally so meticulous and discriminating about her home, her appearance, her social status; none of this seemed to matter anymore. She was diligent in getting Manny to his therapy sessions at Shepard, and massaged his legs every day, as recommended by the specialists.

So absorbed by her son's well being, she neglected to pay attention to the many day to day things, like opening the mail. Finally, one day she took the time to go through the bundle of correspondence and bills that had accumulated over the past month. As she opened one piece of junk mail after another, interspersed with holiday greetings for clients and acquaintances, she came across a letter from Gloria. Immediately, Deidre brightened up. With all that had taken place in her life the past few weeks, she'd completely forgotten about Gloria. Although their schedules didn't permit it, the two always managed to get together for the holidays.

Opening the envelope, she discovered an invitation Gloria had sent for a New Year's party, (which of course had passed by then). The interesting thing was that Gloria, in her note to Deidre, mentioned that she was planning to get married. 'Ms. Castle, you remember Hilliard. He's the one that came to town many years ago.... my beau from Trinidad. Well, we're going to be married this summer. I hope you and Mr. Castle can make it. I'm so happy! Please come to my party if you can. We're leaving for a three week cruise after New Year's. I miss you. Love, Gloria.'

Deidre felt the same sentiments herself. Though she had several pretty close friends in town, Gloria had become like a sister to her over the years. Whenever she needed a confidant about things that really concerned her, she could talk to Gloria. And Deidre wished she could talk to her now. But at the same time, she didn't want to ruin the joy Gloria was experiencing. Before things became so busy, the little moments they spent together seemed to be just that, insignificant. But now, she really missed those times of sharing, of letting their hair down. Deidre remembered the time, one summer evening at Gloria's over slush, that she told her about Sam Case.

Gloria had asked Deidre how and why she and Edison had ever gotten together. *'I met Sam following a sorority rush on campus,'* Deidre related. *'I was pretty isolated most of my freshman year at Spelman... I didn't really know where I fit in. I got along well enough with most of the girls, but I still was pretty much of a loner. One of the Deltas finally convinced me to get involved, so I went to a meeting. Afterward, we were eating some ice cream in a shop on Fair Street. Sam was there. He seemed pretty popular, as several of the older sisters knew him. He was a sophomore at Morehouse, and at the time I didn't know it, but he was best friends with Edison. Sam was kind of tall and well built, but not disarmingly handsome. He just seemed to be in control of himself, and I liked that.'*

'About two weeks later, I ran into him again at the library. He explained that he was taking a class at Spelman, and we just started to get to know one another from then on. Before the semester break, he introduced me to Edison. I knew the two of them were close, as Sam would mention him a lot when we were together. Nothing very exciting happened until the following semester. We had corresponded a bit that summer, and I was anxious to see him when we got back to school. One evening we were at a little secluded park in midtown. One thing led to another, and we ended up making love on the grass in a small woods. It was so wonderful. I wasn't a virgin at that point or anything, but Sam was so..... powerful, yet he was gentle. He just felt so good... inside me. Well after that, I was pretty much hooked. We spent most of our free time over the next six months in bed. All I wanted to do was screw that man! When he was around, I felt secure. At the same time, I got to know Edison pretty well, as he would keep me informed on Sam's state of mind. I liked Edison well enough. He always knew that he would go into politics, and I guess that was one thing that really impressed me about him.... he knew exactly what he wanted to do, when most of us weren't certain which way was up regarding a career.'

'Sam made extra money by occasionally playing the saxophone with a group that performed at the Underground. At first, I would go see him play every weekend. He was very good. But I couldn't stand the women flirting with him, so eventually I stopped going. At the same time, he was paying more and more attention to the music, and less and less to his studies, which really bothered me. We would get into fights over it, and I'd accuse him of all sorts of things. But I couldn't stay away from him. I loved the man. I often thought of trying to make Sam jealous by coming on to Edison. But Edison, even though I know he wanted me, valued his friendship with Sam more than he did spending the night with me. That's something else I admired him for.'

'As fate would have it, I turned up pregnant. Lord knows, I didn't know what to do. I wasn't sure how to tell Sam, and whether or not I should tell my parents, or what to do. Several of my girlfriends advised me to get rid of the baby, but I knew I should let Sam know.... before anything else. I didn't know what to do, where to go. Fortunately, I could talk to Edison. He told me that I should absolutely tell Sam, that he knew above all else that Sam would do the right thing. Finally, I got the courage up to talk to him. At first, he was quiet. Then he got angry.... that I had waited so long to tell him. He said he needed a few days to get his head together. I didn't see or hear from him for almost a week. At last he called, and we had dinner together.'

'Sam told me that he decided he was going to quit school and make a career out of the music, to support me and the baby. I hit the ceiling! I called him a fool for not finishing college. He only had a little over a year left to get his degree, but he was ready to throw that away... because I was pregnant. Besides, I didn't want some hand to mouth existence..... from some small time musician's salary when he could be a lawyer. It got ugly, and I *ended up cursing him out, and told him I was going to have an abortion.'*

    'He called me all night long, said he needed to see me, that we needed to try and work things out. I refused. The next morning, I found out that he was in a fatal car accident on MLK near I-20. The shock of the whole thing caused Edison and I to draw closer over the next few months. Before the baby came, we were married. I guess subconsciously, I held Sam's death against Asia, all these years. And I was the one to blame.... not her.'

    She remembered how bitterly she cried in Gloria's arms that day. All these years, Deidre wished she could take back the words, she'd wished that God would give her Sam back! The memories brought a fresh flow of tears to her eyes. This time, Gloria wasn't around..... and now she suffered from not only the depression of a broken marriage but her son's calamity as well. Ironically, because of the loss of Sam so many years before, Deidre stuck doggedly to a marriage that had long since lost its fervor. And she desperately wanted the material benefits of the life-style Edison could provide. Until now.

    Sadly, the circumstances and her state of mind had literally driven her to drink. She had always enjoyed a good glass of wine, and loved the slush that Gloria would whip up in the summertime. But now, she was hitting the bottle more often, and quite hard. She had taken a liking to brandy; it seemed to make her relax very quickly, and removed her inhibitions. Soon, that was her late afternoon ritual, two glasses of brandy and a cigarette. Interestingly, in her liquor induced frame of mind, Deidre was much more sultry and voluptuous. She was determined to show Edison what he'd missed all these years from her sexually. She became a wild woman in bed, alternately teasing him, then indulging every passionate whim she could conceive on him. But she wouldn't talk to him, other than to express that she was ready for sex. It was so shocking to Edison, he didn't quite know what to do. But it worked. Even though they didn't have any sort of relationship outside the bedroom, they suddenly discovered how passionate they could be together.

During this time Manny did an admirable job of adjusting to the situation. He went to Shepard three days a week for therapy. He took a job after school at the library. His classmates held a welcome back luncheon for him. And he worked hard to concentrate on his studies, now that his basketball career was obviously a part of the past. Outwardly, he was dealing with things very well. In truth, he was OK in the company of others. But alone at night, his private demons would surface with a vengeance.

One of the worst feelings any young man can have is that of sexual inadequacy. And Manny, now fully recovered except for the paralysis, had trouble coming to grips with the thought of not being able to make love, of being unable to father any children. Often, he would sit crying on the edge of his bed, desperately masturbating in vain, trying to massage himself into erection. And while most of his friends understood what had happened to him, it was hard for Manny himself to accept the cruelty of this fate. Even though his equipment wasn't working, the hormones that drove his male desires were still heightened. This was a strange sort of madness he suffered from.

Even more frightening was what occurred when Manny was finally able to drift off to sleep. Night after night, he couldn't escape the recurrence of the nightmare, the vision of Sandra falling to her death. Just as she would scream his name in desperation, the sound would dissipate and the scene would begin all over again. Again and again, Manny watched this tragic scenario in his sleep..... until at last he would wake up with his heart pounding, chest heaving, drenched in a cold sweat.... from the terror of memories too vivid to hide. Such agonizing filled Manny's nights with a macabre palette of forms, colors, and destructive emotions. Still, he might have overcome such internal struggles, were it not for two events that occurred in rapid succession.

One particularly messy February day Manny didn't feel like bothering with school, so he convinced his mother to let him stay home. He had some reading he wanted to finish, and frankly he hadn't gotten much sleep the night before (as a result of his dreaming). Edison returned to Washington several days prior, so Deidre was very hesitant to leave him alone. But she needed to get to the office and contact some of her key clients she had neglected over the past two months. Manny assured her that he would be quite fine by himself.

Not an hour after his mother departed, the doorbell rang. Although Manny had difficulty recognizing him, it was Haskell. It was raining outside, not storming, but a steady, light rain so characteristic of winter in Atlanta. Obviously Haskell had been out in the weather for some time, as he was fairly soaked from head to toe. Manny hadn't seen or heard from him since that fateful night. He'd often thought about Has, but it was so hard for Manny to bring himself to contact him.

"Can I come in Manny?" Haskell asked meekly.

"Sure Has... make yourself at home." Interestingly, Manny didn't offer him a towel or anything to dry off. Entering tentatively, he followed Manny into the kitchen where he was making himself something to eat. "Do you want some breakfast Haskell?" he offered, trying to remain casual despite the obvious tension in the air.

"No.... no thanks. You know... it sure is quiet in here. Can you put on some music?"

"No Has.... I like the silence. It let's me think.... about things. Do you know how that is, Haskell? Just to have time and quiet to think...... and remember?" Manny noticed how disheveled and aimless Haskell looked, although he was completely recovered from the injuries he suffered.

"Manny.... why didn't you call me?" Haskell suddenly blurted out. "I tried to contact you a few times, but you didn't respond. I know how hard this is for you, but it's even harder for me. I lie awake at night. I can't do anything. You know, years ago when we were younger, even though I wouldn't let on, I always respected you. You seemed to have this kind of inner strength.... and courage. And you were happy with yourself. I thought I knew what I was doing Manny, but I didn't... and I'm so sorry about that. I've been watching you come and go for the past few weeks, trying to get your attention. When I saw your mother leaving without you today, I knew this was my chance."

Manny wondered when Haskell had tried to contact him. He certainly didn't recall any messages that were left him. He could sense the rage and bitterness he felt for Haskell mounting, but he wanted to control himself, he wanted to keep from letting it go. It was strange but those sentiments, negative though they were, kept him going day to day..... kept him energized.... and as such were a life giving agent in his psyche. "What do you mean, this was your chance? Your chance for *what*?"

"To make peace with you Manny. To plead for forgiveness. I'm so responsible for this. But you've got to let me...... have my life back! Please Manny, I don't know what to do!"

It momentarily occurred to Manny that Haskell was losing his mind. But the words he used, they were enough to make Manny snap. "What the hell do you mean.... give YOU your life back? Look at me Haskell..... look at me! Does it look like I'm having a ball here.... like I'm having FUN.... as a paraplegic? Huh Haskell.... HUH!??!" He was shouting at the top of his lungs now. "Do you know what it's like.... struggling to do things that have always come so easily, things that were second nature before? Do you have any idea how it feels to see your friends looking at you.... as though you're some sort of FREAK? And to see the look of pity in their eyes. How would you like to feel dependent on everyone around you, to help you get dressed, to open doors for you, to be treated as something..... less than a viable human being? And how would you like to be around women Haskell, attractive young women who treat me very nice, who are real courteous because I'm in a wheelchair. But none of them really wants to talk to me... to socialize... to know me. Do you know why? They don't want anything to do with me..... because I'm PARALYZED Haskell.... because my DICK won't even get hard! How do you think it feels..... to be a social outcast? And you've got the nerve to ask me for YOUR life back. What about my life Haskell? What about the scholarships, and the basketball? What about MY damn life! I'm sorry.... but I've got nothing to offer you. I think it's the other way around. You owe me..... big time! But you'll never be able to repay!"

The passion and energy flooded out of him; the words, like razor sharp pincers, ripped his emotional flesh apart. It was all he could do to keep from flinging the pewter cookware right through the kitchen window. Manny's anger was tempered by what happened next. Haskell just broke down in tears, pleading with him. "Manny.... I'm so sorry. I love you. Please forgive me..... please, please forgive me!" He buried his head in Manny's lap, crying uncontrollably. As his furor subsided, Manny noticed he felt strangely lifeless.... as though all of his energy were draining away. Haskell just wept pathetically, kneeled in front of Manny's wheelchair, groping for the psychological resurrection.... that would restore his sanity.

Several days later, Manny was returning from a visit to his therapist. She had agreed to give him a ride home, which made things a bit easier on Deidre. When he arrived home, he found his mother and an older man sharing a cup of coffee. He quickly dismissed it as one of her clients or professional colleagues. He was quite well dressed, slightly overweight with silver gray hair that was rapidly retreating from his forehead. Before he could make his way upstairs, Deidre stopped him to introduce the gentleman.

"Manny, this is Mr. Whetstone. He is Sandra's father. He came to talk to you."

With great difficulty, Manny had told his mother what happened the night of the accident, and about Sandra. Mercifully, Deidre kept away from all further reference to the events of that night. But now, his worst anticipations..... were looking right at him.

"Son, I realize this is a difficult situation for you," he said. "I've read all the police reports, seen the documentation.... but I must know what really happened to Sandra. Please understand Manny.... I need your help!"

Manny felt uncomfortable to say the least, about reliving the circumstances of the accident. But he thought that perhaps by telling him what had transpired..... he might absolve himself of the mental torment he endured, night after night. Besides, he felt that it was the least he could do, given that he was the last person to see her alive. Deidre ushered them into Edison's office and shut the door, so that they could be alone. She immediately repaired to her liquor cabinet and a healthy glass of brandy.

Slowly, painfully, Manny played back the events of that night leading up to the crash. He told of the basketball tournament, and how he was scheduled to meet his father, and running into Haskell..... and Sandra. Throughout the description, Mr. Whetstone listened attentively, allowing Manny to pause at difficult recollections of the night. When at last, Manny arrived at the scene where they were thrown from the wreckage, her father began to crack. Undaunted, Manny continued to explain how Sandra died, and about how he lost his momentary grip on her...... when the wrecked car fell on top of him.

As desperate as he felt with Haskell just days before, Manny simply couldn't handle the emotion from Mr. Whetstone. Tears streamed down his face as the older gentleman broke down from the strain. "Oh my God...... my GOD," he repeated. "Why did this happen to my BABY? She was the only child I had! And such a GOOD girl. Why did he do this to me?" Staring directly at Manny, with an extreme look of distress on his face, he kept repeating "Why did you let her GO? Why couldn't you HOLD her? Why did you let..... her..... GO? Why......... did........ YOU?!?"

In Washington, circumstances were almost as stressful for Edison. Since he'd gotten back to work, his concentration was missing. He went absently through the motions of committee meetings, Senate hearings, and partisan fund raisers. His mind wandered often, and he had to be careful that he wasn't misquoted in meetings with the press. In short, his life was not the same, and the brashness and arrogance he once could turn on and off at will had disappeared.

In an effort to protect himself (and the Senator), Lance had taken the precautionary measure of forging an alleged note from Camille, explaining to Edison that she was, basically, dumping him. 'After too many years,' it said, 'of suffering the indignations of.... playing second fiddle... I've had all I can take,' and never wanted to see him again. Surprisingly however, it wasn't nearly the shock to Edison Lance expected it would be, and he knew something else was amiss with the Senator.

What he didn't know was that Edison, privately, was starting to question his own motivations, and wonder if everything he'd worked so hard for..... for so many years to achieve.... the things he thought he believed in.... were really worth it. His beloved Washington.... the Hill, the townhouse in Georgetown, all the publicity and notoriety..... the American political process.... what did it all mean? He'd entered this arena with an idealistic gleam in his eye..... with an attraction to the alleged power of public office. Sadly, he was finally beginning to realize that he'd missed his family life.... that he'd exchanged a real life.... for the pale glitter..... of a caricature of life in politics. And in the process, he was gaining an understanding of the fact that his individuality, his true identity, had been lost in the process. He wondered silently if, all these years, he'd been enslaved by a misconception, a distorted understanding....of what was really important. At long last, perhaps too late, Edison was starting to grow up.

His deepest realization was that the years he'd spent indulging his extraneous sexual tastes were misspent; he had no relationship with his wife, and the woman with whom he had been so infatuated..... hated him with complete and utter passion. And worst of all, the time he spent at home.... with a wife that emotionally rejected him, served only to make him aware that after all they been through, after all he'd done...... that he was still in love..... with Deidre! The fear that immobilized him with such uncertainty.... was the knowledge that she might be totally incapable.... of ever loving him again.

Following the trauma of his meeting with Sandra's father, Manny grew ever more despondent daily. He withdrew from everything; he stopped attending therapy; he didn't go to school. Most days, he just sat, staring absently out the windows, not communicating, not eating, just staring. As the days wore on, Deidre drank more and more, attempting to wash the visage of her son's disillusionment out of her mind. Eventually, Manny found himself thinking....... that he really had nothing to live for. With every day that passed, he found it easier to more clearly rationalize how someone could actually do away... with their own life! Occasionally he would make comments around his mother that hinted of his intentions. Soon, he came around to believe that it was his only remedy.... for the pain he felt, for the hurt he'd caused everyone.... for the despair in which he was trapped.

One day, he wandered out of the house and around to the yard. Moving aimlessly, he soon found himself at the servants' quarters where Enrico had lived. Since Enrico passed away, nothing much had been done inside, and cobwebs grew thick in the sparsely furnished little bungalow. The melancholy of the place fit perfectly with his self-destructive frame of mind. Browsing through empty drawers of an old rolltop desk, he opened one of the lower compartments. Startled, he at first didn't believe his eyes. But sure enough..... there it was, a pearl handled .45 automatic handgun! It was as if that gun had been waiting there for him..... in anticipation of a moment like this.

He could tell the pistol hadn't been fired in a long, long time, but upon visual inspection it appeared to be in good shape. There was even a full round of ammunition in the clip. It made Manny wonder if Enrico had been expecting some sort of trouble. At first, the discovery frightened him. He wasn't used to guns. But day after day, he returned to the servants' quarters, and contemplated how he would carry out the deed. After all, he had nothing to live for.... he was such a burden to his mother, and himself. It was the only logical choice for him to make.

Deidre, at wit's end, couldn't decide what to do. She was afraid to leave Manny alone, but she also had to attend to her practice, which was suffering from her recently developed drinking habits. She interviewed several candidates for a position as a live-in house keeper, but Manny's growing depression scared off her best choices, and she was frankly concerned that the other people she talked to would do more harm than good.

Miraculously one day, her doorbell rang. Deidre struggled to answer it, wrestling herself up from another private round of drinking. She was unkempt and downright sloppy looking, and tired from too little sleep the past few days. Opening the door she was shocked at first, then thrilled.... to see Gloria! Initially, Deidre didn't recognize her. She was stately and professional, in a charcoal grey wool suit and pumps. Gloria looked every bit the school administrator she was. On the other hand, Deidre hardly resembled the tough, successful legal mind she had once been. Mutually surprised at the sight of one another, the two friends nonetheless stood there in the doorway, sobbing and hugging one another. The sight of Gloria was such a welcome comfort for Deidre.

At the same time, out in the servant's quarters, Manny had finally settled the matter in his mind; he was ready to end his life! He picked up the automatic and examined it carefully. He noticed two long, thin cracks that ran the length of the pearl handle. The shaft of the barrel glistened in the twilight that peeked through the dingy windows. Manny held the weapon in his hands for a long time, slowly fondling the handle, then the barrel, and finally the trigger, so as to get the feel... to get to the essence..... of that gun. 'We need to blend together here,' he said directly to the .45. 'If you're to be my fate.... well, then we need to get to know one another.' Manny proceeded to recite all the reasons..... why he deserved the sentencing of this unceremonious execution he was about to administer.

Looking about the room as though he expected someone, Manny nervously took the barrel of the gun and placed it, horizontally, into his mouth. Biting down on the hard steel, the cold shaft filled his jaws. Slowly, carefully, he undid the safety, and fingered the trigger. Uncontrollably, he started shaking as beads of perspiration jerked from his brow. Closing his eyes, he said a silent good-bye, and deliberately began to..... squeeze the firing mechanism..... that would usher him into..... oblivion!

Inside the house, the two old friends were getting reac-quainted, albeit under far more dire circumstances than the last time they were together. Deidre recounted the events of the past few months for Gloria, and the horrific stress she now faced. Gloria, for her part, hadn't heard much about what had transpired. All she knew was that Deidre had been planning to spend the holidays in Washington, partially to see if there was any way she could rescue what was for all intents and purposes, a failed marriage. Particularly distressing to Gloria was the despair and abandonment Manny was experiencing, a victim of events and circumstances far beyond his control. Little did she dream of the tragedy about to unfold just yards away, the disposition of which..... was under Manny's complete control!

WAIT a minute! thought Manny, suddenly realizing he had one item of unfinished business remaining. He knew he needed to leave an appropriate suicide note! After all, it was the least he could do..... for his family. Momentarily laying aside his instrument of death, he groped around for a suitable piece of paper. Quickly Manny scribbled down his last living impressions of this world. Comfortable that he had now satisfied all the requirements of mortality, he again prepared for his untimely departure. Picking up the gun, he rolled himself over near one of the windows to get a last look at the house. Repeating his improvised ritual, he inserted the gun in his mouth... and again made ready to depart. Summoning up all his courage, he shut his eyes tight to fight back the tears. Glimpses of the past flashed before his mind's eye, and he felt the strange sensation of lightness, as though a tremendous burden had been lifted from his shoulders.

Just when he was at last ready.... to let it all go, his concentration was interrupted.... by a scratching noise in the nearby hall closet. Manny was so startled; he actually thought someone might be hiding inside. Immediately wheeling himself over there he snatched the door open, expecting to apprehend an unwanted intruder. Instead, a red squirrel trapped inside for several days and hungry, darted out from among some old boxes. Manny tried to laugh at his own alarm, at his imagination.... that someone would dare to eavesdrop on the scene of his suicide. However, the force with which he whipped open the closet door caused some items on a shelf above him to be unsettled. Glancing upward, he was taken by surprise when an old, tattered basketball dropped down..... landing right on his lap.

Slowly turning the ball over in his hands, he examined the worn signature engraved into the leather years ago. It read 'Emanuel Castle'; immediately he recognized that this was the 'magic' basketball...... his *uncle* had given to him years before! DEREK! He had forgotten all about Derek! Manny was still a kid when he last saw him.... but he quickly comprehended... he knew deep inside.... that in this, his severe moment of personal crisis.... Derek had made a provision for him; he was there, somehow, to show him the way out!

The excitement of discovery began to build, and crowded out the destructive impulses which just moments before had so dominated his psyche. 'Talk to me Uncle D,' Manny silently admonished. Rolling his chair outside, suicide gun still in hand, Manny headed for the outdoor basket not far away from the pool. The net had long since worn through, and the rim was bent and rusted, but Manny didn't care. Parking himself at the foul line he looked up at the goal, and he believed..... he absolutely knew..... what would happen when he shot that ball. The shot went up from his right hand with perfect rotation, and slipped right through the ring; had there been a net it would have made that pleasant swishing sound of the cords rippling as the basketball passed smoothly through. Tucking his pearl handle .45 safely away, Manny rolled around his childhood court, flipping up that old basketball, which couldn't bounce, at the distorted rim. Unerringly, magically, the results were the same.... he made every shot, the same way he'd done the day his uncle had given him the ball!

Suddenly, it was as if all his senses were hyperactive; Manny felt an alertness, a clarity, he hadn't experienced in a long, long time. He knew it had to be DEREK! He was speaking to his nephew now, in the language that could only be understood through the realm of the spirit! His uncle's words came rushing back to him, and his consciousness flooded with a comprehension..... that went well beyond the limitations of normal cognition.

Manny recalled how Derek had told him with perfect conviction years before ".... the words that I speak to you.... may not mean much now; you may be unable to recognize their significance. But there will come a time in your life..... when these lessons, this instruction of the spirit.... and the experience of culture.... will convey you safely past..... your point of no return!" The poignance of Derek's statement catapulted him into a vortex of revelations. All at once, it was as though there were a wellspring of understanding.... that smoldered from within him. Manny remembered the segmented pyramid Derek drew for him that night, long before. It suddenly became crystal clear... what his uncle had endeavored to explain.

'Comprehending the role that culture plays for us is crucial; culture is the vehicle that enables us to properly understand our history and our (collective) experiences; it defines our identity. We are Africans..... among the many that have been dispersed around the globe throughout history. Knowing who we are, and the power of our traditions is the key for us to validate the truth of our spiritual connectedness. Such knowledge empowers each of us..... to act *appropriately*..... to discipline ourselves..... in this world. The only responsible conduct for a man of culture....

for a spiritual man.... is to act with impeccability.... in the face of life's every challenge!'

Racing back inside the bungalow, Manny picked up a dusty bible lying on a shelf in the roll top desk. Thumbing through several pages, he suddenly closed the book and mouthed these words, 'God, I believe you're real; if you are, then reveal yourself to me.... in this Bible.' He re-opened it, and found himself at the Book of Deuteronomy. Manny read from chapter 30, verse 19:

'....I call heaven and earth as witnesses today against you, that I have set before you (this day) life and death, blessing and cursing; therefore choose life, that both you and your descendants may live....'

Inside the house, Deidre had spent most of the past two hours relating her torment and despair to Gloria, who had counseled with her, and laughed with her, and cried with her the whole time. The two were emotionally spent, and visibly drained. As such, several moments of complete silence ensued. Then they heard the gunshots; an initial blast, followed quickly by a second shot. It came from the back of the house. "MANNY!" Deidre shouted. Instantly, she sprang to her feet and rushed outside, fearing the worst, with Gloria in close pursuit.

The two women reached the servant's quarter's simultaneously. Barging in, Deidre could see from behind Manny slumped over in his wheelchair, the gun dangling from his hand. "My GOD...!!" she cried out in terror. Rushing to his side, Deidre shocked herself to discover........ that Manny.... WASN'T DEAD. He **hadn't** shot himself! He was simply crouched intently over his reading. "Oh my baby.... my darling baby!" Deidre exclaimed, hugging and kissing him all over the forehead. "We thought you were....... dead!"

Looking up, incredulous, from the Scriptures, Manny spoke softly. "Dead? Why would you think I was dead? On the contrary Mother, I'm very much alive. I'm alive...... in Jesus!" His words snapped them to an immediate and rapt attention. Deidre recognized in his eyes the warmth of compassion, and the eagerness for life..... that had been so absent..... for so long.

"You know," he continued, "Derek is right. Once you understand what this is about, what we are here for.... then all of our experiences, both good and bad, become meaningful. And there is no middle ground.... we either walk in the fullness of our birthright.... or we are really dead, already, just waiting for the passing of this material existence.'

"And the rich history of our people in this country.... is an ever-present example of the compelling power.... of our cultural interdependence. To have survived the inequity, the injustice, the genocide, the hatred, the dispersion..... and yet to perservere and go on. Do you know we owe such a tremendous debt to those who have gone before..... to those men and women of color..... who have made the opportunities for us.... which we so casually enjoy!"

He looked over, mystified, at the pistol in his hand. "And I offer to them such an enormous apology. I apologize for even considering....... that I had the right to take my own life! You know Mom, this life I hold really isn't just my own. Our lives are bound up with one another; that is the purest cultural lesson of our heritage! Our collective identity has nothing to do with how much we make, or what we do, which are the trappings of material living. The truth is we are all agents and caretakers.... of this sacred process called life. This is the essential cultural principle.... that defines us. And I apologize for allowing myself to think.... that I somehow (because of my misfortune) existed outside that mechanism."

The two women could only stand speechless, marvelling at the depth of insight coming forth from this young man. And the words touched them... with a power they couldn't describe. Calmly, Manny pointed the pistol at the ceiling and fired, adding a third hole to the two already there. "You know," he said with unsettling composure, "for me to have committed suicide.... for me to have done such a deed...... it simply wouldn't have been..... *appropriate*..... would it?"

Chapter 11

The Power Brokers

Dr. Haynes Thursday morning lecture series on International Business and Management was quite popular on the campus at Howard University. Offered as an elective in the graduate program of Management, the class was consistently over-enrolled the past three semesters. Despite such success, Professor Haynes had instituted a guest lecturer program, where various professionals from industry, marketing, finance, and management consulting held a series of lectures on a topic of particular relevance to the students. Far and away, the most popular talk to date in the visiting lecturer program was called 'Cultural Imperatives and the Global Marketplace'.

"Let me first take the opportunity.... to thank all of you who have stuck it out with me these past three weeks," the speaker began, eliciting a not so mild round of laughter from the standing room only audience. "Today I must conclude our discussions. However, before I address my main topic this morning, let me briefly review how we've gotten to where we are, both literally and figuratively. The idea of a global marketplace, which probably had its genesis some twenty-five years ago and was identified in earnest during the late '80s, has today firmly entrenched itself in the thinking of the astute business manager. And rightfully so. Key technological developments of this decade, most notably, the high speed global telecommunications infrastructure now available via your home telephone, have dramatically altered the nature of most basic business processes: distribution, marketing, promotion, merchandising, finance, accounting.'

'In this literally new world, the essential ingredients for successful operation and management of a business, whether large or small, have also changed. And with these changes have emerged tremendous opportunities for insightful players to enter this global venue. But such an endeavor requires new modes of thinking about the very nature of the marketplace itself. This is the area I intend to focus on today..... these new market dynamics, and the *appropriate* response to them.... for business people of color.'

'Let me share a key statistic with you. In just three years, the start of a new century, some 60% of the domestic work force will be made up of employees who are not native born white Americans. Think of it! In and of itself this represents a significant management challenge for all domestic firms. As important, or potentially even more so, this culturally diverse work force will represent three quarters of the retail buying power in this country, and almost 70% of the tax base. With such an enormous economic impact, it is clear that the major opportunity for business, whether domestic or foreign, rests with the ability to provide **high quality,** culturally specific products and services.'

'As such, there seems to me an implicit mandate for the development, manufacture, distribution, and access to products and services by businesses who take the idea of multi-culturalism to heart. Interestingly, the impact of global economics necessarily forces major strides to be made in social venues, where decades of civil activities have failed. Since the days of slavery in this country, repeated efforts have been undertaken to provide a meaningful dialogue on issues of race. Clearly, most Americans simply cannot comprehend our frame of reference regarding racial issues. Concepts of culture also escape a common understanding, for the same reason. But these same Americans **do** understand our frame of reference.... when the discussion turns to money. They know what it takes to generate wealth and economic success. And the long term economic future of the America **they** know and love.... has been jeopardized.'

'The two key tenets, verily the only real beliefs of the American system are capitalism and democracy. Since the dawn of the incorporation of this country, democracy has provided the governmental environment within which capitalism has flourished. But a capitalism that is not participatory, a capitalism that is exclusive, ultimately leads to polarization and anarchy, which is the hotbed of totalitarianism. Clearly economic power and political power go hand in hand. But there have been those who exploited the political parameters of democracy.... to create an environment of increased capitalist exclusivity and extreme wealth, at the expense of broad participation in the capitalist experience. This was the tragic and painful economic lesson of the '80s. However, one of the major positive results of such excess... was the removal of the veneer of supposed equality of opportunity, of the disintegration of the illusion of a level playing field and equal access for all players.'

'When these factors are then superimposed upon a worldwide canvas, the resulting picture is one of immense challenge, but also of immense opportunity. Even as the rhetoric of democracy continues to spread to all parts of the world, the true global rallying cry.... is an economic one. So when you examine the dynamics of the economic market-place domestically, and incorporate the intensely competitive nature of global enterprise, what we in business today are faced with is truly a situation that I characterize as the multi-cultural imperative.'

'In this intensely competitive global marketplace, we (as a people) cannot afford to be defined simply as consumers; on the contrary, we must bring something to the table. We must become and remain those who make; people that have the power to expand, and in many cases define, the global economic pie. And the flavor of this economic pie.... is multi-cultural. Despite the enormity of this challenge, I stand here today to tell you, no.... to remind you, that we are a truly resilient and enterprising people. There is no other ethnic group in the history of this country that has made such extraordinary strides in such a short expanse of time. We must use that same resilience and enterprise to be full participants in the global economic order. And we are uniquely qualified to do so!'

'And the requirements for participation are stringent; we must have something to offer. We must equip and train ourselves and our children to be able to comprehend and understand the universal dialogue of money management and the creation of wealth. We must re-invest that wealth in enterprises that truly embrace a multi-cultural vision. We must use our collective resources to finance institutions and organizations that contribute to the economic revival of American cities, and fully understand the economic merit of educating the children that have all too often been abandoned in these cities. We must encourage trade with, and only with, enterprises who demonstrate commitment to a multi-cultural agenda.'

'Many of you in this audience will go on from here to careers in the corporate world, public administration, and entrepreneurial endeavors. As such, you will have an increasing opportunity to regulate wealth, both of a personal and an institutional nature. Of course, this will occur not in the interest of fairness, or open access to you as African-Americans. It will happen because it has to happen; the very foundations of a Western (e.g. European) oriented economic order are collapsing, even as we speak. And you will become successful, if you use what you have; the tools, the education, the intrinsic drive that has characterized our experience in this country for so long.'

'But be aware.... the road doesn't stop there. This cultural imperative I am describing doesn't end with individual success. In the future, as you walk the board rooms of America, and sit in the council seats, and look out of your penthouse office windows, you will realize that those who regulate wealth, have some say in who shall enjoy wealth. Make no mistake about it; the development of individual wealth on the part of people of color is indispensable to participation in the global marketplace. But the cultural imperative requires new thinking, requires an attitude, that transcends simply 'living the good life.' The approach of wealth for wealth's sake, of success at all costs..... cannot become part of the agenda. And we cannot allow our children to fall prey to the same type of thinking. Such isolationism, such insular thinking has characterized European culture for centuries, and ultimately leads to a lack of discipline; to decadence. This is simply not viable, not appropriate..... for the global, multi-cultural marketplace. For capitalism is not the sparkle of what you wear, but the caliber of your product. It's not what you spend, but what you save and invest. It's not what you crave, but what you create. It's not what you say, but it's the integrity of what you do. Ultimately, these will be the barometers of value.... in the new world economics.'

'As the new leaders and captains of industry, we must condemn every form of personal and economic isolationism and insularity (in the African-American community) that discourages participation in the success experience. These forms of insularity include: the denigration of wealth and success as selling out; the rejection of the importance of education; the focus on immediate gratification; short term acquisitiveness at the expense of long term opportunity; the tolerance of drug abuse.... in any economic strata. We must operate in the knowledge (and teach our children) that success and the development of wealth are not discrete events, but rather processes that must be managed and directed with a continuous flow foremost in mind; even as we gain wealth we must recycle that wealth into our communities and businesses and institutions that foster and develop our educational and cultural enrichment.'

'Contrary to popular belief, the essential factors in the operation of these (success) processes I mention are not derived from pedigree or social background, or even I.Q. The linchpins of these processes, and I want you to know I am closing shortly, are rooted in the experience.... of spiritual illumination and cultural enlightenment. Both these factors are deeply personal in nature, but they have their impact on families, on communities, on businesses, on societies, on very nations themselves. In a Western (European) cultural model, there is a very segmented view taken of reality; intellectual development can somehow occur without spiritual development; scientific theories are articulated without reference to the connectedness of natural forces that give rise to the scientific phenomenon; the continual pre-occupation with the physical, the external, at the expense of any teaching about the growth of the inner being. In short, the process of life is dealt with as a series of separate, stand-alone episodes.... the vital circumstances of which are left disconnected and as such, are incomplete.'

'What the global imperative demands however, is an approach that approximates the true nature of things; we are witnessing a convergence of these supposedly discrete fields into a vital continuum, a continuum that increasingly will be measured in economic terms. I believe that the correct model (of reality), a truly cultural model, can be described as a pyramid... with three layers; the bottommost layer, and the broadest, is the realm of the Spirit. In the middle resides the Soul, and at the top of the pyramid is the physical experience, the material world. Each of us are made up of these same three components; the spirit, the soul, and the body. The processes of life flow from the bottom to the top, from the spirit through the soul, into the physical realm, and not the other way around. The spirit realm is the source of all things, the seat of all creative power; it is the vastness of eternity, the limitlessness of God himself. The soul is the residence of those characteristics that make us individuals; the mind, the will, the intellect, the emotions. And the body is the sensory vehicle that enables us to experience the constructs of the spirit and the soul; namely the physical world.'

'Once an understanding of this critical interrelation-ship is established, then one can fully appreciate the impor-tance of culture, and its dynamics. Culture empowers identity; it equips the soul of man with the tools through which the limitless power of the spirit can be properly focused and channeled into the physical realm. A man or woman devoid of culture.... will have an incomplete view of reality, and is therefore incapable of handling the re-cre-ative power of life! And this has, for far too long, been the state of leadership in this country.'

'The cultural imperative then, demands that we, who are people of color, return to the traditions of our greatness. Even though our tastes have been conditioned by the experience of European values in this country, we are Africans.... by culture. Yet the fact that we have been here for more than five hundred years provides us with a per-spective that when handled properly, uniquely positions us for the global leadership role we must play. We must become purveyors and examples of this three-tiered cul-tural model in action. And each of the aspects of the model.... has a direct correlation to business in the global marketplace. We must develop and understand the principles that govern the realm of the spirit; for from the spirit arise those creative forces that drive the development of new (and needful) products and services for the marketplace. A full appreciation of culture prepares us with insights into culturally driven consumer tastes, and the potential appeal of products for the marketplace. And a full comprehension of the (three-tiered) model will cause us to discipline ourselves to bring to bear all our (considerable) resources to deliver the highest quality products and services possible, to create things that will endure.'

'The challenge of the global marketplace and the new economics is enormous. But that challenge is exceeded only by the enormity of the opportunity it presents. Such opportunity will only be successfully managed by those of us who actively bring the infinite power available through the spirit.... into the material realm. We must prepare each of ourselves individually to handle this dynamic, but just as importantly we must prepare our children and subsequent generations to similarly appreciate a complete view of themselves. We cannot afford to stop at being successful, though successful we must be. The uniqueness of our heritage, the very cultural model itself, is a inexhaustible process that requires an impeccability of attitude and the integrity of action.... from which we cannot shirk. And this (three-tiered) cultural model is both a means and an end; it is at once the most direct and effective way to achieve the true success to which we must aspire, but it is also the most perfect mechanism by which to channel the benefits of our success.... to create a better world for our children, and to empower <u>them</u> to create a better world for themselves. To make an *appropriate* response to the new marketplace dynamics.

I congratulate those of you who will go on from here to take your place in the new, global economic continuum. It is my hope, my sincerest prayer, that you will do so in the knowledge and the power of this cultural imperative..... that we all share! Thank you for your time."

The raucous, sustained applause that ensued confirmed for the speaker that his talk had been received warmly by the crowd. Professor Haynes moved quickly to prevent a mob scene by the students, who were anxious to speak to his lecturer one on one. Many wanted to know when he was coming back. Others, intent on dealing with the practicality of their own situation, were interested in what job opportunities were available within his organization. The guest lecturer was the managing partner of the New York investment banking firm of Couples, Sanderson, and Pratt. His name: Derek A. Alston.

About thirty minutes later the gallery disbanded and Dr. Haynes offered to take Derek to lunch. At the nearby faculty dining room, the two men got to know one another better. "You know," Derek said "it's a good idea to get people from industry to spend time with the students. Hopefully, it gives them a little better sense of the practical nature of what's ahead for them."

"Yes, I've been struck by just some of the rudimentary things they pick up from experienced business people like yourself.... that they don't get in our laboratories or internships. Like the hazards of business travel!"

The two had a hearty laugh, each relating their own horror stories of being stranded in airports, lost luggage, and dealing with disgruntled flight attendants.

"I spend a fair amount of my time traveling overseas," Derek noted, " and I always find it interesting that despite many of the customs procedures you have to deal with and obvious language barriers, that many of the airports are pretty well organized, particularly in Europe."

"Do you have any projects going on abroad now?" Dr. Haynes inquired.

"Well yes... as a matter of fact I'm looking into some power utility projects. Many of the European community countries have begun to privatize formerly government owned industries such as power... and I believe there is tremendous investment potential in such companies. I'll be leaving for Marseilles in a few days, and then on to South America."

As the two continued to speak, they didn't notice a tall, lanky gentlemen, with dark framed glasses ambling toward them. About halfway to the table, he stopped, carefully eyeing the two men as they chatted over some dessert. Suddenly resuming his gait, he nearly ran over to the table where they were seated.

"Excuse me," the man asked, almost out of breath, "but is your name.... Derek Alston?"

Looking up, somewhat startled, at their sudden intruder Derek paused for a moment. The man was tall, nearly six foot five, with dark curly hair sprinkled with gray specks here and there, dark complexion and bushy eyebrows that emphasized his hazel eyes peering through the heavy frames of his glasses. All at once, Derek recognized him.

"Emir... Emir is that you?" he exclaimed jumping up from the table. The two old friends embraced one another warmly. A short round of introductions ensued.

"Emir Richardson," said Derek. "I'd like you to meet Dr. Anthony Haynes."

"Dr. Haynes?" mused Emir briefly, "you're in the business school aren't you?"

"That I am," the professor replied. "You look familiar to me also. Are you on faculty here?"

"As a matter of fact I am," Emir answered. "I teach applied physics and engineering." Glancing over at his homeboy he added, "Derek and I grew up together. In fact, his father got me interested in a scientific career. He teaches physics at Drexel University." He motioned to Derek, "How is your Dad anyway?"

"Dad's doing fine Emir. He retired from Drexel about three years ago, but he still does a little writing from time to time."

"What are you doing down here?" Emir asked.

"Your friend just gave a very moving talk to my graduate management class," Dr. Haynes interjected. "He's quite a businessman."

"Well... who would have ever thought that," Emir laughed jovially, recalling their youth in Philadelphia. "He always wanted to be a basketball player, even though he wasn't very good back then. Are you any better now?"

The three men all had a good laugh at Derek's expense. Dr Haynes subsequently explained that he was sorry he had another appointment which was pressing, but suggested the two of them continue to visit and catch up with one another. "And please be my guest," he said to Emir. "Get yourself something." Not one to disappoint, Emir ordered a rich dessert as Dr. Haynes was leaving.

The two friends spent the remainder of the afternoon reliving good times and catching up on old aquaintances.

Eventually, the discussion got back to careers... and job frustrations. "You know," Emir began "I really love the opportunity to work with these young people, helping to interest them in a technical career and such. But to tell you the truth, I don't feel I'm being challenged. I'm not exploring any new horizons."

"Are you saying you're bored?"

"Yes... I guess that's basically what I'm saying. Why?"

"Well... what are you going to do? You shouldn't talk about something like that... unless you plan to deal with it."

"That's the problem... I don't know what to do about it. I've thought about going into business, but that isn't what I really want."

Derek sensed the dissatisfaction in Emir's voice, and he was interested in hearing his true feelings. "C'mon Emir, even though I haven't seen you in years, I've known you for a long time. Why don't you tell me what's really on your mind?"

Emir quickly scanned the dining room, assessing who was still present. "I don't bring this up with everyone, because I never quite know where people are coming from. But I'm just so damn sick of these drugs! We seem to have such a very relaxed attitude about them. And it's killing so many of our kids; kids with the potential to do something important in life. The phrase I hear so often is recreational drug use. And I seem to come in contact with so many of us.... who are stiff cocaine users. As if we don't have enough of that going on in our communities. I don't want to sound like I'm preaching, but how can we ever do the proper job of educating and protecting our own if we continue to enable such personal destruction? I guess I feel sort of impotent to really do something about it. And I'm frustrated."

"But Emir, you have a talent for what you do... you need to apply it. My father always thought so."

"Maybe you're right D, but I feel I could be using my time more productively.... to try to do something about this."

Derek regarded what his friend said for a moment, then offered his own view. "I tend to look at the picture from a business perspective. The popular approach the past ten or fifteen years has been to try and discourage demand.... by education, by driving home the message that drugs kill. And no doubt they do. But there is always demand for drugs, which is continually stimulated in media and advertising by legalized peddlers of addictions: pharmacuetical companies, tobacco firms, alcohol. Such stimulus will always entice those people who are self-indulgent, or those who believe their situation is hopeless to the point of abuse. So, the first approach in dealing with the demand equation... is to teach people that there is hope, that they can control their own destinies; but in order to do so there has to be a sense of, and commitment to, a life of discipline.'

'However, if you look beyond the demand side of this and get to the root of the problem, you've got to consider the production and distribution aspects of the chain. And this is where the huge money is, and it's where many of our fine and upstanding citizens derive a considerable investment income, and where you run into government who looks the other way because of the enormous dollars that get channeled into so many pockets as a result of the perpetuation of this process. Their prey are these same self-indulgent and/or hopeless parties I mentioned. So if you want to do something about any of this, it most come from an external influence, not from any of the parties, who either dierctly or indirectly, benefit financially from this continued dumping of contraband on our cities. And it will require extraordinary insight to come up with an approach that will work!"

Emir looked at his childhood friend in amazement. "I didn't realize you felt so passionate about these things," he wondered aloud. "Sounds like you've given if a lot of thought."

"Believe me, I deeply share your concerns." Rather than elaborating however, Derek abruptly changed the subject. "Emir... are you familiar with the idea of photonuclear reactions?"

Gazing at him quizzicly, and wondering why he would bring up physics at a time like that, Emir nonetheless rendered his understanding. "The idea of photonuclear reactivity is still theoretical at this point. The quantum theory is defined simply as the designation of a nuclear reaction... suitably induced by photons. Photons are the quantums of electromagnetic energy generally regarded as discrete particles having zero mass, no electric charge, and an indefinitely long lifetime. Photons occupy the upper range of the definable electromagnetic spectrum, which extends from frequencies of 0 cycles per second at the low end to 10^{23} cycles at the high end. Describing this spectrum in terms of wavelength, this would correspond to a range from infinity to 10^{-13} centimeters at the high end. This electromagnetic spectrum includes, in order of descending frequency, cosmic ray photons, gamma rays, x-rays, ultraviolet radiation, visible light, infrared, microwaves, radio waves, heat, and electric currents. Is that what you're talking about?"

Derek chuckled softly as he acknowledged Emir's explanation. "That's one thing I always admired about you, my brother. You really know your shit! But consider this. You realize that all matter, all material things, can ultimately be described mathematically. This is the essence of the atomic model of physical phenomena. A corollary hypothesis suggests that if all matter can be described mathematically, then the composition of all things can be described in terms of vibratory patterns, and these vibratory patterns can be mapped to a specific set of frequencies."

"I don't know where you're headed Derek, but I'm following your train of thought."

"Where I'm headed is.... if all matter can be described in terms of vibratory patterns, and these patterns can be resolved to specific frequencies (in the electromagnetic spectrum), then by selectively manipulating the frequencies.... you should be able to transform the nature of the material itself."

Emir stared at Derek, attempting to absorb the gravity of his assertions. "You know Derek, theoretically what you say is possible. But I just can't think of any practical scenario where something like this could happen."

"C'mon Emir. Look at water. The chemical description is two parts hydrogen to one part oxygen. But when you put water in the freezer, it changes from a liquid state to a solid state, namely ice. But it's chemical composition isn't affected. It's still H_2O."

"But what happens when you go the other way. When you heat water, it turns into steam.... which is dissapated into the air."

"The essential point is that these transformations affect, and are affected, by the molecular vibration rates of the same element. And everything we are discussing is occurring at the low end of the electromagnetic spectrum, namely the level of heat."

"Derek, I understand your theoretical concept, but any nuclear reaction throws off a tremendous amount of waste (energy) mostly heat. What do you do with this waste? Besides that, even if it were possible to establish specific elemental frequencies that different types of matter consisted of, to do what you suggest would still require a chemical reaction at some level to re-establish a new molecular structure. In other words, it would (theoretically) be infinitely easier to break down one material.... than to re-create another. And really, what is all this about? Where does all this lead?"

It was Derek's turn to glance about the room to see who was still present. Fortunately, most of the other diners had long since left. "About four years ago, as the result of some deals I put together, I managed to come into controlling interest of a mining company in South Africa. Several of the former owners were willing to take their money and run when apartheid was finally overturned. At any rate, I was aware of an effort that our government had underway years before, just to the north in Namibia where we were funding exploration and mining of ores that had tremendous superconductive potential. The mining company I bought also owned interests in the mines in Namibia. One of the ores we were able to extract has some very interesting characteristics, to say the least. We called it Xenus ore. One of its first applications is as the raw material used in the production of the alloy called Xenium. Xenium has been applied successfully in experimental treatment of AIDS patients. Unfortunately, the FDA has not yet approved the Xenium implants for widespread availability. We are gearing up our efforts in anticipation of significant production.'

During one of my visits to the mine, I happened to notice some of this ore that had been left out in the sun for a few days. I was startled to discover that a portion of the ore that was directly in the sunlight was transformed into a material that I can only describe as something closely resembling sand. It had a dense, packed texture.... like the wet sand you would build castles out of at the beach. But there was no moisture. I had several of our chemists examine the material, but they couldn't make a determination as to why, or more importantly how, this transformation could occur.'

'So Emir, to get back to your question, I strongly believe that this ore has the potential, in combination with the appropriate energy source, to provide that chemical reaction necessary to re-create a material, which has been reduced to it's elemental vibratory pattern. And the waste from the nuclear reaction you mentioned? Well that's the beauty of a photon induced reaction. As you point out, photons have no electrical charge. Therefore, no net energy dissapation has to be resolved. This is normally the case in conventional nuclear reactivity which results in unstable radioactive waste, and manifests itself in the forms of excessive light and heat. If it were possible to carry out a photon reaction, in the upper end of the electromagnetic spectrum, you would conceivably have an essentially clean process.... with no muss, no fuss. And it would appear to be instantaneous, since at that extreme rate of vibratory interaction, you are beyond the limitations of time and space.... time itself would appear to stand still!"

Emir studied Derek carefully, and he could see that his old friend wasn't kidding. On the contrary, he was completely serious. "Let's say I agreed with your hypothesis," Emir intoned, "which at this point I can't say that I do. To what purpose would all this effort be put, D?"

"The purpose... would be to disrupt the cycle of production and distribution... of these illicit drugs which we both despise, particularly cocaine. To manage the controlled transformation of something deadly and addictive... into something harmless." Derek's eyes widened as the words cascaded from his lips. There was that bright gleam in his eyes like years before, that indicated the expression came from somewhere deep inside, not just the result of mental activity. Again Emir voiced his skepticism.

"But D, we're talking about a worldwide problem... not something that you can effect in a laboratory environment."

Derek noticed the kitchen help coming out to prepare the dining room for the evening dinner crowd. It was after 4:00. "Looks like we've got to get out of here," he motioned to Emir. "I'll be out of the country for about three weeks. Please give these things some thought," he encouraged him. "And let me know what you think when I get back." The two exchanged phone numbers and rose to leave. As they parted, Derek emphasized to his old friend, "Emir, I know this sounds far fetched. But don't worry.... I think I can take care of the worldwide part."

Emir regarded him cautiously for a moment then said, "Somehow, I believe you will D. I believe you will."

Six weeks later, the phone rang in the offices of Couples, Sanderson and Pratt. "Good morning, I'd like speak to Derek Alston please," the voice at the end of the line said.

"May I tell him who's calling, please?"

"Just tell him it's an old friend," the man replied.

"Please hold." Two minutes later Derek picked up the line. "Good morning, this is Derek Alston."

"Derek.... it's Emir."

"Hey E, how've you been? What's up?"

"We need to talk. I've done a lot of thinking about the conversation we had. Can we get together?"

"Certainly Emir, but I won't be able to get down there for a couple of weeks."

"I'll come to see you," Emir said. "I can get a Metroliner this evening."

"O.K." Derek agreed. "I'll meet you at Grand Central."

"See you tonight," Emir said tersely. CLICK.

At dinner that evening, the two quickly got down to business. "Derek, I think I've come up with a technique.... to isolate discrete frequency patterns of different elements." Derek could feel the excitement in Emir's voice. "After you left, I spent some time with one of my students. We ran exhaustive computer timesharing exercises to see if we could come up with a mathematical model which would closely approximate the photonic state. Once we built the photonic model, we then did a refraction analysis on an organic material such as wood. The refraction analysis enabled us to build a visual repersentation of the molecular structure of the wood, in such a way as to illustrate this structure in terms of vibratory frequencies. The fantastic thing is... once we had these two models superimposed in computer memory, I found that as we manipulated the frequency ranges above 10^{23} cycles, we actually saw a change in the molecular model as well! Each time we ran a new refraction representation, the molecular structure was different, although there was no physical change to the wood itself."

"So what you're saying is..... you don't think I'm so crazy after all, eh? It's almost like tuning in another station on your radio, isn't it?" They both laughed at the thought. Despite their momentary levity, Emir's enthusiasm could not be contained.

"Derek... we should publish a paper on this technique. I mean.... we're talking about Nobel Prize stuff here!"

A slight tinge of disappointment shadowed Derek's face. "Emir, I obviously share your excitement at this discovery. However, I must say that I am far more concerned with the constructive application of such a technique, than with the noto-riety of the explanation itself. As I pointed out to you, there is the specter of worldwide drug trade... that is a compelling target.... I feel (our) energies should be focused on. Besides, there is a tremedous amount of work ahead to take this analytical model and build a prototype that will manifest in the physical realm..... what is now a computer simulation."

"But D, we can take our approach to the federal govern-ment. They have far more ability and resource.... than we have."

Disappointed, Derek tried vainly to hide his amazement at Emir's naivete. "As I mentioned to you the last time we got together, to do what needs to be done.... takes an outside influence. The same government that covertly allows and benefits from the trafficking of drugs, certainly is not going to shut that trafficking down. There will be lip service given, and efforts made to slow the trade. But the issue is too enormous, and the political and financial interests too persuasive.... for the government to follow through appropriately.'

'Consider this, Emir. The insight that has led us to this point, wasn't just happenstance. It's not a coincidence. The implications of what we are dealing with are enormous. Because of those implications, we need to focus on applying such (cre-ative) power.... to address problems of commensurate enormity. I don't believe getting your name in the paper, or even winning a Nobel prize.... will accomplish that. I'm sorry Emir. Obviously, I can't tell you what to do. But I know what I must do."

Emir considered what his old friend said, and silently validated the truth of his statements. For several moments, there was silence. Before long, he spoke up. "I've havent been so excited by anything in this field.... in a long, long time Derek. I feel as though I've got something here to carry me forward, something that has restored the thrill of exploration. What do you want me to do?"

"If you're serious, I'd like you to head my research team. As I said, we have to come up with a prototype.... to deliver the power from the photonic realm into material manifestation. And it must be specific. We've got to work with the real thing."

"But that's going to take lots of money and (lab) equipment. And what about the cocaine. We need enough to test. Where will all that come from?"

"Don't worry about the financing arrangements. That's my job. For now, I think you need to refine the mathematical models. I'll get back to you in a month with more news." Derek gazed at Emir, eyes shining and asked, "Well... are you in, my brother?"

"You know I've got no choice. Of course I'm in!"

Over the next nine months, the full dimensions of Derek's plan started to unfold. Under the banner of Global Initiatives Development Corp., Derek put together a consortium of investors that systematically began aquiring controlling interests in electric utility companies around the world. The early thrust of this acquisition activity focused on Venezuela, Columbia, Ecuador, Panama, and Mexico, which happened to be the principal routes of departure and export for cocaine out of South America. Within a year and a half, GID controlled utilities in Southern France and on the Mediterranean coast of Spain.

The final pieces of this puzzle were to acquire control of two key domestic operations, Florida Consolidated Power and

Gulf Coast Edison. And these were the hardest, since he now was faced with the prospect of handling American investors who weren't necessarily in a desparate position, unlike some of the foreign interests he'd dealt with. But the basic rules governing an investment opportunity are the same: if you can show someone that you know what you're doing, and how they can grow their money and minimize their risk, they'll invest.

After addressing a board meeting of Florida Consolidated, Derek was confronted by the President of the company, in the antechamber outside the board room.

"You realize that what you're proposing.... will never be accepted by this board, don't you?"

"No sir... I don't realize that."

"It won't be accepted.... because you're an outsider, you're not one of us."

"What is that supposed to mean?

"You're not interested in helping the citizens of South Florida. You're like all those other corporate raiders. And I won't allow you to disrupt what we've built here.... for the interests of our community."

Derek listen thoughtfully to the passion with which the gentleman spoke. Speaking slowly for added emphasis he replied, "Your community spirit and altruism is commendable. But I believe you are overlooking one thing; my proposal is designed to appeal to that most elemental of human attitudes, which can never be completely accounted for.... and that's greed. This offer will make these board members, and the stockholders very rich, albeit over some period of time. And believe me, when faced with the opportunity to enhance the value of their ownership, greedy people will respond.... every time."

"You're a mad man!" the President admonished him. Just then, the board Chairman emerged from the conference room. "We're ready to accept your proposal Mr. Alston," he quietly announced.

Turning to his vanquished adversary, Derek smiled and asked rhetorically, "Am I?" Immediately he headed inside to meet with his new board.

With the mesh of strategically located power companies in place, the implementation of the plan was moving ahead quickly. Specifically, it called for the development of a photon generation mechanism that would be retrofitted into the power generation facilities at each of the electric utilities. The retrofitted generators were to be designed to initiate a photon reaction.... even as the power that drove the lights and electricity was flowing from the plants and sub-stations. In theory, the photon reaction thus intiated would cause cocaine, in any of its forms, to instantaneously be transformed..... into a substance that closely resembeled.... sand!

Under Emir's direction, Derek had assembled a crack team of design engineers, who undertook the fabrication of the photon generators, which incorporated derivatives of the Xenus ore extracted from the mines in Africa. His team set up the research lab on a tiny island called Bonaire off the coast of Venezuela, not terribly far from Curacao. Through a network of contacts on the South American continent, they were able to negotiate access to some twelve kilos of pure cocaine.... that was to be used in testing the process. The payoff of the elaborate plan came on the eve of their second anniversary working together.

Inside the lab, after repeated failures to effect a physical transformation, Emir was finally able to determine that the amount of Xenus ore required to accomplish the chemical reaction, was inversely proportional to the projected capacity of the generator itself. In other words, what was required was less of the photochemical agent rather than more. With that bit of insight driving him, it was only a matter of weeks before the first successful tests of the process took place.

Responding to a wire received in his New York office from Emir, Derek reached the island retreat within days. Unveiling the photon generator prototype was somewhat underwhelming; the device was no larger than an oversized microwave oven, yet two of these units could (theoretically) generate as many kilowatt-hours of power.... as the enormous turbine generators currently operating in the utility plants they'd acquired. However, when Emir started the photon reaction, what the two old friends witnessed was, for them, a thing of beauty! Emir had his assistant bring in one of the kilos of cocaine, packaged in a clear plastic wrap. As they watched, they saw the white powder undergo a transformation... right before their eyes! Within seconds the cocaine had become particles of sand; there was no audible noise, no perceivable chemical reaction, no residue.

"It WORKS!" was the triumphant chorus of those present. The effect was, well.... it was like magic! They subsequently tried different packaging techniques on the cocaine, to determine if there was any connection between the transformation and the transparency of the plastic wrapping. It worked every time, no matter how dense or opaque the container.

"I didn't think the package would make any difference," Derek mentioned. "The photon wavelengths are so infinitesmal, there aren't any known materials dense enough to block the frequencies."

Later that evening he and Emir sat down to a victory celebration. Over dinner and wine, they reflected on how momentous an occasion it really was.

"Well Emir," offered Derek. "What are you going to call this process you've worked so hard on?"

"As a matter of fact, I have given it some thought," the physicist said. "How does 'inverse synthesis' strike you D?"

Derek mulled the name over for a moment. "Actually I think that's quite appropriate Emir, appropriate indeed!" he replied hoisting his wine glass in a toast. The two friends hugged each other in mutual congratulation. Then Derek spoke again. "We're very close now Emir. And the beautiful thing about our application of 'inverse synthesis'.... is its elegant simplicity."

"What do you mean Derek?"

"Once we can iron out the finishing touches on the prototype, and put the photon generators into production, the real fun begins. Can you imagine what will happen.... when the cocaine cartels find that every drop of narcotic they ship, via all their trusted routes of distribution... turns up as brown and grey pouches of sand? The real beauty of it all.... is that nothing will be wrong with their production or smuggling procedures! And there will be no evidence of tampering; yet everyone in the distribution chain will assume they've been double-crossed... by their own contacts! What do you think they'll do, when it's discover that the hundreds of thousands of dollars they spent.... went to buy beach dirt?" He paused, reflecting on the enormous simplicity of it all. "Do you realize Emir, that within a few short months the massive, worldwide, cocaine distribution mechanism.... will simply choke itself to death!" Gazing out the window at a nearby fog lamp, Derek concluded. "And all we have to do, to bring that irresistable juggernaut to its knees, my brother..... is to turn up the power!"

Chapter 12

Crisis and Conflict

Life was looking very good to Lance. You might even say he was at the height of his powers. He most certainly felt that way. His concerns over the consequences of Camille's videotape turned out to be unfounded. Edison, upon returning to D.C. was continually pre-occupied with matters at home, and Camille's attitude or whereabouts seemed to be far from his mind. Despite such emotional absorption, or perhaps because of it, Edison relied on him as much as ever, and that suited Lance just fine.

He was feeling quite proud of himself, particularly how effective the entire Xenium scam had been. In fact, Lance's organizational skills and savvy were causing him to be noticed by others on the Hill. One of the most highly regarded lobbyists in town was interested in his services. Lance knew how well the influence peddlers were compensated; as a result he was beginning to think about life without Edison. He could sense his own power and influence in D.C. growing, and it appeared that his toughest challenges were behind him. He even intellectually toyed with the idea of mounting his own campaign for office. Besides everything else, the late spring weather was gorgeous in the District, which has to be one of the most beautiful cities in the world at that time of year. Yes, it was shaping up as one helluva summer..... for Sir Lance.

But even in his wildest imaginations, he couldn't have conceived what was about to transpire over the next six weeks. It began early in the month of June. Edison came into his office one evening, quickly explaining that he and three other Senate members had been called away to a highly classified meeting in Toronto, at the urgent request of the President. The nature of the discussions was confidential, and Edison had been instructed to share information concerning the whereabouts of the meeting, only with the most trusted members of his staff. Lance expressed concern over the Senator's safety, but Edison reassured him that the entire trip was under scrutiny by the Secret Service. Other than the location however, Edison was unaware of the nature of the discussions.

His real problem was Deidre. She was scheduled to fly into town the following evening, but he had to leave that night. Edison attempted to persuade her to change her plans, that he would be back in town three days later. But Deidre had staunchly refused, pointing out that she really needed a break from Atlanta; and that she could take care of herself (in D.C.) for a few days without him. Despite such self-assuredness, Edison was concerned about her welfare, and requested that Lance 'chaperon' her.... while he was gone. Lance thought the circumstances a bit unusual, but privately he looked forward to spending some time with Deidre, whom he hadn't seen since Manny's accident.

Tuesday evening Lance met her at National Airport. Over the past few weeks, Deidre had begun to come out of her funk over Manny, even as he had started to recover from his depression. Her appearance reflected the change. She looked quite lovely in a hot pink sundress with a halter collar and plunging neckline. Her bare shoulders were caressed by a delicate silk shawl, enhancing her skin tone, which was bronzed and smooth. Deidre still maintained a taste for her liquor though, and had sucked down three bloody marys during the flight. Hence, she was in a very relaxed and playful mood when she got off the plane.

She looked even better than Lance had hoped. He was determined to maintain the position that he was there representing her husband in an official capacity, but had considerable trouble doing so. She greeted him with a warm hug, and the fragrance of her cologne inflamed his senses. He noticed the firmness and familiarity with which she took his hand as they headed to the baggage claim area. For him, Deidre was an exciting woman, regardless of the fact that she was married to his boss. And she seemed genuinely excited to see him, too.

It was gorgeous outside and Deidre insisted they have dinner together, somewhere outdoors. Taking him by the arm, she led her 'bodyguard' to the baggage claim area to retrieve her luggage. Once they had the bags, the duo headed to his car. Lance obliged his guest by taking her to a small riverfront cafe in Old Town Alexandria, which was only a short ride from Washington National. Over drinks, Lance tried to explain the nature of Edison's impromptu commitment, without disclosing his whereabouts.

"Lance... you don't have to make up stories for Edison," Deidre said with a bluntness encouraged by the liquor in her system. "I know he's been running around on me.... for years. This is another of his alibis. But I don't care; it's too late for me to worry about it now."

Lance thought it a little disheartening that she viewed the situation that way, but at the same time he felt bad for Edison, because this time there **was** no other woman. "Deidre, you need to know the Senator was very anxious to see you," Lance offered in support of his employer. "But he was called away quite suddenly by the President." Even as he said the words however, his mind was entertaining thoughts... of discovering what the woman underneath that sundress was REALLY like. Just then, the small pager that Lance carried in his shirt pocket went off. About a year before, he found one the size and thickness of a normal business card, which was very convenient. (It also worked quite well for his drug suppliers to reach out and touch him when necessary). The number that came through on the LCD wasn't one he recognized though. Quickly excusing himself, he headed to the payphones outside the restroom area. The call was from Edison.

Lance informed him that Deidre had arrived safely and that they were about to eat. Edison asked to speak to her. When Deidre came to the phone, she listened impatiently as he explained the urgent nature of his departure. When she demanded to know where he was, Edison reiterated the confidentiality involved with the meeting; he couldn't even tell HER of the specifics. Which didn't help his cause. It just made Deidre angry. But rather than voice her displeasure, she reassured him that everything would be fine until he returned. Edison told her if she needed anything until he got back, to talk to Lance. "Fine. I'll keep that in mind," she said as a closing reply, and hung up.

Returning to their table, Deidre informed Lance that "Edison told me while he's away to get anything I want.... from you." She had a teasing sort of look in her eyes that startled him. He could feel himself becoming aroused as he watched her sit down opposite him. Quickly he gulped down his margarita, and ordered a second. Leaning over close to Lance, she said playfully, "Well, what do think we should do tonight, big guy?" Deidre's question caught him in the middle of sipping his second drink and her expression, and sultry tone of voice nearly caused him to choke on it. She helped out by slapping him across his back, assisting him in catching his breath. The entire episode was quite hilarious, and they both knew it. Each of them tried to keep from laughing, but soon broke down and had a good, from the heart chuckle at the whole thing!

With the tension thus broken, the two went on to have a lovely evening, getting fairly well inebriated in the process. They talked and laughed like the old friends that, in a certain way, they were. Lance took her on a riding tour of the downtown area, which was splendidly illuminated at night. They stopped for ice cream at a little shop near Capitol Hill. From there they took a leisurely stroll through Georgetown, ending up at the river. It was fantastic spring night in the District, and they both knew how such a romantic moment should end.

Deidre checked into a suite hotel overlooking Pennsylvania Avenue. Without hesitating, Lance escorted her to the room. It was a spacious unit, with most of the comforts of home. From a balcony off the sleeping area, there was a spectacular view of the Capitol, bathed in the dramatic incandescence of floodlight. Very few words were exchanged between them; the heavy intoxication of passion simply overcame reason, and the moonlit night made all things seem magical.

They plunged into one another's arms, violently ravaging kisses all over each other. Moments passed as they, locked in sensuous, wet osculation, literally tore their clothes off. The excitement rose as Deidre began biting Lance's throat, and licked his pectorals. He lifted her up powerfully, penetrating deep into her as they fell, naked, to the luxurious king bed. Deidre's passionate screams of ecstasy made Lance go wild, and he thrust himself savagely inside her, even more urgently. Their amorous intensity continued until both collapsed in a heap of semi-exhaustion. The breeze from the open doors of the balcony provided a soothing respite from intense body heat. In the streets below, the sounds of vehicular traffic and activity formed a cacophony of white noise. But the sheer pleasure of the moment calmed any disturbance it might otherwise have caused.

Lying awake in a blissful stupor borne of satisfaction, Deidre thoughts wandered slowly back into reality. Even though Lance certainly proved to be an exciting lover, she wondered if her fascination with him wasn't more of a desire to strike back at Edison, as a kind of slap in his face, than a truly passionate need on her part. She indeed felt an extraordinary sense of emotional release, and the recognition of that fact.... was nearly as stimulating as the physical pleasure she received from Lance. It was almost as if she had been freed from carrying an emotional chip on her shoulder.... against Edison. Whatever the case it was clearly an enjoyable evening, one she would remember for a long time, although she had no intention of ever letting her husband know the truth.

As Lance snoozed happily in peace, she got up to relieve herself. Returning from the bathroom, she happened to notice a small vial of white powder lying beside Lance's rumpled slacks on the floor. Picking it up and examining it carefully, she initially wasn't sure what it was. Suddenly she recalled a criminal law colleague of hers in Atlanta, relating one of his cases, where such a vial (of cocaine) was one of the key items of evidence that helped convict a DeKalb County commissioner in a drug related trial. *Oh no!* she thought. *What have I gotten myself into here?*

The prospect of Lance's cocaine use, or worse, the sale and trade of such, caused her to rapidly sober up. It wasn't that she was naive enough to think that sort of thing didn't occur, particularly in the high pressure world of the nation's capital. But she immediately realized how foolhardy she'd been in allowing herself to get involved with someone so close to Edison. Especially someone who could be as unstable as a coke fiend could be. Thinking fast, she felt the best thing for her to do.... was to get out of there, as quickly as she could. Deidre managed to gather all her things and dress quietly enough not to disturb a sleeping Lance. She scribbled a short note and left him there... in dreamland.

About five thirty (A.M.), Lance awakened with an urgent need to release the contents of his bladder. Groping about the bed, he soon enough recognized Deidre was gone. Looking around the rest of the suite, he discovered all the luggage that he'd brought in for her was missing too. At first, the hangover he wore caused him to wonder if his recollection of the night's events was a dream. *If so,* he thought, *how did he end up in the hotel?* To reassure himself, he picked up the phone and called the front desk. They answered with a cheery "Yes Mr. Powell, can we help you?" Upon her departure Deidre left instructions that they were not to acknowledge her registering, and she had them change the record to read that Lance was in the room and not her, even though she paid for it.

"No, there's nothing I need right now," Lance said absently. Hanging up, he searched his mind, recalling the things that transpired, hoping desperately that he wasn't going crazy. He was certain he'd met Deidre at the airport, that they had been together all evening, that he had talked to the Senator before dinner. None of the pieces quite fit together however, and Lance felt disarmed by an inability to fully reconstruct the circumstances. He even considered calling Edison's house in Atlanta to see if Deidre were there. But he thought better of it. Besides, if she were home, it would only confirm that he WAS losing his mind. Lance felt edgy and uncomfortable. Nervously, he grabbed his slacks off the floor and reached into the pocket.... for his vial of white confidence. Instead, he found the note.

"Lance, you were great!" it read. "I want you to know I had a wonderful, evening. But I realize now there's no future in it (for me). Thanks for showing an older woman... a nice time. You're a good kid."

Immediately his consternation melted in the heat of defiant anger. 'BITCH!' he yelled out to no one in particular. 'Who does she think she is... walking out on me, and taking my blow with her? And who the hell is she calling a KID?' He couldn't decide what hurt most; the fact that she took his cocaine, or his ego at being described as an adolescent. Balling the note into a wad, he flung the paper out the open balcony doors onto the streets below, swearing at the top of his lungs. 'Well you can just go FUCK YOURSELF, Deidre Castle! I'm sick of you... and your lame duck husband! I'm Lance Powell and I can handle you... and a thousand other women like you!'

His anger rose to the point of delirium, but then mysteriously vanished as the violent outbursts subsided. Attempting to gather his thoughts, Lance wrestled with the prospect of what in the world he would tell Edison upon his return. He had no idea where Deidre had gone, and he in no way looked forward to facing the Senator. Lance would have to find out what happened to her, if for no other reason than to cover his ass! The sunrise was coming soon, and Lance tried to control the uneasy sensation he had in the pit of his stomach regarding the new day. Unfortunately, things were about to get worse.

As the days passed, and the development of the photon generator moved ahead flawlessly, Emir grew uneasy and restless. He saw the beauty and elegance of Derek's plan. Yet it bothered him that such an awesome device couldn't be brought to bear on the nation's cities, where within a matter of months they could put all the dope dealers and crack houses out of business. After weeks of soul searching Emir decided he would go to the authorities, in hopes of gaining agreement to roll out his prototype in a systematic urban campaign.

Ten days later, a certified letter arrived in the offices of the Secretary of Housing and Urban Development in Washington. The package outlined the nature of the photon inversion process, and sketchily discussed the basic design of the photon generator. The enclosed letter cited Emir's mailing address at Howard (where he was still officially on sabbatical) and requested a meeting with members of HUD's legislative policy committee.

Emir summarily received return correspondence requesting that he bring a working model of the photon generator for demonstration. He responded, indicating that legally he did not have ownership of the prototype, but would make detail design drawings and related materials available. A committee hearing was scheduled for two weeks later.

At the hearing, Emir passionately articulated why he was taking such direct action in bringing this discovery to the committee. "It is my feeling that such a breakthrough in research needs to be properly introduced into an environment where it will be used to save lives, to help end despair, and to restore livability to our cities." He went on to say that he believed the Federal government needed to take "...a responsible and active role" in speeding development and production of such photon units, and that was the reason he was there.

Unbeknownst to Emir, several 'members' of the committee were actually agents with the DEA and the FBI. They were called in by HUD when the first letter was received. His presentation went along smoothly, actually too smoothly for his taste. There were very few questions, until the discussion got around to the effects the photon generator had on cocaine. Emir was deservedly proud of the process, so naturally he was willing to expound on this area. But when all the questions came from the same surrogate 'members' of the committee, and they were all focused on who the other parties involved in his venture were, on who had 'ownership' of the prototype, Emir began to worry. They were so intent on understanding his 'organization' and where their 'headquarters' was it upset him. At the end of the meeting they seized his drawings and technical papers, brusquely dismissing him with a response of "We'll be in touch with you."

Several weeks passed, and Emir felt worse and worse about his initiative with HUD. Derek was on an extended trip in the Far East, and wasn't due back in the U.S. for another week. For his part, Emir had been splitting his time over the past month between his office in D.C., and the island research center. It was clear that he needed to advise Derek of his actions, but he wanted to do it in person rather than via cablegram. The next day, he received an official correspondence from the HUD committee requesting he meet with several of their 'advisors' to further address his proposal. Emir hoped that it was the breakthrough he had been waiting for. Still, he couldn't help but feel uneasy about the whole thing.

Three days later, a black limousine pulled up outside the Engineering Center on Howard's campus late in the afternoon. Two men entered Emir's office, saying they were representatives from HUD. He thought it a bit unusual that they demanded he not bring any of his materials on the proposed implementation of the photon generators. They escorted him to the car, ushered him in and drove off.

The following day, his body was discovered in a dumpster, bordering a vacant lot at the corner of D and Vermont, the recipient of two bullets in the back of the skull.

Confusion reigned just prior to Edison's return from Canada. Lance still wasn't sure if Deidre was in D.C. or back in Atlanta, or somewhere else for that matter. He'd called their house several times, only to get a recording. Lance knew Edison would have his head if anything happened to her. During the height of his anxiety, he received a phone call from the Senator. Edison seemed to be in a good enough mood, as well he should. The President had requested that he and two of his colleagues lead Senate sponsorship of the White House supported Environmental Protection legislation, which was quite a prestigious endorsement of their Senate floor influence. Lance however, talking without thinking, blurted out that he had taken Deidre back to the airport the day before. "She said she was concerned about your son and decided she ought to head back to Atlanta," he explained. Edison thought that a little strange, since Deidre had told him on the phone that Manny was participating in a two week retreat at the Georgia coast. He decided not to pursue it any further, although he couldn't help but wonder if Lance wasn't trying to hide something.

"I'll be in around 8:45 tomorrow morning," he told his Chief of Staff. "Why don't you take the morning off? It'll give me a chance to get through some paperwork, and then we can sit down and catch up on some things."

"Anything you say Senator," Lance answered dutifully. He silently kicked himself for opening his mouth, particularly since Edison hadn't even inquired about Deidre. But there was nothing he could do about it now. He just hoped to God that she was in Atlanta when Edison called home.

On Friday morning there was a message on Edison's desk when he arrived back in his office. It was from Deidre. She called to let him know she was staying with her mother in Philadelphia for a few days, and would be back in Washington that evening. She explained that she checked into a hotel room the night they spoke on the phone, and since he wasn't going to be back from his trip for a few days, decided to catch an early train the following morning for Philly. Of course, this contradicted the story he'd gotten from Lance. Edison eagerly anticipated confronting his protege upon his arrival later that day.

As bad as the crisis of confidence was becoming with Lance, the situation immediately worsened when Edison opened a letter addressed to him, with no return destination, that lay on top of the pile in his in-basket. The letter was from Camille. He hadn't heard from Camille in months, and frankly had made no attempt to contact her himself. Partly due to this neglect, but more so to misgivings of her own, she had written apologizing for the vindictiveness of the videotape, pledging that she no longer harbored the same vicious anger toward him... that caused her to go to such lengths in an attempt to destroy his career. Camille recognized that their relationship was over, but she sincerely hoped that he and his family would be able to overcome the tragedy they now had to live with.

Edison searched his mind in an effort to remember what Camille could possibly be talking about. He hadn't seen any videotape, in fact....... *Wait a minute,* he thought. His instinct told him there was something wrong with this picture, and that his name was spelled L-A-N-C-E! Edison had trouble putting all the pieces together, but he was sure that he had something to do with it! He was ready to call Lance at home and confront him with these issues, but decided to wait until he arrived. He didn't want him to suspect anything was amiss before he got there. It was incomprehensible to Edison, that after all he'd done for him, Lance could have betrayed him this way.

He left word with the receptionist that he wanted to see his Chief of Staff the moment he walked in. Barely fifteen minutes later, the intercom on Edison's desk buzzed loudly. "Yes?" he spoke into the machine.

"Senator, there are several gentlemen here to see you. They say they're with the DEA. They tell me it's critical that you meet with them, right away." Edison wondered what the DEA wanted with him, but he also knew not to mess around with them.

"Show them in."

His receptionist's description was slightly inaccurate. It was more of an entourage than several people. The group included members of the FBI and CIA as well. They filled up most of Edison's ample office chambers. Recognizing the size of the group, Edison immediately convened the meeting in an adjoining conference room spacious enough for everyone to be comfortable. Dispensing with introductions, one of the CIA officials jumped right into the reason for this unscheduled gathering.

"Senator Castle, several days ago the body of a physics instructor at Howard University named Emir Richardson was found not far from a known cocaine dealer's location here in the District. He had been shot in the back of the head. Upon investigation by the police, an extensive set of documentation and design drawings were discovered that were subsequently turned over to the FBI. These drawings describe a device our people are calling a 'photon generation' unit." At that moment, Lance entered the conference room. He sat down near Edison.

The CIA operative continued. "Our engineering and research people tell us from the documents they've been able to review, that this so called photon generator... has the ability to change the molecular structure of cocaine.... into some other type of substance." Immediately, he got Lance's rapt attention. "We believe this Professor Richardson... to have ties with cocaine smuggling operations in South America."

"But I don't understand," interrupted Lance. "If he were connected to cocaine smuggling operations, why would he develop a device that would transform it?"

"Who are you?" a large FBI agent inquired of the newest entrant to the room.

"This is Lance Powell.... my Chief of Staff," Edison responded. "He has security clearance, for the moment." Lance didn't quite know what to make of that comment, but he didn't get time to dwell on it very much, as the CIA agent resumed the discussion.

"We believe that this Emir Richardson was the point man... in an international conspiracy to gain control of cocaine distribution to the United States. If this device worked as designed, Richardson and his operatives could render any cocaine they chose... to be useless. By doing so, they would naturally make any of the drug in their own possession... infinitely more valuable. Unfortunately, all we've been able to secure are the design specs and documentation. We believe there is a prototype machine already working... somewhere."

Edison, intrigued as he was, still wasn't able to make any reasonable connection as to why they were there. "I must say, I find this information quite fascinating," he said. "But frankly, I don't understand why you're here. It seems that this is something the DEA ought to be handling."

Quickly, one of DEA officials spoke up. "Senator, this entire operation had to be bankrolled and structured by someone other than Emir Richardson, someone with knowledge and access to considerable financial resources. And that person (we believe) has the prototype generator in their possession."

"Sounds like someone very dangerous to me," added Lance. "Certainly a potential threat to U.S. security."

"Exactly!" the CIA official emphasized. "Senator, is the name Derek Alston... familiar to you?"

"Of course it's familiar to me. He's my wife broth... WHAT!!?!" The realization that Derek was implicated in this discussion nearly floored Edison. "You don't really expect me to believe... that (crazy) Derek... is the one behind all this, do you?"

"Senator, we frankly don't care whether you believe it or not. We have been able to secure records of bank drafts drawn by Emir Richardson on special accounts controlled by the investment banking firm of Couples, Sanderson, and Pratt, of which Derek Alston..... I mean, your brother-in-law, is the managing general partner."

One of the FBI agents joined in. "The Securities and Exchange Commission has on file a prospectus for the leveraged buyout of a large South Florida power utility company, by a consortium of private investors, headed by....."

"Derek Alston!" Lance chimed in on cue.

"We have reason to believe the power company was to be used as a front... for the domestic portion of your brother-in-law's operation." There was a pause in the discussion, during which time the gravity of the situation began to bore in on Edison. In a day of startling revelations, this clearly was the most astounding.

"What would you like us to do?" volunteered Lance.

"We need any and all information concerning your brother-in-law's whereabouts. We need to know when he contacts you, or your wife, for any reason."

"We haven't seen Derek in eight years," Edison said. "And I don't believe my wife has even spoken to him in more than five years. I can try to find out where he is, though."

"Senator, I don't think we need to reiterate the security implications of this situation. More importantly for you, consider the political ramifications of what we've discussed. You don't want to be perceived as impeding this investigation, in any way. We're relying on you for your full and active participation."

Edison, still numbed by the disclosure, grudgingly agreed. Even though he disliked Derek, he somehow had trouble believing him capable of what they suggested. "I'll do everything I can.... to help."

"Remember this Senator. I realize this is going to be hard going forward, but I think you understand.... that we cannot have any one man, any one person... in control of the vital interests of our country. No one should have **that** much power." Acknowledging the comment, a stunned Edison could only stare absently at the wall, as the meeting summarily dispersed.

Outside in the antechamber, several members of the 'committee' pulled Lance aside. "I think you understand how important this inquiry is," one of the men said to him. "And we're not certain we can rely on the good Senator to work with us. There are many influential people aware of what we're doing here. It would be a feather in your cap... if you were involved in bringing this Derek Alston to justice. We really need someone like you... to do everything possible to assist in this investigation. Do you understand?"

Lance nodded in the affirmative. "I understand completely. We'll be sure... to get Derek!"

A pleasant evening greeted the members of the New York Symphonic Society at Lincoln Center. The crowd of men and women, decked out in formal attire were there to hear the performance of a Brahms retrospective. The guest conductor was Harrison Rousson, and he was leading a student orchestra from CCNY. The concert had been sold out for weeks, and the line was already beginning to form in anticipation of the doors opening.

Inside, members of the orchestra were tuning their instruments, in anticipation of the crowd. The performance was for the benefit of several arts foundations in Manhattan, and many of the City's dignitaries were on hand. Two of the hundreds that were in attendance... were Derek and his date, Ms. Audrey Mason. He had returned from Hong Kong several days before, and they planned to spend some time together before he left for Bonaire in the morning. Derek hadn't spoken to Emir in over a month, and was starting to wonder what had happened to him. But he determined not to let those thoughts interrupt an enjoyable evening of classical music.

Following the performance, many of those present greeted Maestro Rousson in the Grand Foyer and started an impromptu autograph session. Audrey was anxious to speak with the maestro, but Derek persuaded her that they could better spend their time elsewhere. Hailing a cab, they headed to a quiet French restaurant on the lower East Side for a cozy dinner for two. When they were through Derek flagged a horsedrawn carriage, and the two took off for an exhilarating (and romantic) tour of the town. The evening ended in a mutually gratifying concupiscent encounter at Audrey's apartment.

Around five fifteen (A.M.) Derek arose, showered, and dressed quickly. He said good-bye to Audrey, and headed to his office. Emir was again on his mind, and he needed to pick up some things there before he left for the island research center. Arriving at the office tower, he was greeted awkwardly by the security guard, who seemed very agitated that Derek was there so early in the morning. Watching closely as Derek boarded the elevator for the ride up to his eleventh floor suite, the guard quickly radioed his contacts upstairs as soon as the elevator doors closed.

"Hey, you guys need to hurry it up. He's on his way up... right now!" The guard was speaking to some 'workmen' who had been in his offices for a little over an hour.

"O.K. we're just about finished anyway. We'll use the fire stairs," they replied and signed off quickly.

Derek's office overlooked a plaza with a pool that belonged to a health club in the building, and just beyond that he had a scenic view of the East River and Queensborough Bridge.

Exiting the elevator, Derek felt that something wasn't right, particularly as he thought about the way the security guard acted downstairs. He entered his office suite cautiously; but everything seemed to be in order. He was beginning to think he had just overreacted.... until he noticed a wire filament lying on the blotter on his desk.

Sitting down, he examined it momentarily.... and couldn't determine what it was. Inadvertently, he knocked over a pencil holder and spilled a half dozen pencils on the floor below his desk. Bending down, he saw it, and immediately realized what the filament meant! It was part of a fuse! On the underside of his desk, was smeared enough plastic explosive to blow a hole the size of a crater.... in the Great Wall of China!

'JESUS!!' Derek screamed, and he instinctively dove through the plate glass window directly behind him, just moments before the explosion ripped a gaping hole in that side of the building. Alarms rang out and flames leaped from the orifice of steel and mortar, spewing debris on the plaza below. Miraculously, Derek had hit the water of the pool and managed to save himself. Coming up for air, he could see the enormous damage that had been done far above him. In the background, he heard the sirens of the fire department, signalling the impending arrival of the authorities. Emerging from the water, he now knew that Emir was definitely in trouble, or worse. And he knew he had to reach Bonaire... before **they** did!

Edison still had trouble believing the accusations presented concerning Derek, yet he faced the dilemma of risking his political career... if he spoke up in support of his brother-in-law. It was a curious state of mental inertia he experienced; in the past he was always able to convince himself of an expedient course of action. But this time, such direction escaped him.

Ironically this indecision enabled him, or perhaps more correctly caused him, to share his true feelings with Deidre... for the first time in years. Though she was obviously distraught and upset over how Derek had been implicated, the two bonded to one another unlike at any other moment in their married lives. And while they were together over the weekend, one course of action became clear to Edison. He instructed Deidre to return to Atlanta, and he would keep her informed of things as they proceeded.

Arriving early at his offices Monday morning, Edison was waiting for Lance. For his part, Lance sensed there was something wrong and wanted to avoid the Senator, but the FBI types that were there Friday advised him that he needed to carry on his affairs around the office as normal. He was only valuable to them as long as he was on the inside; that way he could track any information or contact that might be forthcoming regarding Derek. He arrived some thirty-five minutes after his boss.

Edison had Lance come in and sit down. He even offered him a drink.

"Senator, you know I don't indulge so early in the morning," Lance mentioned, attempting to refuse. Ignoring his comment, Edison poured a stiff shot of brandy and handed it to his Chief of Staff.

"Drink it," he commanded him. "You're going to need it." Lance's heart sank when he heard the words. "Politics is strange business Lance," Edison said. "I've been at this for a long time now. During that time, I frankly haven't run across someone as talented as you. And I admire you for that; so much so that I trusted you... as I would my own son." As he spoke, Lance started gulping down the brandy. "I had hopes... that you would someday follow in my footsteps. But now... it's become apparent that my trust, my hopes, were misplaced." With that, Lance polished off the rest of the liquor. "I think you should know Lance, that I feel as though I want to hurt you, to do some sort of physical harm to you. But I'm not going to do that. I'm going to do something worse." There was a sharp knock at the door. "Come in," Edison said calmly. Two secret service men entered, and closed the door quietly behind them.

"What are they here for?" asked Lance nervously.

"They're here to escort you out of the building Lance. You're fired!" The words pierced him, as though an arrow had pierced his throat. The pressure of the moment was so intense, Lance actually crushed the oversized shot glass in his hand, causing blood to spurt through his clenched fingers.

"You can't do this to me!" he screamed, tears streaming from his eyes. Rising up to go after Edison, Lance was bodily restrained by the secret service agents. They actually had to drag him out of Edison's office.

"And Lance, you can forget about that position with the lobbyist. I've already made sure.... that you'll never make another dime... in this town!" Lance strained mightily as the two men dragged him away.

"You can't do this to me Edison," he yelled. "I helped you, I looked out for you. I MADE you, Edison Castle! I MADE YOU!" His shouts slowly faded away.... as he was dragged away from Edison's offices, and ushered out of the building.

The siege began before dawn on a Sunday morning. A squadron of Navy seals, along with some DEA operatives came ashore on the westernmost tip of the island. Derek had done all he could to evacuate as many of the natives as possible. But many of the people refused to leave. In the two and a half years they had been there, Emir and Derek (and company) had taught the people some new techniques in cultivating crops, had built several schools and recreational facilities for the children, and employed many of the young men and women at their research center. And there was no attempt to change their cultural views or proselytize.

As a result, Derek had inspired a feverish loyalty; but he knew that this was to become mortal combat. And he couldn't stand by while innocent people were killed, or worse.

At various locations around the island, they had constructed a sophisticated surveillance system. From a control room, Derek was able to observe the movements of the attack squadron through infrared lenses. Such observations were crucial since there was one other matter of unfinished business.... that Derek had to attend to. In the distance, he could hear the explosions of land mines going off as they were tripped. That was good; but he knew that it was only a matter of time before they identified his location, so he had to work fast.

Outside, the attackers went about their business with chilling savagery. The would shoot children in the head in front of parents, until they got the information they were seeking. Even though there were casualties among them, they still numbered some sixty-five men, armed to the teeth. The squad moved in an ever-tightening circle, slowly enclosing Derek's location.

Inside, he was busy with a series of computer transactions. First, he wiped out all records of the photon reactor construction. Next, he initiated a timing device that would cause the photon generator prototypes to self-destruct. Finally, and most importantly, he went about the business of transferring his ownership interest in the Xenus ore mines.... to Manny. Derek of course, understood the enormous importance of the Xenus compounds, and realized it was critical no one made the connection between the ore and the photon devices. The only person he knew he could trust was his nephew. And Derek was certain Manny would know what to do with the mines years from now.... when he was gone.

It was an involved sequence of transactions that required him to access several different legal archives to electronically file proxy statements and transmit signature verifications. His hands lightly skimmed over the keyboard as he worked feverishly to complete the ownership transfer. He knew the troops would be upon him.... within minutes. Seconds ticked away, as beads of sweat formed into tiny rivulets of perspiration that ran down his face. Just two more commands to complete. As he entered the symbols, he noticed the telltale infrared beam of a sonic targeting device locking on to the display screen. This was it! He had to get away; **NOW!** Diving out of the way of the shot from the laser cannon, he didn't see the acknowledgment that flashed on the screen... just before it was blown to bits; **'TRANSACTION COMPLETE.'**

The troops were inside the compound now. He took a tiny elevator to a sub-level, and made his way to a small arsenal room. Derek strapped on, and loaded himself up with suitable firepower to take on twenty men. But sixty-five? Thinking critically, he decided to bait a trap for his intruders. Stationed just below was a tunnel that joined this sub-level area to a second building. Stationing himself safely beneath this tunnel, Derek set off several electronic indicators that falsely signalled his 'position' to his pursuers. Reacting quickly, they found the entrance to the tunnel.

As row after row of the squad members entered the tunnel, Derek waited until he could tell most of the men were inside. Speaking softly to himself, he said simply, 'Time to turn and burn, D.'

From a small remote control unit, he activated a switch that immediately sealed the entrance to the tunnel behind his pursuers. At the same time, the floor of the tunnel was flooded with gasoline, and vents on the walls released pressurized natural gas into the chamber. Suddenly realizing it was a trap, the attackers vainly attempted to retreat. Recognizing the entrance was sealed, they were too far away from the open end of the tunnel to get there in time. The last image they saw was the backlit silhouette of Derek standing at the open end, flame thrower in hand. With the aperture of the tunnel closing in front of them, they heard him say, "Need a light?" The flames shot inside the opening, igniting the mixture of liquid and toxic gases. The tunnel was inflamed like a broiler, with the continuing pressure eventually inciting an enormous gas explosion. Fifty-nine of the sixty-five men were lost in this furnace.

The hunted quickly became the hunter. One by one, Derek picked off three of the remaining commandos. A fourth returned to the landing party location... to radio for reinforcement. Moving quietly, Derek happened on a small office in the complex. Peering inside, he found a fifth attacker, who had trapped a young native girl and had tied her down to the top of a desk. He had already beaten the girl severely, and while he thought no one was around, was preparing to rape her.

Reacting instinctively, Derek pounced on her attacker from behind, just as he was getting the trousers of his fatigues down around his ankles. Using a machete, Derek administered a slicing blow to the lower back of the rapist, cracking his spine and causing him to keel over backwards. With the attacker thus temporarily subdued, Derek mercilessly grabbed the commando by the hair, and with a swift, decisive motion, savagely decapitated him!

Turning to the young girl, he cut her loose, and commanded her to leave quickly. As the terrified girl departed, Derek held up the head of the mercenary that he had separated from the rest of the torso. Holding the bloody face in front of him, Derek slowly whispered into the dead man's ear, "This Homeboy don't PLAY that!!" On his way out of the office, he took the machete and pinned the dead man's head to the wall, right through the stiff, greasy hair. There the grotesque head hung, a morbid reminder of the carnage that had taken place.

The remaining squad leader, a Commander Pike, proved to be quite a match for Derek's wits. Pike figured Derek would eventually try to reach the laboratory, where the photon prototypes were. Even though he'd initiated the destruct sequence from the computer, Derek had to manually arm the detonators. Once he showed up, as he knew Derek would, Pike would be waiting for him.

Pike maneuvered himself into position about thirty feet from the rear entrance to the facility. He properly anticipated that Derek wouldn't use the front door. As he came in, Pike locked on his target, aimed slowly and fired a single round from his shotgun. The blast hit Derek in the right shoulder, shattering his clavicle. The pain was excruciating; but Derek managed to somehow crawl out of the line of fire. Finding his way to a conference room, he managed to strap his bad arm down to his hip, in a makeshift body splint. Quickly reorienting himself, he knew that Pike would soon discover he'd only wounded, and not killed him. He had to work fast. Making his way to the generators, he quickly armed the detonators on two of the three units.

Coming around to the third unit Derek discovered, to his great dismay, Pike waiting for him. His face was charred by streaks of flame from the tunnel explosion. "I must admit, you've been quite a challenge," Pike said to his unarmed prey. "I've been in Nicaragua, Desert Storm, and never had an entire squadron wiped out..... by one man. But now the party's over Derek, and you're history!" Before he could squeeze the trigger however, Pike himself took a large machete in the back... from the same young girl Derek defended shortly beforehand. She'd returned to thank him, but discovering he was gone, she pulled the machete out of the wall and went in search of her protector.

Bleeding profusely, Derek nonetheless armed the last generator, and yelled "Vamanos!" to the valiant young girl, to be sure she was clear of the ensuing blast. Derek himself made it as far as the beach, before collapsing in a heap of exhaustion and pain, even as the Navy patrol boats approached. The photon devices detonated themselves as planned, with a brilliant flash of light... brighter than a hundred suns, visible miles off shore. But there was no noise, no flame, no explosion. Only the brilliance of light. When the luminosity subsided, the photon generators were gone, as was the laboratory itself.

For someone as innovative and resourceful as Lance had been, adjusting to his newfound unemployment was unusually painful. True to his word, Edison made sure no one hired him, even though he seemingly got to the final round of interviews on several occasions. Never having had to deal with rejection before made the emotional strain unbearable. Without unemployment compensation, he sped through some twenty thousand dollars in savings in just a few months. Of course, feeding his all-consuming cocaine habit had a lot to do with that. He borrowed money from his family, but his frustrations continued. And his habit grew. Eventually, just to try to make ends meet, he had to stop buying the pure coke he loved. All his 'friends' and suppliers left him, and no one was willing to do business with him on credit.

But he didn't know how to stop the need to get high. Eventually, a couple of acquaintances connected him to India, a crack dealer. His cravings overcame good sense; he needed the rush of drugs in his system. And the crack made him feel immediately better. Not better, wonderful! Within a week, Lance Powell, congressional aide, senior administrative assistant, ex-Senatorial Chief of Staff..... was a crack addict.

Three months later, he was arrested for aggravated assault and manslaughter in the beating death of a seventy year old woman... from whom he attempted to steal fifty dollars.

Chapter 13

The Nubian

Derek's trial was to begin on Thursday. The Federal courthouse in Atlanta had been heavily secured. Shifts of city police garrisoned the Russell building during the day while inside, Federal agents and plainsclothesmen were watchful for anything unusual.

Guards at the metal detector stations and the elevators that provided access to the 17th floor were doubled. All of the preparation seemed more appropriate for someone ominous, like Manuel Noriega. But in the view of the government, he was much more of a threat than Noriega.

Derek was to be represented by C. Hassan Danielson, one of the most notable defense lawyers in the country. Danielson had enlisted the aid of a local Atlanta firm, Arlington and Associates, to assist in finding character witnesses and to handle much of the technical research required to prepare the case. Danielson hoped to create the image of Derek as a creative and talented scapegoat, which he was. There were big money interests controlling the prosecution however, and the government was certainly more willing to listen to well endowed influence peddlers than cries of justice for the defendant.

The legal task was formidable. Derek was accused of conspiracy to illegally transport cocaine and impeding international drug enforcement agencies. He was also accused of stealing classified information and turning it over to 'unfriendly' organizations; according to them he was a spy. At best the government's case was contrived. But the image of Derek as a traitor and drug trafficker was being carefully cultivated in the media. If he was to have any hope, Danielson had to somehow convincingly portray Derek's real intentions. But much of the important technical documentation had been (conveniently) destroyed.

The treatment the family received from the media was brutal. Edison was interviewed almost daily about the case, his relationship to Derek, whether he received any campaign contributions from him, etc. He was questioned about his involvement in providing classified information on alternative energy sources. He was asked if he had participated in the power consortium Derek arranged. On and on it went.

To his credit, Edison never once allowed the media pressure to affect his judgment. "Although I do not agree with his methods, I am firmly convinced Derek acted in the sincere interests of humanity.... in his attempts to disrupt the cocaine trade, an effort we should all support." The press would try to ridicule him for supporting Derek in light of the 'evidence'.

Newspeople were constantly in his face, "C'mon Senator Castle. It appears that Alston wasn't really going to wipe out cocaine, but was actually attempting to corner the market. The power company consortium was simply a front."

But Edison was steadfast in his denials of any wrongdoing, and of his support for Derek. It was one of the few times in his life that he actually acknowledged Derek in something of a positive light. It was very hard for him, given his public stature, and the way he had always felt about his brother-in-law. And it was becoming more clear everyday, that he loved Deidre in a way he hadn't understood before.

This trial was terrible for her. She had been sick out of her mind over Manny's disability and suicide attempts. Even as Deidre was coming to grips with the trauma of that ordeal, she was now faced with her brother being labeled a criminal and a traitor. On top of that, everything Edison had worked for so diligently was being questioned in public. But interestingly, all the pain of the past year had somehow made her stronger; she revealed a side of herself no one had seen before.

Deidre was always concerned with how other people perceived her, about making the right impression. Over the years of Edison's political development, she always maintained her composure in trying situations, ever the gallant, elegant political wife. And she did love being the envy of the Atlanta social set. But with the troubles that were afflicting the men who were most dear to her, the buppie attitude had worn off. Real life had set in, in a big way.

She got involved in working with handicapped children, helping with their rehabilitation. Although her initial motive was as much therapy for her, and guilt about Manny's paralysis, there was a genuine pleasure Deidre derived in watching their progress, and experiencing the joy they expressed.... that someone would take the time to support them. It was something that really helped get her mind off the family's problems. She was excited about something again; Deidre found there was meaning in other things slightly more important than her social events and Edison's political mixers.

"Manny, I just love my kids," she'd say to her son upon return from one of her sessions. "That Darnell is beginning to show signs that he might not need his wheelchair much longer. He really has such a great attitude. He says, 'Mrs. Castle, when I get out of my chair, I'm going to come to your house and wash your car for you. I like washing cars. When I grow up I'm going to own a car wash.' And he's so cute, a little doll. The young ladies are going to have trouble with him in a few years. It reminds me of when you were young, how I just enjoyed you so much. Manny, I KNOW there is hope for you. Just be encouraged, have faith in yourself. And you know I'm always here for you. You're my baby."

It was good to see her active and alive and excited about life again. The handicapped children affected her deeply, and she desperately wished (and prayed) for Manny's recovery. But it was hard for everyone, Deidre included, to focus on day to day activities.... when Derek was facing disaster.

Interestingly enough, the circumstances surrounding Derek's trial had the effect of bringing the family together in a way they hadn't known in years. Asia came down to be with the family during the proceedings. Gloria would spend any time that she could get away from school with Deidre. And Edison and Manny even began to have long talks, sometimes for hours into the night.

On one such occasion, he took Manny out on to the veranda in back of the house, a glass of sherry in his hand. Manny knew he was ready to talk by the way he would sit, with his back to him, facing out toward the woods. He didn't look at his son; it was almost like he was talking to himself, you know.... just thinking out loud.

"You know son, for many years I resented Derek," he'd start out. "He represents everything that I feel is wrong with our people; he has a total disregard for what makes this country great, and he doesn't respect authority. My father, your grandfather, was active in the Civil Rights movement; he was with Martin in some of the key protests of the Sixties. If it weren't for men like that, I wouldn't be where I am today, in a position to help determine what course this country takes. And Derek might not have gotten the opportunities he did to go some of our most prestigious universities. He has benefitted as much as anyone from the sacrifices of men like my father. Now I know how strongly you feel about him, but it's important that we discuss these things, man to man."

Manny was impressed how sincere his father was, but he couldn't stomach much of this 'We marched with Martin' stuff. What Edison really meant was that Derek wouldn't sit still for some of the attitudes and materialism and bullshit so many of us get absorbed in. He was trying to do something about it! Derek always said that '... tradition for tradition's sake is useless, unless it focuses us on a course of action.... to deal with our problems, ourselves'.

"Dad, how do you think Derek feels about you?" he asked his father innocently. The directness of the question caught him off-guard. He seemed to be groping for the right words. Manny thought he felt the need to be diplomatic about his feelings. Finally, unable to control his anxiety, all his years of frustration came flooding out.

"Derek doesn't give a SHIT about me Manny! He doesn't give a shit about my position. If he did, he wouldn't have gotten us involved in this whole mess." Edison was breathing heavily; Manny could see the pressure building up in his face; he was beginning to sweat. For a moment, Manny thought his father might be having a heart attack. Minutes passed.

After a while, Edison regained his composure. "Despite how I feel about him, I believe he's innocent. I want you to know that. I don't think Derek is a criminal. The very sad fact of the matter is that the drug trade and drug enforcement agencies.... have become key industries in this country. Tens of thousands of jobs and millions and millions of dollars are tied up in our fight against illegal drugs. Sophisticated surveillance and weapons systems help accommodate drug enforcement efforts. Derek and the process he created are seen as eliminating the need for all that. The U.S. government CANNOT allow that to happen. Do you understand, Manny? There are influential people in Washington who view the drug trade as an undesirable, yet integral part of our economy. I'm a member of the U.S. Senate, and sworn to uphold the interests of the United States. I truly believe Derek's heart was in the right place. But he acted outside the jurisdiction of a private citizen. And in doing so, he violated the interests of the government. I cannot in good conscience endorse anyone, even Deidre's brother, undermining the interests of our government."

It was hard for Manny to believe what he was hearing. Derek was going to be sacrificed because he was seen as a threat to the economy! Never mind about the lives that were being wasted, everyday, in cities all across this country! Cocaine was too important to the economy! This was incredible.

Just then the notion occurred to him that if the drug trade had become such an important economic engine, then why not legalize it. I mean, beside the moral implications of substance abuse, the government ought to be able to regulate and license and TAX manufacturers the same way it does alcohol, tobacco, and pharmaceutical companies. In that way, you at least can impose quality control, labeling and distribution regulations on the 'products'. Even though there was still opportunity for abuse, the legitimate regulation of the 'industry' would provide real jobs in a number of fields. And it would stop the warfare in the streets, just as the end of prohibition ended the reign of mob bosses in the 1930's.

The logic of the solution seemed pretty straightforward to Manny. It appeared the answers to these problems were there to be had, if someone wanted to deal with them. Right at that moment, Manny had the most uneasy feeling; he actually began to get sick to my stomach.

It dawned on him that the government really WASN'T interested in eliminating the illegal drug problem. To a certain extent, drug trafficking had to be encouraged (unofficially of course) in order to survive. Then it hit him. The presence and distribution of drugs in the cities was another subtle, yet incredibly sinister form of genocide, being practiced on the minorities who make up the vast majority of our inner city populations.

The whole vicious cycle of ignorance and economic depravity and welfare conditions that make the inner city an overripe market for contraband was causing entire generations of young men and women to be swallowed up..... in the black hole of drug dependency. And as long as the problem was defined as being criminal in nature, it provided the perfect excuse for the government..... to wage legalized warfare in the streets. It also created the perfect marketplace for the sale of arms, thereby boosting the black market trade in weaponry. And all this existed at the expense of thousands of lives, and the waste of generations of young minds, potentially creative people. Sadly it had to be 'sanctioned' by the government in order to perpetuate itself.

It upset him to think about the terrible social consequences that had resulted. Reports from the Centers for Disease Control stated that a black male between the age of fifteen and twenty-four had a higher likelihood of being killed in this country, than he would have during a tour of duty in Vietnam! Manny's rage grew hotter as he realized that his own father couldn't (or wouldn't) see this; that he really believed this wasn't an issue of human rights.... but of national security and economic policy. Derek knew better. And now he was going to pay the price for trying to do something about the entire mess!

His emotions were so intense, Mannny felt as though he would rise up out of his wheelchair. He was so overcome with anger. His own father was such a large part of the problem!

But then, the strangest thing happened. He was about to let Edison have it about his morals and hypocrisy. But before he could voice his feelings, Manny realized that.... all of a sudden.... it didn't matter. He really didn't care! An intense feeling of aloofness absorbed him. Where moments before he had been so emotional, he was now detached; he couldn't stay mad at his father. It was strange. Manny suddenly became so objective, as if someone else occupied his body, and he was sitting nearby, watching the entire scene!

At that moment, Manny began to laugh. Softly at first, not loud or hysterical. But it kept growing as he recognized how clear this sense of detachment made him feel. Here he was, laughing loudly now, and his father has been spilling out his guts to him. I'm sure Edison thought he must be crazy.

Manny heard himself say, "Dad, you know, you're a real hypocrite. You say you don't believe Derek is guilty, yet you don't speak out against the role the government has got to play, in allowing the conditions that Derek is fighting against to exist. Are you THAT in love with your job?"

He could see Edison get quite restless and irritated by the question. Although Manny was interested in his response, he was more drawn to this tremendous feeling of indifference, and giddiness. Gradually, Manny could perceive everything slowing down, as if time itself were stopping. Strangely, he saw his father forming words with his mouth, but Manny's sense of hearing seemed to be turned off. Everything was happening in slow motion.

Quite unexpectedly, Manny's eyes were suddenly able to see 'everything'; he actually experienced the sensation of perceiving his father as he really was, an intricate vibratory energy pattern. Manny could 'see' the outline of his body, with what apperared to be rays of light emanating from around his abdominal area, radiating in all directions, upward through his head and out into the air.

As he would speak, certain vectors of light would get brighter. Actually, they would brighten BEFORE he said anything. Manny realized that these emanations were the essence of his thoughts which were being verbalized in the course of their talking. He could actually see the process of each thought being generated, and the light emanating as he spoke.

The term 'seeing' is being used here in the broadest sense. Manny couldn't be sure if his eyes were actually involved in the process, or if it was some other part of him that he couldn't articulate. All Manny knew is that the perception was real! He could only recall such a senation once before; when Derek was explaining to him about the role of the (cultural) warrior when he was young.

The experience of these senstions was such a tremendous rush, Manny totally lost track of himself; he became caught up in the movement and intensity of Edison's thoughts. After what seemed like hours, Manny noticed that by focusing his attention on a specific set of these light vectors, he was able to interpret what Edison was about thinking, what he was going to say. It was such a very strange feeling. But... Manny knew.... that... he was READING HIS MIND!

Edison's thoughts were quite revealing. Manny never knew how insecure his father had been about his stammering, and how that had caused him to work so hard.... to be successful as a public figure. He said.... or more accurately, he thought how sorry he was that he hadn't spent more time with Manny when he was younger, and how he felt responsible for his disability. He was supposed to send his limo for him after the All-Star game, but had allowed himself to be persuaded by Camille to go to dinner, and ended up at Antigua Gregory's later when Manny's accident occurred.

It was touching for Manny to realize how much Edison now cared for his mother, how he had neglected the support Deidre had given him over the years. And it really amused Manny to 'discover' how sincerely his father secretly admired Derek.... for being true to his convictions in the face of ridicule and attack. And for how much Manny respected him.

This was GREAT! Manny had such a feeling of clarity, of carelessness that he had never known before. It was then he understood what Derek had told him years before about losing self-importance. The focus and clarity came when Manny was totally unconcerned and unburdened with his own existence. His worries, his cares, his effect on people, his attitudes, his program. Suddenly, Manny wasn't attached to any of that. The entire realm of possibilities was open to him. Manny felt he could comprehend the enormity of the universe. It was such a tremendous feeling of power, as though he were tapped into the very source of life itself! In the midst of all this, Manny experienced an overwhelming sense of comfort.

Just as quickly as the objectiveness came, however, it began to fade. Manny could feel the return of the material world and the restoration of his 'normal' sensory perception. The focus and intense clarity were gone. As Manny became aware of himself back in the wheelchair, he also discovered his father sitting there, screaming at the top of his lungs.

"MANNY! What is wrong with you? Are you having a seizure?" It must have been strange for Edison to see Manny sitting in the chair, just staring at him like that.

"No Dad, I'm OK. I'm just a little BESIDE myself right now." Manny couldn't stop from breaking into a delirious laughter. The entire scene was so ludicrous. He had just been 'viewing' the most intimate of his father's thoughts, and Edison thought he was out of his mind.

Manny noticed the tears in his eyes as he got up. "Son, I'm drained. I've got to get some sleep. Manny, please for your mother's sake and mine, get some help. Please! We love you!"

"Don't worry Dad. I'll be alright. Good night!" Strangely enough, even though Manny acknowledged his father's sincere feelings of love and support, he didn't feel any sympathy for Edison. Manny knew he wouldn't understand what had transpired, even if he told him. Actually, Manny wasn't quite sure if he could fully describe it himself. But it was such a tremendous feeling. Manny didn't care if Edison thought he might be a little 'off'. He was his father, but at that moment Manny had the sensation of an uncharacteristic coldness; not anger or hatred for the things he represented. Not even patience or any sense of kindness. Just indifference. He couldn't care less!

It was then that Manny recalled years ago when Derek explained to him that one of the true signs of a warrior's understanding of how to deal with power, was the process of developing relentlessness. "Manny," he said, "For a man of power to be commited, he must become relentless. True commitment doesn't come from any intellectual or rational process; it is given by the urging of the Spirit. Relentlessness isn't a character trait or an aspect of one's personality. Rather, it is essential to the process of mobilizing the energy necessary for one to 'grip the Spirit'.

Gripping the Spirit is the ability to focus all the dynamic forces of the human spirit on the circumstances of our daily lives. In a state of relentlessness, the warrior loses all sense of pity. Once the pity is gone, the urging of compassion that expresses itself in the spirit of man.... can have free reign, thus moving the warrior to act. These actions, spurred by compassion, become acts of power, acts of commitment. Acts of power keep the soul of the warrior clear. And the warrior's clarity enables him to act with maximum effectiveness."

Manny remembered discussing the cultural heritage of a warrior. He told me that '....one of history's greatest warriors was Jesus Christ. Many times in the Bible it is recorded that Jesus was moved with compassion, a compassion which caused him to manifest the power of the covenant that God had enacted with the Jews. Jesus did not view the human condition as 'pitiful'; on the contrary he taught his disciples that the power of God was at hand for all men to partake of'.

Derek said the power that Jesus manifested in the Earth has been undermined by the development of organized religion. Religions fostered the deception that there were intermediaries between man and the manifestations of the power of the Spirit. The organization of the various religions were based on specific aspects of doctrine or techniques of worship (Baptist, Methodist, Catholicism, etc.). Over time, the nurturing, development and well being of the organizations themselves had become more important than the effects of the doctrine in the lives of the worshippers. Jesus said '....the (false) traditions of men make the word of God of no effect. God is a Spirit; they that worship him must worship him in spirit and truth'.

The result was that, for the most part, modern man had lost the ability to manifest acts of power, of channeling the truth of the Spirit into the lives of people. The essential lessons of culture had been replaced by the deceptions and divisions of organized religion. The degree to which the power of the Spirit was available to man, was in direct proportion to the degree to which clarity was manifest in the soul of the warrior. In this day and time, it was needful for men of power to act in a commited fashion, in order to help restore order to a society bent on chaos and self-destruction.

All of these things which seemed so obscure to Manny years ago, were beginning to make sense in a real and tangible way. Their recollection made him wonder again about his uncle, and how he was dealing with the circumstances of his trial. Somehow Manny felt sure he would face this challenge with conviction.... because he knew Derek's motivation was based on compassion.

Inside the dingy confines of his tiny cell, Derek seemed to be at ease, if a bit disheveled. He had been isolated from the other prisoners since he was considered a security threat. Because of the injury to his arm, it was difficult for him to shave with his left hand and consequently he had stopped. He received decent medical attention, although he refused to take pain medication. At night the pain and throbbing became nearly unbearable and on several occasions shots were administered by the prison physicians to help him sleep.

Derek's bail was enormous; over $1.5 million, and since all his assets had been frozen, there was no way for him to post the bond. He refused to create any sort of hardship on the part of Deidre and Edison, so he sat quietly in his cell awaiting his court appearances.

Two days prior to the start of the trial, Hassan Danielson came to consult with Derek and advise him of the status of the case. "Hello Derek. I need to discuss where we are with your case. Have they been treating you well?"

"Hello Hassan," Derek wasn't in a particularly good mood that day, but he managed to remain civil. "I've been having some trouble with my shoulder the past few nights. A lot of pain." Derek had to have two metal plates inserted in his right shoulder to reconnect bones that were shattered during the seige and battle with Pike.

Although Hassan was empathetic, there was work to be done. "If you get uncomfortable I'll have the guards bring some medication for you. We've got to talk about preparations for court."

Even though he didn't smoke, Derek knew whenever there was a lengthy discussion Hassan would break out his pipe. Actually, the aroma of the tobacco was quite enjoyable, and Hassan, with his horn rimmed glasses looked quite the distinguished college professor, a lot like a dark skinned version of Malcom X.

"You know I'll cooperate in any way I can," Derek responded. "Have you spoken to Deidre? How is she?" He was very much concerned about the effect all this was having on his sister.

Derek relied on Hassan to not only prepare his case, but to also keep track of Deidre's state of mind.

"Deidre is fine. Don't worry about her right now, Derek. We need to talk about you. The Arlington people haven't had much success digging up character witnesses outside of your family. The people they did find haven't seen you in years. It could be difficult putting members of the Castle household on the witness stand. Right now, our position is not that strong."

"What are you trying to say?" Derek's instincts told him that he didn't think he would like what he was going to hear.

Hassan took a long draw on the pipe. "The prosecution has proposed what I think is an attractive plea bargaining deal. If you agree to plead guilty to conspiracy, they'll drop the trafficking and espionage charges. I could probably get you off with 5-7, if you're willing to cooperate."

Derek knew it couldn't be as simple as that. "Cooperate with what?" he inquired."C'mon, what's the rest of the story here?" Derek had read about the prosecutor, Russell Kirkland, and how Kirkland was interested not only in his own conviction, but in his ties to his brother-in-law, the Senator.

"Kirkland wants you to turn over evidence of Edison's involvement in all this. He knows there are classified documents that were in his possession that you used. It may be our only chance of avoiding a stiff sentence if you're convicted. Besides, you'll eliminate any further embarrassment for Deidre and the family."

"So.... that's it. Kirkland's got you on the run."

Hassan looked straight at Derek. He took a long draw on his pipe and allowed a small cloud of smoke to eke from the corner of his mouth. "Derek, I've been in this business a long time. I'm a fighter by nature. But I also know how to pick a good fight. This isn't a good one. They've got the odds stacked against you. You're facing up to thirty years in a federal penetentiary. THIRTY YEARS, Derek! Think about it. I happen to know there's no love lost between you and Edison. You are my client. It is my professional responsibility to advise you.... to act in your own best interest. I think the prosecution's terms are fair, given the circumstances."

The pain in his shoulder had returned. Derek got up to walk around; it seemed to help ease the discomfort. "You're right. I'm not a big supporter of Edison. But he is my family, whether I like it or not. And I'm not going to implicate him in any of this. Besides, the information he had on the superconductor research was outdated anyway. There were already plenty of things written in the public domain that were more relevant and up to date than the documents he had. I just read them as a way of comparing notes. He didn't do anything."

Hassan was shaking his head. "You mean you're going to protect someone you don't like, someone you don't even respect?"

"You're wrong about my not respecting him. I DO respect him; as a husband, as a father, as a provider. He's under a tremendous amount of pressure. I am bound by what I believe, to honor his position in this family. Do you understand?"

Hassan realized it was useless to protest. "OK Derek. We'll do this your way. But you're going to have to start at the beginning, and take me through exactly what happened. All of it. Are you up to that?" The shoulder had begun to ache again, and the pain and throbbing were causing him to tear. "I'll have the orderlies come in," suggested Hassan.

"No, no I'll be alright," Derek gasped. "If they come they'll give me a shot. I need to be clearheaded a little while longer."

Hassan took a small microcassette recorder out of his jacket. "Well, just start talking when you're ready. I've got my tape recorder right here."

"About twenty years ago," Derek began, "I became very interested in some of the research that was going on with laser technology, and some of the new materials that were being discovered and synthesized as superconductors. As an undergraduate, I had been a physics major, although I subsequently changed and received a degree in economics. After finishing the graduate program in finance at the Wharton School, I went to work on Wall Street. All the while, I never completely lost my fascination with physics.

Several years later, my marriage broke up and I felt I needed some time off, a mental health break, if you will. I took a leave of absence and came down here to live with Deidre for a few months. During that time, I came across some documents that Edison had as a result of his work with a congressional subcommittee, on alternative forms of energy. Some of the materials that were mentioned in those documents I knew could be synthesized into highly efficient superconductors."

Hassan interrupted. "Slow down, Derek. What are these superconductors, and why are they such a big deal?"

"Sorry, Hassan. Superconductors are materials that conduct electricity with very little loss of energy. In conventional conductivity, a large amount of energy is lost during the transport or conduction process. Therefore, power generation techniques tend to be fairly inefficient, not because of the generation, but because of the energy lost over the distance transported. Superconductors enable much more higly efficient generation and transport mechanisms to be implemented, and much more powerful applications of this power to be made. But the superconductor discussion is only part of the story.

The important factor is relativity. Einstein's theory of relativity states, essentially, that any form of energy can be generated by vibrating mass, or matter at the proper frequency. $E = mc^2$. This relationship is the basis for atomic energy. An atom smasher is really an enormous centrifuge that accelerates specific types of matter until the atomic structure of the material is broken down; the material becomes radioactive. The atomic bomb is a crude, albeit, highly destructive application of this theory.

At any rate, if you examine the inverse of the equation, it states that a particular form of energy divided by the constant of acceleration equals mass, or matter. In other words, relativity implies that physical objects which are 'real' in a material sense can be transformed into other material forms.... by the correct mathematical application of the relativity equation. All matter as we experience it is really a particular set and concentration of vibratory patterns, or reasonances. From the point of view of relativity, if you can change the resonance patterns you can change the material. The key is LIGHT.

The constant of acceleration C (in $E = mc^2$) is known as the velocity of light. By manipulating the right approximations of the velocity of light, you can generate mathematical transformations that, when properly applied, will synthesize or decompose materials. It was my belief that by properly utilizing such principles, you can cause even organically based materials.... such as cocaine..... to alter their molecular structure, thereby totally changing their characteristics."

Hassan took his glasses off. "Do you mean to tell me that you could cause such a powerful drug..... to be rendered harmless?"

"Exactly. But at that time it was still a theoretical assumption. First of all, you need a very highly efficient form of energy, hence the business about superconductors. But I also reasoned that there was a need to manipulate the characteristics of light in order to set in motion the correct vibratory reactions to cause the transformation.

Completely as a coincidence, about three years ago, I ran into an old friend, Emir Richardson, who was conducting quantum physics research at Howard University. Upon describing my ideas to him, he agreed to do the computer analyses to either confirm or refute my mathematical assumptions. I remember him kidding me about what to call the process; he said he needed something to write down in his laboratory log. I told him it was the inverse of synthesis, so he called it 'inverse synthesis'. Real creative, huh?"

"Yes Derek. I think it's very original," smirked Hassan. "May we get back to the story now?"

"OK, OK. During my years in investment banking, I enjoyed some phenomenal successes and even made a small fortune. More importantly, I developed a following of investors who knew my credentials and trusted my judgment regarding investment ideas. One day I received a call from Emir. He told me that he had finally come up with several mathematical models that could, theoretically, accomplish what I was proposing. He told me he was thinking of taking a sabbatical from the University anyway, and wanted to work on this project full time. It was then I got the idea for the power company consortium."

Hassan was visibly excited now. "Don't tell me. Let me guess. As a result of your contacts in the international banking community, you were able to come up with the financial backing to gradually acquire controlling interests in major power companies. But why power companies?"

"We worked out a plan to systematically retrofit the power plants with specially modified generators and superconduction facilities. These special generators would take advantage of the models he had developed. The inverse synthesis process would have the effect of changing the molecular structure of cocaine.... or any of its derivatives. The power consortium owns interests in every major power generation plant, in all the key cocaine trafficking locations around the world. Each of these plants would be equipped with the special generators."

"My God!" Hassan was standing up now. The utter simplicity of the plan Derek described stunned him. "How would the process be activated?" he inquired, waiting to hear more.

Derek slowly smiled. "It really was simple. The process was activated by..... turning on the power. Or more correctly, as demand for the power was required these specially equipped generators would cause a photonic reaction. The idea was that no one would know why the stuff decomposed; it would just become unusable, literally before your eyes. Cocaine in any of its forms would be rendered useless. Imagine the confusion that would have resulted among the cocaine distributors. The manufacturing sources would be accused of swindling their distribution people. The whole network of cocaine operations would be totally disrupted within six months."

Hassan interrupted. "But the reports said that over 10 kilos of pure cocaine were seized at your island off the coast of Venezuela."

"It was for research. The process hadn't been perfected. We were very close, though. The coke was for the testing necessary to certify the process. You might view it as a quality assurance procedure. We had to get just the right resonances.

Finally, we came up with a technique that caused the coke to be changed to sand. Sand won't burn, and you can't snort it.... well I guess you could snort it, but to no avail. Things were beginning to look very good." Significantly, Derek omittted any discussion of the Xenus ore, and the mines in Namibia. He was careful not to let any information about that come out, certainly not until well after his fate was decided. He didn't want any scrutiny placed on Manny, to whom he had transferred his controlling interest.

Hassan was visibly concerned. "Why didn't you and Emir go to the authorities.... for backing of your research?" It was obvious he was still a bit skeptical.

"C'mon Hassan. Why would we? One of the reasons to seek government support is funding. Money wasn't an issue. The power company business is quite profitable. More importantly, this activity wasn't any of the government's business; we were operating in international markets, outside U.S. jurisdiction. Yes, we had the 10 kilos, but there were no plans, no intent to distribute."

Hassan thought about what Derek had told him. "Do you have any proof, any witnesses who can corroborate your story?"

"The other members of the consortium weren't aware of the entire purpose of the retrofitting. It just so happens that the new generation equipment would also be a much more efficient way of producing power. Their primary concern was a return on the investment. The key people were with us at the island."

"What happened to Emir?" asked Hassan. He was really looking for some way to develop this information into a defense for his client.

"Emir was killed mysteriously. His body was dicovered, I found out, with a bullet in the back of his head on an empty lot in D.C." Derek was visibly distraught at the recollection. "Somehow the CIA got information of our project. Washington obviously authorized the seige of the island. What a tremendous waste!"

Hassan turned off the microcassette. "Tell me something Derek. Why? Why would you risk your success, your reputation, even your life on something like this?"

Derek started to pace the floor, back and forth. "Because someone has got to stop the madness! Someone has got to stop the needless waste of lives, the destruction of families, the poisoning of generations. The drug trade is a ravenous cancer that threatens the viability of modern civilization. It is particularly conspicuous in our cities, where the poor, the disenfranchised and uneducated are progressively victimized by the lure of easy money and, consequently, are being shot down every day in drug wars. These are my people! If not me.... who? Tell me Hassan, who?"

There was silence for several minutes. Finally Hassan spoke. "One other thing really intrigues me. This inverse synthesis stuff. How did you gain the insight to comprehend what appears to be some very complex scientific principles?"

The pain in Derek's shoulder was resurfacing, with a vengeance. "What we know and experience as the physical world is actually concentrated manifestations of the forces at work in the spiritual world. Science is simply the body of descriptions of these physical relationships. The key to understanding the workings of the spirit is the understanding of culture. Culture relates human experience to the totality of spiritual existence. Most ancient cultures of the world acknowledge the wholistic nature of our existence.

In particular, there were a people from the region of Africa which is known today as Ethiopia and the Sudan. In the 7th century B.C., they conquered the people of Asiatic descent who were at that time the rulers of Egypt. In Egypt, the Southern area was known as Kush or Nubia. For nearly five hundred years they ruled Egypt, the territory to the South, and much of the Sinai Peninsula. Most historians believe thay would have ruled indefinitely, had they not become involved in a territorial dispute with the Assyrians which ultimately led to their downfall.

At any rate, part of the body of knowledge and beliefs they developed were a comprehension of the spiritual and scientific principles, some of which we have been discussing. They recognized light as the source of all physical life. Some of the rights of passage for the Nubian princes was the perfection of techniques for manipulating the structure and composition of the material world. Such things as the design of a monumental sculpture which, when coated with special emulsions and placed in contact with sunlight, would be transformed into gold. Things like that.

Much of the history of this people has been lost at the hands of European historians. But the lessons of such a powerful culture are returning."

Hassan was incredulous. "Are you trying to tell me you're a descendant of some ancient African royalty?"

Derek looked at him quizzicly. "No, Hassan. I wish it were that simple. In reality, it's not me. I'm simply the conduit... the guide. A messenger, attempting to explain the traditional passages of a culture... that was once lost. The one you truly seek.... is my nephew, Manny. It is he.... that is the Nubian."

Epilogue

Narrative: 1999   Manny, age 19

I didn't go to the first week of the trial. Mom and Dad were there each day, and Asia even went a couple of times. It wasn't that I was afraid of what might happen to him. I just felt it might be a distraction if I were in court. With the feelings I was experiencing now, it would have been too much of a burden to be around him during the proceedings.

Each night Mom recapped the day's activities for me. The prosecutor, Russell Kirkland, argued the government's case effectively. According to Kirkland, Derek was the head of an international cocaine smuggling operation based off the coast of South America. The prosecution's 'witnesses' testified to seeing private planes taking off from an airstrip near the compound, loaded with uncut cocaine. Over 10 kilos of the drug were found during a raid on the property. The power companies were an elaborate front for the entire operation, according to the prosecution.

The defense case amounted to proving that the prosecution was going strictly on circumstantial evidence, and that the power consortium was, in fact, a legitimate operation. Hassan Danielson was able to produce a patent application for specially modified power generation equipment, which supported Derek's contention. But because of the lack of witnesses to support Uncle D, Hassan would have to put him on the stand to tell his side of story. He knew that would be Derek's only chance to convince the jury of the truth.

Lately, I have been meditating on the meaning of truth. And of reality. And freedom. I've begun to realize that years before, in my conversations and interactions with Derek, what he was really doing was training me, not intellectually, but training my awareness. He was training me to allow myself to perceive things not only through the normal five senses, but with my entire being. What I had experienced that night in the talk with my Dad was an expanded level of perception; I was able to 'see' with my whole being, in the spiritual sense.

What I experienced that evening, was the perception of the radiant forces of his spirit as they emanated from inside. It occurred to me that these emanations were neither good nor bad, right nor wrong. They were manifestations of truth, in the purest sense. Such expressions of truth are conditioned by each individual's internal filtering mechanism, the soul. And the conditioned emanations manifest themselves in the physical world. Probably a good analogy is a movie projector. The light source is the active agent. The film images through which the light is projected condition what is perceived. The screen is the required physical medium which brings the film 'to life', the same as we experience the material world through the interaction of our bodies and physical senses.

Human beings are by nature perceivers. Not only do individuals emanate life forces, so does the Earth and all of its life forms. Perception occurs when the individual's internal emanations align with emanations outside of the person. What is normally referred to as reality is the collective body of perceptions. The forces of the spirit are tremendously powerful. Alignment of the emanations is the passageway to bringing the power of the spirit into the physical realm.... of changing reality.

The problem for the average man is the internal dialogue that is maintained within. This dialogue is the expression of worries, the preoccupation with self-reflection, self importance, ego, etc. These are the things that clutter the soul, that garble the expression of the spirit. The enormous power of the spirit can only be utilized when a state of total (internal) silence is achieved. The power of silence.... is the clarity of the warrior.

Freedom then, from a cultural perspective, is the discipline required to take full responsibility for the totality of one's existence. The challenge of giving full expression to the truth of the spirit, is the essence of being free. And the richness of our cultural heritage makes us uniquely suited to allow the truth of the spirit to reign in the physical world.

That is the challenge for which Derek had been preparing me years ago, for which I finally understood.

Our society today is desperately in need of the creative power of the Spirit. These realizations make me think of the time Derek and I would spend together. What I experienced as 'magic' or daydreams with him, were really instances of his utilizing the force of the spirit to subtly change the alignment of my perception. In that state of re-alignment, I experienced a new 'reality'. So my experiences were, in fact, real and not dreams. And it has taken me the intervening years to begin to appropriate these lessons of perception... for myself.

"Manny," I heard Mom in the distance. "Are you going to eat something?" She looked particularly pretty that night.

"Mom, you know something? You're a beautiful woman. I don't think I've ever told you that."

"No young man, you haven't." She could sense my preoccupation. "Are you worried about Derek?" Even though I'd thought about him often, I really hadn't been focused on the trial. "He means a lot to you, doesn't he?" She sat down and took my hand. Her hair was dark and healthy. The glimmering black was streaked with specks of gray here and there, and her eyes were bright and shiny.

"Manny," she said, "I've spent all of my life trying to please other people, in one way or another. Mostly men. It was as if my value as a person.... depended on male acceptance. First Daddy, then boyfriends in school, your father. Everyone except Derek. He always treated me as though I were responsible for my own life. As though my opinions really counted; I think he believed I could make a difference. Even when we were small, he would take up for me at school, getting into fights to defend me. Sometimes I think he's crazy, but you know, I was so proud of him yesterday when Hassan put him on the witness stand. It sounds a bit farfetched, but somehow I know he's telling the truth. I just wish he'd let us in on it."

I could see the sincerity and admiration she held for Uncle D. As she spoke, it was almost like a rose blossoming in the sunlight; I could see my Mother coming alive, with the excitement of living.

"One thing he's shown me Manny.... is that you can't live someone else's life. The joy of living comes from within each of us. No amount of money or material success can bring us that joy. That's what I tell my kids. We all have something to offer. We have to believe in ourselves. I love Derek very much, and I know he loves me. And you know something.... in many ways you're a lot like him."

Her comment surprised me. "Do you mean.... I'm crazy?" There were a few seconds of silence. Then we both erupted in a roaring laughter. "Thanks Mom, I needed that." We hugged one another lovingly.

"C'mon Manny. Eat something. There's no need to starve yourself. By the way, you should plan to be at the courthouse tomorrow. The closing arguments and jury verdict are due. We're going to spend some time with Derek. I'm sure he'll want to see you."

It was a brilliant day in Atlanta. The dogwoods and magnolias were in full bloom. The air was alive with the aroma of flowers. The federal courthouse was filling up early. Deidre and Edison had requested permission to see Derek prior to the start of court. Hassan arranged for them to meet in one of the judges chambers that wasn't being used. Asia had come down to join her parents.

The room was bright and warm. Enormous rectangular windows framed the downtown skyline. There were two over-sized leather sofas, and a couple of leather wing chairs. Rich mahogany-surfaced end tables flanked the sofas and each of the chairs. The walls were covered in an oriental patterned fabric. The lush charcoal gray carpeting was thick and freshly shampooed. It was quiet, and very serene, almost like a sanctuary.

They had been waiting for fifteen minutes when the guards finally brought Derek in.

He was impeccably dressed in a striped three piece suit and bow tie. He looked strange, however, because of the cumbersome sling restraining his shoulder, and the wrist and leg irons he wore. "Hi family," Derek greeted them cheerfully in spite of his restraints. "How are you?"

"Why does he have to have those chains?" Asia protested. "He's not a criminal." The irony of her statement wasn't lost on the group. Deidre ran over and embraced him warmly.

"Why didn't you tell us what was going on, D? You know we would have supported you. Isn't that right Edison?"

"Of course," responded Edison weakly. He wasn't sure if Derek was aware of the security briefings that took place prior to the siege at Bonaire.

"Deidre," Derek began, "I'm very sorry about this whole mess. I couldn't let you know.... because I didn't want to risk you're being implicated. And I knew that if anyone in the family became knowledgeable, Edison would become a target. It's not his fault." Tears began to well up in Deidre's eyes.

"D, please forgive me. I've misjudged you for many years. Whatever they say, I know you're not a criminal. Let us help you. If things don't work out, we'll appeal. I'm sorry for the way I've acted, the way I've treated you." She was crying profusely now. Asia came over to comfort her.

"I want to apologize too," offered Edison. "It's funny how it seems to take a crisis situation.... to cause one to take stock of the things that are really important. I love Deidre so very much. I'm a very fortunate man to have the love and support of a woman like her.... and a family like ours." It was unusual for Edison to be so earnest about such things. However, his heart was (finally) in what he was saying. "I've never been able to understand you. But

I want you to know no matter what happens Derek, I am proud to be your brother-in-law."

Without acknowledging his apology, Derek addressed Edison directly. "You are a successful public figure. Now is the time for you to utilize your stature and influence to reach our young people. Communicate the importance of education, of responsibility, of self-respect. Get involved in helping young fathers and young mothers commit to changing their own lives. Teach them to channel the negative aspects of their existence into positive energy; to be disciplined enough to give themselves and their children the opportunity to learn. If you're sincere about what you said, then get involved in this struggle."

Just then the bailiff came in. "Time for court, Mr. Alston."

"We're praying for you," said Deidre, as he was being led out by the guard.

Turning back to them, Derek inquired anxiously, "Where's Manny? Is he all right?"

"He told me he'd be here," answered Asia. "I know he wants to see you."

"Good luck, Derek," offered Edison. With that he was gone down the hall to the courtroom.

When I arrived at the courthouse, the place was packed. The media was everywhere. I couldn't get inside the courtroom once the proceedings had begun, but I could hear what was going on via a loudspeaker in a chamber just outside. Apparently, both sides had already made their closing statements. Judge Singletary asked if the jury had reached a verdict. The foreman requested a brief recess to tally the jury ballots. The judge agreed, but decided not to release the court until the final verdict was validated.

Inside, Derek whispered to Hassan, "This is some bullshit, some real bullshit." In his own awkward way, he was acknowledging his realization of everything closing in on him. There was a low murmur around the room, everyone discussing everything that had transpired.

For me, it was just the thought of seeing him again, to be in his company one more time, that was important. So much had taken place in both of our lives since the last time I saw him, yet I knew once we were together..... it would be as though we had never been apart.

I heard the jury returning as they filed back into the courtroom. Judge Singletary immediately asked for the verdict. The foreman stood and said simply, "We find the defendant, Derek Andrew Alston... guilty as charged!" There was an immediate eruption inside, as reporters and spectators rushed for the doors at the back of the courtroom.

"Order! ORDER! in this court," Judge Singletary screamed as he tried to get control of the situation. Outside, I could hear him say over the loudspeaker that the date for sentencing would be June 15.

After the initial flow of humanity, I anxiously awaited Derek. It seemed like forever. Finally, he emerged from the courtroom, the surge of media and lawyers close behind. He spotted my wheelchair at the end of the hall.

Despite what he'd been through, he looked calm, even relaxed. When he got to me, he smiled that crazy smile of his, and I knew he was alright.

"I'm going to jail, Manny," he said softly, his deep set eyes wide with disbelief. It had been years since I'd seen him, but the tremendous sense of exhilaration I felt... made me oblivious to the confusion and the crowd. With his good arm, he reached out and shook my hand, like he always did. We both broke into the biggest grin.

And there we were, amidst the gaggle of onlookers, enjoying each others' company..... for the last time. Just grinning and grinning.... madly!